SEARING SEDUCTION

Seething with anger and jealousy, Lucien was a man possessed. He gripped Samantha by her smooth, pale shoulders and whispered huskily, "I want you. What the young men of Paris have known, I must experience this night. You will be mine now . . ."

"I am not what you think," Samantha said in a quavering voice, but pride kept her from telling the whole truth. Truth would matter little to Lucien, who was consumed by his desire for her. He reached under her white lawn nightgown and caressed her soft, hot skin. Her nails pressed into his flesh but that only provoked him more. He was intent on making her burn for him.

"Taste my lips," he said. "It will be the first union of our bodies." And as he carried her swiftly to her bed, his hands made her cry out with delight. Finally, lost in the splendid sensations he aroused, she could no longer distinguish between fantasy and reality. There was only Lucien and the magic of his love, taking her to a place she had never been before . . .

MORE BESTSELLING ROMANCE BY JANELLE TAYLOR

SAVAGE CONQUEST (1533, $3.75)

Having heeded her passionate nature and stolen away to the rugged plains of South Dakota, the Virginia belle Miranda was captured there by a handsome, virile Indian. As her defenses melted with his burning kisses she didn't know what to fear more: her fate at the hands of the masterful brave, or her own traitorous heart!

FIRST LOVE, WILD LOVE (1431, $3.75)

Roused from slumber by the most wonderful sensations, Calinda's pleasure turned to horror when she discovered she was in a stranger's embrace. Handsome cattle baron Lynx Cardone had assumed she was in his room for his enjoyment, and before Calinda could help herself his sensuous kisses held her under the spell of desire!

GOLDEN TORMENT (1323, $3.75)

The instant Kathryn saw Landis Jurrell she didn't know what to fear more: the fierce, aggressive lumberjack or the torrid emotions he ignited in her. She had travelled to the Alaskan wilderness to search for her father, but after one night of sensual pleasure Landis vowed never to let her travel alone!

LOVE ME WITH FURY (1248, $3.75)

The moment Captain Steele saw golden-haired Alexandria swimming in the hidden pool he vowed to have her — but she was outraged he had intruded on her privacy. But against her will his tingling caresses and intoxicating kisses compelled her to give herself to the ruthless pirate, helplessly murmuring, "LOVE ME WITH FURY!"

TENDER ECSTASY (1212, $3.75)

Bright Arrow is committed to kill every white he sees — until he sets his eyes on ravishing Rebecca. And fate demands that he capture her, torment her . . . and soar with her to the dizzying heights of TENDER ECSTASY!

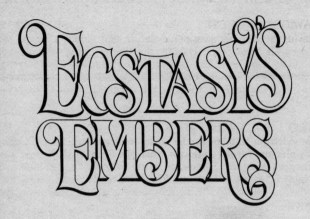

ECSTASY'S EMBERS

BY
VICTORIA
LONDON

ZEBRA BOOKS
KENSINGTON PUBLISHING CORP.

ZEBRA BOOKS

are published by

Kensington Publishing Corp.
475 Park Avenue South
New York, N.Y. 10016

First printing: February 1985

Printed in the United States of America

To My Husband Who Makes Everything Possible

Prologue

Something was wrong. All evening a nagging feeling warned the American that things were not going as smoothly as they appeared. After three years of working as a spy for the new government, Lucien Fraser would not still have been alive if he hadn't been able to sense when trouble was at hand. As he uncrossed his long legs, his midnight blue eyes quickly scanned the room, noting the possible exits. Somehow he had to bluff his way out of this tavern and get back to his ship.

"Are you certain, Mr. Fraser, that these . . . ah . . . how shall I say it . . . acquaintances of yours are interested?" The thin man sat stiffly in his seat trying to gauge the expression of the tall, dark American seated across from him.

"I can assure you that these gentlemen are more than willing to promote His Majesty's cause. But"—Lucien instinctively reached to remove some lint from his black shirt—"they will need the names of the English agents in America." He absent-mindedly leaned into

7

the high-backed chair, away from the glow of the candles on the table which shadowed his lean, rugged features.

The noise from the tavern's patrons blocked the thumping sound the Englishman made as he drummed his bony fingers on the table. The steady drumming of the fingers seemed to be synchronized to the steady downpour outside. He was unusually nervous.

The large mantle clock chimed ten times. A serving girl hurriedly brought another tray of ale to Lucien and his companion. She had noticed the two earlier when they first had entered the tavern, particularly the tall one who towered above all the patrons. As he casually unhooked his flowing gray cloak, she saw the rest of his body clad in a black shirt, tight black breeches, and boots that outlined his long legs and muscular thighs. He was the most strikingly attractive man she had ever seen. And she would wager a year's meager pay that he knew how to satisfy a woman. This one, she sensed, was special. Even the dim light of the tavern could not completely obscure his handsome face.

Standing deliberately in front of the American, she winked. His slow smile warmed her body as she bent over to lower her tray, giving him an unobstructed view of her buxom chest. Despite the powdered wig he wore, she could tell from his dark, arched brows that his hair was as black as his ruffled shirt.

"Later?" she whispered hopefully and sauntered away.

"Are you staying until Friday?" asked the Englishman, changing the tempo of his drumming fingers. "I believe we will have the rest of your money by then."

"And the names."

8

"What? Oh, yes. The names of the British contacts in Washington." He removed a neatly folded piece of paper from his pocket and handed it to Lucien. "This is a partial list. Will you stay?" He smiled, looking in the direction of the serving girl. "I am sure she will wait."

Glancing at the mantle clock, Lucien answered, "A few more minutes will not matter." But he knew that this man was trying to detain him. Why? Lucien wondered to himself. Weren't those two burly men seated at the table to his right large enough to coerce Lucien into complying with the British? Whatever the reason, Lucien had no intention of waiting to find out. He tucked the paper into his boot.

Suddenly a loud clap of thunder echoed through the damp tavern, distracting the patrons.

"Damn," Lucien muttered aloud. "I believe I've dropped my cravat pin. Sweetheart," he called to the serving girl whose eyes were riveted on him, "can you help me?"

The girl sashayed to his side, still balancing a tray full of drinks. No one saw his booted leg moving toward her. She tripped over his feet, and the tray slid out of her hands onto the other man's lap. With a loud cry, he jumped from his seat, ineffectually wiping his breeches with his hands.

"Why you stupid, clumsy girl! Did you see that?" he asked Lucien, ignoring the girl's tearful apologies.

No response. The Englishman looked up. Gone! Lucien Fraser was gone!

"Hawkins, Daniels!" he called to the men at the next table. "You let him escape! After him! I must have his signed confession!"

Lucien ran through the dark, winding, London

streets toward the dock, knowing exactly where his ship, the *Newport Wind*, was located.

"There he is! Over here, mate!"

The voices were getting close, but, impeded by the blackened sky and the blinding rain, Lucien knew his pursuers would be having as much trouble seeing the way as he was. He quickly ducked into a doorway, removing his wig and long cloak. Minutes passed, yet he stood still until he heard the footsteps pass him. Only then did he expel a long breath. For a few instants a jagged streak of lightning illuminated the black and gray sky.

Wet, dark hair plastered to his head, water dripping off his face, dressed completely in black, Lucien Fraser, with eyes shining, blended into the shadows of the wet London night.

Chapter One

Charleston: September, 1805

"Samantha, I want you to marry me," the young man announced.

"Clinton, I . . . thank you. This is a bit sudden, don't you agree?" She turned her leaf green eyes up to him and his pulse quickened. Her well-modulated voice blended culture with just a trace of a Southern accent.

"I am not interested in marrying—not yet. And might this proposal have anything to do with that awful duel you fought the other day?"

The late night air was filled with the scent of jasmine and magnolias, and the heat and humidity made more than one young couple wander into the gardens behind the Thornton's charming townhouse. The front of the house faced Charleston Bay. The sound of laughter and chatter from inside the crowded ballroom reached their ears as Clinton Davis moved her toward the far end of the gardens, near the fountain, where it was quiet. The path was outlined by finely manicured azalea bushes, and at its end a live oak tree with gray moss stood tall as a sentinel. Two tiny lanterns hung from a low branch.

"I suppose one of your other beaus told you about that duel." He sounded petulant.

"Is it true? Did you not wait for the full count of ten paces before you turned to shoot?"

"That's not exactly true . . . Oh, I don't know. I don't remember!" He rubbed his sweaty hands along his crisp, white coat and pants. Regardless of the situation, Clinton always maintained a stylish appearance. "Besides, it was only a shoulder wound that I gave him."

"Only a shoulder wound! This is ridiculous. Clinton," she demanded, "have you been drinking again? What has happened to you, Clinton Davis? You are not the same person I used to know. People have warned me that you are not a gentleman."

Because of the humidity, her carefully arranged coiffure was loosening, allowing long strands of her coppery tresses to escape. She was not in the best of moods tonight and had no tolerance for the plaintive tone of his voice or the way he possessively held her slim waist.

"It's all because of you, Sam. I love you! I cannot think of anything but you! Your green eyes haunt me. Your body makes me quiver. Why won't you marry me?" he whined. "You are nineteen now—old enough to marry. I will ask your father for your hand tonight."

His grip tightened and for the first time since she had known him, Samantha was frightened by his strange behavior. "Clinton, please. Let go of me!"

"No. You are mine. Why won't you let me hold you and kiss you? You always tease me, Samantha Thornton. Well, this time I will not let you get away

12

with it."

Grabbing her shoulders, his mouth brutally descended to her delicate lips. She tried to free herself from his hard embrace. No longer frightened, Samantha was furious with his bold assumptions. Without thinking, she raised her leg and stamped on his left foot. When he released her, she raised her hand and slapped him across his face with all her strength.

"How dare you!" she stormed. Picking up the hem of her yellow silk gown, she ran blindly toward the house.

Suddenly she felt her body slam into a hard, unyielding object, nearly knocking all the breath from her. Then she noticed the gleaming black boots. Not looking up she snapped, "Can't you watch where you are going?"

"Me, my dear?" replied the "object." "I think you are the one who is somewhat short-sighted."

She wiped the loose curls from her eyes and raised her head. He was so tall and dark—no wonder she did not see him.

"Who could possibly see you, dressed in all that black!" She could not make out his features.

"I think, my dear, your . . . ah . . . friend is coming to look for you."

She recognized Clinton's light blond hair as she saw him approaching. "Well, I have no desire to see him." The man still held her arm but not with the same brutal grip that Clinton had employed. "If you will release my arm, sir, I can go inside to repair my hair."

He lifted an errant strand from her shoulder. "I don't think you should. You look enchanting just the way you are now."

"Why you insolent . . . Men!" She snorted and,

twisting out of his grasp, marched back into the crowded room.

"Ah, there you are, Sam. Father and I have been looking all over for you." Adam's cheery voice annoyed her.

"Me? Where have you been, brother dear? You are aware that you are the guest of honor. I am not getting married next month. It is your forthcoming wedding we are celebrating."

"I was in the library. I had something important to attend to," he replied, not at all put off by her sarcasm.

"Father and I stood on the receiving line for more than an hour, and still you did not appear." She snapped her ivory fan and continued. "Lately you are always closeted in some room. It's a good thing that both you and Father look alike. I can look at his dark red hair and hazel eyes and remember that I have a brother somewhere. Your business cannot be that time-consuming. Doesn't your partner do anything when he is not sailing around the world?" The more she spoke the angrier she became with everyone—her brother, Clinton, her brother's mysterious partner. High color rose in her cheeks.

"What did I tell you?" Adam turned to an approaching figure dressed all in black.

"Oh no," she murmured, wishing she could disappear.

"Sam," Adam blithely continued, "this is my 'mysterious' partner, Lucien Fraser. I admit he often dresses for the part."

"How do you do, Miss Thornton. You are as

enchanting as your brother had said." She did not miss the reference to their previous meeting but appreciated his tact in not telling Adam.

"It is a pleasure to meet you at last, Mr. Fraser. After all the things Adam had written about you in his letters over the last few months, you seemed more like a myth than a man." Her gaze locked with his and, for the briefest moment, she felt breathless.

"Whether you know it or not, Fraser, my sister has just given you a compliment."

The musicians seated at the far end of the large room began a new musical set and Samantha heard the strains of the recently introduced dance, the waltz.

"Oh, Adam. Isn't this lovely? After your marriage, you will be living in Newport again, so"—she reached for his arm and began pulling him toward the dancing couples—"you owe your only sister this dance."

Lucien watched Adam move about the dance floor with his sister. What a lovely young creature, he marveled. The strong-willed, independent baby sister, Adam had called her. He had expected to meet a flat-chested, short-haired girl who looked more like a boy, not this lovely vision dancing away from him. When Adam had introduced them, Lucien was sorely tempted to reach out and touch those fascinating strands of red-gold hair. But no, she would probably turn on him. Her behavior in the garden hinted of a tempestuous nature.

As she twirled past, the yellow lace hemline of her silk gown rose above her calf. Lucien heard her laugh, a pleasant warble, like a nightingale. Her full mouth, soft skin, sculptured cheeks and small, upturned nose created in his mind the image of a young goddess blossoming into womanhood. For an instant, Lucien envied the man who would be lucky enough to initiate her. He had no time for silly little virgins. But still he walked toward her.

"May I?"

Adam laughed and he released his hold. "If you need me I will be closeted in the dining room, eating all the food you saved for me, Sam. Careful, Fraser, she may step on your toes."

Lucien saw her faint blush and grinned. "Come, green eyes, I am sure I can manage."

She was embarrassed by the teasing but still allowed Lucien to lead her to the middle of the now-crowded dance floor. From half-lowered lids she took the opportunity to study him as he skillfully whirled her about the brilliantly lit room. She had always considered herself to be too tall, yet she did not even reach Lucien Fraser's chin. She had to look up into his deep blue eyes.

"You dance very well, Miss Thornton."

"You're not so stodgy for an older man. And a New Englander, too." The words escaped her lips before she could stop them. He was smiling down at her, which made her feel all the more ridiculous.

"I assume," he said dryly, "that that was another one of your compliments. I hope your 'friend' over there is not unduly upset." His dark head motioned to where Clinton was standing with a glass of whiskey in hand, glowering at them.

"Oh, Clinton. He has no real claim on me."

The words "real claim" inexplicably irritated him. As they moved toward the back of the large room, Lucien inquired, "Do you trust me enough to go

16

outdoors, little dove? I promise you that I have better manners than your friend over there. Especially," he chuckled, "because I am an 'older man' and a 'New Englander,' too."

"Why, of course." Her voice was oddly stilted. "I hope I did not offend you, Mr. Fraser." Again she looked up at him. He was far more handsome than Adam's description of him—and far more arrogant. That curious combination of rugged and fine features must make him attractive to women, she decided, noticing the stir he caused among the women they passed. What woman could be oblivious to those sensuous lips which, according to Adam, experienced the touch of many others? "Your reputation is known to all of us. Adam has also told me of your success in business. Yet Fraser Shipping and Imports has become more prosperous since my brother became your partner, hasn't it?" As they reached the veranda, he offered her a glass of punch from the large crystal bowl standing near a table that was full of food.

Amused by her loyalty, he said, "Yes, your brother is indeed an asset. But I have always known that. I think, however, that it was my sister's eyes that induced him to remain in Newport. Are you sorry that he is marrying a 'New Englander'?"

"No." For some reason she could not look into his dark face. "Tell me, Mr. Fraser, how many times have you been to Europe?" It was a stupid question. Samantha never before had difficulty conversing with a man. All her witty phrases seemed to have evaporated into the humid Charleston night.

"I have been abroad several times. You know, of course, that I sailed the *Newport Wind* to China."

17

It was obvious that he was humoring her. After all, Samantha knew enough about Lucien Fraser to make her wonder if she should have a chaperone. She knew he was thirty, only a few years older than Adam. And she also knew that he was a notorious rake with no desire for the more romantic side of love. Adam said it was unnecessary, seeing the way women threw themselves at Lucien. Obviously, she concluded, things came too easily to him. Samantha decided that she did not like this man's manner, and she felt that she had to put him in his place.

"We were supposed to go to Europe three years ago for my sixteenth birthday. But"—she looked into her champagne glass—"that was before Mother died."

"Yes, I know." He was looking at her with piercing blue eyes that seemed to have the capacity to bore a small hole in her heart. Even if she had known nothing about Lucien Fraser, his firm jaw surely suggested a strength of character few men possessed.

"We will be going to France after Adam's wedding."

He did not appear to hear her. Perhaps she was boring him.

"Do you have many romantic attachments in Europe?"

"No, little dove, I make sure never to have 'attachments' but only romances. A woman in every port—as the saying goes—can be quite tiresome." He paused, looking for her reaction, imagining the green eyes flashing brighter. He was right. She was taken aback by his blatant display of arrogance yet instinctively knew there must be some truth to his statement.

"Are you trying to impress me with your conquests,

18

Mr. Fraser?" she inquired while snapping open her ivory fan.

"Impress you, green eyes? Why, I'll wager you have never been kissed by a man—a man, my dear, not those foppish gentlemen friends of yours."

Angered and flustered now, she tartly replied, "Of course I have—many times."

"Then show me what you know," his deep voice challenged.

She was trapped. On the one hand she wanted to kiss him and wipe that insolent look off his face; but on the other hand, she knew that if she did, her inexperience would be obvious to him. She stepped closer to his tall, muscular frame, closed her eyes, and lifted her head. She tentatively placed her arm on his shoulder, stood on her toes, and beckoned for his lips.

There was no question that Lucien saw through the charade. Yet, he impulsively pulled her nubile body closer to his and said, "This is going to be your first lesson in kissing a real man." He bent his head and pressed his lips firmly against hers. Samantha, not knowing how to respond, mimicked his actions, thinking this was no different from kissing Clinton. But when his tongue penetrated her closed lips, she felt an unfamilar tingle slowly spreading down her body. When he wrapped his arms even tighter around her body, she felt herself unable to breathe. As abruptly as he had embraced her, he released her, bringing her to her senses and making her aware of her ignorance.

Lucien smiled down at her. "There, little girl. That is something you won't soon forget."

"Won't forget? Why, Mr. Fraser, I have forgotten already." Her cold response surprised him. She would

19

not dream of giving him the chance to see her humiliated.

Lucien started to reply, but Adam and his father abruptly appeared on the veranda.

"It is good to see you again, Lucien," drawled Robert Thornton as he clasped Lucien's hand. "Your reputation, as usual, precedes you."

"How odd. We were just talking about that, Father," said Samantha sardonically.

Ignoring her now, Lucien responded, "Mr. Thornton, after meeting your family, I have some sense of whom your son takes after. But I must admit, I am still perplexed about whom your little girl resembles." After a moment's hesitation, Lucien turned to a furious Samantha. "No offense intended, my dear."

If looks had the power to kill, that blue-eyed devil would be entombed. He's not heard the last of me yet, she vowed.

"Sirs"—she moved toward the brightly lit doorway—"if you will excuse me, I have sorely neglected my duties as hostess. I must see to our guests." Stiffly, she walked into the ballroom.

"I suppose I angered her." Lucien smiled at the amused faces of Robert and Adam.

"Lucien, my daughter has a very temptestuous nature and occasionally has difficulty controlling it."

Adam grinned broadly and clapped Lucien on the back. "What did I tell you, Fraser. Sam is anything but sweet tempered and docile."

Chapter Two

"I am sorry I could not join you in Washington for your meeting with the President. But, as you can see," Adam grinned, "I would have had a hell of a time explaining to my sister why I could not be here for my own party."

"Yes, I noticed how docile she is," Lucien said. "Adam, you did not warn me about your sister."

"Oh, come on, Fraser. Her temper is no worse than yours."

Lucien was about to explain what he really meant but thought better of it. How could he tell his partner and future brother-in-law that his sister made him think of more than just engaging in polite conversation? How could Lucien admit that he desired Adam's sister?

It was almost dawn. Lucien and Adam were alone in the library, all the guests having long since departed or fallen asleep in the Thornton's guest rooms. Lucien sat in a dark brown leather armchair near the window. Looking out of the high French windows, he watched the rising sun as it came up behind the thick, dark clouds, casting odd shadows on the water of Charleston Bay.

"Tell me about your trip to England. Were our suspicions correct?" Adam asked.

Lucien leaned forward in the chair as he recounted all the events in England, including his escape from the London tavern.

"So, Adam," he concluded, "I am positive that the British want to establish a spy network in our Southwest—and I have the names to prove it. It's also clear that war with Napoleon will continue and the Louisiana Territory is a perfect area for the British to gather information about both the Americans and the French."

"What do President Jefferson and Mr. Madison want us to do now?" Adam was still smiling, but Lucien was not. What the President was asking them to do would surely interfere with Adam's marriage to his sister.

Conflicting emotions warred within Lucien: loyalty to his President and country and his feelings of responsibility for Adam. It was his old friend Thomas Jefferson who had instilled in him the sentiments of patriotism and who years ago had introduced Lucien to Adam Thornton. And it was Lucien who got Adam more involved as a government agent. Not that Adam balked, he reminded himself. In fact, Lucien knew long before he and Adam became business partners, that Adam was involved in a few minor government assignments. But they worked so well together in their dual roles as businessmen and United States agents. Lucien trusted Adam with his life. Now that Adam was marrying his sister, how could Lucien ask him to get more deeply involved in what could be a very dangerous yet extremely challenging game of intrigue?

"I know what you're thinking, Fraser." Adam watched him stand up and walk about the room, pretending to be engrossed with the leather-bound books that lined the walls. "Let me decide if I want to take the next assignment." Adam's voice was firm.

"You are right, Adam. I apologize." Lucien turned to face him and smiled. "And that is not something I do too often."

They could hear the sounds of the servants as they began to prepare for the new day's chores.

"If you don't speak quickly, I am afraid you will have my father and a household of guests to explain our new assignment to," Adam teased.

"Not to mention your charming sister." He did not mean to speak of her again. Adam knew Lucien well enough to know when a woman interested him.

"She's usually not up this early the morning after a party."

"Good. I will try to make this brief then." Lucien reached for the half-empty decanter of brandy and poured himself another drink before sitting down.

"The President believes that our former Vice President, Aaron Burr, may be involved in some intrigue of his own in, of all places, the Southwest."

"That is not new. It is no secret that Burr has consistently maintained that the Southwest—particularly the Mexican Territory—be separated from Spanish rule. A lot of westerners agree with him."

"True, Adam. But now with the Louisiana Purchase, so much land is out of the Spanish and French hands

23

and into ours. The exact border lines have not yet been determined, but why is Burr interested now?" Lucien asked rhetorically.

Moving to the armchair opposite Lucien, Adam added, "Well, we know a few things about Burr, but the man is still an enigma. He has many powerful friends. His daughter is married to a man who wants to be the next governor of South Carolina. However, Burr is perpetually in debt—that could be a problem. Since the duel with Hamilton, there is still a warrant out for his arrest in both New York and New Jersey."

"Therefore, Adam, there are very few places left where he would be welcome. One of them is the western territory."

A servant entered the library and carefully placed a tray of hot tea and freshly baked scones on the table.

Lucien was still lounging on the armchair, his black shirt opened at the neck, his jacket and waistcoat long since discarded. Both men were tired, but before there were any more interruptions, they had to decide whether to accept this new assignment.

"What do we have to do, Lucien?" Adam knew that despite Lucien's relaxed manner he was as interested and excited in a new challenge as Adam.

"Well, my soon-to-be brother-in-law, what do you think of another office of Fraser Shipping and Imports in the lovely city of New Orleans?"

"First"—Adam stood up to stretch his long legs—"why New Orleans? And—forgive the practical side—second, how much will it cost us?"

"According to Mr. Madison, New Orleans is the most likely place for Burr to stir up trouble among the westerners and the Spanish. He could raise an army in no time. Once a man like that has an army—ostensibly to fight the Spanish—what's to stop Burr from establishing his own nation? If that's true, it is treason, Adam. So our first assignment is to find out as much as we can before the situation gets out of control."

Lucien was looking out the window again when a darting movement caught his eye. Walking over to the window, he saw Samantha Thornton running toward the stables, trying to tuck her long, thick, red-gold hair under a boy's hat. She was wearing a loose fitting top and wide skirt that rose above her booted legs as she ran. Underneath the skirt, Lucien was sure she was wearing breeches!

"Fraser, what is so funny?"

"I thought you said that your sister never gets up this early. Tell me, Thornton, who is that half-dressed boy/girl out there running toward the stables?"

"Oh, no! I did not think she would engage in this little trick with all the people in our home. Sam loves to ride astride, and whenever she thinks no one will see her, she puts on an old pair of my breeches under her skirt and goes riding. I told you she was different, didn't I?"

They watched her mount the horse without assistance. Then she swung the horse in the direction of the Battery.

"She must have been some hellion growing up," Lucien wondered aloud.

"Worse. But"—Adam tried to draw his attention away from the window—"you were talking about far more serious matters. Treason, for example."

Running his long fingers through his wavy hair, Lucien immediately returned to the main topic. "Look,

25

if we open an office in New Orleans, it would serve us well in a number of ways. New Orleans is the center of the Southwest. It has one of the best ports in the world. We could make a profit buying and selling cargoes while keeping an eye on Aaron Burr and identifying his followers."

"Not to mention the British and French, too," Adam remarked. "Well"—he slapped Lucien's shoulder—"it makes sense. How soon after the wedding do we leave and can I take Meredith with me after my first trip there? She still has no idea of our other activities, and there is no reason for her to know . . . not yet. Besides, perhaps I will enjoy the domestic side of married life so much, I shall want to retire from spying." He shrugged. "A situation I suspect you will never encounter."

"I like my freedom too much. I will leave married life to romantics like you. But, I can assure you, Adam, if you keep traveling, my sister will insist on joining you just to find out what you do on all those lonely nights." He smiled even while trying to stifle a yawn.

"Enough, Fraser. You'd better disappear before my sister returns. Believe me, if I were still living here, Sam would have found out about everything within two weeks. And probably would have wanted to join in, too," he laughed. "She adores Jefferson, you know. He has always treated her as his darling niece. Even spoils her like the rest of us."

A loud bang at the servant's entrance broke the conversation and, with a silent nod and a handshake, the partners went to their rooms.

He never would have seen her if he hadn't gone back

to the library for his jacket.

Samantha was quickly sneaking into the house, her hair partially tucked under her hat.

"Did you have a nice ride, Miss Thornton?" His voice was barely audible, yet she was startled by it.

"Oh, you surprised me," was all she could manage to reply. As she lifted her head up, she remembered something and quickly removed her hat.

The sight of her rich coppery tresses slowly settling around her shoulders and down her back fired his passions. He wanted to be the one to loosen her hair, to arrange it about her body, along the sides of her soft, slender neck, down her shoulders and lower, to her firm breasts. He wanted to gently stroke her nipples, awakening them to the arousal he was now feeling and trying to hide with his jacket.

"Late night, Mr. Fraser? I can smell the brandy from here. You do look a little unkempt. Or did you have to dress in a hurry? Who was she, I wonder," she taunted. "There were so many women paying attention to you last night."

"Jealous, Miss Thornton? Aren't you a bit disappointed that I did not choose you?" His blue eyes remained focused on the outline of her breasts.

Before she had a chance to reply, loud voices emerged from the bedrooms above, obviously heading toward the staircase.

"I cannot let anyone see me like this." She panicked. Seconds later she darted into the music room, unaware that Lucien was right behind her.

"Why are you following me? Go away."

"If I do, I assure you I will not be alone," he replied, reaching for her hand.

27

But she turned her body at the same moment and found herself securely wrapped in his strong arms. Anger blazing now, she twisted in his embrace. "Let me go or I'll . . ."

"What? Scream and bring your friends into this room? I wonder what they would think of you and me hiding in this room at such an early hour."

He felt her body relax, but her mouth was firmly set and those green eyes revealed what she really thought of him.

Impulsively, Lucien's mouth lowered to her temple. He wanted to inhale the fragrance of her hair, to touch her in the way he previously imagined he would.

"I want to kiss you, Samantha."

It was a command she did not want to refuse. Lucien's hands pushed her hair away from her shoulders and she felt a sensation like petals being applied to her skin. It was a soft caress. Not the kind of roughness she expected from him.

When she lifted her eyes to his, they both became unaware of the voices just outside the music room door.

"I want to kiss you," he said again with a greater sense of urgency. His lips searched for her neck. She felt his breath as his mouth found hers.

She lost all will to refuse Lucien. When his lips tenderly claimed hers, Samantha knew she could never compare him with anyone else. Everything about Lucien Fraser was strong and so very masculine. Yet his gentle touch aroused her as no other had before.

As he explored her mouth with his tongue, his fingers made a pathway up and down her arms. She did not know when her arms had wound about his neck, or when her fingers had begun playing with his dark hair.

The deep kiss did not stop. As her body warmed to his touch, Samantha knew she wanted more. His hand slid up her loose shirt, slowly stroking her soft skin, moving inexorably toward her breast. The warmth of excitement made her feel as if every nerve ending was exposed.

"You are so ripe, so lovely," he murmured. "I want you, Samantha."

As he eased her toward the satin sofa, she suddenly regained her sanity.

"No, not like this. Not here."

But Lucien pretended not to hear her. Once more, his mouth captured hers while his hands continued an irresistible stroking.

There was no way of knowing whether Samantha would have let him continue, for her father's booming voice at the foot of the bottom stair jolted Lucien upright.

Looking at the door and then at her desirable body, he sighed, "How I wish we were aboard my ship. I could have you all to myself for hours. But"—he gently pushed her flushed face away from his—"not this time. Perhaps when you are not wearing breeches."

How could she have let him touch her? How humiliating that he could so easily control his emotions while she could not. Samantha irrationally reasoned that she must have been suffering hallucinations.

His smile revealed a partial triumph. Unfortunately, Lucien forgot that she was still wearing her riding boots. Her heel came down on his foot hard enough to make him want to put her over his knee and spank her.

"Stepping on a man's toes seems to be a favorite device of yours."

Slowly backing out of his once-hypnotic embrace, she snapped, "Keep away from me, Lucien Fraser. I will try to remember that my brother respects you a great deal. I, however, do not." She pushed her tangled hair off her face and looked at his bemused smile. "I hope I never see you again."

"That might be difficult, my dear. I assume you will be coming to my home in Newport for your brother's wedding."

She did not answer. Smoothing her skirt, she opened the door, regally turned her back to him, and walked up the stairs to her bedroom, unseen by anyone.

Lucien would have laughed if his foot hadn't throbbed so much.

They did not see each other after that morning.

Lucien remained in Charleston a few more days before taking his sleek, four-masted schooner back to Newport, Rhode Island, and his home, Kingscote.

Anxious now to be home, Lucien wondered how frantic his mother and Meredith must be over the wedding arrangements. The wedding was to be in four weeks—October 15th. He had many business matters to settle and plans to make before assuming his new assignment.

Standing at the rail of the schooner, Lucien stared at the calm sea. The gulls overhead indicated they would be docking by early morning. Running his hand through his wavy, black hair, his thoughts drifted back to an early southern morning and the feel of soft skin against his calloused palm. How well she fit against him when he pulled her into his arms and kissed her ripe lips. And then he remembered those angry green eyes flashing at him, and Lucien laughed aloud.

"Why am I thinking about that child-woman? I simply need a woman," he decided. Soon he would see Caroline . . . Ah, yes, he thought, Caroline Prescott. She would cure what was ailing him.

"Captain Fraser?" The sailor's voice was hesitant. "The first mate wants to know if you can see him now."

"Yes. Tell Mr. Cole to join me in my cabin." Lucien straightened his tall, muscular body and went below to finish the ship's log.

Chapter Three

In the next few weeks Lucien was very busy catching up on business and social engagements while trying to avoid his mother's last minute wedding arrangements. According to her, Meredith's and Adam's wedding was going to be the event of the Newport fall season.

One morning at Kingscote, as Lucien stood by the sideboard filling his plate with eggs, bacon, and freshly baked blueberry muffins, Elizabeth Fraser charged into the dining room. Her usual energy always overwhelmed him. Elizabeth's dark brown hair was neatly pulled back in a bun. Her dress, made of the finest wool, was his most recent gift to her from the continent.

"Lucien, my dear. This is all so exciting. I am thoroughly enjoying every moment. The wedding will surely be a success and knowing that Meredith and Adam plan on living here at Kingscote makes me look forward to the future with anticipation."

Lucien was certainly tired of this talk but was secretly pleased to see his mother so animated. Ever since his father's sudden accidental death some years ago Lucien had been worried about his mother.

"Are you still working on these plans, Mother?" came a voice from the other side of the dining room. Meredith casually walked toward her brother. Superficially, the two younger Frasers, although ten years apart, looked very much alike. They both had dark black hair and blue eyes. At twenty, Meredith was a strikingly tall and lovely young woman. Meredith's features were much softer than her brother's. Her eyes were a less intense blue, the oval face fuller, the lips rounder. Lucien's face was often a study of contours and moods. His blue eyes were a barometer of his temperament. His finely chiseled nose and high cheekbones gave him an aristocratic air.

"Lucien, Mother is truly amazing. The wedding plans are in order, the feast all set, the housing arrangements for our distinguished guests settled. There still is one minor problem, however . . ."

Lucien became alert, knowing his sister and mother long enough to surmise that he was about to be cajoled into doing something.

"Get to the point, Meredith."

"Well, you know there are quite a few pre-wedding festivities. Mother and I do not think it proper for Samantha to attend these parties without an escort. . . ."

"Oh no, Mer, I adore you, would do almost anything for you, but I cannot escort her. You have not met her. I have. It was not a friendly meeting. How can you expect me to squire her around when I know we will argue?"

"I am afraid, Lucien, you have little choice,"

interrupted Elizabeth. "Be a dear, won't you? I do not want Samantha to cause any more gossip than necessary."

"I promised Caroline Prescott that I would be her escort. How can I get out of that delicate situation?"

Meredith knew how difficult Caroline could be, particularly when she had her claws showing. Caroline wanted to marry her brother, conniving to catch him whenever the opportunity presented itself. Meredith was positive that Lucien had never taken any relationship with a woman seriously. But he had led her on and she was sure that Caroline had shared his bed more than once. The thought brought a faint blush to her face.

"Lucien, if I promise to find another escort for Caroline—perhaps one of Adam's friends—would you reconsider? Caroline would love to try to make you jealous with a southern gentleman."

He thought that perhaps the evenings might be amusing, if nothing else. It was bad enough to be near Caroline when she was in one of her snits, but to have both Samantha Thornton and Caroline in the same room could provide much entertainment, he concluded. Then he remembered the feel of Samantha's smooth skin and the lavender-fresh scent of her copper hair.

"Lucien . . . please?"

"Oh, all right," he sighed. "I don't know if I can get through one evening, let alone several. However, if this wedding is going to be smooth, I cannot be a fly in the ointment."

At that magnanimous gesture, Meredith walked over to hug her big brother. "You really do have a soft spot—more than one. But I promise never to reveal your more human side to any of those young ladies who would do anything to get you to notice them."

The Frasers had begun to enjoy a leisurely breakfast, when the butler softly knocked. "Madam, a coach is coming up Breton Drive, and a rider has come to announce the arrival of the Thorntons."

Lucien knew it was too late to escape. I'll see them now and get it over with until the next social event, he decided. Meredith excused herself to change into a more appropriate day dress, while Lucien went into his study to retrieve some papers for Adam, leaving Elizabeth Fraser to welcome the future in-laws.

Adam Thornton was first to jump from the carriage, and he ran into the house, anxious to see his fiancée. He walked right up to Elizabeth, kissed her hand, and smiled. "It's good to see you again, Elizabeth," he said warmly, but his eyes were searching for someone else.

"She decided to change, Adam. Be patient. In the meantime you can present your family to me," Elizabeth instructed.

Robert Thornton soon appeared in the doorway, looking a bit tired but not unaware of the impressive surroundings.

"Madam, I am most honored to meet you," he said after Adam's introduction. "Your son is a shrewd businessman and has shown himself to be a true friend to Adam." He bowed and took Elizabeth's hand. "If your daughter looks anything like you . . . well, I know if my wife were still alive, she would be as proud as I am."

Lucien walked from the study just as Samantha came into the house. Their eyes briefly locked, and

Samantha turned away, wondering why she felt a fluttering in her stomach. She concentrated on the opulent surroundings, anxiously waiting to meet Meredith and her mother. She calmly walked toward Mrs. Fraser and curtsied.

"It's a pleasure to meet you, Sam," Elizabeth smiled warmly.

Samantha knew from the soft tone and friendly use of her nickname that at least this Fraser was full of charm and warmth. "I am so happy to be here, Mrs. Fraser. When can I meet Meredith?"

"She'll be down shortly, green eyes," Lucien directed himself toward the beautiful young woman dressed in a fur-trimmed russet cloak. "You look as lovely as when we last met, my dear." He turned his head so that only Samantha could see him wink at her.

He cannot fool me. He takes perverse pleasure in mocking me, Samantha thought. The war between us is only now beginning!

"Oh, hello, Lucien. I am so thrilled to see you still have your most arrogant manner. Why, I knew this day would not be complete without your delightful witticisms," she drawled.

Lucien recognized the affected southern drawl and was about to say more when Meredith appeared, rushing toward Adam and greeting the Thorntons with grace and friendliness. Then, just as swiftly, she ushered Samantha to her room upstairs, so that the two girls would have ample opportunity to get to know each other.

Samantha instantly fell in love with Kingscote.

37

Although the house was a bit larger than her summer home at Thornton Hill, each room was impeccably furnished. Since summer here was not a problem—as it was at the Thornton Hill plantation—most of the rooms on the first floor were decorated in the rich, colorful shades of fall; accented by dark mahogany wood furniture, Persian carpets, and print wall coverings. It was such a comfortable environment that over the next few days Samantha often paraded from room to room. The upstairs bedrooms, sitting rooms, and parlors seemed to have been decorated with a specific personality in mind. Although she had not seen Lucien's rooms, Samantha imagined they were furnished in simple but elegant, masculine taste, not like the frilly lace and bright colors of Meredith's present rooms. Meredith was currently supervising the renovation and redecoration of one of the large guest suites to accommodate her and Adam.

Samantha and Meredith were constantly together. They learned more about each other in two days than most friends learn over five years.

"Sam, I do hope you plan on long visits here at Kingscote. Adam and I will be here for some time. He travels a great deal, you know. In fact, he plans on a business trip to New Orleans in a few months. It would be wonderful if you could stay with me. Adam has told me so much about you that I felt as if I knew you before you arrived."

"I would love to spend more time with you, Meredith. Perhaps you'll come to the plantation, after our trip to the continent. We plan to leave next month. It's a belated gift. I'm afraid since Mother passed away none of us has felt like going anywhere outside of

38

Thornton Hill or Charleston. Maybe you and Adam can join us in France? We will be gone six months."

Meredith considered the proposal, then shook her black hair. "No, Sam, I don't think so. Lucien and Adam are traveling so much of late, always in different directions. I do not think that a trip to the continent is in their plans."

At the mention of Lucien's name, Samantha looked away. She did not want her sister—for surely Meredith was nothing less than that—to see Samantha's dislike for Lucien. They were sitting on Samantha's bed, examining Meredith's trousseau.

"Now, Samantha, you don't really know Lucien. He's not the ogre you think. Certainly Adam must have told you how kind my brother can be. When Adam was so unsure of himself four years ago, it was Lucien who suggested he come to Newport and try his hand at running the company with him. He certainly needed Adam after Father's accident. Now they have a successful partnership. Adam loves his work and he loves me!" She twirled around the room with her white lace chemise held up to her neck.

Samantha laughed, knowing that this was an ideal match. "All right. I shall try to think nice thoughts of that blackguard brother of yours. After all, he will be my escort."

Meredith looked worried. She had only known Samantha for a short time, but from Adam's description of his sister's headstrong personality, Meredith was sure that Samantha would not be agreeable to an arranged escort.

"You did not have to bother. Surely you knew that Clinton Davis accepted the invitation." She did not know why Clinton's name popped into her head.

She realized it would be awkward to see Clinton again. She had heard a few more unpleasant stories about him since their last encounter. But he was Adam's friend, and they were bound to meet again at future social functions. Perhaps with Lucien Fraser as her escort, she would have a buffer against another compromising encounter. Reminding herself that she was obliged to be with Lucien and could not disappoint Adam or Meredith, she announced determinedly, "I will try to enjoy myself. I am only sorry that President Jefferson cannot attend. It would have been the first time all of us were together. Oh, but do not worry, Meredith—everything will be fine."

In the next few days everything did seem fine. Lucien was a perfect gentleman. At the parties they attended together, he danced frequently with Samantha, spoke politely and on occasion frankly about his business plans. He never mentioned their last encounter in Charleston. He complimented her on her choice of dress and brought her champagne punch when she asked. When they danced, he did so at a respectful distance. Samantha knew this couldn't go on much longer. The strain was becoming too much for her. She waited for the other Lucien to emerge. He's going to lull me into complacency and then, when I am unaware, he'll insult me, she reasoned.

Though Samantha could not know, Lucien was feeling a different sort of strain. Too many times he was tempted to pull that curvaceous body closer, feel her warmth against his chest. Once a stray red-gold curl got caught in the lace of Lucien's cuff. He was suddenly indecisive. Did he have to help her loosen the shimmering curl? His desire was to loosen all the curls and watch them cascade down her slender spine. He wanted to cup her lovely face in his hands and watch her innocent eyes fill with desire when he claimed her mouth.

But propriety would not permit such an outlandish display. Samantha would probably scream at him to release her. Out of frustration and a sudden need to escape his home and house guests, Lucien decided to make a late night visit to his ship, and then perhaps to Polly's House. Her girls knew how to satisfy a man.

He went down Thames Street to Coddington Wharf where his ship was docked. There was a lone sailor on board for the night, taking his turn at watch.

"Good evening, Captain Fraser. I surely didn't 'spect to find ye here."

"I just wanted to check on the *Wind*, Sims. I shan't disturb you."

He walked around the schooner. The stars seemed to be more bright against the pitch black heavens.

He decided to map Adam's next trip and went below to his cabin. He pulled out a good bottle of port and settled himself at his desk. So engrossed was he in his task that he neglected to hear the patter of light footsteps coming toward his cabin.

"Lucien, my love," a voice cooed. "When you didn't meet me at the greenhouse as you promised, I decided to come after you."

Lucien recognized the silky voice even before he turned. "Caroline, you should not have followed me here. I must attend to my business." In the last few weeks he realized that he was tiring of her and secretly hoped that she had understood his hints about avoiding long term relationships.

If she sensed the annoyance in his voice, she chose to ignore it. She walked closer to Lucien, letting her velvet cloak slide from her shoulders. Leaning over his shoulder to see what he was doing, she knowingly let her pale blond tresses brush the side of his face. Lucien tried to ignore this gesture but felt the kind of longing that had prompted earlier decisions to visit Polly's House.

When he turned his face toward her blond curls, his lips met hers in an explosion of passion.

"You see, darling, I knew you wanted me here."

His tongue moved deeply into her mouth, triggering the tight hold that she had on his body. He roughly pulled her onto his lap and gave his hands free rein over her secret crevices. Her nipples hardened in response and, as Lucien's hand slid up her long legs, he could feel the moisture of her sexual desire.

Caroline got up, stood by the porthole, and slowly dropped one garment after another to the floor, teasing Lucien with her sensuous movements.

Knowing he should not use her this way, yet finding his urgings uncontrollable, he walked over to her and brusquely threw her on the big, wood-framed bed. He spread her legs, thinking only of satisfying that pulsating need inside his body. She was vibrant with desire. His fingers were moist with her lust when he rubbed her, and she begged, "Take me now . . . please."

Lucien thrust himself inside her as Caroline widened to receive him. He was lost in the heat of her, enraptured by the pleasure she afforded. Caroline felt a sexual zeal that only Lucien could elicit in her. Her legs moved rhythmically to his pulsating movements, and she alternately screamed and sighed while demanding still more of him. Their erotic wrestling led to an exchange of positions which only heightened the ecstasy, and she clawed his back so hard that she almost drew blood. "You are a bitch, Caroline," he whispered. His words merely increased her need for him until a tide of orgasmic release burst with a cry from her lips even as the warmth spread through her body.

Lucien looked down at her, his deep blue eyes eager for satisfaction. "Now it's my turn." He rolled her over and with two more thrusts felt the release he was seeking.

A few minutes later, while they were still resting, Lucien wryly noted, "You're as good as Polly's girls."

Caroline looked at him and smiled. "Why, if they were as good as I, sweetheart, they wouldn't be Polly's girls. When we marry, you can have a steady diet of this bed play."

Lucien laughed, ignoring the latter comment, realizing that he must be wary or be trapped.

While she dozed off, Lucien swiftly dressed. He left the cabin and arranged for her carriage, which was waiting in the darkened street, to take her home.

Furious that he would so easily dismiss her, she stormed from the cabin, and Lucien sat back down at his desk as if he had never been interrupted.

Chapter Four

Samantha awoke early the morning of the wedding, wanting to have the opportunity to walk alone in the gardens. The air was crisp but not cold, and the leaves on the surrounding trees had turned to the glorious shades of red, yellow, and orange which contrasted sharply with the deep blue sky. She felt the crunching of the leaves beneath her feet, picked up an orange leaf, and twirled it in her hands. Samantha gloried in this beautiful New England day and wondered who—if she ever married—her husband would be.

As she was about to take the sandy path that led toward the beach, Samantha stopped abruptly. She was not alone. The wind rustled the high reeds but she could see that they were being parted by a stronger force. Thinking it was foolish to run, Samantha stood still and waited.

His tall, lean shape emerged from the high reeds. Hands dug deeply into the pockets of his dark brown leather breeches, with a plain white lawn shirt opened at the neck, head bowed as if he were contemplating the path before him, Lucien was completely oblivious to her until he noticed the tips of her riding boots.

"Good morning, Samantha. I am surprised to see you up so early, especially today." His tone of voice confirmed a controlled calmness that she knew she could never feel if their situations were reversed.

"Didn't I frighten you?"

"It would take a lot more than that to frighten me." He smiled, not at all aware that she would consider this statement further proof of his arrogance. "But I confess that I detected your lavender scent a few feet back."

They fell into step, Lucien leading her toward the beach. "Do you often walk here alone?" she asked.

"Every morning. I try to plan what must be done for the day. But of course things change once I arrive at the shipyard."

Samantha lifted her bright green eyes to the sky. "Such a lovely day for a wedding," she sighed. Without thinking, she added, "I wonder what my wedding day will be like."

If she saw him stiffen, she did not say so. Lucien looked into her wind-kissed face and held in the caustic comment he was about to make. Obviously she had not meant to speak aloud.

"I am sure your day will be lovely too, green eyes," his voice softened.

"Oh, I hope so," she said dreamily, and again Lucien was reminded of how innocent she really was.

"Every man will be fighting just to dance with you this evening."

Bending down to pick up a broken seashell, she said, "I don't know. Oftentimes I am as tall as they are. I must not seem very graceful to them." The rough-edged shell was tossed into the surf.

Lucien could not believe that Samantha could ever lack confidence, but her downcast eyes and lost expression was not of a woman seeking compliments.

"Sweetheart," he chuckled, bending down with her, "you underestimate your charms." And your beauty, he thought. He found a deep pink shell and handed it to her, thankful that he found some distraction. For she was so close, so vulnerable, and Lucien fought the urge to take her into the protective and comforting circle of his arms.

Samantha too fought the same urge and succeeded for the moment. She stood up and ran along the water's edge. Lucien laughed and caught up with her.

"I love the sea, Lucien." Her smile seemed to be brighter than before.

"So do I, more than most. I often feel most relaxed aboard the *Newport Wind*."

"Is that why you travel so much?"

"No." His answer was curt and Samantha noticed a hard glint in his eyes. The carefree, unguarded moment was lost along with the pink shell that dropped into the sand. "Come." He took her elbow, changing the subject. "We should turn back now."

Their conversation was forgotten during the last-minute rush to Trinity Church. But sometime during the wedding ceremony, Samantha looked up from her bouquet of daffodils and met Lucien's thoughtful gaze. Was he remembering her wistful words from their early morning conversation? No, she decided, dismissing the notion. Lucien Fraser was certainly not a sentimental man.

There was some time between the ceremony and the

47

evening reception. Adam and Meredith were safely ensconced in their new room, so Samantha decided to take a short nap before her bath. She stretched out on the long, burgundy velvet chaise and thought about how truly happy she was for her brother and Meredith. The female Frasers were so warm, sensitive, and such good company. Elizabeth Fraser invited confidences with her calm and sympathetic nature. Samantha missed a motherly presence and found that her discussions with Elizabeth filled a void. I shall enjoy future visits at Kingscote, she mused and promptly fell asleep.

She awoke later than she had planned and now Samantha and her maid were quickly finishing last-minute touches to her dress and hair. Her dress for the evening reception—an embroidered plum crepe with satin and pearl trimming—was carefully placed on the bed. She knew the dress was a perfect fit and would surely enhance her best features. It was in the latest style from Napoleon's Paris, called the "Empire."

The Thorntons and Frasers were already downstairs on the receiving line. It was coincidental that as Lucien's eyes looked upward, Samantha was descending the stairs.

Her gown clung seductively to her body and the high neck, short sleeves, and gathered bodice revealed Samantha's well-developed figure. The full skirt, looking as if it were draped around a statue, made more than one pair of eyes look upward as she gracefully came down the stairs. Her red-gold hair was piled on her head with small ringlets surrounding her face.

Lucien was enraptured. The fiery colt striving to become a woman had unquestionably achieved her goal. She was a young lady, but her ripe body revealed something else.

Lucien and Clinton Davis, each on a different side of the room, walked over to greet her. Lucien reached her first. Grasping her hand and raising it to his lips, he said softly, "My, what a vision you are. You will save a few dances for your escort."

Not caring for his bold assumption, she declared, "Dear. Mr. Fraser, I appreciate your sentiments, but you're my escort, not my master."

Clinton reached for her hand as Lucien loosened his grip. Samantha spitefully displayed a warm, affectionate smile for Clinton—a smile that was directed at Clinton but designed to disarm Lucien.

"My darling Samantha, you look radiant this evening, like the moon in a southern sky."

Before Samantha could respond, Lucien broke in. "I am sure you will excuse us, sir, uh . . . Mr. Davis, isn't it? Samantha and I must appear on the receiving line." He took Samantha by the elbow and led her away.

"Why are you so arrogant? How dare you be so rude to Clinton?" she hissed.

A wry smile crossed Lucien's lips. "Your looks are deceiving, dear Samantha. It's apparent you have not changed very much. In case you could not smell the fumes, your 'beau' has not been without a glassful of whiskey all evening."

This unexpected sarcastic exchange set the tone for Lucien and Samantha for the rest of the evening and broke their undeclared peace treaty. Samantha was intent to prove to Lucien that she was indeed a full grown woman with more than one admirer. She treated the young men like her colorful hair ribbons—

to be discarded after being used. But her attention kept returning to the other side of the ballroom, where Lucien was deeply engaged in conversation.

She put her fan closer to her face as she observed him. He was resplendent in finely tailored buff trousers, dark blue velvet waistcoat and jacket. His fine white linen shirt was trimmed with flat pleating down the front. A silk cravat wrapped over his neckcloth and was knotted once.

Her opinion of Lucien was influenced by Caroline Prescott, who stood too closely by Lucien's side, as if he were the magnet and she the metal. Caroline was never too far behind him, Samantha thought. Her pale blond features and alabaster skin contrasted sharply with Lucien's dark and suntanned features. Remembering their first meeting, Samantha knew she had already made an enemy out of Caroline.

Apparently, as soon as Caroline had discovered who the Fraser's houseguests were, she lost no time in paying Meredith a visit. Thanks to Meredith's warning, Samantha was prepared to face Miss Prescott. Caroline had not been so lucky. When both Samantha and Meredith greeted Caroline in the sewing room, Caroline's mouth opened in surprise. Her blue eyes turned frosty as she looked at Samantha and said, "Oh, so you're the little girl Lucien mentioned. I must say that Lucien was not talkative at the time—he is such a demanding lover. Yet he was right. You are such a pretty little girl."

Samantha looked directly at her and smiled, then replied, "Yes, I quite agree with you, Caroline, about Lucien's descriptions. Why, you are much older than Lucien suggested. But I am sure you have been around long enough to know how men are poor judges of a lady's character. Oh, I almost forgot, I must find my brother. We have an appointment. Please excuse me, Meredith and Caroline."

As Samantha turned to leave, she called over her shoulder, "It was a real pleasure meeting you, Caroline. I do hope we have a chance to chat again," and left the room, leaving Meredith to contend with a flushed and flabbergasted Caroline.

Thereafter, Caroline and Samantha had tried to avoid one another, but if they were together—which usually meant Lucien was nearby—the sparks flew between them in their looks and their words.

Samantha was so absorbed with her past encounter with Caroline, that she did not see Clinton Davis's approach.

"Dearest, I have been looking for you. I believe you promised me this waltz." He did not appear to be too steady on his feet and she could distinctly smell the liquor on his breath.

Samantha looked at her dance card, hoping he was wrong. She apologized. "I am sorry, Clinton. I have been so involved with the preparations that I forgot. Please forgive me."

As they danced, she looked up at him and realized that Clinton's light blond features were a perfect match for Caroline's. She started to laugh. When Clinton pressed her for the source of her mirth, Samantha tried to make some excuse for her rude behavior.

"Samantha, I think that the heat in this room and anxiety over the preparations are wearing you down. Why don't we take a walk in the gardens? The cool night air should revive you."

51

Not thinking because she was still trying to make amends for her behavior, Samantha accepted and allowed herself to be led outside.

Samantha did not notice Clinton's triumphant smile or the look on one man's face across the room.

That flirt hasn't learned her lesson yet, Lucien thought angrily. As her escort, he probably should do something. Yet as Lucien was about to excuse himself, Caroline, observing the source of his interest, pouted. "Darling, this is our dance. Please dance with me now?"

He was outmaneuvered. He had to dance with Caroline, but he would quickly excuse himself afterward and go after Samantha.

Samantha knew Clinton would try to kiss her again. Remembering the last incident with Clinton in Charleston, she decided to stop it quickly.

"Clinton, I am walking with you unchaperoned because I know you are a gentleman. I have forgotten our last little argument . . ."

"I, however, have not. I have always found you irresistible. I simply must have you." He reached for her and pulled her body to his in a strong embrace. When his mouth came down on hers, Samantha became angry and pushed him away.

"Clinton Davis! How could you do this to me? Haven't we been through this before?"

He did not hear her protestations. He only knew he had to have her and was tired of waiting for her to notice him. He reached for her again and the abrupt movement caused a ripping sound.

"Please, Clinton. Stop pawing me! You are tearing my dress!"

"I don't care, Sam. I want to rip that clinging material off you, to see and kiss everything that is underneath. Nothing has been good for me since you rejected me. I need you to make me lucky again."

"I shall have to scream, Clinton, and that will embarrass us both." She started to back away, frightened by his odd statement, but Clinton still had a firm grip on her arm.

"Oh no, my darling, I cannot let you scream." He put his free hand over her mouth as he again pulled her body closer to him and led her further away from the house. "I intend to have you tonight. Tomorrow I will announce our betrothal. But tonight I have my carriage waiting around the side of the house and—ouch, Samantha, do not fight me."

"Oh, but I will fight you." She bit his hand and tried to kick him, but her dress impeded her. "Clinton, you must be reasonable. This is absurd. You cannot . . ." But Clinton was beyond reasoning as he brought his palm hard across her cheek to stop her from speaking. He was about to hit her again when his raised arm was caught by a stronger one.

"Is this how you persuade women, Davis?" Lucien was furious with both Clinton and Samantha. His voice, however, was cold and impersonal. Pulling a dazed Samantha toward him, he continued, "This is my home, Mr. Davis. I shall not permit this behavior. I want you to leave it at once. Since this is a happy occasion, I shall not ruin my sister's wedding reception by shedding your blood. I never want to see you near my home or find you alone with Samantha again. If an incident like this were to occur, I would not wait for a duel to find an excuse to kill you. Is that clear?"

Clinton looked at Lucien with such hatred that he did not see Samantha or the tears silently running down her bruised face. He bowed and quickly went to the carriage awaiting him.

One look at Samantha's face caused Lucien's anger to disappear temporarily. He pulled out his biege silk handkerchief and gently touched her face.

"Samantha, why won't you learn? You are not a child any more. You cannot lead a man on because you want to learn how to kiss. Be thankful you are only losing tears."

"Damn you, Lucien! Why did it have to be you who found us? I know how to kiss and I know how to handle men." He was about to laugh and raised the handkerchief again to wipe her face when she slapped his arm away.

"I am crying because Clinton's slap caused my eyes to tear. Anyway, I am more angry with myself for letting this matter get out of control. He promised he would act like a gentleman and I believed him."

"You little fool. Don't you know that your body, your smile, and the seductive way you move makes a man forget he's a gentleman? You are a tease, little lady. A man likes to taste what is offered." He was angry again and convinced she still needed to learn a lesson. He took her face in both his hands and bent over to prove to her how easy it could be. "Don't you see yet? You can't invite a man to engage in private conversation and assume you are not leading him on." Her clear, bright eyes widened in anticipation and he forgot himself. He gently placed his mouth on hers and kissed her with all the longing he had hidden these last few weeks of being near her. He kissed her bruised cheek and touched her hair, surprised by his own gentleness.

Samantha too was shocked. She was momentarily lost, but when she opened her eyes and found his arrogant smile, she snapped, "Why Mr. Fraser, you do not even kiss as well as Clinton. Perhaps you need a few more lessons. I am sure Caroline would be happy to oblige you."

He wanted to strangle her. A muscle in his cheek twitched in anger but again he kept rigid control of his voice as he responded.

"Let us hope the courtiers in the European capitals you visit can teach you something about proper behavior as we in Newport failed to do. I surely hope, my dear, you do not lose your virginity to the first Frenchman who asks you to visit his apartments."

"You can be sure, Mr. Fraser, that if I give my virginity to someone, it will be a person of my own choosing. Which, naturally, leaves you out." Samantha curtsied and, gathering her pride about her, walked toward the house to repair the damage to her dress and cheek. She said aloud to herself, "I can't wait to get away from him. Even Caroline would be better company."

Chapter Five

Samantha strolled toward the rail of the French passenger ship. They had been at sea for a few weeks, yet she still exulted in this ocean voyage. This trip to France was what she truly needed. As far as she was concerned, she had to be away from Newport and Charleston—away from Lucien. Whenever she was near him she lost control of her emotions. One moment she wanted to scratch his handsome face, the next to feel the security of his strong arms around her.

"Oh, good riddance, Mr. Fraser," she called to the swirling dark green waves of the sea. "I will consider your last words and enjoy myself completely. Who knows? I might marry a marquis."

The thought made her laugh. But then, why not? She could do whatever she wished. "But damn you, Lucien," she fumed, "why do you always make me so angry?" Every time he had stared at her she could sense his silent mockery. "Well, it does not matter now," she thought. "For the next six months I refuse to think about you or Newport at all."

She walked to the other side of the deck, nodding at her fellow passengers. Her father was standing near the quarterdeck, deep in conversation with an elderly gentleman.

A brisk, chilly wind swirled across the deck, causing some of the female passengers to wrap their shawls tightly about their shoulders. But Samantha enjoyed the feel of the breeze upon her face and body. Her peacock blue, long-sleeved muslin gown kept her warm against the sea air. It was too bad she couldn't have worn her breeches underneath, she thought. Ordinarily the wide blue skirt hid her curves, but the wind molded the material to her body.

Robert Thornton noticed the longing gazes of the sailors she passed and vowed to keep her within his sight. Robert suspected that his charming daughter underestimated her effect on men.

"Father, I cannot wait to see Paris." Her voice held a trace of the excitement she felt for their new adventure.

"Come"—he excused himself to the other gentleman—"let's sit here and I will tell you more about the Emperor Napoleon and Paris."

They were not sitting for more than ten minutes when a young man approached them.

"I hope I may join you, sir, Miss Thornton." His voice was pleasant and friendly.

"David, Father was just about to tell me about Napoleon."

"I am sure you know much more, Mr. Parker. I must congratulate you on your promotion. After all, you have a very important government position now."

The tall, thin man smiled. This was a major assignment for him. As the new American attaché to

France, Mr. Madison wanted David Parker to complete the negotiations for the Louisiana Purchase.

David sat down across from Samantha, next to Robert. "This will certainly be an exciting time to be in France. Napoleon has many grand visions."

"The British do not care for his visions," Samantha stated, aware from her father's conversations with Adam that war between the two countries has always been a certainty. She had grown up with politics, her father never having discouraged her interest. As a young girl she often visited then Secretary of State Thomas Jefferson who included Samantha in his political conversations with the rest of the family.

David was not used to such a straightforward young woman. Samantha was a very intelligent and quick-witted lady, and David took great pleasure in their conversations, particularly about literature. Yesterday Samantha had returned a book she borrowed—Adam Smith's *Wealth of Nations*—which led to a two-hour, heated exchange about moral philosophy. He found Samantha's companionship as comfortable as he knew his friendship was to her. Lately, however, he had to admit that his feelings for her were more than platonic.

Another strong breeze loosened the matching blue shawl that Samantha wore over her hair, and David noticed a few red-gold curls uncooperatively flying across her face. Her soft laughter made him forget what he was about to say.

"David, Father and I would like to know what you think of the Louisiana Purchase." Her eyes reminded him of dewy grass in the early morning.

"Well"—he nervously pulled his unpowdered brown queue—"I think it is one of the greatest opportunities

59

our country has had. Do you realize how much land is involved?"

As he explained the political significance of the Purchase, Samantha could not help but think of her brother who was planning to leave for New Orleans to start another office. Why wasn't Lucien going? she grimly wondered. Adam and Meredith had spent less than two months together. It did not seem fair, and Samantha found one more reason to dislike Lucien Fraser.

". . . fascinated by this man Aaron Burr, aren't you, Samantha?" Her father's voice interrupted her private ruminations.

"I am sorry. I was just thinking about Adam."

"He's probably in New Orleans by now," Robert said. "He will be in the heart of the new land."

"What were you saying about Aaron Burr?" She was aware that President Jefferson had never liked Burr, and she did not understand what the former vice president had to do with the Louisiana Purchase and asked David about that.

"Oh, but Burr seems to be very interested in the new land, too. So much so that it has been rumored that he intends to travel to the area."

"Why?" she asked, removing the shawl completely from her head. Samantha did not notice the appreciative gleam in David's eyes, but her father did and smiled before he excused himself to join the captain for a game of chess.

David was explaining much of the political history of the Southwest when Samantha suddenly remembered something Adam had said. "David, Aaron Burr has always believed that the Spanish should be out of the Americas completely. So"—she smiled, pleased with her memory—"that is why Mr. Burr is going to the territory."

"Precisely. Aaron Burr is going to conduct his own investigation of the area. He has, according to our office, been in touch with General James Wilkinson, one of the governors in that area and Commander of the United States Army." David grimaced as he mentioned Wilkinson's name. "I met him once and I did not like him. Nor do I think he can be trusted. I've heard he's a scoundrel. Yet, it was President Jefferson who appointed him. The General knows the West, but . . ."

"You still do not trust him?"

"No." Again he tugged at his hair. "I think there is undiluted evil in that man. And from what we can gather, Burr and Wilkinson may be planning something together. We have a few 'agents' or 'contacts,' people who actually work for the Secretary of State, gathering information about unusual political activities."

"I wonder," Samantha mused, rapidly piecing together some of her brother's more recent statements and actions, "if Adam is involved as one of these spies."

"Samantha"—David's voice rose—"I can assure you that these people are not spies and believe me, no matter what they get involved in, there is bound to be some danger to it. I do not even know who they are. I expect to be contacted by someone while in Paris."

"But why Paris, David?"

"Because we believe Mr. Burr has contacted the French ministers for reasons that could only be defined as treason."

*　　　*　　　*

After an uneventful arrival in Paris, the Thorntons found themselves caught up in a world of social gaiety. Even Robert, still grieving over his wife's death, had begun to enjoy himself again. He renewed old acquaintances and with the help of his hosts made some new ones.

Jean and Corinne Debache were so delighted that their cousins were coming for a six-month stay that they took special care to arrange for each of the Thorntons to be comfortable in Parisian society. When Robert suggested that he and Samantha rent a home near their cousins, Jean became adamant about having them stay with his family. His son Philippe was only a few years older than Samantha and was delighted to be her escort. He insisted that the Thorntons were not displacing anyone and were most welcome in their large home. And large it was. Each person had a private bedroom, their servants and staff were easily accommodated in the servant's wing, and the dining and entertainment rooms could rival any southern townhouse. Of course there was the Debache's summer residence in Saint Cloud which was not far from the Emperor's estate. The Debaches were thriving under Emperor Napoleon's reign, but Jean, being a clever businessman, knew that all this was temporary.

Early one morning before the ladies joined them for breakfast, Jean confessed his concerns to Robert.

"I tell you, Robert, the caprice and disregard for hard work of my fellow citizens cannot go on indefinitely. The French want to forget the time of the Terror and Napoleon gives us a new sense of pride in ourselves. The French have gone through so much in the last twenty years, and the Emperor has given us back our self-esteem. There is a new social class. Paris is being transformed from an old-fashioned, small city to the modern capital of the world. Behind everything there is the hand of Napoleon."

"But Jean," asked Robert, "how many more wars can you fight? How much more can he tax the French?"

"I worry about this, my cousin. We will do what we can. If the Emperor persists in the notion that he can rule the world and demand our financial and moral support for his dreams, there could be another revolution."

The concern in Robert's voice was evident. "Jean, promise me that if anything happens, you will immediately join us in America."

"I have some money safely out of the country . . . Bah!" He waved his hand. "You are probably listening to the words of a man who finds things to fret over. This is a special time in Paris and I am delighted that you and your beautiful Samantha can share it with us."

The conversation ended with the arrival of Samantha and Corinne. Samantha was excited. Corinne was going to take her shopping and arrange for Samantha to have some gowns made. Samantha ran up to her father and hugged him. "I am so thrilled that we are here. Do you think we will meet Napoleon during our stay?"

"I am not sure, *ma petite*," answered Jean. "After the Emperor's coronation, plans were made for his trip to Italy. However, he does try to come to Paris often. After all, he has made the Tuileries his home and the balls the Empress gives are fantastic—beyond description—as you shall soon see."

Adapting to the elite social life of Paris came easily

to Samantha. She attended afternoon teas, cultural events, lavish balls, and evening theater parties.

One night her cousin Philippe took Samantha and his mother to see a new production of Moliere's *The Misanthrope*. It was so enjoyable that Samantha was reluctant to leave their box during the intermission. Philippe and Corinne went for their refreshments. Samantha lifted her opera glasses to view the opulent environment of the theater and its patrons, particularly a well-dressed, very attractive young man in the box below and to the right. At the same time he lifted his glasses. She should have blushed at her own boldness, but strangely, when the man lowered his hand and smiled at her, she smiled back. She was still looking in his direction when he stood up and quickly left the box.

"Sam, here is your champagne. It was so crowded out there that you would not have enjoyed yourself," Corinne announced. "Philippe met a friend of his and will be back shortly."

As she turned toward her aunt, she noticed her cousin and, immediately behind him, the man from the box!

"Samantha, may I introduce my good friend, Stèfan Turreau?"

"*Enchanté, mademoiselle.*" His voice was slightly husky. He reached for her hand and lightly kissed her wrist.

"*Bon soir, Monsieur Turreau.*" Without realizing what she was doing, Samantha quickly studied Stèfan, mentally comparing him to Lucien. He was not as tall as Lucien, but she was suddenly positive that Stèfan's chestnut hair, large, light brown eyes, and broad grin revealed something in his personality that Lucien

64

certainly did not possess: warmth.

Over the next few weeks, Stèfan and Samantha were discussed at many engagements given by the social elite. Because Philippe and Stèfan were good friends, it was not thought unusual to find Stèfan at the Debaches' home. The three of them were often seen around Pais.

"Samantha, you are so different from any woman I have known," he stated. They were walking in the gardens of the Palace of the Luxembourg. The afternoon was unusually warm for early spring, so Samantha unbuttoned the heavy, gold velvet pelisse she was wearing. The unexpectedly sweet scent of the various flowers in the beautifully sculpted gardens made her sneeze a few times.

Wiping her nose on her white silk handkerchief, she laughed. "No, I am not very ladylike either." She remembered her friends taunting her about being tall and awkward.

"That is not true, my pet." Stèfan knew he was falling in love with her. She was different from most of the flirtatious, empty-headed girls he knew. She did flirt, of course, but Samantha was also frank and engaged in conversation easily.

"Samantha, when I come to the United States, I would like to spend time with you." He reached for her ungloved hand. "I intend to ask your father for permission to court you."

Stèfan kissed her forehead and his gentleness made her forget that other dark face with piercing blue eyes that occasionally haunted her dreams. Yes, she concluded, Stèfan would be good to her.

"Well, I have not left Paris yet!" she playfully scolded

him. "My father would like to learn much more about you before we depart."

"Such as?" His light brown eyes twinkled with good humor.

"Well"—her brows creased in thought—"does a gentleman like you, whose father is the newly appointed Ambassador to the United States, enjoy politics?"

"Yes, indeed, *ma petite*. In fact, my father often discussed the possibility of my joining the diplomatic corps. I never thought seriously about it, or much else, until I met you."

As they walked toward the high-hedged gardens, they realized that they had quite innocently found themselves separated from the others. Looking about, Samantha saw quite a few couples embracing in some of the more remote sections of the gardens. Feeling a little embarrassed, Samantha allowed Stèfan to lead her to a marble bench near a small duck pond. The heat from the bright rays of the sun reflected on Samantha's shoulders. Unaware of the effect it would have on Stèfan, Samantha removed her pelisse. At the sight of Samantha's creamy breasts pushing up from the bodice of her green satin and brocade dress, Stèfan felt exhilarated. He had tried to avoid any untoward advance, but the sight of her smooth white skin and beguiling green eyes was more than he could bear.

He reached over and touched her shoulder, more like an explorer of the unknown regions of her body rather than a man filled with desire. His lips followed the path.

"No!" She sat upright, pulling away from him. Her shocked response surprised him. "Please Stèfan. I cannot . . . I mean, this is not right!" Her voice rose in indignation.

"Why, *ma petite*, I had hoped you felt the same way about me as you know I feel about you." His hand caressed her lovely yet innocent face, but her undemonstrative response gave him an unequivocal message that he could not help but understand. "Perhaps I am going too fast for you, no?"

Grateful for his understanding, she nodded, allowing him to kiss her palm. Before they could resume their earlier camaraderie, an anxious Philippe found them, insisting that they be off.

Chapter Six

As their romantic involvement continued to develop, Samantha began to spend some time with the Turreau family. Stèfan's father, Louis, had recently returned from the United States for a short visit with his family, and his stories of America made Samantha homesick. However, after a few more discussions with Monsieur Turreau about America, Samantha became annoyed. Louis Turreau was very critical of American policies, particularly those of Jefferson and Madison. Soon her fierce pride and loyalty were revealed whenever he spoke about America.

One evening at a dinner party the Turreaus gave in the Thornton's honor, Samantha again found herself in the position of defending her dear friend Thomas Jefferson. Fortunately she was not alone, for David Parker was among the small number of dinner guests in the elegant home. By the end of the dinner, she realized that the Americans were squared off against her French cousins and the Turreaus.

"I tell you, Mr. Parker, your Mr. Madison is alienating the French. Emperor Napoleon was most generous with the sale of the Louisiana Territory and yet we still squabble over boundaries and dollars."

"Nonsense!" interrupted a now-exasperated Samantha. "You know as well as we that the Emperor had to sell the land because he could not control the area, and, most importantly, Napoleon dearly needed our money to finance his wars!"

"That is partly true," resumed Louis, only slightly amused by Samantha's anger. "We have always known both our countries share a mutual dislike for the British. The sale of this land which doubles your present size presages great national wealth in the future. That is, as soon as a more realistic president assumes the leadership of your country. Really, my friends"—he gestured with a sweep of his hand—"how can your President continue to ignore the interests of your merchants in the northern states? Why does he continue to favor the farmers? Your daughter-in-law's family is from New England. How do they feel about this?"

"Well," said Robert, "the Frasers are an exception, but I do know from Adam about the political unrest in New England."

"But that was two years ago. Tempers have cooled considerably," added David, ever mindful of his political duty.

"That may be true," remarked Stèfan, aware of Samantha's look of approval as she smiled at David. "But the Emperor would never deliberately alienate any French faction."

"Oh please, Stèfan," bristled Samantha, "you French are too cowardly to speak out against anything Napoleon does. He has you in the palm of his hand." As Samantha gestured with her own palm, her emerald eyes became darker with ire.

Jean, noticing the anger and imminent dispute between Samantha and Stèfan, decided it was time to switch to a safer subject.

"Tell me, Robert, have you heard from Adam?"

"Yes, in fact one of Fraser's ships docked yesterday and brought a packet of mail from home. It seems, my friends, that I am about to become a grandfather in a few months."

Samantha's expression immediately softened at her father's mention of Meredith's pregnancy. She, too, received a letter from Meredith, and her sister-in-law's happiness and love for Adam and their coming family was evident. Meredith was longing for Samantha to stay with her at Kingscote before the baby's arrival. Samantha also detected some sadness, too, because Adam was traveling a great deal between New Orleans, Washington, and Newport, and Meredith's doctor had forbidden her to join her husband.

"Yes, in fact," said Robert, "Samantha and I have decided to leave Paris in a few months so the family can be together in Newport."

Stèfan's stricken look suggested he knew nothing of Samantha's decision.

"I, too, shall return to America soon," said Louis, "for there is much to do, especially with the departure of Aaron Burr from Washington life."

Both Samantha and David looked at one another at this strange reference to Aaron Burr.

"Why would Mr. Burr's departure have anything to do with you, Monsieur?" Robert Thornton was clearly baffled by this too.

Louis's expressionless face revealed very little about

71

the matter, and being the true diplomat, he replied, "Why we French are always interested in you Americans, particularly the remaining true statesmen. Mr. Burr is an excellent statesman and I believe there is still a future for him."

Later on, as the men returned from the library, Samantha cornered David, truly concerned by Turreau's strange comment. "I tell you, David, he knows more about Burr. I wonder if that is why he came home at this time? You know he was not scheduled to come home for another month."

"I know. I received a letter from Mr. Madison today. Something is happening, but whether it has anything to do with Turreau's early arrival I cannot tell. Our American contact will be arriving shortly. Perhaps he will know more."

"Well, I hope we can find out more so we can help this mysterious contact. And I intend to get the information from Stèfan or his father."

"Just remember, Samantha, you are not playing a game, and I would hate to see your relationship with Stèfan adversely affected by this intrigue," David grudgingly added. Since his friendship was what Samantha sought, David wanted to remain a true friend.

"Don't worry, David." Samantha linked her arm through his, as they walked into the parlor to join the others. "I intend to be most discreet."

Stèfan rose to meet Samantha and sat her next to him on the satin couch. She flashed her warmest smile—all anger forgotten now—and Stèfan's heart sang.

"Adam was impressed with New Orleans," her father was saying to the others. "He found the people most helpful. In fact, Lucien joined him for a few weeks before he went off on a new shipping adventure."

Samantha's attention quickly perked up at the mention of Lucien's name. Meredith's letter had said very little about Lucien's activities and Samantha found herself mildly disappointed. I'll bet I know what kind of adventure he's off on, she thought wryly. He's probably chasing after some woman.

"*Mon coeur*, I hope you are not angry with me still," Stèfan interrupted her reverie. His concerned look caused her to smile.

"Oh, Stèfan, let's forget it. I just want to enjoy your company. Perhaps you will come to America sooner than you planned."

"Perhaps I shall, *ma petite*, and I hope you are waiting for me."

The Paris social season seemed to become more frenetic as the spring wore on. The Thorntons were seen at tea parties, early suppers, the theater, and at most of the balls. Naturally Samantha wore an appropriate outfit to each social event. But the constant social pressures were beginning to wear on her, as did Napoleon's insistence on French nationalism. She longed for Charleston and Thornton Hill. Even Newport seemed appealing, for Meredith should be in her fifth month and would surely be lonely without Adam. Still the Thorntons were planning to leave Paris within six weeks and Samantha was as determined as ever to find out why Louis Turreau was in Paris and what, if anything, his appearance had to do with Aaron Burr. She tried, unsuccessfully, to pry the information out of Stèfan; however, his evasive manner only convinced her that he might know something.

She expressed her frustration to David over lunch one day. They were comfortably seated in the garden of a small restaurant near the Tuileries. Her father stopped to chat with some friends, giving Samantha the chance to talk freely to David.

"Samantha, erase that notion from your mind. I believe you. Louis Turreau is up to something, but we have to wait. I do not want to antagonize him. After all, I am still involved in negotiations with the French Ministry. And my contact is due in Paris any day now with an important missive from the President himself!"

"David," she pouted, "I am tired of waiting. I hope to get some information this weekend at the hunt my cousin has planned. We are all going to Saint Cloud. It is sort of a pre-farewell party. When Cousin Corinne asked whom she should invite, I deliberately suggested people who are well connected with Napoleon."

"Samantha, again I warn you to be cautious. Mr. Smith—at least I am told to call him 'Smith'—will know what to do when he arrives. I promise to arrange a meeting between you two when he does settle in."

"David, I intend to have some information for our Mr. Smith *before* his arrival." She smiled smugly. David recognized confidence in her look and secretly hoped she would not get into too much trouble.

In the next few days the Paris weather became very humid and hot. By the time of the hunt, Samantha was more than anxious to leave for their stay in the country.

She was successful in gaining bits of information from Stèfan about Monsieur Turreau's knowledge of Aaron Burr. She started a diary to record the information accurately for David and Mr. Smith.

The Saint Cloud estate was quite lovely and Samantha enjoyed long rides through the grounds as often as she could escape social duties. The long rows of trees and hedges reminded Samantha of her Thornton Hill plantation.

The stone house was large enough to accommodate the many overnight guests who were staying for the party after the hunt. Samantha knew that Corinne Debache had excellent taste, despite jealous gossip about her gaudiness. Although the furniture was made of the finest mahogany, the usual ornate gold trimmings were understated. The *meridienne* sofas in the sitting rooms were upholstered in pale blue satin. Samantha especially liked these sofas, whose ends were of unequal height and were joined by a sloping backrest. Next to the sofa in the music room was a mahogany pianoforte that she took particular delight in. But Samantha was most attracted to the wide, curving bay window at the far end of the room that had a plush, crimson velvet window seat, and it was there she found herself on the morning before the day of the hunt. The window looked out on the front of the house, and one could view approaching carriages without being seen. It was like the large bay window and seat at Kingscote, she realized. But that was in the library. Lucien's library, she remembered and wanted to pinch herself for conjuring up his dark image. Instead she went immediately to find her cousin and promised to join him on an afternoon outing.

It was on this excursion that Samantha discovered an important piece of information. Samantha's horse had stumbled on some rocks, so the pair decided to rest awhile by a nearby brook. They passed the time companionably, and after a delightful picnic lunch Philippe announced that regrettably he had to leave her, not wanting to be late for a rendezvous with his latest lover. Samantha was happy to remain alone to enjoy the country air and lush greenery. The area was surrounded by tall trees which made it impossible for approaching riders to see her. She was about to mount her horse when she heard the loud voices of approaching riders. One voice clearly belonged to Louis Turreau and the other, Samantha discovered, belonged to a French nobleman.

"Louis, what do you think the English will do about Aaron Burr's request for money?"

"I think, *mon ami*, that they will not be too hasty. How do they know if Mr. Burr can organize an army in a short time, or if he can truly establish a nation in the Louisiana Territory?"

At the mention of the words "establish a nation" Samantha almost choked.

"No, *mon ami*, the English will not support him. After all, they are being asked to finance a large military expedition against the United States and the Spanish. Nevertheless, President Jefferson would be most unhappy if he knew what was happening." Turreau laughed.

Samantha swiftly put her hand over her mouth to stifle a gasp. If Monsieur Turreau discovered her now, she knew she could never explain her eavesdropping.

"... and so if the English are not interested in lending money to the former vice president for his revolution, perhaps he will contact the French ... if he has not contacted us already, *n'est-ce pas*?"

"Ah"—and Samantha knew Louis Turreau was gesturing with his hand—"we shall soon find out, for I am to speak with the Emperor next week."

The gentlemen laughed as they resumed their outing, leaving an astounded Samantha behind to assimilate the shocking information.

She returned to the house and immediately sought David. He listened intently, then told her what she was hoping to hear.

"Samantha, Mr. Smith will be here tomorrow. I will arrange for you to meet him after the hunt. People will be resting then, so I am sure we can meet quickly and quietly."

Chapter Seven

What transpired the following morning was a ritual which held no meaning for Samantha. She participated in the hunt but was so anxious for the meeting that she left the group to ride at her own faster pace. She rode with such speed that her hair was loosened by the wind and fell around her shoulders.

She realized that she would not have enough time to bathe and change her clothes, so she smoothed down her dark blue velvet riding habit and ran her fingers through the coppery curls, trying unsuccessfully to put them back in place. Mr. Smith is probably an old man anyway, she thought. He will not take any notice of me.

She walked quickly to the library and spotted David by the window. She walked up to him and gave him a light kiss on his cheek.

David was clearly flustered, but Samantha sought to ease his discomfort and laughed. "Oh come now, David, I am sure Mr. Smith, wherever he is, has seen young people kissing." The curtains were drawn, so Samantha could barely make out the back of a gentleman seated near the fireplace.

"Samantha, let me introduce you." David took her

arm and walked her toward the sofa.

Samantha was tired of hearing about the mystery man. She deliberately walked over to the window and pulled the curtains aside to get a good look at him. As she did, she declared, "I am happy, in fact most anxious to meet you, sir."

Mr. Smith walked toward her. Taking note of her stunned look of disbelief, he smiled.

"You!" she stammered. "What are you doing here?"

He laughed and she had to close her eyes, for the image before her of the tanned face, black, wavy hair, and slate blue eyes that had haunted her dreams was more than she could comprehend.

"Samantha dear, you cannot faint. I have come specifically for your information."

Lucien reached out to steady her. He was delighted with her reaction. When David Parker had told him whom he would be meeting, Lucien suppressed his excitement. He obviously had not told David that he and Samantha were well acquainted.

He noted her disheveled appearance, but it did not matter, for she was even more entrancing than he had remembered. Lucien had been made aware of Samantha's activities all these months, for Meredith and Adam had read their letters from the Thorntons aloud.

When President Jefferson had suggested that Lucien time his latest shipping venture with a trip to Paris, Lucien had almost laughed, knowing that old Jefferson was completely unaware of Samantha's involvement. Lucien knew about Parker from Mr. Madison's reports, knew he was a good man and could handle most diplomatic situations. But Samantha's letters to Meredith about her relationships with Parker and this

Stèfan fellow had strongly influenced Lucien's decision to comply with Jefferson's request.

That morning Lucien had received a written report about the Turreaus from his personal contact. Young Turreau sounded pleasant enough, but what Lucien read about a certain amorous encounter in the Palace of the Luxembourg with Samantha made him uncharacteristically angry. *That flirt is meeting him secretly, just as I predicted*, he thought. *And kissing Parker, too!*

Samantha observed the sudden and short-lived flicker of emotion on Lucien's face and recognized his angry scowl. *Damn*, she fumed, *what was he so angry about! I am the one who should be angry. Whoever would have thought that that arrogant brute was working for the American government.*

"So, Mr. Fraser . . . I mean Smith, have you come to check up on me, or are you really interested in Aaron Burr? And how long have you been involved in this whole affair?" she asked accusingly.

"Long enough to know that you should not be," he snapped. Then his voice softened as he walked toward her and held her small hand in both of his. "We will talk about this later, green eyes." His touch caused a curious warmth to spread through her body.

David, also trying to recover from the shock, interrupted.

"Lucien Fraser. My God! I should have known you were my contact! Mr. Madison was so circumspect in this matter I did not think of making further inquiries. Well, I am happy you are here now. Let's get down to business, shall we?"

All three sat down and revealed everything they

knew to be fact or rumored to be fact. Samantha's latest information seemed to put into perspective Lucien's earlier suspicions.

"Well, I intend to pass the information on this afternoon. One of my faster ships is returning to Washington tomorrow." He stood up and paced around the room, serious now, but with complete confidence in his ability to handle the situation.

"Samantha"—he turned to her—"I want you to introduce me to the Turreaus. Parker, can you get me into the French and English embassies? Oh, and Samantha sweet, do you think you could refrain from telling your paramour about my mission?"

She wanted to strike him for that slanderous accusation but thought better of it. Let him think the worst. He does not deserve a civil response, she thought, inwardly fuming. She gave him her most innocent look as she replied, "Yes, Mr. Fraser. I know my Stèfan and I have more interesting things to discuss. And I'll arrange for you to meet him this evening."

Much later that day, Samantha had the time to analyze the entire situation. As she was preparing for the evening's festivities, she tried to think dispassionately of Lucien. He looked tired, as if he had ridden a long way, but his tanned face seemed as rugged as ever. His body—she shivered in spite of her warm, rose-scented bath—was as lean as the last time she had seen him; and she had not been able to help but notice his strong muscles rippling under his tight black breeches and black lawn shirt.

"Oh, why did it have to be him?" she cried aloud. "Why must he appear when Stèfan and I need no more reminders of home and my departure? Damn him. I hate him! Well," she announced to the empty room, "I shall ignore him. He will not mar my happiness."

If Lucien could have seen her determined look, he might have been glad, for at least she was affected by his presence. He stood in one of the many guestrooms thinking of the cool, innocent-looking woman he had greeted in the library that afternoon. "Innocent-looking." He laughed aloud. Lucien was positive she had given herself to that Turreau chap. And maybe, he realized, Turreau was not the first. Hadn't she said she would meet eligible men?

He started to pace the bedroom, his increasing anger matching his desire for a strong drink that might drown his thoughts of her.

Lucien fell asleep for an hour but awoke with a start when he realized that he was late for dinner. His head cleared and he made sure to keep it that way for the rest of the evening. He quickly joined the others and spent a good deal of time with Robert, who was delighted to see him again.

"Robert, I do not have any deadlines to meet. I would be happy to delay my departure for a few more weeks and I insist that you and your daughter sail back with me on the *Newport Wind.*"

"Lucien, I don't really know if I should accept. But I, for one, would certainly prefer having you at the helm of any ship."

"Good." Lucien smiled at Robert. "It's settled then. We will leave in three weeks."

Samantha was watching this exchange from the side

of the room and could not understand the cause of Lucien's satisfied smile. If she had noticed his drinking or that he spoke for a long time with the Turreaus, she made no indication of her interest. She knew Lucien was here to conduct his business and depart quickly, leaving others to make explanations for him.

As if it were mutually agreed in advance, Lucien and Samantha steadfastly appeared to ignore each other all evening. They would, however, glance each other's way when they were sure no one noticed, and only twice did their eyes meet in anger.

Lucien was well aware of the almost intimate way Stèfan held her around the waist, and when they walked outside, he was tempted to follow but sought another drink and a pretty female companion instead.

That night, alone in the gardens with his intoxicated thoughts, the enticing silhouette of Samantha in Stèfan's arms haunted him. He could not help but assume that the ingénue had experienced the physical joys of womanhood and the thought enraged him. Seething with anger and a feeling he refused to recognize as jealousy, Lucien vowed that he would take her that very evening. His face was flushed and unresponsive to the chilly evening air. The long walk did not cool his anger, and he strode purposefully and with stealth into the house, heading directly for Samantha's room.

She was seated at her vanity, brushing her hair and preparing herself for sleep. Lucien stood outside her door, examining the hallway for other guests. When he put his hand on the doorknob, any sense of propriety was finally dismissed. His passion took control of his thoughts.

He opened the door swiftly. Samantha turned and stood up, so shocked by his presence that she could not speak. Before her lips could form a word he was upon her. His face mirrored his desire for her, but she was determined not to succumb. Lucien pinned her arms to her sides and began raining kisses on her neck. She tried to remain impassive, but the faint odor of liquor mingling with the clean lemon scent of him excited her senses. Her body felt warm and limp even as her thoughts remained rigid and angry. She was torn between desire and the preservation of her maidenhood, but her body demanded that she give herself to Lucien, only to Lucien, and her fears vanished in the presence of his passionate assault.

Lucien was a man possessed. Her hair spilling across his face was a firebrand igniting his actions. He could not control himself. He whispered huskily, "I want you. What the young men of Paris have known, I must experience this night. You will be mine now—you will taste the joys of a real man."

Somewhat frightened, Samantha replied, "I am not what you think," but pride kept her from telling the whole truth. Truth, of course, mattered little to Lucien, who was consumed by his desire for her. He reached under her white lawn nightgown and caressed her soft, hot skin. Her nails pressed into his flesh but that only provoked him more. He was intent on making her burn for him.

"Taste my tongue," he said. "It will be the first union of our bodies." As his tongue searched the inner cavern of her mouth, she felt a warm moistness at her core which signaled her sudden sexual awakening. He carried her from the dressing area to her bed so quickly that in her mind's eye it was a tick of the clock. His tongue, in long, sensuous strokes was painting her skin with caresses while his hands stroked her sensitive nipples erect. Lost in the splendid sensations he aroused, Samantha could no longer distinguish between fantasy and reality.

Lucien was blind with desire—a desire Samantha could feel as the hardness of his manhood pressed insistently against her thigh. It made her remaining resistance disappear, and she embraced him eagerly. His impatient hands tore away her nightgown to reveal her naked body, softly illuminated by the one remaining candle near the bed. His own clothes seemed to fall from his muscular torso, and Samantha watched spellbound as his bronzed form hovered above her. He lowered himself slowly using a gentleness which she readily invited. He found her pulsating with need. "Now," he whispered, "you will be mine. You will always be mine." She wanted to cry out, but no sound came from her throat. It was a moment of indescribable anticipation—a moment that utterly surpassed her adolescent fantasies.

He did not penetrate her immediately, but slowly rubbed her secret hollow with his shaft. Her body ached for something more. Through half-closed eyes, she admired the size and strength of his member and her thighs willingly separated, forming a pool of inviting warmth. At that instant he pulled her to him and they were joined as naturally as tree and earth. He felt the resistance of innocence meet his thrust as she tried to stifle a cry of pain.

Suddenly he realized that all his assumptions about her were wrong. For the moment it did not matter because now he knew he wanted her more than ever. With fast, hard movements his manhood taught her to respond to him.

Like a tidal wave responding to the moon's command, Samantha felt the building rapture flood through every cell in her body as pain vanished in an explosion of ecstasy. "Lucien!" she cried. "Lucien!"

The sound of his name on her lips swiftly transported him to a paradise of unparalleled fulfillment, and as their breathing slowed, the delights that both had discovered now translated into the softness of relaxed sharing. He stroked her hair, kissed away a tear from her cheek, and whispered, "Samantha, my sweet, I am sorry for so much."

The stillness of the night was undisturbed. They lay there without speaking, and Samantha's mind was filled with the wonders she had experienced. The only witness to their act was the night, a guardian that utters no words and keeps lovers' secrets.

Chapter Eight

The faint light of dawn eased through the windows. Lucien awoke with a start, realizing he was not in his room, nor was he alone. His arm was wrapped securely around Samantha as she nestled closely in his shoulder. Her arm was draped across his chest and red-gold locks were spread across the pillow and under his arm. Lucien looked down at her peaceful face. She still has the look of an innocent, he thought. Innocent—my God—what have I done! How could I have behaved like such an animal? How could I have betrayed my good friends who trust me? Will *she* ever forgive me?

Samantha unknowingly snuggled even closer and Lucien instinctively put his free arm around her curves. As fiercely as he had felt passion the night before, he now felt a strong sense of protection toward her. The thought of any man touching her infuriated him. He thought a long time and finally decided there was only one thing he could do. He must marry her! He, the bachelor who swore never to marry. He chuckled to himself. Caroline Prescott would be furious and it might be worth it just to see that pretty, pale face frown. Yes, marrying Samantha was the only gentlemanly thing to do and he knew that his mother and Meredith would be thrilled.

Samantha stirred and opened her eyes. The deep green eyes found themselves looking directly into his midnight blue ones. She smiled at first, remembering the passion and the tenderness he had awakened in her. She looked at his tentative smile and felt a tingle not unlike the warm glow of last night.

"Good morning, my sweet. I hope you will forgive me. But I had no idea what a passionate little vixen you are. And"—his look became serious, almost angry— "you did not tell me you were a virgin."

"Lucien," she sighed, "would you have believed me if I had told you? You thought the worst of me, as usual. When will you ever take me seriously?"

"Well, green eyes, I start today. After we are married I have no choice but to take seriously my wife."

She sat up, and the covers slipping down her breasts caused Lucien to catch his breath at her loveliness.

"Your what?" she shrieked, surprised by his arrogant assumption. "What makes you think, Mr. Fraser, that I have *accepted* your proposal? It is a marriage proposal, isn't it?"

"Samantha," he drawled, "I think that under the circumstances, you and I have no choice. I admit my error in judgment and this is the least I can do for you. Now, as long as we are to be man and wife, let's start our honeymoon." He pulled her face toward his and bent his head to capture her lovely lips. What started as a sweet, almost chaste kiss became a warm, demanding one. He was anxious to have her again.

Samantha almost succumbed. But his lack of consideration for her feelings stiffened her resolve. She pulled away from him and snarled, "You arrogant bastard, what makes you think I want to marry you?"

He didn't know whether or not to laugh. "Samantha, I am willing to do the most honorable thing I can do under the circumstances. I dishonored you. I am sorry. And"—he tried to pull her into the protective circle of his arms—"I want to make it up to you. Being married to me will not be so bad. I am sure you will get used to it, perhaps even learn to love me."

At first she thought he meant that. But his mocking smile cast some doubt. "Lucien, you presume too much. Yes, you dishonored me, but I do not love you. I will not marry without love and what about Stèfan?"

His hands dropped to his sides. This was unbelievable—she was turning him down! "You don't love Turreau any more than you love Parker. I know what you want. You are like every other conniving little . . . You only want his title and the glamour of French society." He grabbed her roughly and pulled her to him. "From this moment on, miss, I owe you nothing. I offered you my name, and you have declined. We are even. But before I go, let me remind you of what you will not have with any other man."

Before she could comprehend all that he said, she was underneath him. His large hands roamed over her body in smooth, sensuous strokes. His mouth kissed her lips then traveled downward, sucking her nipples, licking her; and still he traveled further; his hands never stopping their smooth motion. He reached her passionate center which was covered with the same red-gold-colored hair. His hands began stroking her breasts and his tongue sought her sexuality, as first gently then roughly he sucked her tiny bud.

It felt so good. Unknowingly Samantha's hands grabbed his black hair and pulled him down as she groaned. She was swept away by the same passion as the night before. She could not get enough of him, yet she begged him to stop. "Lucien," she groaned, "I cannot stand it. Please!" He ignored her at first, sucking harder and faster. Then he abruptly paused and looked at her. "You want me, don't you, Samantha? Don't you? Do you want me to stop?"

She was lost and knew it. "Please Lucien, don't stop."

He smiled triumphantly and lifted his body onto hers, pushing his member against her parted thighs. "You will never forget me, my sweet." He entered her slowly and deliberately, and when she moaned again he was tempted to let himself go. "No, my sweet Samantha, you can never forget me. Each time your Stèfan enters you, you will remember me and what we shared. You are wanton, my lady, and will never be satisfied with anyone but me. Do you understand?" He plunged deeper and lifted her up to take all of him.

She scratched his back and reached for his buttocks, pushing him deeper into her. "You will miss me too, Lucien." She looked directly into his eyes. When he pumped deeper and faster, she could no longer hold back her release. She closed her eyes and clutched him. Again she cried his name.

He waited for her to finish before he turned her over and pulled her on top of him. He showed her with his hands what he wanted and she quickly complied, feeling hot all over again. He never stopped looking at her. When he thought she could no longer stand it, he rolled her over again and plunged deep as he vowed,

"You will always be mine, Samantha." They both let go at that moment, each feeling a deep sense of regret when it was over.

Samantha must have dozed off, for when she awoke her hand automatically reached out to touch Lucien; but that side of the bed was empty and cold. Then she remembered his words and felt an incredible sense of loss. Her mind and body were playing tricks with her. How could I have let this happen, she chided herself. I would not marry that conceited bastard even if I were with child! The thought made her stomach turn and she fought the desire to cry. Unfortunately, Lucien's masculine scent which still permeated the room and the memory of his lips roaming freely over her body caused the tears to flow. And for an instant, Samantha wondered if she had made the right decision.

Finally, she promised herself to forget the last twelve hours. She quickly pulled the quilt off her body and jumped out of bed. Her nightgown was still where Lucien had discarded if after he had practically torn it off her. She placed it on the bed and almost lost her composure again as she looked at the bloodstained bedsheets. She would simply have to explain to the maid that it was her time of the month. As she ordered a very hot bath, Samantha found herself hoping it would relax her sore muscles and cleanse her every pore of Lucien. With renewed strength Samantha pledged to avoid Lucien Fraser at all costs.

After a lengthy bath Samantha dressed for lunch and found her father waiting for her arrival.

"Samantha, I want to discuss a few last-minute

changes with you." Robert was smiling, much to Samantha's chagrin, for her own mood was not exactly cheerful. He took her arm as they strolled toward the gardens.

"Samantha, I have great news! We are going to leave for home two weeks earlier than I had originally planned. The best part is that we will not sail on a passenger ship." Samantha looked at her father in confusion.

"Father, please talk slowly. I think my brain has not cleared from last night's champagne. Are we going home to Charleston?"

Robert shook his head. "No, dear. We are going directly to Newport, to Kingscote!"

"That's wonderful! But how did you manage passage for us?"

Robert kept smiling as he said, "Samantha, we are going to have a private escort. Lucien graciously offered us passage when we are ready to go!"

"No!" she shouted. "I will not sail home with that . . . with him! Father"—she tried to calm herself—"you do not understand. Lucien and I cannot get along. The thought of being with him, on his ship, at his mercy, for six long weeks makes me sick." She clutched her stomach for added effect. "Father, we might kill one another!" She looked at him imploringly, but in Robert's cheerful state of mind he did not notice the frightened look in her eyes.

Damn! Samantha cursed to herself. How could she avoid him? She was certainly not ready to see him. That rapist might try to attack her again, she decided. Whatever would she do? She could not break her father's heart. He had had heartache enough. And he liked and respected Lucien so; and though she herself hated Lucien, she realized it was not for her to turn others against him. She debated silently back and forth and after seeing her father's warm expression began to relent.

"Father, can I think about this?"

"Of course, dear. However, I have to give Lucien an answer in a couple of days."

She could tell that her father was disappointed by her lack of enthusiasm, and suddenly she felt very selfish and very disheartened.

"Oh, all right. You win. But"—her voice could not hide all of her anger—"I warn you. Keep that fiend away from me." She raised her hand and pointed to the house for emphasis. "I want nothing to do with him." She was ready to stalk off, totally disgusted with herself, but her father restrained her.

"Samantha, maybe things will get better between you. You could try. I will talk to Lucien myself and perhaps he will try, too."

She spun around to face him again. "Don't you dare speak to Lucien on my behalf! I can handle things. In fact, I will tell him myself what I want."

"But Samantha, Lucien's gone! We won't see him again until we are ready to sail."

He did it again, she thought wryly. That man always manages to have the last word. She relented and walked away, leaving a thoroughly perplexed Robert in her wake.

The next three weeks were a blur to Samantha. She and Corinne made all the preparations for the departure. Lucien, probably sensing her distress, stayed away from Samantha. On the two occasions when Lucien came by to meet with Robert and Jean, Samantha was out with Stèfan. Messages were relayed through Lucien's first mate, Roger Cole. Knowing that Cole and Lucien were close friends made Samantha uneasy, because she concluded that Lucien was probably the type of man who bragged about his conquests.

Saying goodbye to Stèfan was harder than Samantha had ever imagined. Now that she had experienced the sexual joys of womanhood, kissing Stèfan had as much appeal as a warm glass of milk before bedtime. Stèfan's touch did not make her tingle the way Lucien's long, tan fingers did. Perhaps, she sighed, I need the time away from Stèfan.

"*Mon coeur*, I shall be devastated when you leave." Stèfan's golden eyes looked so sad as he spoke. "I want you to think of me . . . to think of us." Stèfan held Samantha's cool hand in his warm ones and delicately kissed her palm. "I shall arrange with my father to visit your country within the next few months."

At the mention of Louis Turreau, Samantha perked up a bit. "Stèfan darling, when will your father return to America?"

"He is leaving shortly. But he may first go to Spain for a meeting with the other Bonaparte." He gave her no time to ponder this new bit of information, for he pulled her into a tight embrace. When Stèfan bent his head to touch her warm lips with his, Samantha was eager for his kiss. It was long and tender, but the fire in her blood was not stirred. No, she cursed inwardly, Lucien cannot be right. Through misty eyes, Samantha bade Stèfan goodbye and returned to the Debache home for the last farewells to her cousins.

The day of departure was sunny and warm. The Thorntons were ready at last. Their luggage weighed twice as much as when they arrived. Samantha alone had a new wardrobe fully stocked with the latest in Paris fashions. The silks were the finest, and the heavy velvets and brocades were in the most dazzling colors any American woman would dare to wear. Samantha would wear them and, of course, shock every southern matron.

Roger Cole escorted the family to the schooner. Each person in the entourage was excited, albeit for different reasons. Samantha did not quite know what she felt except nervous. She was very apprehensive about seeing Lucien again and she made up her mind to stay out of his way as much as possible. But she would be polite when they were obliged to be together.

Lucien observed the approach of one of the carriages as he was leaving his cabin. He, too, had mixed feelings about this voyage. Since the *Newport Wind* rarely accommodated passengers, Lucien had to rearrange cabins. The first and second mates would double up so that one cabin would be available for Robert. There was an extra cabin for Samantha.

There would be much more space, he knew, if Samantha "doubled up" with him. But that he dismissed as being preposterous. Now that she had turned him down ... Well, he thought, that was a relief. He no longer owed that termagant a thing. He must have been more than slightly drunk that day to even consider marrying her.

Unknowingly, Lucien was pacing back and forth like a tiger stalking its prey. His black leather breeches and white cotton shirt emphasized his lithe body. The wind ruffled his long black hair, and the red scarf tied about his neck and pistol securely tucked into his waistband made him look like a pirate.

Samantha took one look at him and shivered. Robert noticed and asked if she were cold. "It's nothing, Father. I guess I'm just tired from rushing so much," she quickly responded.

Recognizing her reluctance, Lucien's eyes twinkled merrily as he noticed her warily approaching the deck.

"Are you planning a mutiny, green eyes?" His voice hinted at the amusement he felt.

"Why, hello Mr. Fraser, or should I call you Captain Fraser or Mr. Smith?"

She extended her hand and he bowed, kissed her hand, and murmured so low she could barely hear, "You can call me Lucien, my love." The intimate tone was unmistakable. His tongue briefly flicked across her palm. She felt her face flush with embarrassment and yes, excitement. Looking directly into his eyes, she smiled in a most winsome way. His face froze. He expected anger and sharp words but not that dazzling smile.

What was she up to now?

The *Newport Wind* had been at sea for five days, yet Samantha and Lucien spent no more than five minutes alone. It was, Samantha convinced herself, the way she wanted it to be. But it was difficult to overcome the restless feeling she had. She had not felt this way on their voyage to France. Maybe it was because she had other passengers for companions.

On this sixth day at sea she was strolling alone along the main deck sorting her thoughts. The weather was unusually mild for a sea voyage. There were clouds off in the distance, but there was no breeze. Samantha carelessly tied her woolen shawl about her slim waist, exposing her thin, white muslin dress. Still somewhat naïve about her effect on men, she did not realize that the warm sea breeze was molding the dress's thin fabric to her contours. The skirt too blew about her, revealing her long, slim legs.

The sailors attending to their chores on deck stopped to observe her. Their ribald comments would have made any woman blush, but in this case the comments enraged their captain.

Lucien, also, had been observing Samantha from his position on the raised quarterdeck. That witch *can* cause a mutiny, he thought angrily. He resolved to do something about her strolls but was interrupted by Roger.

"Lucien, a ship's been sighted on the horizon. Should we wait for her or keep to our course?"

"Stay on course, Roger. For all we know, she could be a British frigate. I don't think we could engage her with passengers aboard." He continued pacing and looked out in the direction of the other ship, suddenly noting the dark gray clouds gathering, moving toward them. "I believe we are about to sail into a storm, so prepare the crew. Perhaps the storm will increase the distance between us and that ship." He turned back to the main deck to see if Samantha was still there. She was talking to two sailors, laughing at one of their comments.

Samantha was enjoying their attention and attempts to humor her. Both sailors looked to be as old as her own nineteen years.

"Miss Thornton, you should have seen Ben here on that Caribbean island. The captain was entertaining some pretty woman—not half as pretty as you—" He bowed. "I think she was some diplomat's daughter . . . or wife. Anyway, old Ben here tried to sneak his own doxy aboard. Ah, excuse me, I mean woman . . ."

Samantha was laughing at the innocent manner of speech and the way each of the two young men good-naturedly punched each other.

"Oh, do go on, Mr. Hooper. I have not enjoyed myself so in . . ."

"In what, Miss Thornton?" boomed a deep voice behind her, emphasizing the word "Miss." "You did seem to be enjoying yourself the last time we met at your friend's estate."

She blushed at the reference to their night together.

"Gentlemen," he addressed the sailors, "we have a lot of preparation before that storm hits us. Now get back to your duties immediately or you will each be assigned extra work."

They scrambled away quickly, leaving Lucien alone with Samantha. He reached for her arm as if to continue strolling along the deck with her.

"Listen, you witch. Keep away from my men. This is a long trip for them. And . . ."—he caressed her arm—"they will be without the charms of willing women. I would hate to be responsible if they molest you, my dear. I do not think your Stèfan would approve of a very soiled bride."

His words stung deeper than she cared to admit. "Captain Fraser, I assure you I meant no harm. I shall remain as unobtrusive as possible for the rest of the voyage."

They continued strolling arm in arm. Anyone observing the two would have thought they were engaged in polite conversation. What an observer could not notice was Samantha's tension or the hard glint in the captain's eyes.

"There will be a storm tonight. Since I am responsible for your welfare, I want you to remain in your cabin tonight." He bowed formally and walked off.

"What got into him? Could the noble captain be jealous?" she wondered aloud. She smiled as she walked back to meet her father.

The storm proved to be much more severe than first predicted. Men were desperately holding onto the rigging as they tried to loosen the sails. The wheel had to be tied securely to avoid the ship's being blown off course.

Lucien was in the middle of everything—giving orders, organizing groups, and even climbing the rigging to secure a sail.

Joining Robert in his cabin, Samantha tried to sit out the storm calmly, although the rocking of the ship turned her stomach. They were both concerned about the welfare of the crew—particularly the captain.

"Father, do you think Lucien can pull us through? Do you think we should go above to offer our help?"

"Samantha"—Robert looked up from his book— "we were told to remain together and indoors. I am

101

sure Lucien will pull us safely through this storm. He reassured us before that this is not unusual for summer storms. Now what do you say we play a game of checkers?"

Samantha, however, became very nervous. For some unaccountable reason, she wondered if Lucien were safe. She had heard his voice bellowing above the others for the last two hours. Now she did not hear his voice at all. She could only hear the wind lashing at the ship.

"I don't feel like playing checkers tonight." Her voice was deceptively calm. "I think I'll go to my cabin. I am rather tired and maybe I can try to sleep through this storm."

From the passageway she could hear loud voices, but Lucien's was not among them. She made up her mind to investigate. Rather than going back to her father's cabin for her oil slick, she wrapped her shawl tightly about her head and went above.

The intensity of the storm momentarily disoriented her. The rain pelted her body, saturating her clothes. She made her way up to the quarterdeck, knowing she would have a better view.

No one seemed to notice the hooded figure slowly groping along the rail. Where was he? Why couldn't she see him? As she reached the quarterdeck, she heard Roger Cole shout.

"Captain, Ben is snarled in the rigging! We have to get him down . . . No, Captain, I'll go. You must not risk it! You have already been up there twice!"

"Damn it, Roger! I'm going. You run the ship if anything happens to me!" He was off again.

Samantha, initially relieved to hear Lucien's voice,

became terrified when she saw him climb up onto the rigging that was swaying in the wind. She saw Ben desperately hanging onto the mainmast.

"Oh God," she prayed aloud, "please let them be all right."

It was almost unbearable, but her eyes were riveted to the spot where two bodies were swaying precariously in the wind.

She screamed Lucien's name over and over. He seemed to lose his footing momentarily before reaching Ben, but he quickly recovered and disentangled Ben from the rigging.

Samantha did not realize that she was crying or that she kept screaming for Lucien to be careful. She imagined that he looked down toward her but could not be sure. How could she possibly have been heard above the din?

When she saw both Lucien and Ben climb down safely, she was so relieved that she blindly ran toward them. As she reached the steps, her haste prevented her from looking around.

Suddenly another voice shouted, "Look out!" She was about to look up at the rigging again when something flat and hard slammed into the back of her head. All the noise of a moment earlier ceased as she became aware of the flashing colors before her eyes and then . . . blackness.

Lucien could not believe it! He thought he had heard her voice while he was climbing but could not imagine why she would be on deck. Again he heard her call his name, but when he turned to look for her he was blinded by the rain. After Lucien quickly made his way down with a dazed Ben in hand, he headed toward the quarterdeck. There she was, fighting the storm as she tried to get to him.

Roger shouted to Samantha to "look out" as Lucien ran toward her. He felt as if there were lead weights on his legs. Suddenly, a large piece of wood from the mainmast came sailing through the sky and hit Samantha with such force that Lucien feared she would be hurled overboard.

He saw her tumble down the stairs and collapse in a heap. "No!" he shouted. But she could not hear him. He reached her side and gathered her fragile body into his arms.

When Roger ran to them, Lucien ordered him to find the second mate who sometimes served as the ship's surgeon. Meanwhile, Lucien gently picked up her head which he cushioned with his body. When he brushed his hand across her hair, he noticed the blood.

The second mate, hearing the urgency in Cole's voice, rushed to Lucien's side. Samantha was still unconscious but breathing evenly. After a cursory examination the second mate concluded that she had suffered a mild head wound.

Lucien gently cradled her against his wet body and brought her to his cabin. So absorbed was he in her condition that he neglected to call her father.

He placed her on his huge, wood-framed bed and slowly removed her wet clothes. At any other time, he thought wryly, this act would have been sexually arousing. The cabin boy quickly arrived with more towels and hot broth for the two of them.

Trying to take the chill out of her body, Lucien

vigorously rubbed her now-naked limbs with the towels. His long, heavy nightshirt was placed gently over her cold body. He dried her wet hair and fanned her red-gold locks over the white pillows. She looked like a marble statue.

After she was tucked under the quilts, Lucien took care of his own needs. Roger Cole checked to see if the captain and the lady were all right, then told Lucien about the damage the ship sustained from the storm.

"Lucien, the storm will pass. I can handle things now and there is no sign of the other ship. Why don't you stay, help Samantha, and get the rest you sorely need."

"Thanks, Roger. But report back to me if anything unusual happens."

He looked back at his patient and, seeing no movement, sat by his desk to record the events in the ship's log.

Half an hour must have passed before Lucien was startled by the muffled cries coming from a now semi-conscious Samantha. Before he reached her side, he heard her sob, "Oh Lord, no, please let him be all right. Don't fall! Why must you climb up there? Don't . . . Lucien!"

Cradling her body once again, Lucien tried to soothe her. He smoothed her still-damp hair away from her eyes and kept stroking her face.

"Samantha sweet, it's over. I'm here. Everything is fine." He kept stroking and talking to her, trying to calm her down. Slowly, Samantha relaxed and instinctively responded to the soothing voice in her ear.

"Lucien, are you all right?" Her whisper was barely audible. She looked like she was sleeping, for she lacked the strength to open her eyes.

He smiled at her lovely pale face. "Yes, my love, everything is fine. You have a very nasty bump on your head. It's a minor wound." He resumed stroking her face and hair. "You need to rest, that's all."

He started to disengage his arms, to allow her some sleep, but she snuggled close to him and sighed, "Please don't leave me." She promptly fell asleep, secure in his arms.

Observing her slumbering form, Lucien was aroused. She's beautiful even when she's asleep, he mused. The irony of this compromising situation struck him as ridiculous. Here he was with this beautiful, submissive creature in his arms and all he could do was watch her sleep! Who would believe this?

The single burning flame in the pewter candlestick holder on his desk went out, and with the room suddenly darkened, Lucien felt all the weariness of the last six hours overcome him. Wrapping his arms tightly about Samantha, he stretched his long body beside her and instantly fell asleep.

Samantha gradually emerged from her deep sleep and found herself warmly ensconced in Lucien's arms. She pieced together the events of the last few hours, and now, finding herself once more in a compromising situation with Lucien, tried to slip out of bed.

"Samantha, what's wrong? Do you feel well?" The concern in his voice melted her desire to leave. But her father would never forgive either of them if he knew where she had spent the night.

"I am feeling much better. In fact, I think I should leave now. Lucien, you know how my father would react at my being here!"

His grin brightened as he teased, "Samantha sweet, I am captain of this ship, correct?" She nodded slowly as she felt his hand move from her back to the swell of her breasts silhouetted under his night shirt. "I will take care of everything. Are you learning to trust me yet?"

She wanted to say "no" but if she did, he might stop massaging her breasts. Reluctantly she admitted to herself that she indeed craved his firm yet gentle touch.

"Samantha my love, you have the mind of an innocent, but your body responds to my touch like a born courtesan," he murmured in her ear, appearing to have somehow read her own troubled thoughts. "Relax my sweet. I want to make love to you."

His hands chartered their own course over her stimulated body. He nibbled her ear and slowly, methodically, his mouth went lower to her neck and breasts. He fondled and sucked.

Samantha thought she would faint from the pleasure he was giving her. Instinctively her hands reached for him. "Lucien, teach me to make love to you."

He guided her hand to his manhood and showed her how to manipulate him. "You don't need any lessons, my love," he groaned.

Lucien reveled in her touch, encouraging her to continue. Too soon he realized he needed to envelop her and positioned himself above her. He entered her abruptly, and she welcomed him. She matched him thrust for thrust as she continuously stroked his hair and back. Before his tongue invaded her warm, inviting mouth he said more to himself than to her, "I've never wanted any woman the way I want you, my love."

The words "my love" sounded so tender that all lucid thoughts left her mind. Her body and mind screamed for more of him. She urged him to plunge deeper and harder until they both exploded suddenly with a violent surge, crying out their release and their need for one another.

Gradually they both returned to the present. Lucien kissed her lightly on the cheek and once more pulled her pliant body toward his.

"Samantha, I will exchange cabins with you. You still need to rest for a few days and I would feel better if you stayed here. This way I can say I have to check my charts, and I will have the pleasure of viewing your lush body in my bed."

She was about to object, but he placed his finger on her ripe lips. "By the time you awake I'll be on deck and your father will be told what happened to your lovely head . . ."—he smiled—"but not your lovely body." She realized he was right and simply nodded as sleep began to overtake her.

Over the next few days Lucien's kindness and consideration gave Samantha another dimension of his personality to examine. Samantha, resting in Lucien's bed at the orders of the captain and her father, began to look forward to Lucien's daily, late-afternoon visits. Most of the time he made sure to be alone with her. Even when Robert was present, Samantha found Lucien's companionship pleasurable. They played checkers, whist, and chess. Most delightful of all, however, were their conversations. As if by silent agreement, neither of them mentioned their night of lovemaking. The ease with which they laughed at one another in trading stories about growing up made

Samantha realize that Lucien could be quite charming.

The combination of good sailing weather and camaraderie made the rest of the voyage pass quickly for everyone. Since the speed of the *Newport Wind* saved them a few days in sailing time, Lucien revised his plans. He decided to sail to Charleston, make a few repairs, and give the Thorntons an opportunity to settle business and family matters. From there the family would sail on to Newport.

Samantha had little opportunity to see her friends or to attend parties in Charleston. She reluctantly accepted an invitation to Marianne Davis's dinner party even though she never wanted to see Marianne's brother, Clinton, again. But Marianne was her friend and Samantha did not want to insult her. However, she found herself without an escort.

She was informed that Lucien was suddenly called away on an important business matter to Washington. Samantha knew what that meant. He was probably giving his report on Mr. Burr with her information. Oh, how I wish I could be involved, she silently lamented. He could have told me what his plans were. All of the pleasant feelings she had had for Lucien began to evaporate, yet an inner voice warned, He does not owe you any explanations. You are not married and you wanted it this way.

It was true, she sighed. But instead of giving in to self-pity, Samantha decided to go to the Davis's party alone.

Samantha wore one of her new French fashions, a robin's egg blue watered silk Empire gown with tiny seed pearls bordering the bodice and forming the ribbon tie down the front of the gown. The dress had short, capped sleeves bordered with pearls, and a matching shawl. Her only jewelry was a ruby pendant on a short chain around her neck.

Unfortunately, Samantha could not avoid Clinton. It seemed he had been drinking all day and each time he leered at her she felt as if she were being methodically stripped. Never before had he frightened her so much.

"You know, Samantha, that Clinton has deteriorated since that duel," commented a friend. "Rumor has it he has been gambling a lot, and his father refuses to support him. Oh, and Sam, the men he gambles with! They are the meanest looking characters I have ever seen. Clinton is seen at the races and coming out of the hotel with them. It's such a scandal! Everyone says that Clinton has become 'touched,' if you know what I mean."

Samantha skillfully avoided being alone with Clinton, but immediately before she left Clinton found her. Anticipating her departure, he had brought her pelisse. His blond hair was falling into his bloodshot eyes and his hands shook as he placed the pelisse around her shoulders.

"Samantha, I know what you are trying to do." His words were whispered and unclear. "You will not always be able to avoid me, dearest. I promise you that." It sounded like a threat and his hands lingered on her shoulders as he snapped, "Your precious sea captain cannot always be around to protect you!"

"Clinton, you are mad!" She slowly turned to face him, her green eyes blazing with anger and the realization that he did indeed look crazed. "If you ever

110

touch me again I shall not hesitate to use the pretty little dirk I keep in my bag!" She walked away slowly, head held high with all the aristocratic demeanor she could summon so that no one would suspect her fear. She was looking forward to leaving Charleston, and, she reluctantly admitted, to seeing Lucien again.

Chapter Nine

Newport

If only he had known what was in store for him at home, Lucien would have stayed in Washington. He would have gladly suffered through the endless meetings with the President and Mr. Madison, answering questions, speculating about the future.

Lucien and the others had agreed on a new course of action for gathering information about Aaron Burr in the Southwest. As soon as Adam returned to Newport from New Orleans with his valuable information, Lucien would be on his way.

That is, if Adam returned.

Luckily, Lucien stopped by his shipping office before going to Kingscote. The urgent messages were there waiting for him:

Lucien: I am in trouble. Something to do with the General J.W. and a French military officer. . . . You were right. Will leave for home immediately. Adam.

Another message was worse:

Dear Mr. Fraser:
We regret to inform you that your partner, Mr.
Adam Thornton, was arrested and charged with
spying against the Spanish Territorial Govern-
ment. His whereabouts are unknown. We will
contact you as soon as we receive further
information.

Sincerely,
Governor William C. C. Claiborne
New Orleans

Angrily, Lucien shoved the letters into his coat pocket and hurried home. How could he explain this to the family? He agonized over the decision as he recalled the President's parting words:

"Lucien, I am reminding you of what I have said before and what Adam has also been told—you are on your own once you leave American territory. If you are caught, you will be charged with spying. May God help you. Oh, one more thing—keep Samantha Thornton out of this!"

Easy for him to say, Lucien mused.

Riding home, Lucien again revised his plan of action. He had to go after Adam. He would tell the President after he got a head start on finding Adam. But first things first.

The family greeted him warmly. Meredith, in an advanced state of pregnancy, looked as beautiful as the last time he had seen her. Elizabeth seemed to have

114

found a new purpose in life with the preparations for her grandchild's arrival.

Only Samantha held back. The distance gave her the opportunity to observe Lucien dispassionately. She saw something the others did not: he was tense and something more. Lucien was nervous. Why should he, always in control of every situation, be nervous?

It seemed his eyes were searching for her among the family members. As if drawn to a magnet, Samantha moved forward to greet him and her green eyes were full of concern. Am I that obvious? he wondered.

Extending her hand she said, "Hello Lucien. How was your business trip?" She smiled and in a lower voice whispered, "What's wrong? Is it something to do with Mr. Burr?"

He squeezed her hands and winked. "What makes you think something is wrong, green eyes?"

"There is and I know it." She continued smiling so that the others would think the two were engaged in polite conversation. "Now either you come out with it or I tell everyone you are the bearer of bad tidings."

"Shall we go for a walk toward the beach . . . witch?" The last word, of course, was muttered.

Suddenly he felt the need to talk to her. It would be cathartic being able to share his concern about Adam. By the time Lucien finished, Samantha was considerably paler than before. She had not realized that she had dug her nails into her palms in an expression of fear for her brother.

"What are we going to do? Are you going after Adam? When are you leaving?" The questions were delivered rapidly. "I can be ready in two hours."

He wasn't quite sure he had heard what she had said,

so he asked her to repeat the last statement.

"Lucien, I am going with you. He's my brother and if anything happens to him . . . Look"—her eyes misted with tears—"I could not bear to lose Adam . . . not after my mother's death." She was visibly shaken. Her hands reached up to clutch Lucien, imploring him to understand.

"Listen to me, Samantha. I understand your concern for Adam. God knows I feel the same way." He put his arm around her slim waist in a comforting gesture. They continued walking silently along the beach for several minutes before he resumed talking.

"I have a plan. But I cannot tell you, nor can you come along. That, my sweet, is a direct order from our President."

Samantha did not appreciate Lucien's light dismissal. "I don't give a damn about what you, or Thomas Jefferson, or anyone thinks! I"—she gestured for emphasis—"am going to do something!" And as the information Lucien gave her was assimilated, Samantha reached a new conclusion. "Lucien"—she stared up into his eyes—"was Adam also involved in this 'Government business'? Is Adam an agent too?"

He tried to feign indignation and was about to deny her accusation. However, Samantha saw through this ruse.

"Don't bother to deny it. It all makes sense now. All the secrecy, the half-answers to my questions. I know you and Adam are involved in some way. I bet Roger Cole is, too. Have you been working together a long time? This must be another dimension to your business partnership and this Aaron Burr thing is your latest assignment," she concluded.

116

"Okay, you green-eyed witch, I won't deny it. Adam did go to New Orleans for two reasons. One was to investigate the possibility of our opening an office there. The other . . . well, the other was to find out whatever we could about the activities of the Spanish government and certain people in the Southwest."

"Thank you." He looked at her inquiringly. "Thank you for not treating me as a child."

With that body, how could I? he wanted to say. He reached for her, then thought better of it. He had to make her understand that she could not be a part of this search for her brother.

"You have to take care of Mother and Meredith. I will tell them about Adam, but I cannot tell them everything, nor can I stay. They will need a strong person to emulate. You, my sweet, are the one." The gentle look on his face did not affect her determination.

"I will try, Lucien. I won't go . . . yet."

It was getting chilly now as the sun began its descent.

He pulled her body toward his in a rough embrace. A curious warmth spread through her at his touch. She wanted him as much as he wanted her. He bent his dark head to kiss her softly. The softness, however, swiftly turned to passion. His tongue parted her lips to explore her mouth as his hand seductively moved along her back, around to the front of her dress, where it slowly began caressing her breasts. His fingers gently teased her nipples to life and Samantha pressed her body closer to his.

Slowly, reluctantly, Lucien let her go. "Come with me to tell the others." Samantha was startled back to reality and responsibility and heartache came flooding into her thoughts. Neither of them could turn back.

117

The bad news was received stoically with the family trying to comfort Meredith.

"I suspected something," she said sadly. "Adam has not written in so long. And I thought it odd that before he left, he told me of a will he had drawn. He also told me that if anything should happen to him, you, Lucien, could reveal certain facts. What did he mean?"

"My brother gets maudlin for no reason, Meredith. I am sure he did not mean anything at all," Samantha quickly inserted, fearful that Meredith would guess too much.

"I do not believe he is dead," Meredith announced with conviction. "I would feel it. Adam will return to see our child."

The Thorntons and Frasers tried to make each other as comfortable as possible. In the weeks that followed, final preparations were made for the birth of Adam's child.

Unfortunately, conditions were not peaceful. Upon learning of Lucien's return, Caroline Prescott made a number of appearances at Kingscote. Her haughty personality had not improved in the last year. Samantha, in fact, found it even more difficult to be in the same room with Caroline.

One afternoon Caroline swept into the parlor where Samantha and Meredith were playing cards. Since this had been an unusually hot July in New England, the ladies had discarded their shawls and donned their lightest dresses. Caroline wore a rather revealing pink cotton dress trimmed with a flower print embroidery. Her full breasts were clearly outlined by the low cut of the bodice and her pale blond hair was piled high on top of her head.

"Hello darling Meredith." She bent to kiss her cheek. The voice took on a sickeningly sweet tone as she addressed Samantha. "Hello Samantha. My, you do look grown up today!"

Samantha wondered what Caroline would look like with long scratch marks on her pale face. "Your perfume announced your arrival, *dear* Caroline," she responded acidly.

"Did I hear Lucien's horse outside? I wanted to thank him for the delightful tour of his ship last ni . . . I mean yesterday."

I am sure you do, thought Samantha. "You just missed him, Caroline dear. Isn't it funny that whenever you arrive, Lucien is not here!" Her innocent smile remained as she continued, "I will make a point of telling Lucien about your charming visit. I am sure he will be sorry that he missed you . . . again."

Pretending to ignore her, Caroline directed her questions to Meredith. "Have you heard anything about poor Adam?"

Meredith became wistful. "No, nothing since the last message Lucien received last week."

Caroline looked surprised. Samantha took the leap. "Caroline, didn't 'darling Lucien' tell you? Governor Claiborne sent another letter to us. He believes Adam was sent into the Mexican territory. Some American army officers have identified a young man fitting Adam's description being held captive by a Spanish regiment."

"What is important," Meredith interjected with conviction, "is that Adam is alive! Lucien will get

119

him released."

Caroline chose her words carefully. "Oh, I am sure that if anyone can solve this awful mess, *my Lucien* can."

Meredith's tolerant smile showed that she had no interest in taking issue with Caroline's announced possession of Lucien. Samantha, of course, felt differently.

"Dear Caroline," she mimicked, "I too have confidence that *our Lucien* can get Adam released. I just hope he does not take too long." She repressed a giggle. "After all, it might take a bit of maneuvering to replace the empty spaces on your social calendar."

Caroline's scowl revealed her hatred. "We will see, darling child, which one of us gets to the altar with him. You would not know how to keep a man like Lucien satisfied for very long!"

The two women were facing each other, waiting for the first one to make a move. "Caroline . . . I give him to you. I am not interested in anyone who could seriously consider you for a mistress."

The tension crackled in the air. Caroline raised her hand to slap Samantha, but the arm was caught in midair. "I may not look very strong to you, dear, but I have been known to wound a gentleman or two. I would be pleased to demonstrate how it is done." Samantha's grip tightened. Caroline realized the truth of Samantha's words.

But the mood was suddenly altered when Meredith exclaimed, "Ooh!" and held her rounded belly. Samantha ran to her side. "It's nothing, Sam. I think the baby's kick is a lot stronger lately." She struggled to rise. "Perhaps you can help me upstairs. I am so sorry,

Caroline, that we have to cut our visit short."

While Samantha was bantering with Caroline, Lucien was experiencing his own angry confrontation.

"Harrison, you are being paid to give me any information you can about my partner's whereabouts." He paced furiously about his office. "How can you present a report that tells me nothing. Are you daft, man?" He threw the papers down onto his desk.

Mr. Harrison's expression paled as he shuffled his feet. "Mr. Fraser, I am doing the best I can. The City of New Orleans is buzzing with rumors. General Wilkinson is running the city, not Governor Claiborne. I spoke to the president of a local political association who formed a group called the 'Mexican Association.' The association was formed to promote independence for the Mexican territories. Naturally, they work against the Spanish government. But your partner and Mr. Clark were friends. I think—"

"Damn it, man!" Lucien burst out. "I am not paying you to think! I want Adam free and alive. In order to do that"—he grabbed Harrison's arm—"I need solid, reliable information. Do you understand, Harrison?"

"Yes . . . yes sir!" he stammered.

"Good. Now, go back to New Orleans. Tell the governor I will be there within the month. You'd better have more information including dates, names, and places."

Lucien was getting nowhere. The men he hired to get him the information he needed before he went to New Orleans came up with nothing but false leads. His problems were compounded by his having to be in

Newport to supervise the building of his newest ship and meeting family obligations at the same time. Although Robert Thornton was a very capable fellow, he couldn't be expected to handle all these women. Meredith was doing as well as could be expected, but her forlorn expression tugged at his heart. Then there was Caroline Prescott who was busy campaigning to become his wife. Her possessiveness was no longer tolerable.

Lucien walked over to the window which gave him a clear view of Newport harbor. He poured himself an ample glassful of whiskey and sighed. An uncalled-for image appeared—the green-eyed witch! Now, as if the other problems weren't enough, *she* had to enter his life.

Samantha was continuously badgering him for information about Adam. Her threats to do something on her own could not be taken lightly. His nagging fear was a belief that she would indeed do something which in the end would endanger herself and Adam.

Being near her yet unable to touch her soft body was driving him mad. Too many people were around them. For the sake of propriety he could not make any more advances. He was almost tempted to accept Caroline's numerous offers to resume sharing her bed. He chuckled, wondering what Samantha would do if she realized Caroline was only her substitute. No, he had to leave Newport.

The family did not have to wait long for the newest family member. Meredith's and Adam's son entered the world two weeks later. The birth was an easy one, making Meredith's recovery quick. But the jubilation was overshadowed by the sad fact that the father of the child could not be a witness. He had been named James after Lucien's and Meredith's father.

"Adam and I discussed names before he left," she told the family at the first dinner she was able to attend. She lifted her wine glass. "I want to make a toast to Jamie's godparents: To Lucien and Samantha!" The look of genuine surprise and delight on both their faces was what Meredith had counted on to lift everyone's spirits. Continually looking at Samantha's engimatic expression had upset Meredith. Oh, she knew her family was trying to hide its true feelings from her, especially Samantha, but whenever she caught a glimpse of her sister-in-law, Meredith saw the truth.

"I think we should have an old-fashioned New England celebration," she announced. "So dear godparents, after dinner let's share a few more toasts, and let's dance!"

No one refused. Elizabeth took out her music box which played a waltz. Meredith and Lucien danced first. Even the servants joined in. And eventually someone remarked that the godparents had not danced together.

"Shall we, green eyes?" The smooth, deep voice brought back the curious tingle she had felt before. When he put his arms around her waist, she wanted him to hold her tighter so that she could feel those strong arms caressing her, protecting her. However, they remained at a respectable distance. Lucien's eyes revealed that he felt the same way. The spark was ignited once more. She recognized that look and was grateful that they were not alone, for there was no way she could have resisted his overtures.

In spite of the gaiety, Samantha could not overcome her sadness. She missed Adam and felt so sorry for Meredith. And since Lucien had been unable to make any headway with his search, a plan began to form in her mind.

Samantha made up her mind that she was going to New Orleans. She did not know how to accomplish this goal yet, but remaining at Kingscote was simply impossible. The rigors of another sea voyage so soon after her European trip were not something to which she looked forward, yet her decision to do something had been formulated over the last few weeks. Now that James was born, her departure could be rationalized.

Long after everyone was asleep, Samantha stayed awake ruminating about her trip to New Orleans. Once she got there, she knew she could stay with her mother's cousins, the Bonnards. Surely they would help. Meanwhile, she had to invent a plan for an unmarried, unchaperoned lady to travel alone.

Unable to sleep, Samantha wrapped a light woolen shawl around her nightgown and went downstairs. She thought a small glass of brandy would help her to think. She quietly opened the library door and made her way to the bay windows. The moon's light outlined every contour of her body as she poured the brandy and stood gazing at the moon and stars.

Lucien sucked in his breath at the sight of her silhouette. He too had been unable to sleep. Reclining on the dark blue velvet couch, he had been thinking about being aboard his ship. Its rocking motion always managed to soothe his nerves. So deep in thought was he that Lucien did not hear Samantha enter and first noticed her as she stood by the window.

Startled by the sound of his indrawn breath, she dropped the brandy glass.

"Why must you always sneak up on me?" she accused. She bent down to pick up the shards of glass scattered about her bare feet.

"I should be asking you the same question. After all"—he stretched his body—"this is my library and I was here first." He walked over to where she was crouched and helped her pick up the glass.

"I do not want your . . . ouch! See what you made me do? You made me so jumpy, I did not notice this piece of glass." She held up her bleeding fingers for Lucien to see. He placed her fingers in his hands and wiped the blood away with his handkerchief.

"I am sorry, sweetheart." There was a trace of sarcasm in his tone. "I do believe this isn't fatal." Long after the bleeding stopped, he still held her hand and looked longingly into her emerald eyes. They both knew what would come next.

"Lucien," she whispered, "please don't." But she was powerless to resist as he pulled her into the embrace she had experienced before.

He gently picked her up and carried her to the couch. His sensuous lips and strong hands started exploring her body before she could free herself and protest.

"Come now, sweet. Do not fight me any more. I want you as much as you want me." He teasingly kissed her ear as his fingers fondled each breast.

She tried to resist him one last time. "Please, Lucien. We cannot go on like this. You don't want me. I am just a substitute for Caroline."

He picked up his dark, wavy head, looked into her

lovely face, and smiled. "If only you knew, my love," he murmured. Their mouths met in a rapturous kiss which left both of them breathless. Her desire for him was obvious and her protests ceased. "I think, my love, you are ready for a new lesson in lovemaking."

He gently turned her soft, pliant body so that she bent over the sofa, her back facing him and her copper hair spilling over the velvet side arms. Never stopping the caresses, he placed soft, tiny kisses along her back. When it was clear she was ready for him, Lucien gently entered her moist center from this new position. She moaned with pleasure. "You need me," he huskily whispered in her ear.

His movements became faster and harder as Samantha cried out for more of him. "Lucien, I want to hold you," she gasped. He turned her about and resumed the passionate, insistent rhythm. Her legs wrapped about him as she clutched him closer, kneading his back muscles with her hands.

"My love," she cried, the unfamiliar words being torn from her as they both climaxed in a Niagara of passion. They held tightly to one another, each the other's lifeline to reality.

His soft fingertips smoothing the loose strands of hair away from her face brought her out of a half-sleeping state.

"What are you thinking about, my sweet?"

She turned her face to look directly into his eyes. "I am thinking that this is the only way you and I can ever get along. Why do we always disagree, Lucien? Yet," she puzzled, "I love to feel you kissing me, making delicious love to me."

He smiled, wondering the same things. "I don't

know, my love. Maybe we are too much alike, too headstrong, passionate, and independent for our own good."

An almost childlike look enveloped her face as she asked, "Do other couples feel the same way . . . I mean . . . do other women enjoy making love the way I do? Or am I as wanton as you seem to suggest?"

Suppressing a smile was difficult, but he did not want to ruin this tender moment or embarrass her. He knew it took much courage for her to ask. He reached for her once more, stroking her face. "I do not know what your mother taught you. But no, my love, there is nothing wrong in feeling the way you do. So many women are hypocrites by pretending indifference." He became more thoughtful. "Most women never have the opportunity to experience such passion."

Not wanting to press the intimate topic any further, Samantha changed the subject. "What are we going to do about finding Adam?" She sat up to arrange her clothing while she smoothed her messy hair. The dizzying passion of minutes before was passing into sobriety. "I have to do something. I have been thinking—"

"No," he cut her off sharply. "I had a feeling you would not remain patient for long. There is nothing you can do." He grabbed her arm, ignoring all the tenderness they had just shared. "Do you understand, Samantha?"

"No, I do not!" she declared, trying to pull her arms free. "I want to see President Jefferson. I am sure he would help us." In an exasperated voice, Lucien explained the delicacy of the situation and why the President of the United States could not interfere. "He is the President first, Samantha. He must avoid an international incident at all costs."

"Then *I* must do something!" She was standing now, about to pace, unknowingly imitating Lucien. "I am going to New Orleans." She stopped in front of him, watching him light up a cheroot, waiting for him to explode. The light from the flame outlined the hollow planes of his handsome face.

He deliberately took his time before replying. "My dear, how do you expect to get to New Orleans alone? If you are not molested by the time you board a ship—I assume you would go by ship since that is the faster method of travel—you would surely be some man's plaything once you reached your destination."

"I would rather be 'some man's plaything' than yours!" she spat. "You owe it to me to help. Adam would never have become involved if you hadn't forced him."

Lucien was enraged by her accusation. "Just wait a minute. Your brother is not the simple-minded fool you think him to be. He's a man with a good mind, Samantha, and possesses that same stubborn independent streak you have! Now just forget this nonsense and let me handle it!" he thundered.

As much as she hated to do it, she resorted to her last, "emergency" plan. Forcing herself to be calm, she sat down, took his hand in hers, and smiled her dazzling smile. It had disarmed him once before, she mused, so why not again?

"All right, Lucien. Maybe I could not go myself. But I could go with you . . ." she hesitated, "as your . . . ah, wife."

"My what?" He roughly pulled his hand away.

128

"Haven't we played that little scene already?"

"Don't you see? We don't have to marry. We can just tell everyone we are married," she answered, becoming even more enthusiastic over this plan.

"Hold off, sweetheart. What do you propose to tell our respective families?" He began to pace furiously about the room like an animal sensing a trap. "Do you propose to tell them that we are only pretending to be married, so we may travel together and live together once we get to New Orleans? What do you think your father would say? And what would you intend to do about your reputation if we ever came back?" He was satisfied now that her bubble had been broken. One look at her crestfallen face told him so.

"I did not think about that," she barely whispered, feeling disappointed. She thought a few more seconds and decided to take the plunge. She stood up to meet his gaze, her arms akimbo. "Why do we have to *pretend* to marry? You asked me once before. Well"—she touched his arm almost imploringly—"I accept."

This couldn't be happening to him. It was a bad dream. Lucien looked down at her serious face and started to laugh. The idea was so ridiculous that the more he thought of her asking him to marry, the harder he laughed. He sat down again, sure that his legs could no longer support his shaking body.

"You want to marry me now? Woman, you are truly mad!" He wiped the tears from his eyes. "I told you before, I almost made that mistake with you. You turned me down, remember? And now you tell me you have reconsidered?"

At any other time she would have cried from this humiliation, but never, she vowed, would he be a

129

witness to her tears.

"We could be married in name only. Call it a marriage of convenience. We would do what we have to do in New Orleans. Once we found Adam, we would divorce." It was stated flatly, without emotion. "You owe me, Lucien Fraser."

"Once I did, my love. But you canceled that debt. Now"—he reached for her to sit next to him—"forget this. It won't work. I do not want to be married to you any more than you want to be married to me." He tried to kiss her neck, but she pulled back.

"You are a bastard, Lucien. And I will never forgive you," she answered hotly. Angrily, Samantha stood up and walked toward the door. "I will," she vowed, "go to New Orleans—with you or without you!" The door slammed before he could reply.

Why don't I ever learn? Lucien thought. Once again he had made the stupid mistake of underestimating Samantha.

She was gone.

He had thought the matter was forgotten. By the time he had seen her again Samantha appeared resigned to leaving things as Lucien wanted. Of course, he could not be sure, since she refused to say more than five words to him. However, his keen observation of her had led him to the conclusion that she was content.

"Damn that green-eyed witch!" he cursed aloud. It had all been a charade. She had deliberately misled him and he had been so sure of her that he had taken a business trip to Boston. He now realized that she had been planning her escape all along.

When Lucien had returned from Boston, he had found his home again thrown into confusion. Samantha, pleading a stomach ailment, had refused to leave her bed for three days, and in fact, the only person she had allowed in her room was her maid, Maria. This subterfuge had given her plenty of time to make her escape.

Meredith had calmly tried to relay the facts to Lucien, knowing how furious he would be. Not only did her brother display a peculiar sense of responsibility for Samantha, but whether either one of them cared to admit it, there was deep feeling as well. And, she surmised, that feeling was mutual. Although Samantha had steadfastly refused to talk about Lucien, whenever someone else did—especially Caroline—Samantha's face became quite flushed and her body more erect.

Somehow, Meredith sensed that Lucien was indirectly involved in her sister-in-law's abrupt departure. It had been a bizarre thing for Samantha to do. Everyone knew that. Robert was beside himself with worry and Samantha's brief letter of explanation didn't help much; yet they all agreed to wait for Lucien, as if he could magically clear up the problem.

"When I see her again, Meredith, I swear I am going to spank her for acting like such a spoiled child," he growled, "and then I will strangle her. How could she be so foolish, and worse, how could I assume she was a conventional female? My God!" He slapped his knee for emphasis. "How could I have been so stupid?"

"You knew all along, didn't you, that she might try something?" Meredith queried.

"Yes, but what good does it do now? Someone—

131

namely me—will have to go after her and bring her home, like the errant child she is. I only hope she doesn't get herself or Adam into more trouble." He poured himself a drink before continuing. "She got her way. She wanted me to go and now I have to set everything aside to chase her down! Hell," he exclaimed, "I'll bet she planned it this way!"

Meredith let him curse, pace and shout. Finally, after he calmed down, they planned for his departure.

"I was going at the end of the month anyway. But I still must go to Washington first. I hope that brat can manage without me."

Chapter Ten

New Orleans

Until now Samantha was, in fact, managing quite well. She was again aboard a ship—not one of Lucien's—and posing as a woman recently widowed. Between sobs, she had told the captain that she simply had to board his ship in order to reach her family in New Orleans. She could not take the heartbreak alone, especially now that she was expecting. Her performance was brilliant and secured her a place aboard ship.

That was a week ago. Now the port of New Orleans was in sight. Samantha recalled the seven days she had planned for her forthcoming adventure. She giggled to herself, wishing she could have seen Lucien's expression when he found her gone. She hoped the note she left her father would allay his fears. But all that was in the past. She had made up her mind to find her brother, and find him she would. Unconsciously her chin lifted in a defiant pose. *I hope that by the time that bastard gets here, both Adam and I will be waiting and gloating,* she silently prayed.

Her cousins had a city home that was generally open all year. When Adam had been corresponding, he had mentioned the magnificent house in which he had spent several nights. Because she wasn't sure if her letter would reach the Bonnards before her arrival, she planned to continue her widow's charade and go directly to the hotel in town.

Mentally, Samantha had made a list of the names of people to be contacted. Number one was General James Wilkinson, who seemed to be involved in everything. Even her fellow shipmates confirmed this fact. Numbers two, three, and four were, respectively, Daniel Clark, a local American resident, Governor Claiborne, and the Spanish Minister, Don Carlos Martinez Yrujo. Satisfied that everything was falling into place, Samantha smoothed her black crepe dress, pulled the black cape about her, and waited for the ship to dock.

She could not have known how poor her timing was, for Samantha unwittingly walked into a town seething with turmoil and political unrest.

There was an unnatural flutter of activity near the hotel. The coachman Samantha hired had to fight his way through the crowd congregating near the main entrance. Too preoccupied with her own problems, Samantha failed to note the many people surrounding the hotel until she tried to obtain a suite.

"Madame, I am sorry but we cannot accommodate you," said the polite but quite harried concierge. "This town is falling apart. Most people are trying to leave, but the port is closing and the roads are blocked."

134

Unsure about what this gentleman was babbling, she asked him to please repeat himself.

"Madame, don't you know?"

"Sir, I am recently widowed," she replied, dabbing her eyes with her handkerchief for effect. "I do not understand. I am here to stay with relatives."

"I am sorry, dear lady, for your loss," he bowed. "But the General has declared martial law in New Orleans. It is feared that the city will be invaded by revolutionaries. These pirates are trying to separate us from the rest of the country! And who knows? Maybe the Spanish are involved too."

The incredulous look on her face prompted him to continue. "Dear, dear lady, I think you picked a terrible time to visit our beautiful city."

"Sir, who is behind this seditious plot?" She already had a pretty good suspicion but needed confirmation.

"Why, it is rumored that Aaron Burr, our former vice president, is the leader."

This is it, she thought. If this man's ravings are even partially accurate, all the events of the last few months—Louis Turreau's interest in Burr; Adam's and Lucien's activities; the elusive Mr. Burr's travels—fit neatly together. All the intrigue ends here in this city of New Orleans. Somehow Adam knew that and much more. She realized that someone desperately wanted Adam disposed of. Maybe her arrival was not so poorly timed, for by being in the middle of things, she could find the information she had been seeking. Amidst the confusion, there might be some individual eager to talk about political plots.

"Madame," interrupted the concierge, "I could give you a very small room until the departure of some

135

guests. People are coming and going very quickly these days."

After thanking the gentleman, she turned to leave, then a thought occurred to her. "Monsieur." She lowered her lashes. "My departed husband's cousin might have stayed here. A southerner, I believe. His name is Adam Thornton."

"Why, yes. He was here. A nice gentleman, too. Always polite. It's a shame about what happened to him."

She stiffened. "What happened to him? I have some familiarity with his family, you see."

"He was taken quite ill, suddenly. I do not know what the ailment was. One night he did not appear for his key, nor the next. We were concerned."

Oh God, she prayed, let this be a good lead. "Yes monsieur, please continue."

"There is not much more to tell you. Two military officers came by the third day. They said Mr. Thornton was too ill to leave a friend's house. He had asked them to bring his belongings. If I had known you were arriving, I would gladly have held his things."

I wouldn't wager on that, she thought. "You let the officers have my cousin's belongings?" He nodded. "Did they leave anything to be shipped to his home?"

"No Madame, I am sorry. I have no idea if your cousin is still alive. Several weeks have passed."

"Thank you for your information. By the way"—she tried to smile—"do you know which company these military officers were from?"

"Yes, yes, I do. They were from General Wilkinson's special brigade."

Person number one must be contacted immediately.

136

If General Wilkinson knows what's good for his reputation, he will see me . . . or dispose of me, too, she thought grimly. Considering that possibility, Samantha decided to establish contact with her real cousins at once. As an afterthought, she also decided to contact Governor Claiborne. As loath as she was, she knew she must also write Lucien. If she did find herself in trouble, he might as well know it. He could look for Adam and for her.

After a well-deserved nap, she freshened up and was determined to find the infamous General Wilkinson.

She arrived at his crowded temporary military quarters, not far from Governor Claiborne's offices. The clerk took her name and curtly told her that if she would like to wait for a few hours with the other people seeking the general's counsel, she could. Unaware of the faces looking at her, Samantha turned around to see at least five other people waiting.

"Tell the general that Samantha *Thornton* is here to see him about an urgent matter. Thornton—Adam's sister!"

Not recognizing the name, the clerk shrugged and said he would give the information to the general.

She sat next to an older gentleman who promptly explained why he was there.

"The general knows many people, Madame. I was hoping that he might have news of my son, Harvé, who disappeared a few days ago." The man looked at her with big, sad eyes.

"Do you know why he disappeared?" She did not want to pry but wondered if there were many other people in New Orleans whose friends or relatives had mysteriously disappeared.

"Oh, Harvé has always been a bit impetuous. Most of his friends were rumored to be wild. Harvé challenged the wrong man to a duel."

"Wrong man?"

"Monsieur Gaspar. The second most important man in the Louisiana Territory. He is also a very close friend and advisor to the general."

The gentleman would have told her more but the clerk appeared before her, motioning her to follow. So, my name must mean something to the general, she thought smugly.

The room she entered was garishly furnished. The furniture looked like a combination of French and Spanish design. Two men in uniform stood by a window. One was short and quite plump with graying hair, while the other towered over him. The taller gentleman was somewhat attractive. His long, dark hair contrasted sharply with his white and blue uniform. His lean, swarthy face had the lines of experience and the passionless look of childhood deprivation. But his eyes made her shiver. They were the coldest steel gray she had ever seen. Instinctively she knew this fellow could be a formidable enemy.

The shorter man broke the silence and stepped toward her. "How do you do, Miss ah . . . Thornton, isn't it? I am General James Wilkinson, Commander of the Army of the United States and Governor of the Territory of Louisiana." His voice was firm. He bowed and extended his hand. The other gentleman remained behind. "Let me introduce you to my aide, Major Henri Gaspar." She hoped they hadn't heard her sudden gasp at the mention of his name.

Forcing herself to remain calm, she curtsied and

looked at her two adversaries. The general's blue eyes twinkled with what—anticipation? Major Gaspar's slight smile never reached his cold eyes.

"Sirs, I am truly grateful that you have agreed to see me so soon. Why, this heat and activity are overwhelming." The southern belle tactics were feigned, but she felt they would do for now. Let them think that I am a simple-minded ingénue. Instinctively she knew she would need time to outwit them.

"Miss Thornton, are you in mourning?" Gaspar's steely eyes bored into her.

"Oh, you mean my silly disguise?" She sat strategically on the gold satin couch, taking her time arranging her black skirts. "Daddy would never approve of my being alone in this big city. So we compromised on my traveling as a widow . . . Mrs. Fraser." She deliberately mentioned her father's approval but cursed herself for using that name. Perhaps they might think twice about disposing of her, if they were aware her family knew her whereabouts.

"Fraser, you say? Isn't that the name of your brother's partner?" asked the General.

These two were well informed, she realized, trying to think fast. "Why yes, gentlemen, it is. My sister-in-law suggested I use the name. Her family did not mind at all." Except Lucien, she grimaced inwardly. He would kill her anyway, so why not add this to his list of grievances. "I plan to move to my cousin's home tomorrow. Do you know of anyone who might assist me?"

"I am sure I can arrange something. Now tell me, how else may I be of assistance?"

"Well, I simply do not know where to begin," she

139

drawled. She removed her fan from her reticule to cool herself. "We have had no word from my brother in months. His darling wife just had a baby, and poor Adam does not know of the blessed event." The handkerchief was dabbing at her eyes again. "Why, he seems to have disappeared." She quickly decided not to mention the concierge's information. "I don't know where to go. Most of the people I have spoken to said that you, General Wilkinson, would know of some way to help find my brother."

"In fact, Miss Thornton, I know a little of your brother. He was taken quite ill and remained at the home of one of my officers. I will ask Captain Richards to report to me immediately. You certainly did the right thing in coming to me first."

The general appeared to be taken by her beauty. Certainly her flirtatious behavior could not hurt her cause. She lowered her lashes and smiled. She caught a glimpse of Major Gaspar, who continued to stare at her without moving a muscle in his body. He turned to pick up his riding quirt which had an unusual silver handle. Still staring at her, he began to slap the quirt against his palm. Over and over, like waves slapping against a rock, the quirt struck. It was an unstated warning. Samantha began to quake inwardly. I will not show him any fear, she vowed. A man like this would love to see me tremble. She looked directly at him and smiled. His brow lifted, as if saluting his worthy opponent.

"I am so sorry we had to meet under these circumstances, General. I have heard so many fine"— she almost choked—"things about you. You know my dear cousin—well, he's like a cousin to us—Thomas, I mean President Jefferson, holds you in the highest

140

regard. I will tell him about our meeting and send him your greetings if you like." Samantha flashed her sweetest smile.

The general was clearly impressed. "I would be honored, Miss Thornton. Perhaps after you have moved to your cousin's home you would do me the honor of being my dinner guest?"

How could he have a leisurely dinner in the middle of all this chaos? she wondered. This General Wilkinson is someone quite unique. She stood up and extended her black, gloved hand to the general which he kissed without any hesitation. Then she reluctantly turned to the major. He took her hand, holding it in a firm grip. As he bent to kiss it, his unflinching eyes never left her face. She shivered.

"I enjoyed our meeting, Miss Thornton. Perhaps I shall see you again soon. I certainly hope to have more news for you. Good day."

She only wished she could have hidden in the room to hear what they would say about her. If she had had any inkling of what they were planning for her, she would have wanted to remain hidden.

Samantha was cordially received by Governor William Claiborne a few hours later. The governor was clearly distracted. His city was in turmoil and rumors were traveling through the city like a cholera epidemic. Whatever influence the governor had had with his constituents was seriously being undermined by the presence of General James Wilkinson and his army.

Governor Claiborne insisted she join him and some friends for dinner. Why not, she thought, hoping that someone would know something about Adam. Realizing that the widow's garb was no longer necessary, she decided to return to her hotel to change.

The hotel room was dark and damp. Ignoring a feeling of anxiety, she walked to the oak desk to light a lamp. A sixth sense warned her to look around. She thought she saw the silver edge of a familiar object, but her conscious thoughts never had a chance to surface. She was grabbed from behind and her arms pinned to her sides. Samantha frantically tried to kick her tormentor as a horrible-smelling cloth was put over her mouth and nose. Within seconds Samantha lay limply in her attacker's arms.

He smiled then and placed her on the bed. Seeing her inert form brought on a rush of desire. His hands stroked her hair then searched for her breasts.

"Soon, my pretty, you will be mine. But I do not care for you to sleep while I enjoy the pleasures of your body," the voice whispered passionately. "I want you to see me and writhe with the pleasure I'll give you. Not this time," he said regretfully, "but we shall meet again. No one will stand in my way." His gray eyes glinted with lust. Placing a dark, hooded cloak over her body, he roughly pulled her up, tied her hands, and shoved the foul-smelling cloth in her mouth. Two other men swiftly entered the room to help remove her body. It was so easy.

Chapter Eleven

Her dreams were so strange. It felt as if she were swinging in her hammock at Thornton Hill. Someone—a tall, strong man—walked toward her. The face was shrouded in fog. He kept coming closer. When he reached her, he bent down to touch her hair. She became frightened, begging the man to identify himself. She tried to move her arms to keep him at a distance, but her arms wouldn't move. Suddenly the fog began to clear. She could see the face. Black wavy hair, deep blue eyes . . . Lucien! "Lucien," she cried, "please help me!" He smiled as he reached for her. She was almost lifted into the security of his arms when the fog enveloped him again. She blinked a few times to clear her vision. Looking up into his face she screamed in terror. That face . . . it was just a trick! It was not Lucien. The eyes were metallic gray; the thin lips were set in a tight smile. A flash of silver . . . a riding quirt lifting to hit her . . . Major Gaspar!

"Help me Lucien. Someone please help me." Her head thrashed from side to side. A hand began gently to tap her cheeks.

"Miss, please wake up. You are safe now." A

pleasant voice. "Please, you were having a nightmare."

Ever so slowly, she opened her eyes. Sighing with relief, she looked into the face of a young gentleman. His light brown hair matched his eyes and his words suggested concern.

"Who are you?"

"I am not the man you appear to be terrified of . . . although I think I know his identity. Nor am I, I am sorry to say, this Lucien you have been crying for."

He helped her to sit down. The cloak was so tangled around her arms that she needed assistance to free herself.

"My name, beautiful lady, is Samuel Swartwout."

As he extended his hand, he continued, "In answer to your next question, we are aboard a military ship bound for Washington. I think that whoever wanted to be rid of us"—he smiled and pointed to a corner of the room—"wanted to be rid of you, too."

Looking to where he pointed, she saw another man who appeared to be sleeping. "That fine gentleman is Dr. Erick Bollman. We have the misfortune of being Aaron Burr's friends."

"Aaron Burr? But I thought Mr. Burr was marching into New Orleans."

His laughter confused her more. "Oh no, dear lady. That is what some people—namely General James Wilkinson—would like others to think. Mr. Burr is an honorable man. We have been friends for many years. He is a loyal citizen." Mr. Swartwout was most serious now.

"You see, it's the general and his henchman, Major Gaspar, who want the President to believe Mr. Burr is conspiring against the U.S. Government. Dr. Bollman

144

and I came to New Orleans before Burr's arrival to make the way easier for him. He doesn't know many people in this city."

It was difficult for her to conceal her excitement and confusion. "Why, sir, did Mr. Burr decide to come to New Orleans?"

"He was to meet the general here. You see, Burr was organizing . . . well, I guess you could call it an army— wait, let me finish." Samantha had been about to interrupt. "Aaron Burr was going south . . . to Mexico. He wanted to liberate Mexico from the hated Spanish."

"Do you mean that he was not trying to separate the Southwest from the rest of the country?"

"That is correct," said the now awake prisoner in the corner. "How convenient it is for General Wilkinson and Major Gaspar to be playing both ends against the middle."

"Let us continue this later. You look faint."

"I never faint," she protested. "And I guess I should introduce myself." Here were these kind men caring for a stranger, having no idea who she was or why she was with them. It was an embarrassing situation. "I am sorry, sirs. My name is Samantha Thornton. I was here looking for my brother, Adam Thornton. He mysteriously disappeared and I suspect the general knows a lot more than he cares to admit to me." She quickly decided not to tell them everything—particularly of her family's connection to the President.

"Was Major Gaspar present at your meeting?"

"Yes, he was, Mr. Swartwout." She shivered at the mention of Gaspar's name. Her hand reached for her head as memory flooded back. "Of course. The silver riding quirt! I knew I saw a flash of something silvery before I passed out. It was the major's riding quirt. He did this to me!"

"Yes, I thought so," Swartwout said smugly. "This fits into their plan. You see, all potential informants had to be removed from New Orleans before any word got to the President about Wilkinson's nefarious activities. Your brother—I believe I met him once—had to be removed. I hope he was only temporarily removed—like us."

The other gentleman came forward. "I think, Miss, since we are to spend the next two days together we might as well be less formal. Please call me Erick."

"I am called Sam by my friends." She smiled sweetly.

"So am I," Swartwout laughed. "Why don't we use my Christian name, Samuel."

The two men presented a point of view about Aaron Burr, the President, and General Wilkinson she had never considered before. Samuel insisted that Aaron Burr was a loyal citizen, willing to give his life if necessary for his country. The stories he related about the last five years in Burr's political life were fascinating. Mr. Burr was somewhat eccentric—loved intrigue—yet his devotion to his family and friends was most sincere. Against her will, Samantha began to appreciate Aaron Burr.

They painted a picture of a lonely man. His daughter was in South Carolina; his political life had been cut short by Thomas Jefferson and the Federalists; the duel with Alexander Hamilton had ruined his reputation. Burr had allowed friends to persuade him to travel so that he could investigate the possibility of freeing the Spanish territorial possessions. It was something he was prepared to do. He could prove to his countrymen that he was not ready to retire. After all, he was only fifty.

Much to her dismay, Samantha learned of another dimension to Thomas Jefferson. Erick and Samuel told her about his vindictive side. Jefferson had been furious when he learned that Burr had received the same number of electoral votes in the election of 1800. Having Burr as his vice president was a constant reminder of that humiliation. Burr was also well connected. Too many politicians relied on his opionions, rather than Jefferson's—especially those from the North—which increased the President's antagonism toward his vice president.

Didn't Samantha think it strange, they asked, that a man like Wilkinson could be appointed to such high positions as Commander of the Army of the United States and Governor of the Territory of Louisiana *simultaneously*? It was a strange appointment. She had to concede that. Their argument continued. If—as everyone seemed to know—Wilkinson was such a scoundrel, wasn't it likely that the President knew this too? Wouldn't the President also be aware of the rumors linking General Wilkinson to the Spanish Government? Wilkinson was, in fact, in the employ of the Spanish Government! The President must have known. Yet it was easy for him to ignore his principles when it came to getting even with Aaron Burr.

It bothered her to think they might be right. Samantha was eager to talk to someone about these issues as soon as she reached Washington.

Samuel and Erick vowed to clear their names. They had been illegally arrested by Wilkinson and could prove it. The general had to be stopped. If the President did not know what was really happening in New Orleans, they were going to enlighten him. Ironically, Wilkinson's declaration of martial law was aptly being called the "American Reign of Terror." Samantha promised her friends that she would sign a statement attesting to the abominable conditions she had observed.

As soon as the ship docked, five military officers appeared to remove two prisoners. They were astounded to find that there were three—one a woman.

"If these gentlemen are to be considered prisoners, then so am I. You cannot put them in prison. They are innocent men. Why, they weren't even given the right to a trial!" Samantha would not move.

The senior officer stepped forward. "Miss, I do not know what you are doing aboard this ship, or why you are here. I will be happy to take you to see my commanding officer." He signaled for the prisoners to be led off the ship.

"Wait a minute, Sergeant. I demand to see your superior officer who will, I hope, understand the situation after I explain how well my family knows President Jefferson."

If Samuel and Erick were surprised, it didn't show. Their new friend deserved respect. If she said her family knew the President, they did. She was undoubtedly a very special woman.

It took a few hours to convince the commanding officer of who she was, but she finally succeeded. It was late in the evening by the time a dirty, disheveled

Samantha was ushered into the Secretary of State's office.

Looking as regal as possible under the circumstances, she walked unescorted into the room. Jefferson and Madison were waiting for her arrival.

"How in God's name did you get involved, Samantha Thornton?" Jefferson was obviously angry with her. Nevertheless her bedraggled state reminded him of her youthful tomboy days. He couldn't resist hugging her, relieved that she appeared unharmed.

"This is Lucien's fault. I warned him not to let you get involved. I told him he was responsible for your well-being."

"Wait a minute, Mr. President," she interrupted. "I am not responsible to anyone. Especially not to that arrogant man. He owes me nothing. I am not married to him, nor do I have any intention of marrying him or anyone," she indignantly declared. Arms folded, she continued. "And I will not discuss anything with you until you do something about releasing Samuel Swartwout and Doctor Erick Bollman. They are innocent, Mr. President, and you know it."

"You are still a stubborn child. Let me assure you, however, that your friends are being released right now. I have every intention of personally apologizing to them for what they have suffered."

"They have suffered at the hands of your Commander of the Army and his henchmen. You must do something," she pleaded. "Innocent people are myseriously disappearing or found dead."

The two men looked surprised.

Mr. Madison stepped forward. "Samantha, suppose you tell the President and me exactly what happened from the moment you decided to go to New Orleans alone."

She did. For two hours Samantha told them everything that had happened. They listened patiently, asking questions after she finished her tale of despair. Too exhausted from the events of the last few days, she no longer had the strength to ask those important questions about Aaron Burr. The Madisons insisted that she be their house guest while she made plans for her departure to Kingscote. It seemed to Samantha that no one wanted to let her out of his sight, fearing she would go back to New Orleans.

Go back she would. Going alone wouldn't do. She realized she had to have protection. If only she could have worked something out with Lucien. If only they had had a better understanding. If only . . . such foolishness, she decided. Nothing could ever change between them. He disliked her so.

Over the next two days, Mrs. Madison took Samantha under her wing. Exhausted by the recent events and her trip from New Orleans, Samantha had hardly noticed her elegant surroundings, particularly the Madison's lovely house on F Street. No other drawing room in Washington received as much attention as Dolley Madison's. Since President Jefferson was a widower, Mrs. Madison often found herself acting as the official hostess at most social functions. Samantha was in very capable hands and did not mind being pampered by the warm and endearing Dolley Madison. When she saw that Samantha had regained her strength, they shopped together, attended teas, and were guests of honor at a dinner given by friends. Days and events blended into a continuous social whirl.

Samantha never had the time to discuss the political events in the Southwest with the President or Mr. Madison. Nor did she suspect that plans were already in the making for her future.

The days were getting much cooler with winter approaching. The morning of Samantha's fifth day in Washington was one of the dreariest she had seen. The sky was darkened with the threat of an impending rainstorm. Samantha lazily moved about the bedroom. She had lost all desire for flirtatious encounters at parties. Realizing that both the President and Mr. Madison were avoiding her, she made up her mind to try once more before she left Washington.

The blue silk nightgown clung seductively to her body. A satin print wrapper kept out the wintry chill, but she shivered inwardly as the sky reminded her of a time, not too long ago, when she had experienced terror during a similar storm aboard Lucien's ship. A sudden clap of thunder made her stomach quiver as she recalled watching Lucien sway in the ship's rigging. Sitting by the window seat, she saw the storm play havoc with the Madison's garden, and it was a relief to observe the rain from within a warm, comfortable house.

Out of the corner of her eye she noted what appeared to be a horse and rider rounding the entrance to the house. The rain kept pummeling the window, making it impossible for her to get a clear view. Out of curiosity, she struggled to get a better look from the window when a loud knock at the door interrupted her. "Miss Thornton, would you care to join Mrs. Madison for a game of whist? She thought you might want some company, what with this horrible storm and all," the maid informed Samantha.

Bless Mrs. Madison, Samantha thought and smiled. The lady has the warmest heart I have ever seen. "Please tell Mrs. Madison I would be delighted to join her as soon as I change my clothes." The maid curtsied. Before the maid closed Samantha's bedroom door, a loud disturbance from downstairs couldn't help but be overheard. Within seconds loud voices echoed through the house. It must be that rider I saw, she assumed. Samantha moved closer to the door to steal a glimpse at the cause of the commotion when Dolley Madison appeared downstairs, near the staircase.

"Sir, you cannot go upstairs. I insist you wait here for Samantha."

A sick feeling permeated her body. Her first thought was of the evil Gaspar. He must have followed me, she despaired.

"Out of my way, Mrs. Madison, or I refuse to be responsible for my actions. She will see me now whether she is dressed or not!" the voice thundered.

She wanted to vanish. Of all people, she never expected to see Lucien here! He was going to kill her. She had no doubt about his intent.

Gathering her wits, she dashed back into her room, slamming the bedroom door shut. Quickly she pulled a chair under the doorknob. She was looking for a place to hide, but it was too late.

"Open this door now, Samantha. For if you do not, I swear I will break it and everything in this house." He was no longer shouting. The voice was cold, ominously direct. How could she allow him to ruin Mrs. Madison's lovely home? Defeated now, Samantha removed the obstacle from the door.

The water was dripping from his hair and coat, like snow melting from a mountain crevice. Afraid to look directly at him, she turned to find a blanket to shield her exposed body from his eyes.

"Get dressed. We are leaving right now, Samantha. If you say one word, I promise to hit you—just hard enough to temporarily render you unconscious. You are going with me, willingly or not. Right now, Samantha." He planted his body in front of the door, preventing any would-be rescuer from entering.

"I will not dress with you in the room," she hissed. Before she realized what was happening, he shoved her toward the armoir. He raised his arm, as if to strike her, then abruptly dropped it. Shocked that he really meant to carry out his threat, she stood frozen in place, eyes haunted by fear. Gingerly she touched her sore arm where he had cruelly held her.

"Don't make me hit you. I said get dressed, Samantha." Never taking his eyes from her, Lucien removed his coat as he sat in a chair near the warm fireplace.

Taking her time to dress, she taunted him with momentary glimpses of her partially revealed body. Only a muscle in his cheek twitched—nothing else. Without expression, he watched her.

Minutes later, Lucien pushed her out of the room and apologized to a dumbfounded Dolley Madison who was waiting at the foot of the stairs. Securely wrapping Samantha in her cloak, he led her to the door.

"You cannot take her outdoors now, Mr. Fraser. She will catch a cold," Mrs. Madison protested.

"We have been summoned by the President and your husband, Madam. I was told they must see us immediately. I regret"—he adjusted his own coat now—"being outdoors and forcing my horse to brave this weather because of this brat!" His grip on her arm would have forced any other person to scream with the pain. But Samantha was simply numb. What, she wondered, would the President want with them now?

"Nevertheless, Mr. Fraser, I insist you take my carriage. I have ordered my coachman to bring it around."

Samantha's eyes revealed her gratitude as she stood near the door.

"All right." He almost felt sorry for Samantha. But then he thought about the hell she had put him through the last few weeks. "No more delays. We must leave." The sound of the coach stopping in front of the house cut off further objections.

They rode in complete silence with the sound of the rain pelting the carriage. She had never seen Lucien like this before. There were many sides to this devil, she realized as she tried to sneak a look at him. His cold, dark blue eyes were looking right through her. But she refused to show him her fear. She moved as far away from him as she could, and she turned her head in another direction.

Thankfully the ride lasted only fifteen minutes. There was someone waiting for them at the entrance to Madison's office. Lucien practically propelled her out of the carriage, pushing her into the warm office.

There was no time for pleasantries. Before Samantha had the chance to vent her anger on all three of them, the President spoke.

"I am sorry to inconvenience both of you. I know each of you has been through a lot recently. However, I too feel somewhat responsible for what has occurred. Samantha," he gestured to her, "please hear me out. I have already told Lucien what I believe must be done to rectify matters. Your reputation, Samantha, is ruined."

She was shocked by this claim. "Sir, that is none of your business," she declared.

"Oh yes it is. It is also Lucien's business. You see, I hold him equally responsible for your welfare. He was well aware of that."

She turned to look at Lucien. Again, no expression. His eyes were fixed on a portrait of George Washington on the wall across the room.

"You and Lucien are to be married tonight. All the arrangements have been made. Your father would agree, Samantha, that this marriage must take place before you return to Kingscote. Sit down, Samantha. There is nothing to be said about your impending marriage that I have not already heard from Lucien."

The response was barely audible. "I refuse to marry someone whom I loathe, who surely loathes me."

"You are absolutely correct, brat. However, it is time you thought of those people you have hurt, instead of concentrating on yourself. Our friends here have made themselves perfectly clear. You, dear child, have forfeited the right to choose a husband. I seem to have lost a few rights, too," Lucien grumbled.

Madison broke the silence that followed. "There is nothing left to do. We will all go back to my house to ah . . . meet the minister."

Fury consumed her. "Just who do you think you all are? No one"—she stood up, her body rigid with suppressed anger—"can force me to marry against my wishes. Lucien"—she turned imploringly to him—

"you have to do something. If not, I swear I will run away after we are wed."

For the first time since she had seen him today, he smiled. "Will you excuse us a moment, gentlemen?"

They walked out of the room, leaving a smiling Lucien with a molten Samantha. "Sweetheart, you try any more of your schemes and I promise you will be placed in the chains reserved for the mentally deranged. As your loving husband, I can do that, you know." He grabbed her by the hair, making any movement impossible. Once again she felt herself powerless in his hard embrace. As she stood motionless, his lips crashed down on hers, bruising her mouth. Slowly, as if he knew what would happen, his tongue gently parted her lips, seeking her tongue. Caught unexpectedly by his gentleness, Samantha allowed herself to respond. Suddenly his tongue probed deeper, exploring her mouth as if he had every right to claim her mouth and more. Unable to pull away from his iron embrace, she suffered through the kiss. Her humiliation was not complete, though. Pressing her body against the wall, yet refusing to release her lips, Lucien's hands roamed the familiar curves. He was sure of her body and of her response to him, and Samantha was unable to deny him as she seductively moved against him, wrapping her arms about his neck, reaching for more. His hands slipped under her bodice, first gently, then harshly rubbing, pinching her nipples. Her eyes may have been closed, but it was crystal clear that she and this man taking liberties with her body would soon be tied, as long as either one lived, in marital union.

Chapter Twelve

Washington: Winter, 1807

It was over in what seemed to be an instant. If Samantha had to describe her wedding to anyone, she could not. One moment she was dressing, the next she and Lucien stood before the minister, repeating vows. She must have blinked once more, for Lucien's cold lips chastely touched hers, then people congratulated them. So fast. So simple. Samantha Thornton Fraser. Her new name was silently repeated over and over.

Lucien was experiencing a similar reaction, but not for the same reasons. His rage at himself, Samantha, the whole situation was blinding him. How could he have let things get so out of control? Why had he ever trusted her? Now they were irrevocably tied in wedded bliss. "Bliss." He almost laughed aloud at the word. Their relationship will definitely not be blissful—stormy, frustrating—but never blissful.

Allowing his mind to wander, the events of the last few weeks which had ultimately led him to the altar quickly flashed before him.

Lucien had left for New Orleans four days after Samantha's furtive departure. Although the *Newport Wind* was probably faster than the schooner Samantha traveled on, he was unable to catch it. Upon docking, Lucien and Roger Cole had immediately set out to find Samantha. Even with the advanced messages Lucien had received about the American "Reign of Terror" in New Orleans, he still couldn't believe what he had found. Chaos was the mildest term that could describe the situation.

Thinking it best to work separately, the two men had divided up the tasks. Roger went to the hotel and Governor Claiborne's office, while Lucien contacted the Bonnards and, finally, General Wilkinson. They were able to piece together Samantha's arrival but were mystified by her sudden disappearance.

The concierge, it seemed, received a note informing him of her decision to go to her cousin's home. After checking the handwriting, he knew it was not Samantha's hand. A knot of fear for Samantha's life grew in the pit of Lucien's stomach. When the concierge told them about Adam Thornton's "illness," Lucien thought that Samantha might have met the same fate.

Within the first two minutes of their meeting, Lucien evaluated Major Henri Gaspar and saw a hateful foe. General Wilkinson he thought to be a clever, wily man. Not as mean or violent, though, as Gaspar. At that moment, Lucien swore if Gaspar had touched Samantha, he would slowly kill Gaspar and not feel the least bit remorseful.

"Yes, Mr. Fraser, we met the charming Samantha," Wilkinson smiled. "A lovely and spirited lady, I think. Did you know that she was using the name 'Fraser'?"

No, he had not, but nothing could surprise him when it came to Samantha. "Yes, I did, General," he lied. "She's quite independent. Her father is most anxious for me to return her safely as soon as possible. But"—he looked directly at Gaspar—"she seems to have disappeared—like her brother." There was no reaction. These men were dangerous—he could feel it. "It is odd, gentlemen, that both the concierge and her cousins received notes from Miss Thornton, each one believing she was staying with the other. I am sure her disappearance was carefully arranged."

He knew that he couldn't accuse either of them . . . yet. But time was running short. If he couldn't find any traces of her now, it would be impossible later on. "Even in the Louisiana Territory, kidnapping is a serious offense. Especially," he smiled, "if the lady happens to be as close as a daughter to the President of the United States. Since you are the highest ranking military officer, General, I believe that makes you responsible. You see, a military officer was last seen leaving her hotel room on the night of her disappearance."

"Mr. Fraser, I will put the major and his staff at your service. I regret that I do not know what happened to the young lady after she left here." The General looked somewhat concerned.

"She went to Governor Claiborne's office. However, I am sure you already knew that. The Governor invited Samantha to dinner. Samantha decided to go back to her hotel to freshen up first. She was seen going in . . . but not leaving." Lucien's fists clenched. "In fact, everything in her room was left untouched. Samantha is willful, but I assure you, General, she wouldn't disappear without taking her purse or some clothing."

The General looked uncomfortable but not the major. A silver-handled riding quirt was continually toyed with in his hands. The man was truly irritating Lucien. He wanted to find an excuse to pummel him. Maybe that arrogant bastard wouldn't be so sure of himself if his arms were broken.

Lucien had prepared for this meeting. It was not difficult to get the information he desired about both Wilkinson and Gaspar. Wilkinson's story was public information but Gaspar was a mysterious fellow.

Although born in New Orleans, his family was descended from lesser known French nobility. Being the second son, Paul Gaspar and his wife emigrated to New Orleans where he sought his fortune. However, life had not been fair to Monsieur Gaspar. Not possessing any particular skill except for gambling, he relied on the reputation of his family's name. The Creoles admired anyone with even a hint of nobility in his blood, so the Gaspars managed for a short while. Within three years, there was no one in New Orleans willing to extend credit to them. By that time there was a child to worry about. Paul desperately wanted his son to succeed where he could not. Henri was destined for the army as a way to seek his fame and fortune.

Paul had gone back to France to try and raise funds—actually to borrow from his relatives. There was a storm at sea and the ship and all its passengers were lost. Widowed and tired of being poor, Yvette Gaspar lost no time in marrying a very wealthy American while Henri was sent abroad to pursue his military studies. A position in the rag-tag American

160

army awaited him upon his return to the now American-controlled Louisiana Territory. Henri, while abroad, had developed a well-defined sense of his goals. Obsessed with restoring the name of Gaspar to its rightful high position, Henri made sure that nothing—and no one—stood in his way. Wealth and power were the only things that mattered. Working for General Wilkinson served to promote this aim.

Fortunately, Lucien knew what type of man he was. He had neither honor nor morals. Lucien had dealt with many such men before while working for the government as well as those he came across in business. They were ruthless. Get to them first, he knew, for you will never live to have a second chance.

"General Wilkinson, I plan to stay in New Orleans for a few days. My crew will waste no time in searching for me if I happen to 'disappear' like the Thorntons."

Although Lucien was addressing Wilkinson, his cold, blue eyes never left Gaspar's expressionless face. Lucien was covertly daring Gaspar to try something. "It was a pleasure meeting you both. Thank you for seeing me on such short notice." As he stood up, his hand caressed the pistol handle secured in his waistband. Lucien was taller and more muscular than Gaspar. "I sincerely hope, gentlemen, that you will have information for me about the Thorntons before I make my report to President Jefferson." His threat was clear: Either they gave him some indication of Samantha's or Adam's whereabouts, or their positions could become quite unsettled.

Over the next two days, Lucien and Roger had

checked every possible lead—even the old man Samantha had met at Wilkinson's office. Through his own sources, Lucien was made aware of the unorthodox arrest and departure of Swartwout and Bollman. Suspicious now that Samantha had been kidnapped, Lucien knew he needed proof. All the while he was worried about Samantha, but furious with her, too. The fury would wait until he caught up with her—if he caught up with her. Roger and Lucien were seen everywhere in town. People expected to see the two tall, dark men around the city at all hours, asking questions or simply watching the street scene.

The break came one night when they were drinking in a tavern near the wharf. A nervous young sailor approached them.

"Are ye the two looking for a woman?"

Roger asked him to join them for a drink.

"I am not sure, mind you, but one night, about five days ago, I was on duty aboard me own ship. I saw two men—their hands were tied—put on board the American military ship. I learned later they were the ones arested for treason."

"Go on man," prodded Lucien, anxious to hear the rest.

"Well, ya see, what I thought was really strange was the late night goings on aboard the ship. I know it was late—it was almost the end of me watch—and I saw two army men carrying something aboard the ship. The ship was due to leave soon. It seemed mighty odd that other people would go aboard." He quickly gulped his drink before he continued. "Anyways, this object they was carrying moaned. I thought the sound was made by a cat nearby. But then I saw her hair. The thing covering her head fell off and all this red hair fell out. I knew it was a woman, but before I could call someone to help, they disappeared. Now I know they probably left her on the ship and ran away—like cowards."

Lucien's suspicion was confirmed. There was no need to check further. Samantha had been abducted and put on tht ship bound for Washington. It was useless to stay in New Orleans any longer. The *Newport Wind* was made ready for immediate departure, and there was no mistaking the captain's apprehension.

After Lucien's interview with the President, his fury was almost uncontrollable. He was told about everything that had happened to Samantha even though there was no news about Adam. Yet, he was relieved that she was safe and still in Washington. However, when Jefferson informed Lucien of his imminent marriage, something snapped. He was no longer in control of his destiny. People were issuing orders and planning his life. That was something Lucien could not tolerate. Samantha was responsible for this entire mess . . . and she would pay for it.

They were finally alone. Somehow Lucien's desire to sleep was greater than the necessity to talk to her. They would have a whole lifetime together now and he blanched at the thought. What he did not care to know was that his bride felt the same way.

Gradually, the numbness Samantha had felt all day was replaced by awe. How did this situation get out of control? Why did Lucien permit this to happen? It must

163

be his way of avenging himself. It was impossible to distinguish the pounding of her heart from the sick feeling churning in the pit of her stomach. There was no escape. It occurred to her that she might be more secure if she were still imprisoned aboard the military ship rather than in Lucien's grasp.

Probably because he wanted them to have privacy, Lucien insisted they spend the next few nights at the home of an old school friend who was currently abroad. As with the Madison's house, Samantha hardly noticed her surroundings.

"Lucien, we have to talk about this horrible situation we find ourselves in," she suddenly announced. Her husband was already stretched out on the big canopied bed. Unwilling to lie near him, she thought to avoid the bed. She quickly looked around the unfamiliar room for a place to sit.

Delighting in her discomfort, Lucien said sarcastically, "Come now, sweet, sit by your loving husband. There is no need to avoid me."

"Always mocking me, aren't you, Lucien? Well, I will not let you make me angry this time. I want to talk to you," she insisted, flinging her cloak aside. She would not, however, get undressed in front of him. Still wearing the elegant gold and pink brocade dress she had worn for the wedding ceremony, Samantha advisedly sat next to Lucien on the large bed.

"I apologize for causing you all this trouble. I know you were planning to marry Caroline."

"I was? I suppose Caroline gave you that bit of information."

Unfortunately, Samantha misunderstood his look of anger, convincing herself Lucien was angry, as usual, with her and not with Caroline. Sitting as stiffly as one could on a soft bed, she continued her prepared speech.

"As I was saying, I apologize for ruining both of our plans for the future. I have an idea I would like to discuss with you."

Intrigued more with her delicate profile than the idea, Lucien nevertheless propped himself up on the pillows. "Please continue, my sweet."

"Well, I think our marriage should be the same arrangement proposed in Newport." She saw his brows rise in confusion. "When I was in Paris, I met many couples who had this arrangement. That is, they . . . ah . . . stayed together in name only. You know, a marriage of convenience." The latter part of her statement came out in a rush. For some reason she felt Lucien had to understand that she did not want this marriage any more than he did. Actually, she could not even predict this marriage would last beyond the week. Visibly tense now, a light sheen of sweat appeared on her brow, in spite of the chilly night. Turning her body to face him, she went on.

"You must understand, Lucien. I am still going to find Adam. I have to go back to New Orleans. If you won't accompany me, I will find someone who will—perhaps Father."

His hands were itching to strangle her. Instead, he restrained himself by folding them behind his head. "We keep coming back to the same issue, don't we? Well, wife, you will now do as I say. Your father is in no position to contradict me." Reaching for a loose strand of her hair, he resumed in a cool monotone. "I have made plans for both of us to return to New Orleans in a few weeks. I have hired men, under Roger's supervi-

165

sion, to get any information they can—any way they can."

How relieved she was to hear that. "Oh, I am so glad, Lucien. We can go home to make arrangements. But Lucien . . . about the other matter." It was dangerous being close to him. Quickly she rose to walk to the other side of the room. As she turned to face him, she was startled to see him right behind her, towering over her.

"There is no other matter. You are my wife. There will never—do you understand, Samantha?—*never* be an arrangement or a divorce." Automatically, his arms reached for her waist. Looking directly into her emerald eyes, he bent his head to kiss her.

Twisting her head away, she gasped, "Stay away from me! I am tired of you using my body. I am not Caroline Prescott! If you want someone to fall into bed with you each time you command it, find some other victim." She panted. She tried to run toward the door to escape his touch. Once more his muscular body reached the door before her.

"Are you deaf, madam? I told you that you cannot escape me. Now stop this foolishness!" Again his arm reached to imprison her, but like a deer caught in a trap she kept struggling for her freedom. Hairpins scattered about the room as her hair tumbled down around her shoulders and across her face, temporarily blinding her.

"No, you beast! I don't care if some minister says we're married. Stay away from me!" Her voice sounded hysterical. "I don't want you to touch me!"

"Whom do you want, woman? Do you want Turreau, Davis? How about Major Gaspar?" His eyes

166

hinted at the white hot fury in his loins.

At the mention of Gaspar's name, she froze. "How dare you? That man is as much an animal as you are. I don't need you, dear *husband*, to hand-pick my lovers. I am perfectly capable of selecting them myself. Do you understand me?"

"Perfectly." He grabbed both of her wrists, cruelly twisting them behind her back. With his free hand he reached for the neck of the dress. "Now wife," he said chillingly, "you are about to understand me." With his eyes never leaving her face, he slowly, methodically tore the dress away from her body. Still struggling, Samantha tried to kick, then bite Lucien, but his determination was overwhelming. Tears welled up and fell from her shocked eyes.

"Are you mad, Lucien? Let me go!" Somehow she managed to free one hand from his grasp. With her remaining strength, she brought her hand full force against Lucien's cheek. Only her stinging palm felt the impact. Lucien merely smiled down at her.

"You will pay for that, wife!" He bent his head to her neck, alternating kisses and tiny bites. Her resolve was shaken but she couldn't let him subdue her. Again her hand reached for his face. He pulled her closer to his body, molding her to his form. Her nails dug into his hair and went further as she scratched the side of his face. The blood trickled down his cheek, but still his eyes never left hers. Clad only in her pink silk and lace chemise, she was horrified when Lucien swiftly tore that from her body. He put it to his face to stem the trickle of blood. Her every thought was in the grip of fear.

"Thank you for that lesson, Samantha sweet. I shall

not give you a chance to maul me again." He roughly lifted her off the floor, throwing her onto the bed. Not giving her time to recover, Lucien lowered his fully clothed body onto her now naked one. Her hands were pulled above her head.

"No," she whimpered. "Don't Lucien . . . please."

He was beyond hearing or caring. His mouth came forcefully down on hers. The brutal kiss took her breath away. Suddenly, his free hand masterfully roamed her breasts, then lower to her stomach. Still seeking, the hand lowered to her red-gold sheath, rubbing, stroking. It was ironic that the hand was making love to her body, while his mouth ravaged hers. His legs locked her thighs in place, precluding escape, while his hand bore deeply into her center, crashing down the dam which held back passion's fluids.

"So you want me, don't you, Samantha?" His tongue found its own way to her ear. "I think you want me to take your unwilling body. Feel yourself, Samantha." He brought one of her hands down to her secret hollow. "You are wet, my love, with desire . . . for *me*. You will never have another enter your body, not while you have me . . . my mouth . . . my hands . . . my body."

"I don't want you, Lucien. I would rather bed a snake than you!" she spat.

"We shall see, my love."

Still not trusting her, Lucien swiftly tied her hands to the bedpost with her torn chemise, while he took his time undressing. His desire for her was obvious. He would wait, though; her agony must be prolonged. He would teach her a lesson she would never forget.

"Oh, get it over with. Rape me and be done with it." Her eyes appeared large with fear, but her voice was full of stubborn pride.

"How could I leave my wife dissatisfied on our wedding night?" he mocked. "That would not do, my sweet." He lowered himself into her.

She did not think she was ready for him, but as always with Lucien her body seemed to be independent from her mind. Not only did she receive his maleness, but she involuntarily opened up to him. Why, after this brutality, did she still crave his touch? Her punishment was not being allowed to touch him. Lucien would not untie her hands. Instead, his hands and mouth carefully continued their journey over her writhing body, while he rhythmically pounded into her flesh.

"Untie my hands," she moaned.

"Why, my love? Do you want me? Tell me." He moved as if he were pulling himself out of her.

"Yes—I want you," she said huskily.

"Do you want another? Will you give yourself to other men? Tell me Samantha!" He eased himself out of her.

She couldn't bear not feeling him. Her eyes pleaded with him as she murmured, "I only want you, Lucien."

"That's better, my love." He tore the restraints off her wrists, easing himself slowly back into her waiting body.

Her arms wrapped around his neck, searching his sinewy form. A swift, sharp sensation traveled down his back. "You will have my mark, too, husband. Don't ever tie me again," she threatened.

He should have struck her. Instead, he softly chuckled, "Don't forget, Samantha, even wild horses know taming. And you should consider this the first in the many lessons I will give you in domestication."

With that, he rolled her onto her side, pulling her smooth buttocks closer to him, never stopping his rhythmic motion. They both lost themselves in their mutual need.

As if this night were their last time together, they loved each other until the light of dawn seeped through the windows. Curiously, each felt more relaxed in the other's arms than they had at any other time.

"I fear, Lucien, that I am getting used to you . . . brutality and all." She smiled dreamily, all anger and fear now forgotten after their blazing hours of passion.

"That's because you need me. You may not know it here"—he lovingly kissed her forehead—"but I think you know it here." His hands rhythmically stroked her breasts. "Who knows, maybe you will come to love me." It almost sounded wistful.

"As soon as you admit you love and need me," she teased. "Well, we are together. I propose that we try to make a success of our marriage, starting now." Her voice was full of determination.

"What a chameleon you are. First you swear your hatred, you leave scars all over my body, you fight me . . . and now this!" He sat up to look at her ripe body, his face softening. "What shall it be? Will I ever understand you?"

"No. Nor will I you. And that's why we might stay together—for a while." She sighed, pulling his hand back to her chest.

"Did you have any idea how we all worried over your departure? After I got to New Orleans and found out you had disappeared . . . my God, Samantha, you surely unnerved me."

A soft, tinkling laugh escaped from her lips. "Come now, Lucien, nothing frightens you. But I must admit, after meeting that awful Gaspar I was more than a little frightened." She shivered slightly then relaxed as her husband gathered her into his arms.

"I hated that bastard on sight. Did he harm you, Samantha?" His voice became harsh.

"I am sure now that he was the one who hit me on the head and arranged for my departure. I recall seeing his silver riding quirt before I blacked out. Every time he looked at me, I felt I was being examined like a slave at auction."

"If that bastard so much as looks at you again, I swear I will kill him."

"No! But I am positive that he is responsible for Adam's disappearance. I don't want him to be responsible for yours." She sounded truly concerned.

"You see?" He laughed. "Already you speak like a devoted wife." He kissed her brow. "Tomorrow—or shall I say today—we will make our plans. But now, my love, I want to feel your body nestled in mine."

Chapter Thirteen

Within a few days the newly married couple was once again aboard a ship. Of course, Samantha was far more comfortable in the captain's cabin of the *Newport Wind* than in the deplorable accommodations on that military ship. The ship's crew members were pleased to see the captain's wife. They had a special fondness for her. None of them knew the circumstances of this marriage, so they assumed the couple to be madly in love and unable to wait to return to Rhode Island before marrying.

Roger Cole knew the truth but was still delighted with the marriage. Never liking Caroline Prescott, Roger feared his friend would be ensnared by that cold bitch. It didn't take much effort to like—even to admire—Samantha. Nor did it take long for an easy camaraderie to develop between them. Too bad Lucien had found her first. Surely if anyone had the potential for taming Lucien, this untamed tigress did. Certainly she could use a little taming herself, he observed. As the days slipped by Roger became convinced that if this temporary truce between the Frasers could take root, the marriage would be a happy one. The sly glances she often cast at her husband when he was occupied with the responsibilities of running a ship were not unnoticed by Roger. Her eyes lit up—brilliant green sparkling eyes—watching her man's graceful movements. Those two care for each other, Roger noted, more than they are willing to admit.

At dinner, to which Roger was frequently invited, the playful banter of the couple was refreshing. Even the relaxed manner of his friend, who laughed more frequently, foreshadowed the bright future they could have together if Caroline stayed out of their lives, and if these two could learn how to cope with their tempers.

One day while Lucien was supervising some men who were having trouble with the rigging, Samantha approached Roger. "Roger." She smiled sweetly, admiring his handsome face. "If you ever decide to marry, you must get my approval of the lucky lady first."

"Samantha," he replied, his dark brown eyes hinting of levity, "did you ask for my approval before you married our rotten captain?"

"Oh, but Roger, I know you approve of me," she laughed.

"I do, but I did not say I approve of your husband." He pointed to Lucien who was no longer supervising but actually doing the work.

Remembering the circumstances of their marriage and first night together, Samantha could only blush. The isolation of the voyage provided Samantha with plenty of time alone. Often she found herself wondering about Lucien: What is he really like? His crew idolizes him. Adam and Roger obviously respect him. Even Father thinks the sun rises and sets on

Lucien Fraser.

"Tell me, how did you and Lucien meet?" she asked, interested in learning about the friendship between Lucien and Roger. Roger walked her to the quarter-deck which was still bathed in afternoon sun.

"Well, my family is from Boston. My father was more interested in financial matters than ships; he is a financier. Needless to say, he wanted me to follow his path, but I couldn't. Perhaps some day." His sun-bronzed features were lost in thought. "I always loved the sea. The thought of staying in a room all day, handling other people's money did not appeal to me. Eventually my father realized as much and had me apprenticed to James Fraser, a business associate. He was a wonderful teacher. I enjoyed those years with the Frasers. Lucien was also apprenticing at the same time. He never minded my presence. I was always treated like a brother." He laughed at a new thought. "Well, almost. We didn't always share—especially when girls became a part of our lives."

A small frown appeared on her face. "Oh, did that include Caroline?"

Roger became more serious. "Sam, you must not believe anything that woman says. Don't under-estimate her. She gets exactly what she wants. I never liked her. Why Lucien did—well, she was convenient, I guess," he asked and answered the question himself. "She will give you trouble. You know she always fancied herself as the future Mrs. Fraser," he warned.

"I suppose Lucien had wished for that as well. Now he's saddled with me," she said softly.

"You are dead wrong. Have you looked in the mirror? Lucien was not obliged to marry you. There was no pistol at his head. He never does anything without wanting to. He could have easily removed himself from the situation." Roger was never so sure of his words as he was now.

Samantha, however, could not be convinced. "He was obeying orders, Roger. He doesn't want to be married—especially to someone he does not love."

He tweaked her nose playfully, trying to get her out of this dark frame of mind. "You are young pet, but you will see." He touched her hand. "Remember Sam, if you ever need a friend . . ."

"I know, Roger . . . and thanks." She stood on her toes to kiss his cheek.

"Hey, what's going on over there. My wife and best friend kissing?" Lucien's deep voice boomed across the deck. In three long strides he joined them. His dark blue breeches snugly hugged his muscular thighs. Samantha's eyes were immediately drawn to his rippling chest muscles which were accented by the mat of curly black hair escaping from the opening of his white linen shirt. Being near Lucien made her breathless and she blushed with memories of their passion-filled nights.

"Roger is simply telling me about some of your nastier habits." She smiled, trying to regain control of her emotions. Quickly she lowered her eyes, for if she had looked into Lucien's—which was her impulse—he would have known her deepest sentiments. It was odd that more often than she cared to admit, Lucien had a knack for reading her mind.

"Tomorrow we will be home. I can't wait to see the greeting we will get, my love." Automatically his arm reached protectively around her slim waist as he led

Samantha to the cabin—and hopefully to the big, wooden-framed bed.

Their homecoming was more joyous than either would have predicted. The newly married Frasers agreed not to tell of the events leading to their sudden marriage. They wished to convince everyone this marriage was an impulsive decision made by two anxious lovers.

"We must have a party to celebrate," Elizabeth gushed. "I am so happy. You must tell me how this came about. Later, though. Let's get you settled in Lucien's room first."

Everyone was pleased—almost everyone. Caroline, not knowing that Lucien was married, quickly arrived at his office that afternoon. She sailed through the door, ignoring the protests of Lucien's clerk, and wrapped her arms about a startled Lucien's neck.

"Darling, you are home at last. I can't tell you how lonely and boring it has been without you," her silky voice echoed in his ear.

Embarrassed to be accosted by Caroline in front of Roger, who could hardly control his mirth, Lucien disentangled the fur-clad arms from his body. He held her at arms length. Unaware of what he was doing, Lucien found himself comparing the pale, possessive Caroline to his fiery Samantha. "His" Samantha. He smiled inwardly. I'd better not let that minx get to me.

"Lucien, darling, I am talking to you. Are you feeling well? You seem to have a faraway look in your eyes."

"He does have a faraway look, Caroline." Roger was actually laughing. "He is dreaming about his lovely wife who is waiting for him to come home."

Caroline's mouth dropped in an unflattering manner. A murderous look flashed across her porcelain face, distorting her features. She laughed, convincing herself that Roger, who had never liked her, was enjoying a cruel joke.

"You are a tease, Roger. Lucien, he is joking, isn't he?" she inquired, her hand still possessing Lucien's arm.

If he had been able to blush, he would have. Instead, he gave Caroline an affectionate squeeze of her hands as he smiled.

"Well, yes and no."

Hatred and anger began to consume her. She persisted. "I do not understand, Lucien"—she pressed her body closer—"did you marry someone else?"

"Yes . . . yes I did. Samantha and I were married two weeks ago." I wish Samantha could see her face, he thought, seconds before Caroline raised her palm and slapped his cheek.

"How dare you!" she growled. "And to that horrid child! What can she possibly offer you that I have not and cannot?"

If you only knew, he thought, as he looked soberly at Caroline. That slap seemed to have cleared his brain. He stared at her icy features, twisted with jealousy and hatred which were directed at his wife. Yes, Caroline was attractive, but she lacked warmth and sincerity. Her feelings, if she had any, were masked behind her cold, calculating smile.

"Caroline," he drawled, beginning to find this scene annoying, "I do not like the way you speak of my wife!

178

As for our relationship, we never had anything more than lustful encounters. I never made you any promises."

"You are a beast!" she shouted. "You were going to marry me. Not that little slut—"

Before she could catch her breath to continue the tirade, her arm was cruelly grabbed by Lucien.

"I warn you, Caroline, stay away from Samantha. I was never your possession. I can assure you I never had any intention of marrying you, and you certainly knew that." His dark, midnight eyes first flared with fury then transformed to amusement. "After all, Caroline, if you don't stay away from my wife, I cannot be responsible for what she might do to you."

Roger's bellow of laughter rang through the room. Pulling her fur cloak tight, she coolly replied, "I shall not forget, dear Lucien. I will see you in hell! When you become bored with your sweet little passionless wife, remember how I have pleased you. And if you beg on your knees I may consider taking you back."

"Dramatic, aren't we, Caroline?" Lucien queried. If she heard him, she didn't reply, for she exited swiftly without a backward glance.

"She must be on to her next conquest," said Roger. "Thank God, it won't be me. I hope you really can keep Samantha away from that cat."

It was not possible. Since Caroline's family was among the most prominent in Newport, Elizabeth had no choice but to invite them to the wedding reception.

It might have been easy for Samantha to accept Caroline if she had known what had transpired in Lucien's office. But the confrontation was so insignificant to Lucien that it was forgotten as soon as Caroline had swept out of the office.

The reception was going to be a splendid affair. Even the weather cooperated. February in Newport was usually quite cold, but this particular night was mild. The large ballroom at Kingscote was brilliantly lit by crystal chandeliers filled with candles of different sizes. The musicians sat off to the side playing various melodious tunes for dancing and listening. The women were dressed in the latest fashions, though no one could match Samantha.

On any other woman the deep, emerald green gown would have looked vulgar. The color perfectly matched her eyes. The dress was a long-sleeved combination of satin and velvet, interlaced with delicate gold threading. Whichever way she turned, she sparkled. The neckline was daringly low, causing Samantha's firm breasts to sit precariously on her bodice. One large emerald comfortably nestled between her breasts while matching earbobs offset her glorious hair. The jewels were Lucien's newest gift to her. Her coppery curls were ingeniously styled by Maria. Layers of curls were piled high and highlighted by a matching green ribbon intricately woven through her hair.

As soon as Lucien saw this vision he fought the temptation to bar her from leaving their bedroom so that he could possess her luscious body.

"Lucien," she laughed, "you must stop. Otherwise my dress will be wrinkled." His arms enfolded her waist as he pushed her against the bedroom wall, crushing

180

her with his own obviously aroused body.

"Samantha, love, at this moment I do not give a damn about this party. How can I spend the evening watching you and not being able to caress those ripe, inviting breasts?" He bent his head to nibble at her emerald-studded earlobes, then bent lower, teasingly kissing her tempting breasts. Placing his body fully against hers, Lucien slowly rotated his hips. If he continued in such a manner, Samantha knew her now tingling body would not let him stop.

"Lucien," she whispered huskily, gently pushing him away, "couldn't we continue this later, when I do not have to worry if someone will interrupt us?"

"At least I know you want me too. I can feel it . . ." His hand hiked up her skirt and found the moist junction between her legs. The layers of undergarments could not hide her obvious arousal.

A soft, insistent knocking at the door confirmed Samantha's fear.

"Come, love, let's greet our guests. But not until I taste your lips." His dark head lowered to her lips, kissing her thoroughly, enveloping her mouth.

"Now," she pouted, trying to smooth her hair, "everyone will know what we have been doing."

"Don't fret, my love, we're married. And the color in your cheeks enhances your beautifully swollen lips."

They were late to their own soirée. People greeted them, wishing them happiness together. Samantha's flushed face did not leave much room for doubt. The gentlemen indulgently smiled, wishing they could have been lucky enough to bed such a beauty. The women jealously tittered among themselves; nevertheless, the attractiveness of the couple was not unnoticed. Lucien's tall, dark looks perfectly offset Samantha's diminutive and fiery beauty.

For the first time since she had known him, Samantha was enjoying herself at a party. At previous parties they had either avoided or fought each other. This evening they even looked lovingly at one another. "Lovingly" was too strong a word, she corrected herself. Watch out, Samantha, she thought. Do not lose your heart to him. For if you do, he will take advantage of it. Resolving to enjoy each moment as it happened, she drank the champagne, laughed with her guests, and stole a few sober moments alone with Meredith. Her sister-in-law seemed to be happy, but Samantha wondered how much of her laughter was contrived.

She, and everyone else, obviously could not forget Adam. In fact, Samantha and Lucien had decided to return to New Orleans within the month to continue their search. They had already obtained a small house in the American section of town in anticipation of their return. Finding a place was easy. Who would want to settle there, given the current political situation? They could have rented the governor's home.

Since Lucien was still in the service of the U.S. Government, he would have to obtain approval for his revised plans and get new orders from Washington before going to New Orleans. There was no question Samantha would accompany him. Surely Mr. Madison could not reject her offer of assistance now. And the Frasers had already decided upon their course of action in New Orleans. Their stay depended entirely on locating Adam. If, at the same time, they were able to obtain valuable information about Aaron Burr's or the Spanish Government's involvement in the Southwest, such information would be passed on to Washington. No one would know their real reason for residing in New Orleans. The shipping office that Adam ostensibly went to establish in New Orleans still needed to be opened. Privately they hoped this "cover" would work.

Samantha had convinced Meredith to go to Charleston with her father. Meredith thought a new setting might boost her spirits and certainly a woman's presence at Thornton Hill was sorely needed. Robert could no longer delay his departure for home. Too much needed to be done at Thornton Hill. Having Meredith and his grandson with him was his greatest wish and tomorrow they planned to start south.

Elizabeth Fraser had accepted their impending departure. At least her son and new daughter-in-law would be staying for a few days. Wanting to give the newlyweds more time alone, Elizabeth had made plans to visit her sister in New York. Everyone could be contacted if needed, particularly if word of Adam's safe return reached them.

Yes, things might work out, Samantha said to herself as she looked around the crowded room for her husband. She found Lucien deep in conversation with Roger and a few other merchants.

He caught a glimpse of her sensual form gliding toward him. At that moment all he could think of was feeling her warm, vibrant body in his arms.

"Samantha, Mr. Withers was just telling us about the newest developments in the Southwest." She could tell from Lucien's unenthusiastic tone that they had been listening to more nonsense.

"I hope, Mr. Withers, that when Lucien and I go to New Orleans we have the opportunity to meet this General Wilkinson of whom you speak so highly." Without thinking, her arm linked through Lucien's, causing a tiny tremor in his body at the contact.

"What a charming domestic scene we have here," interrupted Caroline in an unusually high, sarcastic tone. She was dressed in a bright red, clinging satin gown which left nothing to the imagination. And Caroline certainly had not been lacking in male companionship this evening. Well, Samantha thought, she's not wasting any time in finding another lover.

"Have I offered you my congratulations, dears? Lucien can be quite lustful, Samantha. I hope you can manage to hold him." Caroline stepped closer to Samantha as if she were about to kiss her cheek. "If not, Samantha dear, he will know where to find me," she whispered.

Not wanting to display her anger at Caroline's audacious remark, Samantha coolly leaned toward her and purred, "Dearest Caroline, if Lucien ever gets involved with you again, it will be because he has forgotten what the seamier side of life is about." With her lips firmly closed, Samantha smiled into Caroline's shocked face. "Thank you so much for your good wishes. No hard feelings. I do hope we can be friends."

Her rival was not satisfied. Grabbing Lucien's arm, Caroline said, "I believe you owe me this one dance. For old times, Lucien?" Her eyelids fluttered with her false coquetry.

"Oh, Lord," Lucien muttered. "That spiteful bitch has me trapped." One look at Samantha's emerald eyes, now spitting with fury, told him what her feelings were. Yet if he turned Caroline down, an embarrassing scene would disrupt the evening.

Roger at once assessed the situation. "Samantha, you cannot deny me my dance any longer." He smiled into her angry face, lightly touching her arm as he led her off to the dance floor.

"Roger, how could you do this to me? Don't you know that . . . that . . . brazen whore wants Lucien? Why, she wishes me dead and you know it!" She was panting. The combination of anger, humiliation, and pride were explosive and Samantha found it difficult to catch her breath.

"Look, you saw the position she put Lucien in. He had no other choice, Samantha. I think it's time you learned to trust your husband." Her doubtful look pressed him further. Whirling her about the dance floor, Roger finally got her to smile. "Sam, that husband of yours is thoroughly infatuated with you."

"Roger, there is no need to exaggerate. All right, I understand. I will not let Caroline make me angry with my husband. If you keep whirling so fast I'll be too dizzy to notice."

They walked over to the buffet. Casting her eyes about the room, Samantha saw a flash of scarlet. Wasn't that Caroline being led off to the gardens? Who was that with her? She froze. It couldn't be! Why would he do this to me, on the night of our reception with everyone watching?

"Roger, don't tell me that my husband can be

trusted." This humiliation was too much. But it was not all she would have to endure. "Roger, would you please take me outside for some air?"

They walked toward the fountain. Again Caroline's scarlet dress disappeared before her eyes. Determined now, she walked toward the scarlet form, a puzzled Roger trailing behind her. Staring straight ahead like a statue, Samantha's lips formed a bloodless smile. Roger followed her gaze and saw them, too. The two shapes near the fountain were locked in a tight embrace. Caroline's lips were waiting for Lucien's to accept them.

As if suddenly jolted by a clap of thunder, Samantha's hand flew to her mouth. She gasped and turned around, fleeing toward the bright, warm lights of the ballroom in the house that was to be her home.

Caroline was positively triumphant. This meeting had gone exactly as she had planned. She strolled back into the ballroom, leaving the men behind her. Lucien, however, was in a murderous rage, mostly directed at his wife who had run away from him instead of waiting for him to explain; at Caroline, who had deliberately planned this awkward confrontation; and at Roger, who was looking disappointedly at him!

"For God's sake, Roger, stop looking at me like I am a snake," he almost shouted.

"Why not? You deserve that much and more, my friend. How could you choose that strumpet over Samantha?"

"Not you, too! Do you think I would rendezvous with my former mistress—I said 'former,' Roger—in my home, with my wife so near?" He was incredulous. "Roger, I was tricked. Caroline asked me to dance. You and Samantha were witness to that."

"Yes, and I finally managed to calm Sam down, enough to look for you, and what do we find—"

"Look," he interrupted. "You are not giving me a chance to explain any more than that red-headed, hot-tempered virago."

"All right, I am sorry, Lucien. Please go on." Roger would not move, however, from the defiant stance he had taken. His arms were folded across his chest and his foot annoyingly tapped the stone floor.

"After Caroline insisted I dance with her, she asked if we could stroll outside because she was warm. She also said it would be a nice gesture on my part—for old times' sake." He angrily slapped his thigh, recalling his own stupidity. "I know, it was sheer idiocy. I should not have let her talk me into it. But she started to cry, and I could not stand another scene, so I relented. When we got here, she asked if she could have a good-bye kiss—again for old times' sake. I put my hands on her shoulders to push her away, but she persisted. She kissed *me*, Roger. I did not want her cold lips on mine—not after Samantha'a kisses. Unfortunately, it was at the very moment that Caroline reached to kiss me that Samantha and you appeared."

"Well, I don't see how you will explain this to Samantha." Roger relaxed, for Lucien's agitation convinced him of his friend's innocence. "I am sorry," he said contritely, "for not realizing from the start that you couldn't be that stupid." They both grinned at that last comment. However, Lucien's smile almost immediately disappeared as he got angry with his wife all

187

over again.

"Why can't she trust me? She should know better. I'll be damned, Roger, if I apologize to her now. In fact, I do not owe her a single explanation. If she wants to be stubborn, I can be just as stubborn. Come on, Roger, I think I need a strong drink."

"Lucien, there's going to be hell to pay."

Chapter Fourteen

The rest of the evening was a blur to Lucien. He was too drunk to care about anything. When he went back inside the house with Roger, he noticed his wife laughing and flirting with half-a-dozen men who surrounded her, vying for her attention. Ignoring him completely, Samantha did not notice Lucien's return. She did, however, see Caroline, who made a point of dancing near Samantha, smiling at Samantha's recent humiliation. There was no need for words. This was Caroline's victory.

Lucien and Samantha had to stand together long enough to bid their guests good night. Each was gracious and charming. None of their guests suspected how angry the new Mrs. Fraser was, or how drunk Mr. Fraser had become. After the last guest departed, Samantha lovingly made her good-byes to her family who were leaving early in the morning.

"Meredith"—tears welled in her eyes—"I promise we will have information about Adam for you soon. Before we sail to New Orleans, we will stop for a few days at Thornton Hill." They hugged and cried in each other's arms.

Robert kissed his daughter as he wished her well. "I am so happy for you, dear. I know you and Lucien are right for one another." He shook Lucien's hand. "Take care of my daughter."

"Yes, sir." Lucien smiled. "I plan to." Samantha could have sworn that sounded more like a threat than a promise. Who cares? It doesn't matter any more, she thought somewhat sadly.

Afraid to stay with Lucien any longer than necessary, Samantha swiftly returned to their bedroom. It was clear to her that Lucien had been drinking heavily. He was in such a state that he would probably spend the rest of the night drinking as well.

Preparing herself for bed took less time than usual, for she hoped to be asleep by the time her husband returned.

Hours later, a loud thumping awakened her. She sensed that Lucien was having a difficult time finding his way about the room. She pretended to be asleep, but a loud "Oh, damn," followed by the sound of his boots flying across the room startled her.

"Did I wake you, my sweet? How clumsy of me," he said rather clearly for one so drunk.

"Lucien, I have no desire to talk to you tonight"— she lowered her voice—"or ever."

"Aren't we a bit touchy. Well, I will tell you something, Samantha." He stood over her prone form. "I have no desire to talk to or even live with someone as mistrusting or hot-tempered as you. But," he shrugged, "it appears I do not have a choice."

Scampering off the bed to stand next to him, she lashed out. "Don't talk to *me* about mistrust, Lucien. You couldn't resist taking what that . . . evil blonde

190

was offering, could you?" She faced him defiantly before she continued shouting. "Well, I have news for you. You cannot have everything you want. If you want to continue your dalliance with her, that will be fine with me. But, Lucien"—she paused to catch her breath—"it goes both ways. I thought we decided to try in Washington. If you are ready to turn our marriage into more of a mockery than we both know it to be, well, then so am I."

Without warning he grabbed her arms, pinning them to her sides.

"Stop it! You are hurting me!" she protested.

"I warned you once before, Samantha. I have no intention of calling out every man who kisses your sweet, luscious mouth." His fingers traced the curve of her lips. "You are mine. If I must kill every one of your lovers, dear wife, I swear I will! Think about that before you select your next one."

"Why is it permissible, my husband, for you to flaunt your affairs while I remain passively in the background waiting for you to come home?"

His forced smile frightened her. "That is because I *am* your husband. You will do as I say, while I do what I please. Do you understand?"

The smack of her hand across his cheek was her answer.

"I see that you need a few lessons first." His hand reached up to the same cheek she had scratched in an earlier battle of wills. "You seem determined to scar me, my love." With one sweeping motion Lucien lifted and flung her onto the bed.

"Stay away from me. Didn't you get enough from Caroline tonight?" She was too angry now to measure her words or to be frightened by the hard set of his mouth. She should have noticed his cheek muscle twitching with suppressed anger.

"Samantha, you are begging to be beaten or raped, or—" he looked suggestively at her body, "both."

All the rage and humiliation she had once experienced, she felt again. "I hate you, Lucien," she cried with that pent-up fury.

"On second thought, madam, I think I would rather bed a willing woman than a hot-tempered shrew. Good night." He looked directly into her eyes. She searched his face for some emotion, but he appeared devoid of any feeling. Backing away from the bed she snarled, "Good riddance, then. I hope you never come back!" She rolled onto her stomach, burying her face in the pillow.

If he heard her, he didn't show it. Lucien swiftly gathered his boots and left. She didn't even hear the door close.

There was no word from him for the next two days. Finally, on the third morning one of Lucien's clerks delivered a terse, handwritten note:

Madam:

I have chosen to remain in town aboard the Newport Wind *until we set sail for New Orleans. My manservant, Whitman, will come by later in the day to pack my things.*

If you still want to accompany me to New Orleans, send a reply with Timothy, who has been instructed to wait.

You are under no obligation to join me. I am perfectly capable of handling the situation alone.

Lucien

No warm wishes or apologies. She crumpled the note and quickly wrote an angry reply:

Lucien:
I have every intention of going to New Orleans with you. If you give me one week's notice, I shall be ready.
Your mother left for New York yesterday. She said she was planning to stop by your office before her departure. I hope you had a chance to see her off.

Samantha

"There! If he can be cold and impersonal, so can I," she muttered. She sent the clerk off with her reply. The house was empty except for some of the servants. She missed her family, even the cries of her nephew. What was she going to do in this house, alone, while she waited for her husband's summons?

She decided to redecorate her room. Actually, it was Lucien's room, but once she made some changes the room would look more like hers. The next few days were spent following through with her plan. As long as she was alone, Samantha did not see the need to wear her frilly dresses. She found an old pair of Lucien's breeches and a shirt that she cut down and altered to fit her much smaller frame. Her hair was securely wrapped under a linen scarf. She enjoyed this freedom from dresses so much, she took to riding one of

Lucien's horses on the beach in her new outfit.

At night, too exhausted to even worry if her husband was occupied with Caroline, she had a light supper—usually in her room—took a leisurely bath, and sometimes read a book before sleep.

By the end of the week she received her first guest, Roger Cole. It amazed him to learn that not only was she totally self-sufficient, but that she could still look beautiful disguised in men's clothes and covered with paint.

"Sam, this isn't right. There is really no reason for the two of you to be acting this way."

"I don't care any more, Roger. I can take care of myself. If Lucien wants Caroline, that's fine, but I won't give him a divorce." She laughed. "You know, he once told me the same thing." They walked into the downstairs parlor. Samantha tried to wipe off the dirt on her clothes before sitting next to Roger on the window seat.

"Listen to me, Sam." Roger felt compelled to help them settle their differences. "He's not interested in Caroline. He never was. Do you know what Lucien is doing?" Samantha shook her head. "He works like a dog every day, supervising the loading of two ships. When he's not doing that, he's working in the office on the design plans for three new ships. Most evenings he spends with me. I watch him drink himself into a stupor. He is not a happy man, Sam. He misses you, but he won't admit that, any more than you can. You do miss him, Sam, don't you?"

Sighing heavily, she wanted to deny all the other feelings she held for Lucien. She knew she couldn't. She missed his presence, his masculine scent, his arms comforting her . . . his lovemaking.

"Yes, Roger. I suppose I miss him. But," she added defiantly, "it's too late for us. He doesn't love me."

"Do you love him, Samantha?"

The question was one she had asked herself quite often recently. She looked into Roger's dark eyes. "I honestly don't know, Roger. Maybe if we had more time together without arguing, we could afford the luxury of thinking about love. I am too busy hating him, being angry with him, to think about anything else right now."

"Come into town with me, Sam. See for yourself. Since you are still determined to go back to New Orleans with him, you might as well settle your differences." He thought his words were melting her stubborn exterior. "Sam, what difference does it make if you approach him first? Forget your pride just once."

"I don't know, Roger. I am afraid that whenever I get too close to Lucien, somehow Caroline will get in the middle of things."

"Then fight for him! For God's sake, Samantha, I know you know how to get what you want."

"Is he what I want, though?" The question was really directed to herself. "All right, Roger. You always manage to talk me into something I don't want to do. But if Caroline's cloying scent is anywhere near, I am not staying."

It took less than an hour for Samantha to get ready. The dark blue woolen dress made her feel a little more feminine than the breeches she had become used to. They reached the shipyard late in the afternoon. Since

Lucien wasn't in his office but aboard the *Seafarer*, supervising the loading of gunpowder barrels, Samantha strolled around the area. She had remembered to dress warmly, for the threat of snow was evident and the winds especially cold. Casually strolling over to the site where a new ship was being constructed, she greeted the men who were diligently working.

"Hello, Mrs. Fraser," they shouted. "Congratulations. Boy, is he a lucky man." She couldn't help but smile in response.

Suddenly a loud boom rent the air. All eyes turned to the site of the explosion.

It was the *Seafarer*!

"Hey, there's gunpowder aboard her!" one of the men shouted. "Captain Fraser is on board."

"Lucien!" No, she prayed, fighting hysteria, don't let him be hurt! I could never forgive myself for telling him not to come back to me. She didn't care about anything but his safety. Another explosion . . . Screaming now, she ran toward the flames that were consuming the *Seafarer*.

"Somebody help! Roger, where are you?" she cried.

"Sam, come over here!" he shouted in reply.

At the sound of Roger's familiar voice she felt slightly relieved. She ran to him, her skirts and hair flying. The smoke from the flames made it nearly impossible to see. But when she saw the large hole in the starboard side of the ship, she panicked.

"Where's Lucien!" She grabbed Roger's jacket, clawing him. "Is he aboard that inferno?"

"Calm down, Sam. Yes, he is. I don't know which part of the ship has been damaged, but I can guess." He pulled his jacket off, took the wet blanket that was offered him by one of the crew, and ran toward the dying ship. Samantha was right beside him.

"I am going with you."

"No!" He stopped to face her. "You will be needed here! Sam, Lucien is not the only one aboard that ship. You will be needed to help the injured. Get others to help." The stubborn set of her chin was offset by the tears flowing down her smoke-stained face. He hugged her to him as he choked, "I'll find him, Samantha, don't worry." Before she could wipe the tears, Roger was gone, shouting orders to the rescue team.

It was silly to stand there like a helpless child. Recovering her wits, she sprang into action, issuing orders to those around her. Makeshift beds were prepared, bandages retrieved, calls for doctors and whomever else was willing to help were sent.

The air filled with smoke and an acrid odor of gunpowder. Her vision was blurred but she kept working to assist the injured. She did not want to stop, to think about whether Lucien were still alive. Three men had already died from the force of the explosion. Some of the injured she treated had terrible burns covering their bodies. Most women would have fainted, but Samantha forced herself to continue, soothing the injured, listening to delirious voices, bandaging, assisting the doctors. She prayed and begged, "God, please keep him alive . . . don't let it be too late," she whispered to an injured sailor in her arms.

"Samantha, come quickly!" shouted Roger above the chaos.

She saw Roger and three other men lifting her husband's body off the ship. She started to perspire, felt cold and clammy, and heard a strange buzzing in her ears. "Is he alive, Roger? Tell me!" she demanded.

"Yes, but he has passed out from the pain. It doesn't look good."

"Dr. Bentley, over here!" she cried. "It's Lucien. He's alive, but he needs help." The doctor rushed over to them.

Heart thumping in her chest, she gazed upon Lucien's body. His face was covered with soot, bruises, and blood. His usually shiny black wavy hair lay plastered to his head. Checking his body, she gasped at what was evidently causing his pain: his left thigh was practically split open by an ugly wound, exposing the muscle.

"What happened, Roger?" she asked in a cool, steady voice which amazingly hid the torment she felt.

"If he had worried about himself and not about the others, he would be standing with us now." Roger moved toward her and offered his comforting hand. "After the first explosion Lucien, who was unhurt, tried to help those trapped by fallen timber. But with the next explosion, he was almost buried alive by the debris. We removed the wood and metal from the gunpowder barrels that were piled on him, but his leg was crushed. A thick, sharp piece of metal cut through his leg almost to the bone." He felt dizzy trying to reconstruct the ugly scene. Samantha's face was considerably whiter than before. "Are you all right, Sam?"

A swift nod of her head was the reply. Trying to swallow the bile rising in her throat, she could do nothing else but move her head.

"Well, I managed to pull it out of his leg . . . but Sam, I don't know if that kind of wound can remain free of infection."

"We will see what Dr. Bentley has to say."

Lucien was brought into his office, away from the crowd surrounding them. Someone had to help Roger take charge of the chaotic situation. Knowing this was the least she could do, Samantha filled the vacuum.

"Roger, stay out here to supervise the rescue and cleanup. Report back to me on the damage in half an hour. I will stay with Dr. Bentley and Lucien," she declared authoritatively.

He smiled with renewed admiration. "Yes, Boss!"

Each time Lucien's wounds were touched, he groaned. Dr. Bentley probed and cleaned his leg. The facial cuts were only superficial, as were the scratches on his arms. Ignoring the sweat and grime on her body and clothes, Samantha tried to retain her equilibrium. After several minutes, Dr. Bentley spoke.

"Mrs. Fraser, I do not believe your husband should stay here. He needs to be in a clean, almost antiseptic environment. From what I can gather, there are still small pieces of metal in his thigh. I will have to remove them. I can't do it here."

"Doctor," she sighed, "can my husband be moved to Kingscote? I can get Roger to cushion a wagon. We can tie Lucien down to prevent his being jolted too much from the ride." Her mind was rapidly planning ahead. Decisions had to be made.

"Yes, Mrs. Fraser, he can be moved. But I will ride

with him."

"Good. I will send someone ahead to prepare for our arrival."

The ride was agonizingly slow. With Lucien's head nestled in her lap, she tried talking to him. This is silly, she thought. He can't even hear me. But what if he could? What if her soft words penetrated the haze of pain? It calmed her jumbled nerves to pretend that her husband was merely sleeping.

"Darling, I wish you could hear me. You are going to be fine. I will protect you, I promise." Her hands smoothed the wet hair from his brow. With a damp cloth she tried to clean his face.

"Please be all right, Lucien. Please. Even if you still prefer Caroline to me. I will let you go . . . only please live." Her tortured sobs were spoken into his ear as she bent to kiss him. By the time they got home, she was emotionally and physically drained. Ignoring her own discomfort, she hastily supervised her husband's move into one of the vacant bedchambers on the first floor of the house. Refusing to let go of Lucien's hand, Samantha quietly sat near the bed while Dr. Bentley resumed his examination.

"Mrs. Fraser, I will have to do more surgery to remove the metal. I cannot guarantee that we can get all the pieces out. I will need your help when I stitch up the wound. Can I count on you?"

"Doctor, don't worry about me," she assured him. "I will be fine." She rolled up her sleeves and sterilized her hands.

"Uh, Mrs. Fraser. There is one more thing I must tell

you." The short, elderly doctor hesitated. "I don't know if I can save his leg. I will try everything I know. If the infection spreads . . . he may lose his leg."

Horror-struck, she stared open mouthed at the doctor. "No . . . you must not say that! Lucien wouldn't want to live if his leg were amputated. I know that, Dr. Bentley." She clutched his arm. "Please don't let that happen," she implored. "Please?"

"The decision will be yours," he replied grimly.

They waited. Samantha sat with Lucien, bathed him, talked to him, cried over him, but still his fever rose. Doctor Bentley tried every remedy—even some of the unorthodox ones—but the wound would not heal. Samantha insisted that the bandages be changed every few hours. Not wanting anyone else to go near Lucien for fear of infecting him, she changed the bandages herself. Fortunately, Dr. Bentley successfully had removed most of the metal pieces. So why was Lucien's fever rising?

Unconscious for two days, he had begun to babble in his delirium. On the morning of the fourth day as the fever raged on, the doctor insisted that a decision had to be made about amputation.

"Your husband cannot physically hold up much longer if the fever rises and the infection spreads. It is remarkable that he has withstood the infection this long. He is young and strong. But . . ." He paused. "I do not think he can remain this way much longer. His leg looks worse."

Wringing her hands, Samantha interrupted. "Perhaps the fever will break soon. He does have some lucid moments." She was looking for any excuse to stall for time. Anything to avoid that moment when she—the woman Lucien never wanted to marry, the woman he despised—had to tell Dr. Bentley to cut off Lucien's leg. She knew one thing for certain: if Lucien survived the amputation he would blame her for his loss.

"Let's wait another day, Doctor."

She was so tired. Her hand swept back loose strands of hair from her forehead. If only he could hear her, help her to decide what was best. She wished Adam were here to guide her. Even Lucien's business interests would not wait. She had met with Roger and some of the employees to discuss, among other concerns, the future of the damaged *Seafarer*. Of the many responsibilities she had found herself saddled with, the business was the most fascinating and not too difficult for her to understand.

Taking her usual place beside his bed, she noted her husband's condition. He was very hot, his body thrashing with pain. The laudanum Dr. Bentley had force-fed him seemed to be wearing off.

"Samantha . . . Caroline . . . Sam . . . go away. No . . . not you . . . I still want you . . ." his voice slowly, painfully whispered.

Not knowing what else to do, Samantha began to apply cold cloths to his fevered brow. Yet, something was dying inside her. He was telling her to go away. He was calling for Caroline.

"Jesus, the pain . . . Roger, is everyone accounted for? Damn, who moved the barrels? . . . No! I cannot see her . . . go away . . . I don't love you . . . I never will . . . go away!" His hand pushed at the image in front of him. He struck Samantha's hand, then seized it

202

with an incredible strength for one so ill. Suddenly, the pain-filled blue eyes opened, focusing on her. She was positive he could see her now.

"Samantha . . ." he whispered clearly. "Don't let them cut off . . . my leg . . ." She moved closer to him, so he wouldn't have to strain his voice. "Please . . . I beg you . . . I know you hate me . . . but don't . . . for the love of God . . . let them amputate." He looked so vulnerable, like an orphaned child, she achingly thought. Somehow, despite his high fever and delirium, he knew what was happening.

"Promise me." Again he begged.

"I promise, Lucien." As she tried to pull the blankets over him, he let go of her wrist. A loving kiss was placed on his brow.

"I don't hate you. I never meant those awful words. Please, my love."

But it was too late. The lucid moment had passed. He slipped into unconsciousness again. There was no way to check the tears that fell down her face onto his. It was too late.

Lucien thought she hated him, but he still begged her to help him. Yet in his delirium he called for Caroline, telling Samantha to go away. That caused irreparable pain for Samantha.

At that moment, Samantha made another promise —to Lucien and to herself. "If you make it through this, I will leave you. You can have her, Lucien. I won't stand in your way. As soon as you are well, I will go away." She kissed his lips and eyes as if to seal the promise. "Only please get well."

By the end of the sixth day it looked as if Lucien was improving. Dr. Bentley, however, refused to be optimistic. After his last discussion with Samantha Fraser, he thought it best to say little or nothing.

The night after Captain Fraser had spoken to his wife, Dr. Bentley once again was summoned to examine his patient. There appeared to be no change in Lucien's condition. His leg would have to be removed. He confronted Mrs. Fraser with his decision.

"Absolutely not!" she practically screamed at him. "You will do nothing of the kind, Doctor. We will continue to soak his thigh and change bandages. That is all."

He couldn't believe she could be so hard. "Mrs. Fraser"—he tried to reason with her then—"I don't think you realize the consequences. Your husband will die if his left leg isn't amputated."

"I do not believe that. I can assure you, Doctor, I will not allow my husband to die. Just leave his leg alone! I will take full responsibility."

And so the good doctor let the lady have her way.

Lucien's fever broke that night. Samantha stood over her husband's bed sobbing with relief. She was joined by an ebullient Roger and the usually stone-faced Whitman, who at that moment smiled with relief.

Chapter Fifteen

God, he felt so sore—especially his left leg. The buzzing in his head slowly cleared. Lucien tried to move his head toward a mewling sound off to his left, but it hurt too damn much! When he first opened his eyes, he could not figure out where he was. Certainly not in his bedroom. But familiar items such as the teak desk near the door and family portraits on the wall, gave him a point of reference. It appeared to be dark, yet he could make out the snow flakes clinging to the windows. Christ! It hadn't been snowing when the accident occurred. He tried to reconstruct the events. The pain in his head and that high-pitched sound kept annoying him, disturbing his ability to concentrate.

Slowly, turning his body to the source of that noise, he could make out a small, huddled shape. As he forced his eyes to focus, he quickly realized who it was. What was Samantha doing here? Again he listened for that noise. Then he saw her place a frilly handkerchief to her nose and blow. The sound was unexpectedly loud for someone her size. The notion of Samantha blowing her nose so loudly made him chuckle. Unfortunately, his chuckle turned into a groan as soon as he tried to move again.

"Damn!"

"Lucien!"

She sounded pleased, he thought. She scurried to his side, a big grin on her tear-stained face.

"Lucien, oh, I am so glad." She bent lower to hug him. "You're alive!"

"Of course I am alive. Why shouldn't I be?" His arm went around her shoulders. A spontaneous hug from Samantha was not a frequent occurrence. He wanted to enjoy it while he could. His hand slipped lower to feel the contours of her backside.

"Lucien. You can't be serious." She pulled his hand away with mock anger. "Do you have any idea what we have been through because of you?"

No, he had no idea of what was going on. He looked at her face. He vaguely remembered seeing it so many times recently, leaning over his, frowning, crying. She looked tired. There were dark circles under her eyes and her face seemed so pale. Her hair, pulled off her face, was loosely secured by a purple ribbon. He raised his hand tentatively to brush away a stray curl. It seemed she had lost some weight, for her brown wool dress hung limply on her frame.

"You look tired, my sweet."

The voice sounded like a caress. A slight tremor chilled her body. She was so tempted to lie down with him. But . . . a promise was made. Involuntarily, she backed away from him and in a distant voice told him everything that had happened in the last six days.

Minutes later she finished her story. "We were all so worried about you, Lucien. Dr. Bentley thought your leg would have to be removed."

"I am glad you were there, Samantha. I appreciate it and will always be grateful." Christ! He felt more than that.

Why did she keep backing away from him? He remembered dreaming about her . . . They were dancing, then kissing . . . their hands roamed each other's bodies. When he opened his eyes to look at her face, the bewitching green eyes turned to pale blue, the hair to blond, and Caroline, not his wife, was in his arms. He remembered trying to push her away, saying, "No, not you . . . ," but Caroline forced Samantha away. Yes, he remembered that now.

"Samantha, did I say anything in my delirium?" He was slightly embarrassed. He must have frightened her somehow. Perhaps he revealed something about his feelings for her.

She looked uncomfortable, as if she were holding something back, but he believed her words. "Oh"—she smiled—"you did mumble a lot. Nothing made any sense though," she lied. "Lucien, don't overdo things. Dr. Bentley will want to examine you now. And don't"—she straightened the bed covers—"think you are getting up tomorrow."

After that, Lucien's recovery was "miraculous," according to Dr. Bentley. Of course had the good doctor known Lucien as well as Samantha and Roger did, nothing would surprise him. Samantha believed that Lucien's stubbornness accounted for the recovery.

It was still not fast enough for the patient. There was no question that Lucien had to remain in bed for some time and confined to the house for at least six more weeks. Plans for their departure for New Orleans had to be delayed until April; messages were sent to the scattered family; business matters postponed.

By the end of the third week Samantha allowed certain visitors to spend a few moments with Lucien in his library. This was the first week he was physically capable of leaving his temporary room. During the initial stage of his recovery, it was a relief to know that Samantha was in charge of all household and personal matters. However, that feeling did not last too long.

"In charge . . . that hurricane I married took over," he grumbled. Easing his body into the soft, dark, mahogany leather armchair near his desk, Lucien's thoughts covered the last, almost violent confrontation he had had with his wife.

It had started with Lucien's insistence that he go to his shipping office to sort out the financial problems incurred with the explosion. There were several business transactions waiting for him, too. His irritation mounted with Samantha's equal insistence that he remain at home.

"Lucien, you cannot leave. You know that the exertion could open your wound."

She looked directly at him, eyes flashing fire and determination. A familiar stirring in his loins at the sight of her beauty told him he wasn't that ill.

"Samantha, love, I am well enough to do a number of things." He shifted his body so she could sit on the bed in the space he provided.

As soon as she sat down, he could tell that she regretted it. It appeared as if she, too, was reminded of the desires repressed over the last few weeks, of times when Lucien's hands had suggestively roamed her luscious body. But this was not yet the time for that . . . and Lucien had no way of knowing that she had her promise to keep. She tried to stand up, but Lucien's strength still outmatched hers, and he slowly moved her head closer to his. His mouth found her ear, eyes, and kept probing until his tongue gently, then firmly explored her mouth. She was becoming aroused yet tried to hold back her response. Struggling to disengage herself, she reminded Lucien of his wound.

"Dammit woman!" He was frustrated. "I will tell you if I am not well." His anger subdued his desire. He pushed her to arm's length but would not yet release her.

"I appreciate everything you have done for me, but I am well enough now to handle my own affairs. That includes, dear wife, my business—you know, the thing that provides you with your clothes, jewels, and comforts."

"There is nothing to worry about. Your business interests have all been taken care of." Again she tried to loosen his tight grip on her arms, knowing that his grip might leave a bruise.

"Is that so?" he mocked. "And whom do you think put everything in order while I was forced to remain here?" God, she was infuriating.

"I did." The reply was low but firm. The next thing she knew, she was pushed off the bed. Recovering her balance, Samantha stood up and moved out of his immediate reach.

He could not believe what he had heard! She sounded so damned sure of herself.

"How, madam, did you manage to take control of the shipping business?" His voice was as cold as his icy stare. The fury he felt threatened to obliterate all rational thought.

"I did not see any reason why I should not get involved. I knew you would not have liked all business to stop while you were ill . . . Adam is not here. . . ." She said that sarcastically as she gestured with her hands. "What did you expect? Should I have cried on every available shoulder begging for advice or bemoaning our dreadful situation?" The more she thought, the more annoyed she became and told him so. What nerve he had to be angry with her for keeping his business functioning smoothly.

"You only created extra work for me," he shouted back. "Now I will have to spend twice the time undoing the mess you have created."

"Mess! How do you know? Do you have so little faith in me?" She was dumbfounded. Her rage was visible for anyone to see. The usually rosy cheeks were scarlet from her anger and her body appeared to be shaking. An intricately carved wood replica of a ship that had been on his desk was suddenly hurled through the air, narrowly missing Lucien's head.

"You ungrateful bastard," she cursed. "Why, your account books are in better shape now then when you tried to organize them. I have had enough of your . . . yes, your childish behavior, Lucien Fraser." She stomped toward the door but paused with one last remark before departing. "If you should ever find yourself in this position again, I assure you that I would rather watch you bleed to death than help you."

His eyes would not let go of her. "I think, madam, I would prefer anything to your unreasonable temper."

*   *   *

210

So here he was, days later, still confined to his home with a wife who was barely speaking to him. Since he couldn't walk without assistance, he reached for the cane that he kept by his side to ease himself out of the chair. Limping over to the window, he observed the scene outside. It was beginning to snow. Servants seemed to be scurrying about to do last minute chores. Lucien heard a carriage pulling up the long drive. It would be Samantha. The only way he seemed to know her whereabouts was through his ever-faithful manservant, George Whitman. She must have gone shopping in town, he thought. Not only did Samantha emerge from the carriage, but Roger was right there helping her. As Roger lifted her fur-clad body out of the carriage, Lucien became more than a little annoyed. It had been almost two months since he had so much as touched his wife. And here was his best friend holding her about the waist with a certain familiarity. As Samantha laughed at something Roger said, Lucien reached for the rum. God, she's beautiful. The white fur cloak he had impulsively bought her before his accident complimented her coppery hair. Tonight, he firmly decided, I am moving back into our bedroom whether she wants me there or not.

Roger's knock on the door brought him back from his daydreams.

"Why so glum, friend?" He accepted the glass of rum Lucien offered. "You should be happy that you are recovering so swiftly."

"Not swiftly enough, it appears," he cautiously remarked. "My wife seems to be doing very well in my absence . . . in more ways than one."

"What is bothering you? Samantha told me how angry you were with her because she involved herself with your business. She's got a good head, Lucien, and she filled an important void during your convalescence." Roger looked puzzled because Lucien was frowning. "But what of it, Lucien? So she has proved to be a competent manager. The men respect her. Part of that is because she is your wife." Lucien's dubious look prompted Roger to continue. "Sit down, Lucien, won't you?"

"I do not need another nurse, Roger." But he sat anyway.

"Lucien, she is not taking your place. *You* are Fraser Shipping. She does not want to, for one thing. Every decision she made was with the same overriding concern: What would Lucien do?" Roger chuckled when he remembered something she had done recently. Lucien would not appreciate it yet.

"I am still not convinced, Roger." He drained his glass and quickly refilled it. "That witch dislikes me so much, I don't know what she might do to get even with me. Especially," he remembered, "after that little scene with Caroline."

"You know, you are not always smart. Now don't get angry—it's not healthy, you know." Lucien's expression did not soften. "Did you know," Roger rushed on, "who spent days at your bedside, bathing you, changing bandages, not allowing visitors? Why she acted like an overprotective mother hen. She sweated over you, Lucien, and cried over you, too. But not once did she waver from her decision to prevent Dr. Bentley from cutting off your leg."

"She was only fulfilling her obligation to me," Lucien grumbled. "She only wants me to be well

212

enough to go to New Orleans with her."

Roger stood up and looked sadly at his friend. "You are crazier than I thought. I only hope you two manage to come to a better understanding before it is too late and you lose her, Lucien. Somehow I do not believe you would be happy without her."

Chapter Sixteen

It was past midnight by the time Samantha was ready to go to bed. In the last few days—because of their recent argument—she had made a point of staying away from Lucien. She regarded his behavior as thoroughly obnoxious. Perhaps he could not wait to get back into Caroline's bed, she reasoned. As Samantha slowly ascended the winding stairs to their bedroom, she knew she could no longer postpone her departure from Kingscote. She had made a vow to give Lucien his freedom, even though she felt disinclined to do anything for either Lucien or his blond mistress. Slowly opening the door, she was surprised by the sight that greeted her.

"Hello, love," he grinned. "Surprised?"

"No. I knew it was only a matter of time, Lucien." She sounded resigned, almost defeated.

"That is very noble of you, wife. I do own this house, you know." His deep blue gaze swept the room. "But these rooms do look a bit different. More feminine, I think."

Again he smiled at her, the same mocking smile she detested. Turning her back to him, she began to undo

215

the wide belted sash of her dress before entering her dressing room.

"It has been a long time since I last saw you disrobe for me. Please don't let me stop you. Don't go in there, Samantha. Stay here."

Hoping that she might bore or tire him, Samantha took her time undressing. One glance at his desire-filled eyes, however, told her how incorrect she was.

Propped up on the white pillows, leaning against the mahogany headboard with the sheets neatly arranged across his lap, his naked upper torso was clearly exposed. His wavy black hair looked recently washed, even though it was clear from the way it curled below the nape of his neck that he needed a haircut. In spite of Lucien's confinement and forced inactivity, his body still looked tan. There was no excess weight on his frame. His muscular chest and arms reminded Samantha, however reluctantly, that her husband was indeed a very handsome man.

If only she knew, he thought, how much self-control it takes pretending to be unconcerned while she taunts me with her various stages of undress. The evidence lay underneath the sheet.

Finally, after what seemed to him like hours, Samantha came to bed. Her sheer pink silk nightgown did not conceal the sensuous body he had longed for these last two months.

"Come to me, my love," he whispered hungrily. He gently pulled her into his eager arms. "Let me hold you. You have no idea how I have missed sharing this bed with you."

She was all set to fight him once he began his sexual demands. But his gentleness and the almost pleading tone in his voice unnerved her. Without deliberation, she melted into him, experiencing the need to hold him as keenly as he needed her.

"Have you missed me too, green eyes?"

She could not speak, fearful of revealing her true feeling, so she nodded her head. If only you knew how much I need you, Lucien, she thought. But the more rational side of her warned not to give him ammunition. To freely offer her love would only be used against her, not now perhaps, but during another time when he was more sure of his ability to make her respond to him—when she would be far more vulnerable than she was now, because she would care that he was using her, turning her into another one of his mistresses who eagerly sought his touch.

"Let me make love to you, Samantha. I have thought of nothing else these last few weeks. I want to feel your hair, kiss your body—"

He did not have a chance to finish, for his hands and mouth claimed hers, deftly exploring her body over the cool silk nightgown. Then he slowly unbuttoned the tiny row of seed pearls, pushing aside the material, sliding his hand inside, caressing her rounded breasts. The anticipation of feeling him inside her was so great, she moaned with impatience. But Lucien savored this moment. He wanted to prolong every touch and kiss, make her wild with passion. He moved his hand away from her breasts, slipping it underneath the gown, warming her ankles, thighs and feeling his way higher until he found her center, now liquid with desire for him. Claiming her mouth once more, Lucien felt her hand freely roam along his chest, flat stomach, then lower.

Suddenly, feeling quite brave and reckless with their mutual passion, Samantha moved her head to where her hand was. Tentatively she kissed his erect member, and hearing his murmur of delight, placed her mouth over it. She became so aroused by his response and her sense of power that she barely noticed when she was roughly pulled over onto her back.

They tossed about in a frenzy of excitement until Samantha remembered his healing leg.

"No Lucien, your leg. Let me make it more comfortable for you," her love-filled voice whispered. He kept his head back with a sense of satisfaction as he positioned her willing body above him. She was writhing in the full blush of passion. They could contain their desire no longer. It erupted like a geyser filled with all the love her body had contained in the last weeks. The ecstasy came in waves. First, a soft, shallow lifting of the spirit followed in ever-increasing intensity by deeper realms of passion, until the torrent made her collapse in a pool of satisfaction and exhaustion. Without thinking, she cried, "Lucien, I need you." He responded by touching her cheek. She lowered her head to the hollow of his neck and slept. Her last conscious thought was that she would tell him her plans tomorrow.

The servants were unwilling to awaken the slumbering couple. After all, it was their first night back together again. Lucien awoke first, quickly realizing that they had overslept. As he glanced down at Samantha, a lazy smile grew on his face. If he had known how passionate and free she was, he would have

218

married her without hesitation. She lay on her side, one arm securely wrapped around his stomach. Her cheeks still retained the rosy glow of their rapturous lovemaking. Impulsively he bent his head to kiss her pert nose. The long, coppery eyelashes fluttered, then lifted. She looked directly into his dark, loving eyes and smiled demurely. A sweet rush of warmth and satisfaction enveloped him.

"I fear, my love, that we have overslept."

With a soft cry of "Oh dear," she threw back the sheets and started to jump out of bed. His long arm checked her movement.

"You are allowed to rest. Even the mistress of the house is permitted to oversleep," he cheerfully said.

"Yes, I know. But I have so much to do before . . ."

"Before what? Are you planning another business meeting in my absence?" He meant to sound casual, but a note of suspicion crept into his voice.

"No . . . oh, what's the use? I might as well get it over with now." She sat up on her knees before continuing, so she could face him.

"Lucien, last night was wonderful, but I am afraid it never should have happened." He was ready to protest. "No, wait." She lifted her hand. "Let me say what I have to, then you can speak."

"How diplomatic of you," he drawled.

"Lucien, I am sorry for so many things. But most of all, for allowing the President to push us into marriage. I know how awful it has been for you. When you were bedridden and your very survival was in doubt, I made a promise to myself and . . . to you." It was impossible to hide her uneasiness. She twisted the sheets in her hands, waiting for his response.

"And what kind of promise was this?" The earlier feeling of warmth cooled considerably, making him insensitive to her obvious distress.

"To give you your freedom. Eventually a divorce, if you want it."

The room was so quiet. They could hear each other breathing, first softly, then increasing in tempo.

He could not understand what or who gave her this crazy notion. Yet seeing her stubborn look of determination, he knew she was not joking. His eyes studied her. There could be only two plausible reasons, he thought, for her decision. One, of course, was that she really was telling the truth, believing he wanted his freedom. What could give her that idea? Then he remembered Roger's warnings about how stupid and blind he had been in those areas concerning his wife. Yet in the last few months, they had seemed to be adjusting to the idea of marriage.

The other reason could very well be that *she* wanted her freedom. How very clever of her to turn the tables by placing the blame on him. He would have to wait and see by going along with this silly plan . . . for a short while.

His ice blue gaze kept her frozen. She saw the play of emotions across his face. Minutes passed with neither one moving or speaking. Finally, feeling more uncomfortable with each passing second, Samantha broke the silence. Still on her knees, she shifted her weight. "Well, Lucien. Aren't you going to thank me?" She did not mean the words to come out that way, as if she were annoyed. He responded by moving his hand along her thigh. The soft stroking gave her goose bumps. Bewildered by this display of affection instead of fury, she lifted her eyes to look at his face. Now he was smiling! This man changes moods more often than I change dresses, she decided.

"Samantha, sweet, you are most kind. Your generosity warms my heart. I must admit," he chuckled, "that I was getting used to our present arrangement. I will make a pact with you." She looked somewhat wary, but he was beginning to enjoy himself now and did not want to stop.

"What kind of pact?"

"Let's follow through with our New Orleans plans. I think I can be ready within the month—by the end of April, I think. After we learn more about Adam, let's talk again. If either one of us wants our freedom then, we take the legal step. Agreed?"

Why did he want to postpone the opportunity to have Caroline and be rid of her? It made no sense to Samantha. Although she still felt she needed some time alone, she was secretly relieved to hear Lucien's words.

"Agreed." A smile formed on her lips. "But I have another favor to ask of you." At his look of consternation, she hesitated.

"Go on, Samantha, I can hardly wait to hear."

"I want to leave as soon as possible for Thornton Hill. You can resolve your business and uh . . . personal matters. At least I won't be in your way. You can just as easily meet me in Charleston and we could sail to the port of New Orleans from there."

"You have it all figured out, don't you? How will you get to Charleston?"

She laughed. "Knowing about our business operations helps, dear. We have a ship due to sail within three days. The *New Englander*'s destination, as if you

221

did not know, is Charleston," she saucily replied.

He liked the way she referred to "our business." She had outwitted him, and he grudgingly respected it. It would not be as easy, he realized, not having her at home with him, but maybe this short separation was what they needed to put things into perspective.

"It appears as if the matter is settled. Be warned, my love, that I am allowing you to have your way this time."

Reaching under the pillow, he withdrew a small box. "I intended to give this to you weeks ago, before the accident." He smiled, handing the box to her. "Even while we were living apart, I still thought of you."

Her eyes brimming with unshed tears, she opened the box and softly exclaimed, "Oh, how lovely, Lucien." The gold and diamond bracelet lay in her hand, the diamond initials S.T.F. glittering in the morning light. He fastened it around her small wrist.

Why, she wondered, had he thought of her when he had Caroline Prescott to comfort him? It was too confusing to dwell on at the moment, not with his lips exploring her neck.

Holding her arm up, she said, "It's beautiful, Lucien. You truly amaze me. Thank you. But what about Caro . . ."

"Not now, sweetheart," his husky voice distracted her. "Now"—he pulled her into his arms—"I fear my love-starved body needs you once again."

Without having the opportunity to reply, Samantha lost herself in the tides of their rapture.

It never occurred to him that he would miss her. In

his thirty-one years, he had rarely needed anyone, let alone a woman who did not want him. After Samantha's departure, Lucien spent the rest of that week and the following one settling his own business affairs.

The first day he went into town to his shipping headquarters, he was greeted enthusiastically by his employees. The crew of the *Newport Wind* had organized the other crews of Fraser ships that were still in port, and the shipyard workers, to throw a party in honor of Lucien's return. By the time the drunken party givers left, it was late in the day. Lucien sobered up enough to tackle the papers on his desk.

After the first twenty minutes of sorting paper, Lucien came to the realization that Samantha had been very efficient. She had left neatly penned notes explaining what was and was not completed, organized columns recording income and expenses, and payroll deadlines to meet. In short, he discovered that there was not as much work for him to do as he had anticipated. And when he remembered how he had accused her of making more work for him by interfering, he flinched with self-disgust. Not only was she a terrific bedmate, but she was a good business-woman besides.

In the following days, he learned from others how well she had represented the name of Fraser Shipping. The one contract he had wanted but had never been able to get was with a Boston-based textile firm. Samantha cleverly negotiated a tough deal with this company and, according to Roger, had the owner eating out of her hand.

He drank to her and cursed himself at the same time

for being a fool. He never should have allowed her to go off without him.

Caroline threw herself at him a number of times, but he could not bring himself to bed her. Instead, he went home, occasionally inviting some male friends over for a game of cards, and drank himself to sleep.

"Roger, this celibate life is not for me," he complained one evening in his library. "I think I may have to pay a visit to Polly's House. That, or," he added, "leave for Charleston right away."

His friend merely smiled. "When will you admit that your wife means a great deal to you?"

"I admit nothing," he shot back a trifle too quickly.

"Have it your way. But if I were you, friend, I would not let my beautiful wife out of my sight for too long. I am ready to sail whenever you are, Captain." He saluted Lucien.

"All right, Mr. Cole," he smiled as he returned the salute, "we sail in two days. We must make a quick stop in Washington first, then be on our way to . . . I don't know what."

Chapter Seventeen

Charleston: Spring, 1807

Since her arrival at Thornton Hill, Samantha had
spent most of her time outdoors, riding. The weather
was very warm and humid for South Carolina in April.
She furiously rode her mare, Dawn, over the hills into
the woods for hours, always alone. The dark auburn
mare had a touch of red and in the early morning sun
the blending of the horse and rider was breathtaking.
Dawn's color was only a few shades darker than her
mistress's locks. The animal always seemed to sense the
moods of her mistress, knowing when to race through
the woods or sedately trot along familiar paths.

It was as if Samantha were trying to run away from
something . . . or someone. She knew what was wrong
with her. Try as she would, she could not forget his
mocking face, his deep blue eyes fired by anger then
passion, his arms securely wrapped around her during
the night. She knew the feeling of it all. She could
almost forget in the daytime as she admired the
countryside she knew so well. But the night became her
enemy now when instinctively her arm reached across

to an empty side of the bed.

Dawn stopped at her usual spot. It was a secluded area surrounded by succulent cypress trees in various shades of green. There was a small clearing near a brook, which at this time of the year flowed swiftly, as if looking for a place to go. Like me, she thought. Stop being so melancholy, Samantha Thornton, she chided herself. Samantha Thornton Fraser. "Don't forget Fraser," she again said aloud, correcting herself while staring at her new bracelet.

She could not forget. She missed him. She hated him . . . she wanted him . . . she loved him! Why did I fall in love with that conceited, arrogant brute? The question had burned in her mind these last few days, but she could no longer deny it. How funny, she thought. When I was near him he confused me so much I never really had the time to question my feelings— even when Lucien was so ill. However, as soon as she had sailed out of Newport and had spent her first of many nights alone, that dreadful realization could not be ignored.

"I am so miserable!" she said to Dawn, whose ears twitched at the sweet sound of Samantha's voice. "He doesn't love me. He only wants to fulfill his obligation. That's what I am to him," she despaired, "a burden."

And the more she thought about it, the angrier she got at Lucien, herself, anyone close to her. Her family had begun to wonder about her sudden inexplicable mood swings. Meredith had been so bold as to inquire if Samantha were with child!

"Of course not," she had snapped. Then she quickly, contritely apologized for her rudeness.

People tried to stay out of her way, no longer

226

attempting to include her in conversation. The only meal she shared with her family was dinner. Even then, her mien was distant.

So, here she was by the brook, alone, wondering just what she was going to do with a husband who did not return her love. Should she go to New Orleans with him? She threw a rock into the brook, looking at her own image for some magical answer. Yes, she had to go. She stood up to remove her pale green linen riding jacket, gathering her hair into a severe bun. Should she confess her love to him? Absolutely not! Lucien would only laugh.

The questions swirled in her mind all afternoon. As the sun began to set, Samantha finally gave up. She would wait Lucien out. Divorce was out of the question. She would make a happy life for herself, with him or without him. If and when the time were right, she would tell him her true feelings, but not now.

Feeling more relieved with her decision not to brood over this any longer, Samantha rode back to the house to apologize to everyone for her odd behavior. But when she rode up to the stable, she spotted an unfamiliar horse tethered to a tree. Her heart lurched. Lucien here already? She did not know if she were glad about his early arrival—he wasn't supposed to arrive for a few more weeks—or dismayed about seeing him before she had fully accepted and adjusted to the notion that she was in love with him.

The riding jacket was slung over her shoulder. The crisp white cotton and lace shirt open at the neck accented her lovely breasts. The nervous tension filling her body caused her to march into the hall, almost slamming the huge oak door with an unusual strength.

227

She heard voices in the drawing room. Her father was with another man. But the voice was not Lucien's. She didn't bother to knock, but strode directly into the still-sunlit room.

"Father, do we have a guest?" Her eyes searched the large room and widened with pleasure.

"Stèfan! Oh, how good it is to see you." She rushed over to him, taking both of his hands in hers. "But why didn't you tell us you would be arriving?" The questions came rapidly, barely giving Stèfan a chance to reply. His warm, golden brown eyes smiled at her, but there was a touch of sadness about him.

"Hello, *ma chère.* Congratulations."

Her face fell. "Oh, Stèfan. There is so much you do not know. I should have written you, but there was no time for letters. All I ask is that you forgive me. I never intended to hurt you," she said apologetically. "If you do not want to remain friends, I understand. I deserve no special consideration."

"Ah, but you are wrong, Samantha. I shall always be your most loyal friend." He seemed to be aware of her confusion and depression. "I think you can use one," Stèfan said as he placed a chaste kiss on her cheek.

Tears threatened to spill down her face. "Thank you. I truly appreciate that."

Knowing that an uncomfortable scene had been averted, Robert invited Stèfan to stay at Thornton Hill. Perhaps his presence would lighten Samantha's mood, he reasoned hopefully.

And it did. Over the next few days Stèfan, Samantha, and Meredith went into Charleston to enjoy the cultural events and visit friends. Samantha had worried that she might meet Clinton Davis in

228

Charleston, but after meeting his sister Marianne at a play, she learned he was out of town.

Stèfan's pleasant company was such a balm to her bruised ego that Samantha barely noticed the snide comments some of the Charleston "elite" made about her. Why, they asked, was she parading her new lover so soon after her rather hasty marriage to a New Englander? Since her mother's death, Samantha's reputation had become a matter of public discussion. But now nasty rumors spread widely.

It was easy for Samantha to establish a friendship with Stèfan. Oh, she knew very well that Stèfan still deeply cared for her, but he never made any advances. Nor did he ask about her unusual relationship with Lucien.

Meredith, however, was not to be put off. One warm, hazy afternoon, while Samantha and Meredith were alone outdoors on the veranda with the baby, Meredith decided it was time for some direct questions.

"Samantha, have you heard from Lucien recently?"

It was obvious that even this harmless question made Samantha uncomfortable. She began to fidget with the long yellow ribbons on her cream-colored lawn dress.

"No, I have not, Mer. I . . . ah . . . don't really think Lucien has the time to write me." The reply was soft and hesitant. She couldn't bring herself to look at Meredith, so she focused on the ribbon.

"Are you ready to tell me about it now? You know, Sam, that your father and I have tried not to ask you about this matter. But you cannot keep your unhappiness buried inside for too long. Stèfan cannot take Lucien's place."

Only the sound of Jamie's happy gurgles were heard. It seemed as if the infant was responding to Samantha's uneasiness.

Samantha took Jamie into her arms, thankful for his distracting presence. The baby playfully tugged at her ribbons, then quietly settled down. She smiled down at the tiny face that painfully reminded her so much of Adam.

"What would you like to know?"

"Everything that has happened since I left Kingscote." Meredith reached for her sister-in-law's hand. "I love both you and Lucien, you know. I am not taking sides."

Samantha smiled at her sleeping nephew and did not realize she was crying until Jamie's hand moved to shield himself from her salty tears.

"It is hard to explain a situation that I am not sure I even understand. I do know that Lucien does not love me."

"So why did he marry you? Every time my brother looks at you, his face seems to lighten up or darken. I never saw him act that way with any other woman."

"You mean Caroline." She handed Jamie to his mother so she could stand up. "He was forced to marry me."

At Meredith's stunned expression, Samantha began to tell the whole story of her relationship with Lucien, leading up to the present.

It took two hours. Once Samantha started to talk it was as if an old wound, never properly healed, were opened and then cleansed so that it could heal. She cried, laughed, and vented her anger.

230

Meredith waited for the tale to finish before asking questions.

"So you see," Samantha sighed heavily, "Lucien will come for me, we will play our charade in New Orleans, and then . . . it will be over. I will be twenty, married, divorced, and—I'm afraid—miserable."

"Because you love him?"

"Am I that obvious?" She began to worry. "I can never let Lucien know what a weapon he really has to use against me."

"Is that why you have allowed the rumors to spread about you and Stèfan?" Meredith's sympathy was clearly with Samantha. She fervently wished she could do something, for she knew Lucien deeply cared for his wife, but Samantha chose not to believe that. Knowing how possessive her brother was, if Lucien believed Samantha were having an affair with Stèfan Turreau, there would definitely be a ghastly scene. Lucien had a formidable temper, but then, Meredith reasoned so did Samantha. There was humor to be found in this situation, only no one but Adam would have appreciated it.

Samantha walked to the veranda railing to watch the setting sun. Everything was still emotionally unclear for her. She did not know what she would do when she saw Lucien again. The last time she had seen him, he had been leaning on his cane at the Newport wharf. She smiled, remembering his insistence at seeing her off. It had been a cool day, but he had refused to wear his coat. Instead, he wore a dark brown vest over fawn-colored breeches. She smiled at him, telling him he still looked like a pirate.

231

"As long as I please you, green eyes," he responded. His mouth claimed hers, and only the loud coughing of the *New Englander*'s captain reminded them they were not alone.

"Try to stay out of trouble, sweetheart. I hope you miss me." And he limped away.

"Sam," Meredith's voice intruded on that bitter-sweet memory, "you did not answer my question."

"Oh." She was confused as she came back to the present. "Yes, I remember." She smiled, a bit embarrassed. "About Stèfan."

"Yes, about Stèfan."

She turned to face Meredith and sat down across from her. Samantha's face was truly a reflection of confused, painful emotions.

"I do not love Stèfan. He is a dear friend. I haven't told him anything about the problems between Lucien and myself. Besides, Stèfan is too much of a gentleman to ask."

"Yes, but what does Stèfan feel?" Meredith hated the role of devil's advocate but she had to make Samantha realize the dangerous situation she placed herself in with Stèfan.

"I'm not sure any more. I hope he does not fancy himself in love with me. He says he will be leaving soon." She laughed. "I do not think Stèfan is too interested in meeting Lucien again."

"Smart man," mumbled Meredith.

Jamie awoke. Not wanting to interrupt Samantha when she was talking freely, Meredith rang for one of the servants to bring the baby to his nurse.

"Meredith, I don't know if you can understand. Adam deeply loves you. He would not take a mistress

232

or take advantage of your love. It's good to know that there is someone who wants me"—her hands patted her chest—"who finds me witty, attractive, and who is interested in what I think. I enjoy laughing, having a good time with Stèfan without worrying what it is I do or say that will make him angry, or sarcastic, or ready to tear my clothes off.

"If I want to be alone, I can simply tell Stèfan. With Lucien, if I so much as walk out of his line of vision, he threatens to beat me. But Caroline"—she spat the name—"is always there to remind me of her affair with Lucien. Meredith"—tears once more rolled down her pinkened cheeks—"what would you do in my place?"

Meredith's own tears clouded her vision. "I don't know, Sam. But I do understand."

"Oh God. When will this dull pain inside me stop?" she wailed and fell into Meredith's outstretched, sympathetic arms.

"Let's think about it some more, Sam, before you do anything rash. Lucien won't be here for another two weeks."

Eventually, Samantha tried to smile. She caught her breath, straightened her hair, and with renewed spirit went inside to prepare herself for a pleasant dinner.

After dinner, Stèfan revealed his plans to depart within two days.

"I think it is time for me to join my father in Washington," he announced. As usual, he was smartly dressed in dark blue woolen breeches and matching jacket. Underneath, he wore a quilted waistcoat of various shades of blue. His linen shirt was highlighted by the foulard silk cravat wrapped around a high neckcloth. His light brown eyes twinkled with good humor.

Why, Samantha asked herself for the hundredth time, couldn't I have fallen in love with someone as warm and dependable as Stèfan?

"I do not think Father and President Jefferson are getting on any better these days," he commented to Robert. "He certainly disagrees with the President's passive attitude toward the British, who are still as determined as ever to control the seas."

"What does your father think of the situation in the Southwest?" Samantha eagerly chimed in. As long as Stèfan had mentioned his father first, Samantha did not consider herself manipulative. She was as eager as ever to obtain information before she and Lucien went back to New Orleans. She had to know what to expect. Of course, she reasoned, Lucien would already have this information and much more. However, Samantha wanted to believe that she, too, could be resourceful.

"There is not too much to tell you, *ma petite*. Mr. Burr never did arrive in New Orleans. Father does not believe Mr. Burr is the traitor people have labeled him."

"Yes, I have heard the same thing," she said. Stèfan knew of her disastrous trip to New Orleans, but not everything. He did not know about Gaspar. The mere thought of him sickened her. However, she did tell Stèfan about her attempts to find Adam.

"When I have a chance to talk to Father, I promise to find out if he can get any information from the Spanish Ambassador about Adam." His warm smile lifted Samantha's mood.

Reaching across the card table, she touched his hand and appeared to thank him with her luminous emerald eyes.

The next morning a message from James Madison to Meredith again made Adam's disappearance the main topic of conversation.

My dear Mrs. Thornton:

General Wilkinson has information concerning your husband's whereabouts. The Spanish are holding him prisoner in the Mexican Territory just west of the Sabine River.

We will keep negotiating with the Spanish for his release. Details for future plans have been given to Lucien.

Our prayers are with you.

James Madison

"Well," Meredith laughed, trying to hide her nervousness, "at least they have not forgotten Adam."

Samantha snatched the note. The words "future plans" seemed to jump out at her. They must have discussed something other than a "diplomatic" plan with Lucien when he was in Washington. Dammit, why hadn't Lucien contacted her?

"Come, *ma petite*," Stèfan shouted from the gardens. "It is a beautiful, sunny day. How about a race and then a picnic?"

She clapped her hands with glee at the prospect of an

invigorating ride. "I would love to. I'll just change and meet you at the stables in ten minutes!"

One look at Samantha's riding attire made Stèfan curse himself for promising to be her friend. His passion quickly surfaced when he saw her voluptuous body in . . . breeches!

"Sam, are you sure you are dressed?"

The buff-colored nankeen breeches hugged her lower body, a pair of tight black leather boots hid her shapely calves, and what appeared to be a man's cotton striped shirt had been tailored to her proportions. Her hair was loosely pulled back and secured by a ribbon.

At the sound of Samantha's gay laughter, Stèfan's daydreaming came to an abrupt end.

"Do you like my design?" She giggled again. "I bribed my dressmaker in Charleston into making this outfit. I had to promise her that I would never wear this in public or reveal who made it." She twirled for Stèfan to get the total view. "See? Instead of buttons down the front of the breeches, I have buttons on the side, near the pocket. Oh, this is so much better than those cumbersome riding habits."

"I think," Stèfan gulped, "I understand why women do not wear breeches. If I had to look at them all day I would be hard pressed to be able to do anything else."

As she pulled his arm, leading him toward the stables, he once more felt a powerful urge to take her into his arms. "You will never know, *ma chère*, how good a friend I am," he said to no one.

The day with Stèfan turned out to be one of the happiest for Samantha. They raced—Samantha's Dawn won easily—picnicked, laughed and talked.

"Oh, Stèfan, I shall truly miss you. Must you leave tomorrow?"

He pulled a blade of grass from her hair. "I really should have left last week. But you sorely needed a friend. I hope, *ma petite*, that husband of yours is treating you well."

"He does in his own way, I guess." She did not look too happy now. Whenever someone mentioned her husband, Samantha suddenly became guarded, looking as if she would cry.

"Lucien was very ill recently. He had a lot of catching up to do. That is why he is meeting me here." She felt compelled to say something, so she briefly related the story of Lucien's accident.

"He is lucky to be alive. And," Stèfan added, "very lucky that you were there."

"Yes, I guess you are right." Samantha began to play with her neckcloth. Then she abruptly changed the subject. "How long will you stay in America?"

"Probably a few more months. I do intend to travel. Who knows, maybe you will still be in New Orleans by the time I arrive."

"Perhaps," she said hopefully, "you will meet Adam by then."

"And don't forget that I, too, will help by badgering my father to get some information through his own sources." Before he could stop the words from pouring forth, he added, "If I find your brother for you, maybe you will leave your husband for me!"

"Stèfan, you are a dear." Samantha hugged him as she gave him a friendly kiss on the mouth. "I wish it were so easy."

At that instant, she experienced the oddest sensation along her spine, as if someone were watching. Turning swiftly toward the woods, she saw a bird circling high overhead.

"What's wrong?"

"Oh, nothing." She dismissed the feeling.

"Do you mind, Sam, if we go back now? I have some last minute letters to write."

"Tell you what, Stèfan. You can go back. I would like to ride Dawn a little longer." She saw him hesitate. "Believe me, *mon cher*"—she imitated him—"I do not need a chaperone."

Stèfan watched her gallop away, probably toward her retreat by the brook, he thought as he mounted his horse and rode toward the plantation.

It wasn't necessary to lead Dawn toward the brook, for she trotted there out of habit. Since no one was around, Samantha removed her neckcloth and cravat and unbuttoned the top three buttons of her shirt. If I get any warmer, she thought, I can always take off the shirt. The slip chemise underneath would offer enough protection. Against what or whom? She laughed aloud. No one could find this place unless directed. Putting her things neatly by a large old cypress tree, she walked onto the rocks in the brook. She really wasn't thinking about anything in particular. It was so peaceful watching the water cascade over the rocks, making little waves and whirlpools. The leaves, moss, and surrounding wildflowers gave off a fresh scent that reminded her of her childhood. Samantha felt like a young girl again, without problems or encumbrances. The shadow she cast was wide and she smiled at the off shape. The more she looked at the shape the more she could have sworn it grew in height as well as width. And then the shadow split into another form. She was so startled that she jumped, forgetting she was precariously perched on a rock, and lost her balance. A strong arm reached across her waist to steady her. It happened so fast that Samantha did not have time to be frightened. She clutched the arm for support as she was lifted onto solid ground.

"I hope I didn't frighten you, green eyes."

Oh God. She closed her eyes. He is here and laughing at me again! she thought with chagrin.

"Lucien! Why do you love to frighten me to death?" She was surprised and, yes, happy to see him. He looked so handsome, so healthy. His long, lean fingers protectively held her arm.

"Now what kind of way is that to greet your husband after all these weeks apart?"

Before she could reply, his warm lips captured hers in a hard, demanding kiss. It felt wonderful.

"Did you miss me, my sweet? Or were you too busy with your old beau to think of me?"

The smile was gone. His handsome face darkened with anger, and as she looked up into his midnight blue eyes she thought she detected disappointment. Impossible, she told herself, dismissing the notion.

"I don't understand. What do you mean?"

Lucien pulled the green ribbon from her hair, staring at the long, red-gold curls. How many times have I dreamed of doing just this, he thought, and much more? But he remembered his eagerness to find Samantha, leaving Meredith and Robert at the house staring after him. Meredith had already casually informed Lucien that Stèfan Turreau was also here. "He is only her friend," Meredith warned. But that did not matter now. Nothing did, except this obsessive

239

desire to see Samantha once more.

When he had first found her, she was laughing so gaily . . . with Turreau. She never laughs like that—so carefree—with me, he observed somewhat enviously. His envy was replaced by anger when he saw them kissing. Damn! he cursed. As soon as I am out of her sight, she starts collecting lovers the way others collect stamps.

Being in no mood for a scene, Lucien jerked on the horse's reins and rode back to the house. He swiftly strode to Samantha's room with his bags, looking around to see if he could find traces of another male in that room. The sound of an approaching horse stopped his search. Seeing Turreau alone meant that Samantha was still out riding.

He hastily walked back down the stairs. Only a barely noticeable limp remained, which, according to Dr. Bentley, was only temporary. As Lucien reached the front door, he practically knocked Stèfan down with his haste.

"Hello Turreau," he said curtly, reluctantly extending his hand. "Can you tell me where I might find my wife?"

Sensing Lucien's strained attitude, Stèfan told him how to find Samantha, then quickly added, "Samantha is not a very happy woman, monsieur. I wonder if you have anything to do with it. She needs a lot of love."

"I think, 'monsieur,' I know exactly how to handle my wife—without your advice," Lucien snapped before he walked away.

Now, here he was, holding her in his arms, ready to engage in verbal battle with her again.

"Lucien, what did you mean about my old beau?"

she asked for the second time.

"I mean, Samantha, finding you kissing Turreau!"

At least she can still blush with embarrassment, he concluded, noticing her high color.

"Lucien, you have me confused with yourself. You are so busy being unfaithful you have no idea what it might be like to have a friend of the opposite sex."

Taken aback by her heated outburst, he started to laugh. "So many women, Samantha? Who are they?"

"I do not know, nor do I want to know," she sharply replied, confused by his complete switch in moods. She looked up at him again, realizing something wonderful. A wide, happy smile brightened her sunburned face, reversing her mood.

"You are not using a cane! How is your leg, Lucien? Let me see you walk."

Reluctantly he let go of her to do as she bid. "I still have a limp, and it only hurts when I stand or sit in one position for a long time."

"Lucien," she chided, "no one could notice what you consider to be a limp. Oh, I might, but that is because I know you so well."

"Thank you, Dr. Fraser. Now look what you have done."

"What have I done now?"

"You've made me forget to drop you into the water." He picked up her squirming body, holding her precariously close to the brook.

"You would not dare," she challenged. That was her mistake. The next instant she was sitting in the middle of the brook with a very wet pair of new breeches.

"Oh," she moaned, "you have ruined my boots and breeches." Furiously, she splashed water at his mock-

241

ing face. "You can at least be a gentleman and give me your hand so I can get out."

Still laughing, he reached down for her and was suddenly thrown off balance by a forceful tug.

"You are strong, my love," he commented, no longer laughing, for his expensive Hessian boots were knee deep in water. He bent down and splashed her so thoroughly she looked as if she had just had a bath.

Feeling reckless now, Samantha got to her feet and reciprocated, trying to drench Lucien with her own water attack.

"Truce," he laughed, smitten by her playful spirit.

"Not until you say, 'I give up Samantha. You win.' Go on, say it!" She was laughing with almost as much pleasure as when she had laughed with Turreau.

"Never, you minx." He braved the splashing water, grabbed her wrist, and pulled a protesting Samantha into his arms. Together they lowered themselves onto the grassy land, leaning on their knees. Staring into her beautiful but wet face with its soft, full mouth inviting his, Lucien slowly bent to kiss her.

The wet cotton shirt seductively clung to her curves, revealing her already hardened nipples. The soggy breeches molded to her long, lean legs, giving Lucien the impression that she was wearing nothing but her silk stockings. Oh, how he wanted her!

"Did I tell you, my love, how very appealing you look in those breeches? I think"—he reverently reached to fondle her breasts—"I shall forbid you to wear them for anyone but me."

As if on an arranged signal, their hands slowly, deliciously roamed each other's inviting bodies. Thrilled by his long overdue touch, Samantha would

242

not let his hand leave her, even to unbutton his shirt.

"No, let me," she murmured huskily. Placing tiny kisses on his neck, she moved her mouth lower as each button opened to reveal his sun-bronzed chest. When her hands pulled his shirt out of his breeches and slid under, around to his back, he groaned, pulling her tiny derrière into his hardened body.

"No, Lucien, not yet," she commanded, sensing his urgency. Feeling a recklessness that emboldened her, she pushed him away from her, her mouth finding his nipples, nibbling them. But her hands never stopped touching him, and to Lucien's utter delight and amazement, she undid the buttons of his breeches.

Kissing his stomach, she began following her hands. Where they touched, she kissed, until she pulled down his breeches and found him swollen with desire for her. When her mouth enclosed him, Lucien knew he would never find passion again with any other woman but this fiery angel.

Feeling the need to possess her overwhelming him, Lucien none too gently pulled her into his strong arms, his mouth claiming hers. "I think you have missed me, Samantha," he whispered against her cheek. "And God, how I have missed you."

It was not necessary to say any more. Words could not express what their bodies were saying. Samantha's responsive body told him how much she wanted him.

Chapter Eighteen

It did not take long for Lucien and Samantha to resume their uneasy arrangement. They both knew their relationship was not as good as those early weeks together after they were married. However, this would do—for now.

Meredith knew about the idiosyncrasies in their relationship. If only they could talk to one another, she observed, they both would come to the same conclusion: that they needed and loved each other. There was no one else in her brother's life. Whether he knew it or not, Lucien was in love with his wife. He was such a fool, Meredith mused. At least Samantha admitted her true feelings to herself. It's so sad, Meredith thought, how pride could be such a destructive force in a relationship. Since Samantha had made Meredith promise not to interfere, Meredith could not point out to either of them how foolishly they were behaving. If only Adam were there. Surely he would know what to do.

At that precise moment, Adam Thornton would

have been glad to be anywhere but where he was. Looking down at his soiled, loosely hanging clothes, Adam cursed himself for the thousandth time for being such a jackass. What had made him think that he could handle Major Gaspar alone? Adam had been so close to getting the physical evidence he needed on Gaspar, Wilkinson, Burr—the whole lot of them.

Looking around the sparsely lit room, Adam limped two paces over to his cot. His last escape attempt having failed, not only was he beaten and starved for a week, but he was taken further south over the Mexican border. The tiny cell he was in had little air and there was little contact with the outside world, except when they wanted to question or beat him. His food—Adam grimaced at what his jailors defined as food—was passed through a narrow portal in the heavy wooden door. Adam learned that the two buckets in the cell had different purposes. One was for water and the other for his biological necessities, each to be left beside the door every night to be replaced.

It would be the beginning of April by now, he realized. His child would be a few months old by now. Leaning against the drab concrete wall, Adam wondered about his wife. How was Meredith? Had she survived childbirth? Had she cried for him when he was not there for one of the most important events of their lives? Throughout his long imprisonment, Adam refused to give his captors any information about his role as government agent. Let them rot in hell, he cursed. Over and over, Adam told them he was a shipbuilder and businessman who came to New Orleans to expand his business. No matter how many times he was beaten and threatened, he would not give them names. He had not been formally charged with spying against the Spanish . . . not yet.

But it did not matter, for Adam knew that soon Lucien would find a way to release him. Not for one minute did he doubt that Lucien would come for him—probably with Sam right behind him, he smiled wryly. He hoped that Samantha was making an effort to get along with Lucien, for Meredith's sake. My sister must have torn up the house when she learned of my arrest.

A loud bang suddenly interrupted his musings.

"Señor Thornton. I have a special guest here."

"Oh, is it the King of England?"

"No," answered another voice, much deeper than that of the jailor, but familiar nevertheless.

A bright flash of light temporarily blinded him. Adam's hazel eyes focused on the figure with a silver riding quirt in his hand standing in the open doorway.

"Major Gaspar, isn't it? So good of you to visit me. Excuse me if I don't stand. My leg has not properly healed from the last beating your friends gave me."

Gaspar's smile almost unnerved Adam. "Tell me Mr. Thornton, are you worth more dead than alive?"

Adam never had a chance to answer, for out of the blinding light emerged two of the ugliest, burliest soldiers he had ever seen. And they were headed straight for him.

Lucien was reasonably content at Thornton Hill, although there were, unfortunately, too many reminders of Samantha's "friendship" with Turreau. Once, when he had gone alone into Charleston, he overheard a conversation between two matrons who specifically mentioned Samantha's name and suspected infidelity.

"You know," commented the older one, "I don't see how she manages. Why, just as soon as her devilish-looking husband appears, her other lover disappears."

"Do you think," asked the other, "that her husband killed him?"

Lucien was tempted to shut them up but realized the futility of it. He knew from Adam that Samantha was not well liked because she never cared what those old gossips thought about her. Not that he blamed her for that. He tried to dismiss the matter since Samantha kept insisting that she had not been disloyal. But still he wondered. The thought of her infidelity rooted somewhere deep inside him, and like a cancerous tumor, it began to grow. Sometimes Lucien stared at her, trying to gauge her innermost sentiments. He asked her questions about what she had done at Thornton Hill before his arrival, simultaneously hoping and dreading he would discover a flaw in her recital. And when he found none, he still felt the need to accuse her in any case. But at night when she lay in his arms, when they made splendid love to each other, he realized he couldn't. Not yet. For surely if she had been unfaithful and admitted it, their marriage would end. No, he resolved, not yet.

Samantha and Lucien agreed to leave Thornton Hill for New Orleans the last week of May. There wasn't much to prepare because Samantha had most things ready in anticipation of their imminent departure. With the remaining two weeks, they could relax and enjoy each other's company.

Samantha proudly showed Lucien the plantation and the sights of Charleston. Although they did not accept all the invitations to teas, the theater, and parties, they appeared together often enough to stop most of the wagging tongues.

Three days before their departure, on a hot, sticky Saturday afternoon, Lucien decided to go to Charleston and wait for his latest message from the Secretary of State. Samantha had wanted to join him, but he was so impatient about waiting for her to dress that she sent him off without her. She didn't really care. He had been in such an irritable state of mind that Samantha doubted she would have enjoyed herself anyway. Instead, Samantha decided to spend the afternoon visiting Marianne Davis. The Davis plantation was only thirty minutes away, and it was too hot to ride in an enclosed carriage. Samantha had Dawn saddled while she quickly changed into her stylish blue linen riding habit. Bumping into Meredith long enough to tell her she would be back to join everyone for dinner, she quickly left.

Marianne was delighted to see Samantha. They chatted and laughed about their childhood pranks, and talked much more about the present.

"Oh Sam, you are so lucky to have a husband like yours. He is so dark and devilishly handsome. Why, I'll bet you never get a moment's rest," she giggled.

"He is full of surprises," Samantha commented, hoping Marianne wasn't going to ask any direct questions.

"The last time I danced with him I thought I would faint from the excitement of being so near to him. Does he make you feel that way too?"

"Yes, sometimes he does." That is, when he doesn't make me feel like shooting him, she silently added.

"Tell me again, Sam, about your courtship," Marianne asked innocently.

Samantha gave Marianne a fairy tale version of their courtship and marriage, wishing it were really true. She nevere finished the story, though, for a loud noise startled them.

"Oh, that's probably Clinton," Marianne stated, her tone guarded. "He came back last night. I just don't know what Papa plans to do with him. You know my brother has been having a few problems lately."

Alarmed by Clinton's arrival, Samantha decided to leave. Not wishing to confront him, Samantha quickly excused herself, saying she remembered she had some last minute packing to do before Lucien came home.

As Dawn was brought around to the front of the house, the young women bade each other good-bye. In her haste, Samantha did not look up to the second floor. Standing by the window, with a bottle of whiskey in his hand and a malicious grin distorting his once-handsome face, stood Clinton. As soon as Samantha rode off, Clinton quietly left and followed her.

Ten minutes later, she heard hoofbeats. Quickly looking behind her, she was afraid of knowing yet somehow quite sure of who was following her. She could see Clinton's body leaning over the horse trying to gain speed. She urged Dawn to gallop, knowing she could outrun Clinton. Quite unexpectedly, Dawn stumbled over a log, throwing Samantha high into the air before she abruptly landed hard on the ground and immediately lost consciousness.

It seemed as if hours had passed, but when Samantha came to, the midday sun was still in the sky. She could see the sun through the window... window? Her mind slowly registered that something was very wrong.

Looking around, Samantha could not recognize anything. The room was small—a two-room cabin—and dusty as if no one had been there for some time. The room she occupied was obviously considered a bedroom. Ignoring the pain in her temple, Samantha slowly moved off the bed and peered into the other room. Clinton was sitting near the window with a large bottle of gin in one hand and a long leather whip in the other.

Her stomach churned with fear now. How could she escape unnoticed? Frantically she searched the room for an object, anything sturdy enough to hit Clinton. Glancing out the door once more, it appeared to her that Clinton must have fallen asleep or passed out. For a moment, she almost felt sorry for him. He used to be so well dressed and respected. Over the last few weeks she had heard enough rumors to know he was considered little more than a drunkard and gambler. His clothes no longer fit properly; the once shiny black boots were mud stained; his hair was dirty—what used to be pale blond, looked almost brown now. His lean face was married by dissipation. This was no longer a gentleman.

Out of the corner of her eye, she spotted a brass candlestick underneath a table. It didn't feel too heavy, but she hoped she could at least stun Clinton long enough to get away. Where was Dawn? She looked out the dirty window, searching for her horse. There she was! Samantha could see her tethered to a tree near the side of the cabin, grazing on the grass. Her heart pounding louder than the pain in her head, Samantha prayed for strength.

The door leading to the next room was slightly ajar. The soiled riding skirt hampered her movements, and she silently cursed women's riding clothes, wishing for the freedom of breeches. Her hair fell into her eyes, and she tried to pin it before she managed to get near the door without making any noise. Walking on her toes, she stealthily crept outside the room, the object poised in the air ready to hit Clinton forcefully so she could escape.

He stirred. So frightened was she by this unexpected movement, she did not take the time to aim. The candlestick came crashing down, but she hit his shoulder. There was no time to try again. Samantha dropped the offensive object and ran for the door. Thank God it wasn't locked! She ran outside, hearing Clinton's labored breathing not far behind her.

"You lousy bitch!" he roared. "You can't get away from me."

Still she ran, all the time flinching and fearing that at any moment the whip would slash at her unprotected back. A tangled mess of hair fell about her face and shoulders. But she kept running and suddenly realized that in her panic she was running toward the wrong horse. It did not matter now. In her state, she would ride a bucking bull to be free of Clinton. He was crazed!

"Come back here, whore!"

Panting with terror and exhaustion, she ignored his

threats and the hissing of the whip behind her. Suddenly, she fell to the ground, the long leather whip entwined about her legs. The pain was excruciating. He had deliberately cut off her circulation. Like a fox surrounded by loud, baying dogs, she looked about for any means of escape. There was none. Clinton leered at her with a maniacal look in his unnaturally lit eyes. He's going to kill me, she realized. She closed her eyes and Lucien's image swept before her. Oh please, Lucien, hear me, help me, help me, she pleaded silently.

It was as if Clinton had read her thoughts. "There is no one to help you, Samantha. You are all mine, to do with as I please." He reached for her as she cringed, clawing at the ground, backing away from his touch.

"Don't you touch me," she snarled in a deceptively angry voice.

"Who the hell are you, Miss High and Mighty? Are you too good for me?" Grabbing her arm, he pulled her unwilling body up to his, tearing the sleeve of her riding jacket. He was much stronger than she had given him credit for.

"Look at me. Answer me, bitch! Do you only give your body to your husband and your French lover?" Although he looked at her, she could have sworn he did not really see her face.

Samantha's response was purely reflexive; she spat in his face! He was temporarily stunned. Unexpectedly, his hand released her long enough to come full force across her face. Reeling from the power of his slap, she almost fell, but he grabbed her again, slapping her over and over until Samantha no longer could see or hear. Blackness threatened to engulf her. Yet Clinton kept striking her, holding her sagging body erect so she would not fall.

"Where is your precious captain now?" he laughed, taunting her with his high-pitched voice.

It was impossible to stand still, let alone think clearly. Clinton dragged her bruised body back into the cabin, cruelly grabbing her hair so that she could not move her head. Her vision was blurred because her left eye was swelling shut. In her barely conscious state, she was beyond feeling the pain of Clinton's continuous blows.

Dragging her back into the cabin, he flung her onto the bed. Samantha rallied enough to kick him. She connected, because she heard him grunt. "You will pay for that, my whore," he sneered.

"You are mad, Clinton," she whispered through now-bloody lips. "Let someone help you. You need help, Clinton." Since she did not make any impression, she tried to scare him. "Clinton, believe me, Lucien will kill you."

"That is if he ever finds me. Or"—he looked down at her bruised face—"if your captain ever finds your broken body."

"Don't do it, Clinton," she warned. She almost pleaded but forced herself not to beg. Something was ripping. She could hear the sound, but her body was too numb. Clinton was stripping off her clothes, shredding them in the process. Within seconds, only her lacy under-chemise remained. Straddling her body, he pressed her shoulders into the mattress. His foul-smelling mouth lowered to her neck, savagely biting her.

With her last supreme effort, Samantha freed her

right arm, digging her nails into his face, hoping to blind him. His howl pierced the air but still he did not release his hold on her. The last thing she saw through the bloody fog was Clinton's fist connecting with her jaw. Was that her pathetic voice calling for Lucien before darkness descended once more?

Chapter Nineteen

When Samantha awoke hours later, she prayed this had been a nightmare, that she was in her own bed within the protective circle of Lucien's arms. Her arms! She could not move them. Then she understood why. This was no hallucination. Clinton had tied her arms to the bedposts. It was time to give up. No one would ever find her alive; Clinton would see to that. Every part of her hurt. Yet it was not over. He would beat her some more before raping, then murdering her. She was sure that he meant to torture her before she died.

A groan escaped her swollen lips as Clinton slowly approached the bed.

"I am sorry Samantha. I did not mean to hurt you," he whined. "I only want you to love *me*, not your husband."

He was drunk again. Thankfully, Samantha understood that although Clinton appeared remorseful, his murderous instincts were still evident. Her desire to live prevailed again over her fear and pain. Once more, she tried reasoning with this irrational man.

"Clinton. Why don't we start again? Of all my beaus,

I always liked you best. Let me touch you, Clinton."
She tried to sound passionate. "Please, let me touch
your body." He appeared to soften but Samantha was
taking no more chances. "Please, Clinton, I want you
as much as you want me." She almost choked on her
words.

"Why did you marry him?" he asked, his words
childishly inquiring.

"I don't love him. He forced me to do it." If only the
throbbing in her chest and head would stop so she
could think clearly. Time was not on her side. Keep him
talking, Samantha, she warned herself.

"So you don't love him, huh? You want me?" he
argued. Closing her eyes, she desperately tried to shut
out his image. When she opened them again, Clinton
had that crazed, faraway look in his eyes once more.

"What about that Frenchman?" he accused. "And all
your other lovers? Oh no, Samantha." His shrill laugh
sickened her. "I don't believe your lying, treacherous
words. You are a whore," he shouted, "and must be
treated like one."

Bending down, he picked up the whip, and before
she could open her mouth to scream, it swished down
across the mattress, close enough to sting her bare
thighs. From his muffled curse, she knew that he had
not meant to miss her body.

"This time, I will make sure . . ." His arm rose again
to strike.

"No!" she shrieked and could not stop screaming.

"Shut up, I said," Clinton demanded, expecting her
to respond. "Oh Christ. The only way to shut you up is
to gag you." Shoving his handkerchief into her
protesting mouth, he stared at her bruised, exposed

258

body, realizing his own very aroused state. Dropping the whip, Clinton unbuttoned his breeches and straddled Samantha's prone body, ready to enter her. Her terror was clearly mirrored in her wide, pain-glazed eyes.

"Now you will experience pleasure!"

Suddenly a loud gunshot rang. Clinton howled before clutching his bloody shoulder.

"Stand up, Davis! Get away from my wife," Lucien's voice chillingly commanded. Lucien was dressed completely in black, his blue eyes strangely glittering on an otherwise expressionless face. "Button your breeches. Now turn around, Davis. Because the last thing you are going to see is my face and my pistol that will take your worthless life. I only hope to God that your pain will be greater than what my wife has endured."

Clinton begged for his life, but Lucien was beyond compassion. One look at Samantha's exposed body, her bloodied and swollen face, sealed Clinton's fate.

At the sound of Lucien's voice, Samantha fainted with relief, so she never saw Clinton's cowardice. Nor did she see Clinton grab a knife before he lunged for Lucien.

Reacting instinctively, Lucien shot him in the chest, and as Clinton's life ebbed, Lucien looked at Davis's body and wished he could have killed him again, more slowly. As he looked at his wife—an innocent victim of an insane attack—all of his hatred and anger left him. The pistol fell out of his hand, clattering onto the wooden floor. Tenderly, Lucien removed the bonds and gag, softly stroking her battered face.

"Samantha, please hear me. It's Lucien, my love. I

am here now. He will never hurt you again. He's dead, Samantha. Please, my love, open your eyes." His soft voice was disguised to liberate her from her terror. "I am taking you home, my sweet."

Afraid to touch her bruised body, Lucien gently lifted Samantha's hands to his lips as he lovingly kissed each finger. "Please come back to me. You will be fine." He couldn't wait to get her out of there, to bring her home, and hoped she could tolerate the jolting ride. It was obvious she badly needed a doctor.

The once luminous green eyes slowly opened to the gentle masculine voice she knew so well. At least he thought she had opened her eyes, for her left eye was so swollen it was impossible to tell.

"Can you see me, love?" His gentle tone was forced because Lucien felt so much hatred—for that animal Davis and for himself, because he had not waited for her this morning. And hadn't he also doubted her fidelity? This whole incident was his fault. Now if only he could take her pain away.

When she tremulously smiled back, Lucien was greatly relieved. "I think," he grinned warmly, "I shall never let you out of my sight again."

"Oh Lucien. It was so horrible," she whispered. Now that he cradled her in his arms, controlling her emotions was no longer necessary. Sobbing with relief and renewed fear, she told Lucien everything—every word and gesture she could remember.

He listened as he never had listened before, with all the love and compassion he felt for this fragile, beautiful woman in his arms, admiring her strength. Surely few women would have survived this ordeal. With renewed vigor, Lucien promised Samantha that he would not leave her side. All the while he kept silently praying that all wounds—especially those to her spirit—would quickly heal. Sealing the vow, he sweetly, tenderly kissed her face—every bruise and cut. Her eyes closed and her breathing seemed relaxed. He marveled at Samantha's peaceful sleep, hoping the healing had begun.

Lucien helped her into his buckskin jacket and found a spare blanket in the cabin to wrap around her body. Then he disengaged himself from her long enough to set Dawn free to find her way home then tied Clinton's body to his horse. "This is too good for you," he muttered, viciously pulling the rope.

Knowing that the county sheriff would have to be notified, Lucien decided that Samantha must be protected at all cost. The thought of having her go through any more anguish, especially if there were a trial, troubled him.

It took well over an hour to cover the short distance to Thornton Hill. Samantha was securely nestled in his arms, her head leaning on his broad chest. As he slowly led the horses through the starry night with his battered wife in his arms and the dead body behind him, Lucien again recalled and felt the emotional strain of the entire day.

By the time he had returned to Thornton Hill earlier that afternoon, he was anxious to see Samantha. Lucien felt guilty about not waiting for her in the morning. He ended up waiting in town anyway, for the messenger from Mr. Madison was delayed. The letter Madison sent was not very interesting or informative.

It merely relayed information Lucien already had: Aaron Burr had been arrested and would be tried for treason in Richmond, Virginia; names of people to contact for assistance in New Orleans if he needed it; and the usual final warning that the U.S. Government would deny any knowledge of Lucien's activities, if he were arrested by the Spanish.

Annoyed that their departure had been delayed because of this letter, Lucien quickly returned to the plantation, prepared to apologize to his wife. It was almost time for dinner.

He hurried into the house calling for Samantha. No answer. Instead, a very worried Meredith appeared.

"Isn't Samantha with you?"

"No. You saw me leave without her. Why? Where did she go?" For one very brief moment Lucien wondered if Samantha were secretly meeting Turreau. Of course that notion was ridiculous, since he knew Turreau to be on his way to Washington.

"She rushed out before lunch to visit Marianne Davis. Samantha said she would be back before you. Lucien, there is something else that bothers me."

His sister's agitation became noticeable. Unthinkingly, Lucien's body tensed, sensing trouble.

"Tell me," he ordered, running short of patience.

"I heard from the overseer that Clinton Davis came back yesterday. Lucien, you know as well as I that if Samantha had known he was back she would not have gone to visit Marianne," she said nervously. "I have heard a lot of talk about Clinton. He is not the same man any more."

"Yes, I've also heard." His voice was sharp. "But I am sure Samantha can take care of herself." No, he really wasn't sure at all, but he did not want to upset Meredith further.

"You cannot fool me, brother. I know you are also concerned." She had seen right through him, noticing the stiff way he held his body and the nervous twitter in his cheek. "We both know how frightened Samantha is of him. When she didn't return, I was hoping that Sam went looking for you." Meredith wrung her clammy hands.

"I might have passed her," he speculated, then quickly rejected the notion. "I am going over there. If Davis touches her, he will pay . . ." Without any hesitation he left and rode off toward the Davis plantation.

Marianne Davis was polite but quite confused. Yes, she and Samantha had spent a lovely afternoon together, but Samantha had left three hours ago.

"She said she had some packing to do."

"Was your brother here, Miss Davis?"

"Why, yes, he arrived moments before Samantha left. They did not even see one another." Marianne sounded clearly confused.

"Miss Davis, is your brother home now?" he asked, trying to maintain a calm he did not feel.

"Yes, I have not seen him leave. Wait." She rose. "I will go and fetch him."

At Lucien's affirmative response Marianne quickly left the room to find her brother. Two minutes later she reappeared looking upset.

"I don't understand it, Mr. Fraser. I know my brother was here and was planning to remain home tonight. Something is wrong. I can feel it. Do you think . . ." here eyes revealed her fear, "Samantha is in some trouble?"

He didn't want to waste any more time speculating. A sense of desperate urgency consumed him. Samantha was in trouble. He knew it. If Clinton had stopped Samantha, it had to be on the same road that led back to Thornton Hill. The sky was darkening. Lucien rushed out to retrace the path Samantha should have taken. He had to find some clue to her whereabouts.

If the sun had not been setting at that precise moment, he would never have found her broken diamond and gold bracelet. It lay to the side of the road, the bright diamonds signaling him. Examining the area, Lucien was able to tell that there was more than one horse; that something, or someone, was dragged off the road onto another path. The path was still on Davis property. Perhaps it led to Samantha.

Stealthily, Lucien picked his way along the path. Horses had recently been that way—he saw evidence of that. Finally he saw a cabin. Samantha's horse was not far away. Like a sleek panther, Lucien was poised and ready to strike. And then he heard Samantha's bloodcurdling screams. He froze, his stomach churning, his blood boiling. At that moment, there was no doubt in his mind who would die.

With each chilling scream, Lucien's heart twisted with what he imagined to be her agony. It was as bad as he thought. He noiselessly approached the open window. He could not see Samantha for Davis's body was on top of hers. He had to plan his next move. If Lucien made a mistake, Samantha would die.

Despite his emotional turmoil, he was able to think rationally. After loading his pistol, he went to the side of the cabin. The door was ajar, the inner room dark.

His long, catlike strides were unobserved. He could hear Clinton's incoherent speech and crept close to the bedroom. Clinton was shoving a gag into her mouth; then he reached for the buttons of his breeches. Oh no, that rotten bastard would not harm her any more.

". . . experience pleasure" was all Lucien heard, but that was enough. He stood up and walked into the room, ready to strike. That coward—he almost choked on the bile that rose in his throat. He saw the bindings attached to her wrists. Lifting the pistol, he methodically aimed and fired.

In the melee, the only thing that was crystal clear to Lucien was the bruised, battered face of his wife, his woman. As soon as he saw her swollen face, he felt like shouting at the injustice of it all. She did not deserve this cruelty—no human being did. But he knew Clinton Davis did not act like a sane man.

The sounds of horses' hooves ended his reverie.

Coming onto Thornton property Lucien could see burning torches lighting up the path. As he slowly approached the large brick house, he saw the family and slaves anxiously waiting, then running toward him. Meredith and Robert appeared to be consoling one another.

"My God, Lucien—what happened?" Robert was astonished at the sight of his daughter. He looked further back to the body tied to the rear horse and exclaimed, "Clinton did this?"

Lucien nodded, afraid to speak, feeling that he still could not control his fury. "Here, help me with Samantha . . . Get a doctor. Someone will have to get the sheriff. As soon as she is settled and I clean up a bit, we'll talk." He did not think he was making any sense. His words were confused.

When he tried handing a semi-conscious Samantha down to the waiting hands of her father, she began to moan, then whimper. "No! Don't touch me! Lucien, please don't leave me!"

"It's all right, my love," he crooned. "Open your eyes. Look, it's your father and Meredith." He jumped off the horse and took her back into his arms. "Come sweetheart, I will take you upstairs."

Feeling the warmth and protection Lucien's body offered, she nestled into his hard chest, letting the blackness take her once more.

Meredith had never seen her brother look or act this way before. On the surface there appeared to be a deadly calm about him. But underneath she speculated that there was a smoldering fury ready to erupt. He efficiently supervised the doctor's cleansing of Samantha's bruises and helped to remove her tattered clothes. All the while she tenaciously clung to his arm as if letting go would bring back the nightmare. There really wasn't much for the doctor to do after administering to the bruises, except to give Samantha enough laudanum to put her into a dreamless sleep. Lucien, however, insisted that the doctor stay long enough to tell the sheriff, who was waiting in the parlor, the exact cause and extent of Samantha's injuries. Without any additional prompting from Lucien, the doctor told the sheriff that Samantha could not have defended herself against such a vicious attack.

Sheriff Burton understood but also knew he had to make a thorough investigation.

"Sir," the stocky man addressed Lucien, "I deeply regret any inconvenience this will cause you and Samantha, but I must make a complete report."

"You are not going to arrest Lucien, are you?" exclaimed an indignant Robert. "Surely you know it was self-defense. Lucien told you how Clinton attacked him with a knife. How else could he save my daughter from that . . . madman."

"Robert, I am sorry, but I must speak to Samantha myself. Look," he admitted, "I have known your family for years. I have also known the Davises. Please cooperate with me now and perhaps we can avoid any formal charges or hearings."

"Sheriff." Lucien stepped forward. "I do not believe my wife could withstand the emotional strain of any hearing—particularly a public one." His voice was low but very firm. He reached for the drink Meredith offered. "You may speak to my wife after she has had a few days' rest. And . . . I still intend to leave for New Orleans as soon as she is physically able to withstand the trip."

Sheriff Burton thought otherwise. "Again I apologize, but I must talk to Samantha as soon as she awakens, while the incident is still fresh in her mind. That is my job and I intend to do it." Standing to leave, hat in hand, he added, "Do I make myself clear?"

"Very well," Lucien conceded. "If you think that is the best way to avoid any public scandal, I will do as you suggest." Lucien was having difficulty checking his temper. "Come back tomorrow afternoon." As he shook the sheriff's hand, Lucien grimly reminded him, "I will not allow my wife to be hurt again."

Chapter Twenty

The sheriff was true to his word. The following morning—even though it was Sunday—Sheriff Burton appeared. As it turned out, the man had to wait all day for Samantha to awaken. She remained in an almost trancelike state for nearly twenty hours.

After a few hours rest in between written statements and endless conversation with family and authorities, Lucien tried spending the rest of his time with Samantha. He felt it was important to be with her when she woke up. He solicitously held her hand, bathed her face with cold water, and applied ointment to her cuts.

When Samantha finally awoke, it was with a brief cry of alarm.

"Calm down, my sweet. There is nothing to be frightened of." Lucien held her hand reassuringly. His smile was so warm, despite the dark circles under his eyes revealing that he had had little or no sleep.

"You look like you could use some rest, Lucien," she rasped, for her throat was very sore.

"Don't worry about me. It's my turn to look after you now. And"—he sat down on the bed—"I hope to be as good a nurse to you as you were to me."

"Lucien, you don't owe me anything. Please." She sounded hurt. "There is no reason for you to feel obligated." Tears formed in her eyes—why, she did not know. Before she could think, Lucien gently pulled her bruised body into his warm embrace.

"Don't make me angry, green eyes. I am not doing anything out of any obligation to you. Now"—he kissed her temple—"let's talk about our future plans."

He told her about Sheriff Burton needing her statement, and his plans for them to leave Thornton Hill as soon as she felt able.

"Lucien, they won't do anything to you? I mean, will you have to stand trial?" Her green eyes widened in fright and concern.

"No, not if the good sheriff is satisfied with your statement," he soothed her. She's so beautiful, he thought, even with her tangled hair and bruised, frowning face. He couldn't resist kissing her on the mouth, even though he was unsure of her response. For the last two days he had worried about something. Would she be afraid of his touch—of any man's touch now?

As if the same thought had occurred to her, she briefly hesitated when he moved to kiss her. But she instinctively knew that there would never be any inhibitions with Lucien, not as long as she loved him. Head tilted slightly, she closed her eyes and lifted her soft, still-tender lips up to his warm, waiting mouth.

"I only wish, my love, that I could have prevented this from happening," he told her sadly. "From now on you are stuck with me. You are my responsibility and I promise to protect you. I will take you with me everywhere . . . Well, not everywhere, but as often as I possibly can. I hope you do not become sick of my company." His smile melted all her fears.

Samantha was grateful that Lucien insisted on staying in the room with her when Sheriff Burton asked his questions. Her voice shaking, she related the story in her own words and answered all of the sheriff's questions. Samantha did not want to leave any doubt in the sheriff's mind about Clinton's brutality, for she would not permit any arrest or trial for her husband. Lucien had reacted in self-defense. Lord knows what he would have done if Clinton had not reached for the knife. Deep down she knew.

Earlier, Meredith had helped Samantha into a long-sleeved, high-necked white cotton nightgown with matching bed jacket. Her copper hair was pulled off her face, secured by a ribbon. She looked so virginal. The contrast between the whiteness of her gown and the dark purple and blue bruises had made Sheriff Burton gasp when he saw her. Lucien understood, for when he had first seen Samantha propped up against the pillows, he had difficulty controlling the black rage that engulfed him. Yes, he thought, he was glad he had killed Clinton Davis.

Only Lucien knew how much of an effort his wife was making not to break down. She held his hand throughout the recital, crushing it whenever she mentioned the more terrifying moments. Fighting back the tears, she pressed on, afraid to stop even for a deep breath, as if pausing would make the nightmare real again.

Finally, Sheriff Burton stood up.

"Thank you very much, Mrs. Fraser. I know this wasn't easy for you. I think any further inquiries would be futile."

She anxiously glanced at Lucien's expressionless face. "Are you going to bring charges against my husband?" she asked hesitantly.

"No. Even if your husband did stand trial, what jury would convict a man of murder for saving his wife against a madman? There is also enough evidence to show that Mr. Fraser acted in self-defense." He saw both Lucien and Samantha sigh with relief. After shaking Lucien's hand, he patted Samantha's arm, saying, "I hope you can both forget."

As soon as the door closed, Samantha reached for Lucien and cried. The ordeal was finally over. Tenderly smoothing her hair, he murmured, "You will forget, love. I swear it.

"Lucien"—she turned her large shiny green eyes up to his face—"let's leave in a few days. No!" She noticed he was about to protest. "I will be fine—even better once I am aboard the *Newport Wind* with you."

"Let's see what the doctor has to say." He didn't sound very firm. Actually, he was delighted that her spirit was returning and she was ready for their next adventure together.

"Oh, and Lucien," she added shyly, eyes now downcast, "would you stay with me tonight?"

"Tonight and every night, my sweet Samantha." And he held her securely in his arms again.

Within the week, they were aboard the *Newport*

Wind bound for New Orleans. Samantha's bruises were fading, yet she wore a very wide-brimmed straw hat which practically hid her face from view. The few days aboard the schooner were, for Samantha, peaceful and recuperative. Lucien, in spite of his many responsibilities, was as solicitous of her needs as before. Since Roger was also aboard, Samantha found herself the center of male attention and reveled in it.

It wasn't until the third night aboard the schooner that Lucien decided to talk to Samantha about resuming their physical relationship. Lucien had waited because he had felt that she needed more time to heal—to be away from Thornton Hill and erase the unpleasant memories. The schooner represented a new beginning. Hopefully, she would want to feel his touch as badly as he wanted to touch her. He had resolved much earlier not to make any attempts until she was ready—almost begging him. For then, there would be no more shadows or ghosts, like the ones he had heard her fighting in her troubled sleep.

Samantha was tired but forced herself to wait for Lucien's return to their cabin. He had had some cargo lists to check and wanted Roger to tell him about the Newport shipping office. It was near midnight by the time he returned. Since it was so warm this time of year, Lucien had worked most of the day without his shirt, but had put it on without buttoning it before he returned to the cabin.

As he walked through the door to the darkened room, the glow from the full white moon accented the large wooden-framed bed and its occupant. She was sitting up, her hair cascading down her shoulders, leaning against the mahogany headboard with only a soft sheet covering her breasts. She was naked! He sucked in his breath almost at the same time as she when she saw his muscular body clearly outlined by his tight breeches and exposed chest. With two strides he was beside her, his blue eyes darkened by denied passion, his smile a bit hesitant.

"Are you sure, green eyes?" His hand found the swell of her breasts and slowly began to touch her, sending delightful tremors through her body. As his hand lowered to pull away the sheet, she sighed with anticipation. Looking into his eyes, Samantha communicated to Lucien that she was eager to receive his attention. Her hands reached for his chest, making small circles and patterns before her mouth lowered to his nipples, lightly flicking her tongue over them. Before he could catch his breath, Samantha pulled his loose shirt off.

"Ah, my sweet," he chuckled, "perhaps you will soon be ready for me. But not yet."

He disengaged himself long enough to tear his clothes off and pin her on the bed. His hands led the way for his searching tongue as he explored her ripe body, feeling as if each time with Samantha were a new adventure. She was moaning and writhing to his touch, but Lucien sensed she wasn't ready yet. After this night, he vowed, there would be no more nightmares for her.

To Samantha, Lucien's lovemaking was a delicious combination of mastery and tenderness. The experience was unlike any other with him. And when he slowly entered her, Samantha felt as if she were a virgin tasting love for the first time. Moaning and calling his

274

name, she felt as if she could go on all night. Indeed, they came together three more times that clear, starry night and on into the morning. Finally, exhaustion claimed them both and they slept in each other's arms.

Even with only a few hours of sleep Samantha awoke feeling more refreshed than she had in a long time. Eyes dreamy, she looked over to the muscular arm and leg flung across her body. The covers had been tossed aside long ago, so Samantha could easily view Lucien's sleeping form. His long, dark lashes practically touched his skin, and she thought his nose would have been classically perfect, had it not been for a slight bump at the bridge. His firm chin already showed signs of needing a shave. Once again, she marveled at his masculine beauty. But she doubted he would be impressed if she told him that she thought him beautiful. She couldn't help but smile at his probable scorn. When she looked down at him again, his eyes were wide open, admiring her amused expression.

"I hope you're smiling because you remember your passionate response to me last night," he said playfully before he abruptly sat up, realizing how late in the day it must be.

"My God, Samantha, you must be a witch. I never sleep through the morning aboard ship." He hurried out of bed, reaching for his buckskin breeches.

"I wonder why no one thought to wake me."

"Oh, but Roger tried and," she said impishly as she burrowed under the covers again, "I sent him away."

All Lucien could do was laugh at the absurdity of the situation. No doubt the crew would be wondering about the unusual abilities of his wife. He looked at her radiant but still-bruised face and smugly thought that all would be well for them—in at least one area.

Their arrival into the port of New Orleans was deliberately visible and loud. Lucien had planned to anchor Monday morning. He knew that the port area would be most active then. General Wilkinson and Major Gaspar would know of their arrival well before Lucien and Samantha reached their house.

Lucien wanted the general to speculate on their presence in this city of untamed beauty. He intended to let the general believe that they were here, not only to search for Adam, but to open their new shipping office. Since Wilkinson and Gaspar were aware that both of these enterprises were *against* the expressed wishes of the President and the Secretary of State, Lucien hoped that it would appear as if a "falling out" had occurred which would make him seem a little more receptive—or at least more willing to turn a deaf ear—to certain activities in the Southwest. Lucien really didn't think Wilkinson or Gaspar would trust him enough that he would be privy to information—but who knew? If they let their guard down just once Lucien could get information about Aaron Burr and the evidence he needed to prove their treachery against the U.S. Government and more than likely their involvement in Adam's arrest. Above all, he had to find Adam.

Sensing her presence, Lucien turned toward the main deck to see his wife approaching. The bruises were almost gone, but her lush beauty would never fade. It amazed him to think that minutes after they had made love he wanted to feel her body rhythmically moving with his all over again. Somehow, he resolved, she would be protected from Wilkinson and Gaspar. Although Samantha agreed with Lucien on their course of action, she did not know that her husband planned to restrict her involvement.

"Hello, my love." He smiled. "Are you ready to conquer New Orleans?"

"Not looking like this," she replied, still self-conscious about the bruises. "But I will be in a few more days. I can't wait to see Major Gaspar," she said sarcastically.

"Don't worry, Samantha, he will not bother you. Not as long as I am here. So you see"—he reached to caress her cheek—"you need me, wife."

Her body warmed as usual to his touch. She merely smiled to herself, thinking, more than you'll know, Lucien.

The houses in the new American sector were along the Mississippi River above the Old Tchoupitoulas Gate. The area recently had become known as the Faubourg St. Marie.

The house the Frasers had acquired was a handsome, two-story dwelling on the corner of Poydras Street. Samantha was impressed by the architectural design and furnishings, which were a combination of the older French and Spanish influences. The ground floor had a series of doors and windows, each surrounded by elaborate carvings in the Spanish colonial style. Each room was cheery and bright.

Aside from the bedrooms and parlor, the upstairs contained a gallery along the side which faced the street and the river and had a long, overhanging roof supported by columns. At the rear of the house there was a small, two-story wing with a terraced roof surrounded by a balustrade. The gallery would be a lovely sitting area, thought Samantha, where one could see the activity on the streets below.

"It's perfect," she marveled when Lucien finally found her. "We don't have to do anything but hire some help."

He smiled at her enthusiasm. "That, my sweet, has already been taken care of, thanks to your cousins. By the way, our first introduction to society is in two days. Your cousins again."

"Do you think our 'friends' will be there?"

"Absolutely. General Wilkinson seems to be everywhere Governor Claiborne is. Just for spite, I think. And with the general is his faithful aide."

"Ugh"—she made a face. "I hope we don't have to stay in New Orleans too long before we have news of Adam." They walked along the gallery. "This is a busy town," she commented. "Just look at all those boats and ships."

"New Orleans has become an extremely important and wealthy area for imports and exports," he explained. "While you supervise the unpacking and cleaning, I will go to see our new office. Roger should be there by now. Maybe he has some leads for us."

Before she could protest, Lucien enfolded her in his powerful embrace and kissed her firmly, leaving her breathless and responsive. As her arms came up to pull him closer, a loud cough interrupted them.

"Excuse me, Madam," said an obviously embarrassed older woman. She was short with curly brown hair. She started to back away, but Lucien, still embracing his wife, asked her to stay.

"I was just leaving. You must be the housekeeper, Mrs. Wells." He shook her hand, smiled once more, said a few charming words which Mrs. Wells found ingratiating, then bade the ladies good-bye.

Samantha instantly liked the other woman and knew Mrs. Wells would be much more than her housekeeper.

"Your husband is a very handsome man," she said politely.

"And very charming when he wants to be, except when he doesn't get enough sleep, or when I ask to accompany him to the shipping office." Or when he wakes up angry on a chilly morning because I have accidentally taken the quilt from him, she humorously added to herself.

Within the next few hours the ladies not only put the house in order but found out enough about each other to begin a friendship.

Apparently, Harriet Wells had decided to remain in New Orleans after her husband, a retired Army officer, died. He had been sick for such a long time that most of their money was depleted. At first Harriet had taken in laundry and sewing to remain near her sick husband. She had kept their little house on St. Charles Street after his death but found that the best way to support herself was to do what she did best—run a household.

"Tell me, Harriet," Samantha started, all formalities dropped, "did your husband know General James Wilkinson?"

"*That* one," she sneered. "Bill knew all about him.

279

During the Revolution they were both under General Washington's command. Wilkinson was never a good leader. His men didn't like him. Why, my Bill knew that Wilkinson was involved in many shenanigans. General Washington once told Bill that Wilkinson was not to be trusted. Yet the man is a survivor." She threw up her hands. "How else could you explain his being promoted to Commander of the Army? Poor Bill. He must be turning in his grave."

Intrigued by this information, Samantha wondered why Jefferson had promoted such a scoundrel and thought about her previous conversations with Aaron Burr's friends. They were both sitting in the kitchen now, enjoying a light lunch. Samantha wore an apron over her blue-and-white-striped cotton dress and had tied a scarf around her hair to keep herself from getting too dirty.

"Did you ever meet the general in New Orleans?"

"Oh yes, General Wilkinson visited us when he heard Bill was so ill. I don't even think Bill recognized him. The general and that awful aide of his stayed for a short time."

"Oh, so you, too, have met Major Gaspar."

"You know, Samantha, sometimes I wonder just how much that Major Gaspar tells the general," Harriet added with amazing insight.

"Why do you say that?"

"Well, the general, no matter how incompetent he is, still has a sizable force to command. He cannot do everything or be everywhere. So he has Gaspar handle a lot of things. I just wonder if the good major isn't working hard to line his own pockets."

"You are probably right. Whatever their situation I

am sure that one of them knows exactly where my brother is," Samantha predicted.

Lucien was amused to find his wife in such an unusual outfit when he and Roger came home later that day.

"Samantha, is this what you are wearing to your cousin's house?" he threw laughingly at her.

"Very funny, Lucien." She blushed. "I suppose I don't look very ladylike right now." There was a hint of a smile.

"Come into the library. Roger and I have news for you."

She quickly removed her scarf, asked Harriet to bring in some cool drinks, and joined the men.

"Is it about Adam?" she asked hopefully.

"I finally got a report from that fool I hired to investigate Adam's disappearance. Harrison confirmed Madison's report that Adam is not only alive but is in the Spanish Territory immediately west of the Sabine River." Lucien paused long enough to swallow his drink.

Roger continued. "That's not too far from here, Sam. It seems as if Adam is now being treated more like a guest than a prisoner. He's staying at the home of a Spanish diplomat. He is, of course, not permitted to go anywhere alone." Both Lucien and Roger knew about Adam's imprisonment, guessing the kind of humiliating treatment Adam must have received. There was no point in telling this to Samantha now. The fact that Adam had been moved two weeks ago and his treatment upgraded would mean that something was about to happen. A deal was going to be made.

"So when can we go and get him?" she asked.

"*We* are not going," Lucien corrected her. "Roger and I are going as soon as we get some more information, particularly the exact location of this diplomat's private retreat."

About to protest, Samantha started to speak, but again Lucien stopped her. "The answer is *no*, Samantha. It is not safe for you to go. Anyway, we still must meet a gentleman who may have a lot of answers."

"Not Major Gaspar?"

"No, this time André Fourier is our man. He's a distant cousin of none other than Napoleon Bonaparte. He knows everyone and everything."

"So when do we meet him?" She decided to drop the other matter for now.

"At your cousin's party, Samantha. The Fouriers never miss a party."

"His wife is much younger than he is and I think Monsieur Fourier needs to prove that he is young at heart," added Roger.

"What else do you two know?" she asked, suspicious now of the odd look passing between them.

"Well"—Roger hesitated—"we have heard that Elise Fourier is attractive."

"So?"

"We have heard that she likes younger men," Lucien stated. He wasn't the least bit uncomfortable. In fact, Samantha could swear he was enjoying this.

"You mean she has affairs with men younger than her husband," she said bluntly, trying to shock Lucien.

He was not shocked. Only his brow lifted slightly as

he continued to drink. Roger, however, almost choked on his drink.

"Sam, you don't mince words, do you?" Roger sputtered.

"So now you know what we know, Samantha. The rest you shall see for yourself."

Chapter Twenty-One

Judging from what Lucien did not say about Elise Fourier, Samantha was prepared for the worst. And she was right.

Being the guests of honor at the Bonnard's party, the Frasers arrived promptly at nine. Their house, in the Vieux Carré, was an old-fashioned Spanish-style home made of stucco brick. The Bonnards, an old Creole family, were highly respected in the community. Like most wealthy Creole families, Samantha's cousins maintained a large plantation upriver, just outside New Orleans. The family spent the summer months at the plantation because the city of New Orleans was so hot and the dreaded Yellow Fever epidemics were most common during that time of year. If Lucien and Samantha were still in town by June, they, too, would spend the summer at their cousins' plantation.

The Creoles had a certain sense of gaiety that Samantha had never seen before, not even in Paris. There seemed to be a never-ending number of parties, gambling houses, dances, and duels. Creole honor was not only strong, it bordered on the ridiculous. The slightest insult—even an indirect one—might end with the two gentlemen meeting at dawn under The Oaks, an infamous dueling site.

There was much to learn about the Creoles and Samantha knew there would be plenty of opportunities to observe Creole life. Most Americans who took up residence in New Orleans were socially ignored. The Creoles felt they were far superior to the uncouth Americans whom they slanderously dubbed "Kaintocks." But since Samantha was part French and had Creole cousins, the Frasers would have no difficulty in becoming part of the social scene. Belonging to this tight-knit group was essential if they were going to get information about Adam's whereabouts and other, possibly "treasonous," activities involving Wilkinson.

"Samantha, what are you thinking of? You have such a serious look on your lovely face," her husband observed, bringing her abruptly back to the present.

"Nothing really," she absently smiled. "I was just thinking about how different these people are."

"That they are, my love. But why don't we discuss this much later?" He took her hand and kissed it, smiling down at her. She was wearing a shimmering turquoise Chinese silk dress, cut very low in the front. The wide pearl choker and matching earrings did not diminish the effect of the dress. Lucien was tempted to touch her smooth, lustrous skin. The dress, although gathered in the Empire style, had no other ornamentation. The dress did not, however, flair as much as most dresses of that style, so when Samantha walked, Lucien could see the outline of her enticing body. God, he swore, pulling at his tight cravat, I wish we were home.

All day Lucien had had an uneasy feeling about this evening. Instinct warned him something unpleasant was going to happen. But his instinct underestimated the actual events.

Still holding his wife's hand, Lucien looked up to see a very attractive woman approaching. It had to be Madame Fourier, he thought; she fit the description. The woman was shorter than Samantha, with dark brown hair and equally dark eyes. Her skin was also much darker than Samantha's. She certainly must have had interesting bloodlines in her Creole heritage. Elise Fourier was dainty, yet with what some men called "a well-considered body." Her rounded curves, full face, and fuller chest, barely concealed by her gold satin dress, were attractive now, but she would probably become plump as she got older. Now her ripe body was inviting. No, Lucien corrected himself, her body invited a man to bed her.

He looked sideways again at his wife, whose eyes narrowed as if she were sizing up her opponent. Elise Fourier could never compare to his woman—his Samantha. He would always be possessive whenever it came to Samantha, for whatever reasons he was not yet ready to admit. She was smiling at something her cousin Armand had said. But Lucien knew Samantha better than that. She was on guard, ready to encounter Elise Fourier who was heading for them, arm extended toward Samantha, but looking directly at Lucien, smiling up at him. Damn. He suddenly wished Roger were standing next to him. Perhaps Elise would set her eyes on Roger instead. How he would extricate himself from this one he didn't know yet. André and Elise Fourier knew many people, some of whom were quite influential. Madame Fourier had some valuable information; willingly or not, she was going to help them. Roger and Lucien were counting on that. Knowing a little about her tastes in men, they assumed Elise would be attracted to Roger. After all, he was the one available. Well, Lucien was not going to worry about it now. Plans could abruptly change and he was certainly no stranger to improvising. Besides, his wife's nails were digging into his palm, warning him to watch out for her.

"May I present, Cousin Lucien, Madame Elise Fourier. Her husband André will join us later—some business problem, I think." Armand made introductions, emphasizing the word "cousin."

"*Enchanté*." Her voice sounded husky. "We have heard so much about you, Monsieur Fraser. Oh"—as an afterthought—"Madame Fraser. May I call you Samantha?" Samantha barely nodded. "Your cousins told us of your search for your missing brother." She paused to fan herself, but her eyes never left Lucien's handsome face as her hand reached for his arm. "I hope you find him and if there is anything André or I can do, please do not hesitate to ask us."

She won't hesitate, I'm sure, thought Samantha. That woman cannot take her eyes off Lucien long enough to snub me properly.

"Thank you for your concern, Madame. May I call you Elise?" she mimicked while making an obvious display of linking her arm through Lucien's, practically tearing his hand away from Elise's grip. "My husband and I are most grateful for your kind offer of assistance. Aren't we, Lucien?" She smiled sweetly at him.

He saw the murderous look in her eyes and only wished the moment would pass. No woman had ever made him feel guilty before and dammit, he had nothing to feel guilty about, he angrily decided. It was at that instant that Lucien Fraser began to feel hamstrung by the convention of marriage and totally missed Elise Fourier's calculated manipulation of him in front of his wife and friends.

Quite unexpectedly, he felt the need to prove something to himself and to Samantha: that she would not become such an indispensable part of his life that he would rely only on her—be unable to live without her. For the moment, adventure was his goal and freedom its handmaiden, ends not to be found in the arms of only one woman, he mistakenly thought. Samantha was remarkable, too remarkable and her charms dug deep into his mind and soul.

Feeling the slight pressure of her hand on his arm, Lucien stole a look at his wife and suddenly felt an alien emotion . . . fear. He was afraid of his growing dependence on her . . . he was afraid of falling in love with her! He did not believe in love—that was for fools like Adam, lovesick fools who think of nothing but infernal women, women who twist them around their fingers, bidding them to satisfy their selfish whims. These fools wear silly grins, he imagined, often staring at nothing. Their minds are full of romantic notions. Rubbish! This cannot—no, he corrected himself—this *will not* happen to me!

Yet Samantha was weaving a web around him and he had to break free before it was too late. Why is she doing this to me? She doesn't love me any more than I love her, he thought. I promised to protect her but that was all!

Shrugging with disgust, he decided he did not want

to think about this matter or anything else tonight.

Lucien did not realize that he drank too much that evening. That was Samantha's fault, he rationalized later. Nor did he realize that he danced most of the waltzes, even the quadrilles, with Elise Fourier, leaving Samantha confused at first, then thoroughly furious.

Elise Fourier's feline smile became more smug that night. Monsieur Fraser would be in her bed very soon, she schemed. The thought of that strong man's arms about her, his deep blue eyes glazed with passion, made Elise shiver with anticipation. Never had Elise seen a man as handsome as this American. He was so tall—she did not reach his shoulders—and impeccably dressed. While most Creoles dressed with flashy colors that made some of them look like popinjays, Monsieur Fraser was dressed in dark gray, offset only by his pale blue shirt and cravat, which made his blue eyes even more intense. This was a special man, no doubt about it, Elise mused. Not like André, or the others.

Elise Fourier was bored and had been for some time. Her arrangement with André was becoming routine. She came from a good Creole family but her wealth and connections were insignificant compared to André's. When André had begun courting her, she had ignored him. After all, the man was old enough to be her father. He was bald and not much taller than she. But Elise's father had made some facts very clear. The Fouriers desperately needed André's financial assistance. This marriage was a solution to the negative balance in the family's accounting ledger. Elise's father had made it sound as if she had a choice, but she knew that was not so. André understood and wanted her anyway. That was five long years ago. At twenty-five,

Elise knew she was still appealing to men, and they to her. Strange, she thought, sometimes it was as if her needs were insatiable.

When Elise and André married, she was, miraculously, still a virgin. That was due more to the vigilance of her chaperones than to her virtuous nature. Yet within the first year, Elise knew the sexual side of their relationship was much more boring than a poorly acted play. She flirted with any rakish young men who paid her attention. It did not take long for them to get her message. The affairs followed as naturally as night follows day.

Elise learned to be discreet, to choose her lovers carefully. She never chose men who were close friends, who might do the ungentlemanly thing by talking about her or dueling over her. It was exciting for some time. She had her peccadilloes and André did not appear to be any the wiser. But she was wrong.

He came home very early one evening from a business trip that was supposed to have kept him away for two more days. Her latest lover, a charming young man who was in New Orleans for only a short time, was staying the night—something Elise rarely allowed. But the servants were not there to observe anything and Elise became careless by permitting this exception to her rule.

André had found them in a most interesting position. He must have been watching them for a long time before she noticed him. She almost squealed with terror. However, André, lounging by the door frame, merely smiled at them. But it was the look in his eyes that alarmed Elise. They were alight with . . . she couldn't identify it at first, but she became positive that his look was one of arousal and pleasure. André was enjoying this spectacle. One look below his waist confirmed her suspicion.

The young man did not notice anything aside from where his clothes were, how quickly he could put them on and leave the house.

As soon as the door closed André rapturously moved toward her with only one thought in mind. He never spoke a word nor tried to arouse Elise. Brutally driven by his sexuality, he moved into her unclean body. It did not seem to matter to André; nor did it matter to Elise after a while. The way her husband responded to her adulterous behavior fired her passion. She had never felt like this with André before.

Afterward, André spelled out the rules for this new dimension in their marriage. She could keep her lovers, provided that they were not permanent residents of New Orleans, that she never speak to anyone about her affairs, and that, of course, she would be extremely discreet and selective. Elise had no difficulty in agreeing to those terms; after all, that was exactly what she had been doing, and she certainly did not want André to fight a duel to protect her reputation.

"Oh, and there is one more thing, my darling," he had said, his fingers still stroking her back. "I might come in unannounced again, or"—his eyes again had that strange, demonic glow—"I might privately observe from my dressing room. You will never know when that might happen. Agreed?"

She was speechless. Elise knew that André sometimes stealthily observed her undressing. The dressing room that separated their bedrooms was André's usual path to her bedroom. Sometimes, even though Elise knew she had closed the door, she would find it slightly open. The door was never locked; André forbade that.

Elise considered his proposal, knowing that her husband had often watched her. Secretly, this had even added a little spice to her affairs. If their own lovemaking could be as exciting as this recent encounter . . . why, she would certainly enjoy that too.

"You are so inventive, André." She kissed his cheek, her body still glistening from her two lovers. "I most certainly agree," she replied.

"Elise, I am too good a shot to fight a duel with every one of your lovers. Remember," and his voice became deeper, "be extremely careful when selecting our next lover." She didn't like the way he had used the word "our," but since she was clearly having her way, nothing else mattered.

Their marriage survived; André remained true to his word. But lately, the excitement was diminishing. The arrangement that had aroused her in the past had become tiresome.

Lucien Fraser might be the solution. She couldn't wait to feel his naked, muscular body. As he was dancing with his red-haired, pale-skinned wife, her dark eyes carefully examined Samantha. Grudgingly, she admitted to herself that the woman was somewhat attractive, but Elise doubted Samantha had the fire to hold onto such a man, to keep his interest. She was convinced a woman with her kind of upbringing would surely be prudish about sex. Samantha looked angry, Elise observed, probably because he had spent too much time with her. This affair could last a long time, if I arrange it properly, she thought. Then she vowed to herself that André would not be a part of this encounter. This one would be hers alone. André seemed to be too busy playing politics anyway, she reasoned.

"Lucien Fraser," she whispered his name into her champagne glass, "I cannot wait."

Chapter Twenty-Two

There was no doubt that the evening had become an emotional disaster for Samantha.

It had started when that bitch had seemed to captivate her husband. Samantha kept reminding herself that Lucien was only doing this to obtain information from the Fouriers. But after the fourth dance and many cheerful exchanges between Lucien and Elise Fourier, Samantha had had enough. How would Lucien feel if she—even if it were in the line of patriotic duty—flirted openly with André Fourier or some other very handsome gentleman? Probably beat her, that's what he would do, she decided. How terribly unfair he was. If only she could get even with him. Anger, hatred, love, and pain churned through her head and heart.

By the time Lucien reclaimed his wife, she was fit to be tied. Yet he was not the least bit apologetic; there were no excuses for his actions. Samantha half hoped he would make some excuse so that she could vent her anger while turning him away. She wanted the upper hand. But Lucien acted as if nothing were wrong.

"Come, wife," he humorously called to her, putting

his arm about her small waist, "let us dance this lovely waltz."

Why, she grieved, did he have to look so strikingly handsome? She allowed him to draw her away from some new acquaintances and spin her about the dance floor.

"Did I tell you that you are the loveliest woman here?" His dark head bent to whisper in her ear. His arms wrapped more tightly around her waist, and with each twirl Lucien purposefully, suggestively, let his hand rub her backside.

"Damn you, Lucien," she growled. "Stop this charade." The false smile was still in place as she added, "How could you possibly have noticed me, after the charming Madame Fourier?"

His right hand gripped hers so hard that she almost gasped from the pressure.

"I am sorry, Samantha . . ."

There, she thought triuphantly, he is going to apologize.

"I did not hear you, love. What did you say?"

Deflated, but still angry, she pressed on. "I said, Lucien, I did not think you could notice my beauty when you appear to be so taken by Elise Fourier."

He did not miss a step but pulled her closer, so that now she felt his thigh against hers as they twirled, and it made her more despondent because even now she could not stop wanting him.

His dark blue eyes looked down at her as he said coldly, "That, my dear, is none of your concern. I am not your possession."

Stunned, she almost asked him to repeat himself. His look was absolutely devoid of any warmth or feeling.

"I am sorry I offend you, Lucien," she said meekly, at a loss for anything better to say. He will not hurt me, she kept telling herself over and over; I will not let myself care any more.

Ignoring her obvious withdrawal, Lucien snapped at her with all of the angry frustration that had been welling up inside him all evening.

"What the hell does that mean, Samantha? Don't tell me that you, my aristocratic, haughty wife, are apologizing for your childishness?"

This was too much. She simply stopped in the middle of the room while couples swirled around them. Many people couldn't help but stare in anticipation of their row.

"Samantha," he snarled, "you are making a spectacle of yourself."

"I don't give a damn, my love," she mocked.

Gathering the bottom of her turquoise silk dress in her arm, she turned to leave him. Let *him* make the excuses for this scene, she decided.

She barely walked ten steps. People were still watching, some obviously snickering. Samantha did not look ahead of her, and that was her mistake. If she had, she would have seen Major Henri Gaspar heading toward her. She walked right into him.

"Oh," she stammered, still not looking up, "I am so sorry. I didn't mean . . ."

"A lovely creature like yourself does not need to apologize," the icy smooth voice replied.

Cornered, what else could Samantha do? She couldn't run. Eyes wildly looking for someone, anyone—even Lucien—to rescue her from the major, Samantha unconsciously took a few steps backward.

"I think, my dear, you should not worsen the situation. Your, ah, husband is already occupied."

Indeed he was. Lucien and Elise were on the other side of the room, smiling at one another.

The major firmly took her arm and led her back into the middle of the dancers. There was no time to think. Numbly, Samantha allowed the man she feared the most to touch her. He was neatly attired in his dress military uniform, his jet black hair smoothed off his forehead. His steel gray eyes never left her gaze.

"You look lovely, as always, Mrs. Fraser. Welcome back to New Orleans." Even his voice gave her goose bumps.

"Th-thank you, Major," she finally stammered. I have to regain my composure, she chided herself. I cannot let this man know how much he frightens me. Why, she wished, wouldn't the music stop?

"Are you staying long?"

"Why, yes, Major. My husband has established an office here." And she added as an afterthought, "I am sure you already knew that."

Her fear began to evaporate. After all, what could he possibly do to her in front of all these people? If Lucien wasn't concerned . . . and he was the one who had sworn after her brutal encounter with Clinton that he would never let anyone hurt her again . . . More lies, she thought. Lucien doesn't care; he never did. Didn't he say so? Look at him with his newest conquest. I wonder how long it will take him to bed her, she thought maliciously.

Watching the play of emotions across her face, Gaspar knew she was the most beautiful creature he had ever known. He remembered that night when she lay unconscious on the hotel bed. He remembered everything: what she wore; what her room looked like; most importantly, what her body felt like. And he wondered how her body would respond to his when he claimed her. He felt compelled to have her. That promise was made the first time he had seen her glide into General Wilkinson's office more than four months ago.

"By the way, may I congratulate you on your *recent* marriage? Right after you so hastily left New Orleans, wasn't it?"

Her mind quickly adjusted to this cat-and-mouse intrigue, remembering her charade.

"Oh," she laughed into his impassive face, "I do apologize for those silly white lies I told you. But you must understand, Major"—she fluttered her red-gold lashes—"my being in New Orleans alone was a most silly, if not dangerous adventure," she giggled.

Thankfully the music stopped, but no one came to rescue her. The major led her toward the open windows.

"May I get you some champagne, Mrs. Fraser?"

"No, thank you. I think I must return to my cousins who want to introduce me to their friends." The excuse seemed flimsy, but Gaspar had no choice but to accept it.

"Oh, a pity. I thought we could talk a little bit about your brother."

She stopped. "Do you have more information since the last time I was here?"

"Now you are being coy, my dear." The shiny silver buttons of his blue military uniform twinkled from the candles' glow. Every dark black strand of hair was slicked back in place. Her nostrils filled with his musk scent. He must have bathed in it, she thought. Those cold, fathomless gray eyes seemed to miss nothing as they darted around the room. There was an authoritative air about him even though he was uneasy in her presence.

"I, sir?" Her eyes sparkled with a nervous excitement. A servant offered them drinks and Gaspar took one for Samantha.

"Your brother is in the Spanish Territory. A guest of a certain Luis Herrera. He has a lovely hacienda just twenty miles west of the Sabine River." His expression never changed as he gave her this information. He obviously wanted to elicit a reaction from Samantha, but she, too, was playing the same game.

"Why are you telling me this, Major? Shouldn't my brother's location be given to Mr. Madison or to my husband?"

"I prefer to tell *you*." He stepped closer to her, as if he were about to touch her face.

Instinctively she recoiled, a movement not unnoticed by Gaspar.

"Do I frighten you, Mrs. Fraser?" he asked with just a trace of a smile.

"Only when my back is turned," she shot right back. "Now"—she faced him squarely, every muscle tensing—"is there any more information I should have about my brother, or do you prefer these verbal games?"

He smiled at her clever barb. Just wait—he renewed his old promise to himself—until we are alone, and then I will break you.

"No, madame," he recovered quickly, "I prefer a

different, more physical kind of play. Someday . . ." he promised aloud.

She would have given anything to scratch his wintry gray eyes out. Smiling coquettishly, she asked, "Major, do you know this man, Herrera?"

"A very nice man. Perhaps I could send him a message, through diplomatic channels, of course, and tell him Mr. Thornton's family is prepared to pay whatever is necessary to release him."

What's in it for you, Major? she wondered. She had not dared voice the question aloud, but it did not matter, for she suspected Gaspar would receive a percentage of the ransom money in any case—why, he had probably engineered the whole thing. It was probably easier for him to try this tactic with her rather than with Lucien, she mused.

"Oh, so we are now discussing kidnapping and ransom money." She was hoping for some reaction, for him to betray how much he really knew.

"You should be happy . . . Samantha." He dared to call her by her first name. "At least your dear brother is no longer charged with spying. He is no longer in prison. You have some powerful friends . . . and perhaps I can be another." His cold eyes again surveyed the room, probably checking Lucien's whereabouts, before he continued.

Another servant brought a tray of drinks, but he declined, murmuring, "One must keep one's wits at all times. Don't you agree, Samantha?"

Her blood was racing at this use of her name, but she composed herself as she quietly said, "Please call me Mrs. Fraser. My husband is a very jealous man."

"Yes, I can see," he said snidely. His head swiveled to

the other side of the room where Lucien, still engrossed with Elise Fourier, hadn't seemed to notice where his wife was. Fortunately for Samantha the conversation finally ended with the arrival of none other than General James Wilkinson.

"Ah, my dear, I should have known Henri would find you first." His blue eyes merrily twinkled as he continued chatting, seemingly unaware of the tension between Gaspar and Samantha.

"May I beg a favor, madame?" He, too, was neatly attired in his dress military uniform, brightly adorned with colorful medals and ribbons.

"Yes, General?" She tried to give a friendly smile, but all the while she kept wondering if General Wilkinson knew about the subtle demand for ransom. Could Harriet Wells be right? Was Henri Gaspar calculating enough to be the only one involved in this little scheme? Her hand nervously fidgeted with the turquoise silk of her gown.

"You are the most beautiful woman here, madame." He bowed gracefully in spite of his excess weight. "I want to apologize for the horrible things that happened to you on your last visit to New Orleans. And . . ." he waved off an approaching officer, "I hope you will grant me a favor . . . by dancing this next quadrille with me."

What a charmer, she thought. Well, what choice do I have? My devoted husband seems to have forgotten I am here.

"Why, I would be delighted, sir," she said politely, with a hint of a Southern drawl. "And I accept your apology."

"Major"—she turned toward Gaspar, her hand

already leaning on the general's arm—"thank you for your assistance."

"You are most welcome, Mrs. Fraser." He bowed with the return of all his formality. "Perhaps you shall hear from your friends soon."

The general was a charming companion, telling Samantha various things about the city of New Orleans and its people. He could almost be likable, she thought. *Almost.*

The rest of the evening passed with more introductions and dances with many gentlemen, even Governor Clairborne, who had recently lost his wife to the dreaded Fever. Samantha felt sorry for him. It was easy to see why Governor Claiborne was having a difficult time with the people of New Orleans. They couldn't trust an American—a political appointment of the President—who did not come from the area and made no attempt to learn about the people when he did arrive. No wonder General Wilkinson ingratiates himself the way he does, observed Samantha. Wilkinson, under military guise, makes sure he knows everything about everyone, while poor Governor Claiborne ignorantly imposes American standards on people who still consider themselves French.

She heard talk of Aaron Burr, but he was a ghost whose real behavior could not possibly match the rumors. Apparently Mr. Burr had found out about the double dealings of General Wilkinson and had tried to outfox the military guards sent to arrest him. But Burr finally had been caught in Alabama. Curiously, most of the whispering voices did not hold Aaron Burr responsible for fomenting treason. There was more to learn about this, Samantha knew, but not tonight.

Tonight she had to smile as brightly as possible . . . and leave surreptitiously as soon as possible.

Somewhere her husband was dallying with another woman, with Elise Fourier. And I'll be damned, she swore, if I'll let that bastard know I care.

Roger Cole tried as always to smooth her ruffled feathers before the obvious confrontation occurred. Wisely, he suggested they walk outside where they couldn't be overheard.

"Sam, I know what you're thinking. But before you pass judgment, see if Lucien has anything to say." His words must have sounded hollow. Seeing her false bravado, he hated this whole ugly mess. Roger could not understand why Lucien had not tempered his behavior. He was acting like a lustful adolescent. Poor Samantha.

All these weeks, Roger thought he had seen the developing affection between Lucien and Samantha. Now, however, Lucien was deliberately running away from the best thing that had ever happened to him.

"Roger, don't placate me. And don't you dare feel sorry for me!" Samantha demanded.

Suddenly, she brightened. "Listen, I must tell you what Major Gaspar told me about Adam." She practically tugged at his jacket with renewed spirit.

Roger's dark eyes narrowed in consternation as she spoke. He and Lucien had suspected—were even prepared—for something like this to happen. Surprisingly, it was sooner than expected. At least they now knew for sure what the next move would be.

"Roger"—her voice disrupted his thoughts—"would you be a dear and take me home? I have"—her hand pressing against her temple now—"a dreadful headache."

"Of course. I'll just get your shawl."

"No." She looked a bit frightened. "I do not want to wait alone. I would rather go with you." She tried to look happy, but her attempt was unsuccessful.

They were at the carriage when Lucien finally found them.

"Suppose, madam, you tell me where you are going." His powerful grip on her wrist made it impossible for Samantha to break free. His voice sent chills down her arms.

"I am going home, Lucien. I do not feel very well." She calmly untangled her wrist and turned to step on to the waiting carriage. "You were having such a wonderful time, Lucien, that I hated to disturb you. Roger will see me home safely." Her aloof voice dismissed him.

"You are staying," Lucien ordered, his temper steadily increasing.

Ignoring him, Samantha settled herself into the carriage with Roger, who was looking very uncomfortable.

Before Lucien had a chance to reach for her again, she snapped the door shut, ordered the driver to leave, and, calmly assessing her husband, said, "Good night, my dear."

The carriage quickly rolled down the street, leaving a surprised and then furious Lucien Fraser behind.

Arriving home, Samantha thought sadly that this was the worst night of their brief and volatile relationship. If Lucien wanted his affair, he could have it. But—she turned to examine her face in the foyer mirror, her beautiful features frozen with determination—so shall I.

How dare she act like the poor, vulnerable wife,

Lucien stormed as he watched the carriage in the distance. He kept telling himself that Samantha had no rights at all; that what he did was no concern of hers. Elise Fourier was a combination of business . . . and yes, dammit, pleasure. All of his other assignments had included a little pleasure. Something was seriously bothering him this evening. In the last eight months, only one woman—Samantha—had been the focus of his sexual desires. He had never thought about another. Absolutely disquieting! What's wrong with you, man? a voice persistently repeated in his ear. Can't you enjoy any woman but your wife? Maybe you can't enjoy sexual encounters with another woman. Maybe you are not capable . . .

Somehow he could not shake the little demon inside his head. Unwittingly, Elise Fourier had helped him make a decision. As soon as he had seen Elise Fourier smile seductively at him he had made up his mind: this woman was going to give her body and her information to me—not to Roger Cole—but *me*. And damn Roger if he didn't understand. But most of all, damn you, Samantha, for making me doubt my own capabilities. How that copper-haired, hot-tempered witch did it, he could not say. Maybe she was a witch. Losing control over his emotions because of a beautiful woman was not going to be his destiny. Seeing her surrounded by young men all vying for her attention, Lucien felt his resolve weaken and his passion flare—passion for her, his dear but undeserving Samantha. But I will not be exclusively yours, he silently told her. When I want to feel your body, I will. But yours will not be the only body that grants me pleasure.

The more he had argued with himself that evening,

306

the stronger Lucien's reckless determination to undermine his marriage vows became. And when Elise Fourier invitingly touched him, Lucien made his decision to take what she was offering. This would be a twofold mission. He would get the information the government needed, and he would prove his total independence from Samantha.

It was evident to him that Samantha was furious, a fury that gave Lucien preverse pleasure. The same way you innocently taunt me, dear wife, he reflected. If he had given people the impression that he was unaware of his wife's whereabouts all evening, so be it. As soon as Samantha stupidly walked into Gaspar, Lucien started to move. But, he decided, nothing could happen to Samantha in a crowded room and she deserved a little scare for deserting him like that. A little well-deserved punishment, Lucien told himself. But he missed nothing. Pretending to be thoroughly enamored with Elise, Lucien was able to watch his wife with all the men who approached her that evening. The brittle smile she gave Gaspar and Wilkinson and the way she fidgeted with her gown communicated her discomfort to Lucien. If anything untoward happened, he would have been at her side instantly. If Samantha had known that Lucien wanted to use her to "bait" Gaspar, forcing him to make a move, she would have resisted; indeed, she probably would have refused to do it. And if she had acquiesced, she might somehow have revealed herself to Gaspar.

No, this way is better, he firmly decided and gritted his teeth at the thought of the major touching his wife.

By the end of the evening, Lucien knew that Samantha was so angry with him that she would never have believed his plan, or, if she had, forgiven him for using her with Gaspar. So why should it matter? Remember, he thought, she does not own you and you do not owe her any explanations.

When Samantha left him staring after the carriage, however, Lucien no longer believed he was in command of the situation. He could have killed her for acting like a haughty bitch! Roger, too! Why was Roger taking her side?

It was impossible for Lucien to think straight any longer. When Elise coolly requested that Lucien see her home, he readily agreed, knowing full well what this request meant. André was to be occupied in a long meeting with one of the leading businessmen in the town. Lucien wished he could be a part of that meeting, knowing that Fourier's activities and associations were highly questionable. If he had not had Samantha to worry about, he would have infiltrated that group by now.

Perhaps sweet Elise would know something, Lucien mused. Later, much later, I will ask her.

Elise was no ingénue. Her hand wandered along Lucien's firm thighs as soon as the carriage left the Bonnard's home. There was something electrifying about her touch. Maybe because Lucien felt like a small boy who was disobeying his mother's orders, his responses had an urgency to them. Lucien wanted to take her immediately, with no preliminaries or soft kisses. Yet, when she boldly kissed his neck, then his mouth, he saw another face, smelled a different perfume, and angrily pushed a very confused Elise away.

"Something wrong, *chèrie*?"

"Elise, I would prefer a more romantic atmosphere, wouldn't you?" As usual, his firm, deep voice gave the impression that he was not in the least bit embarrassed about refusing a woman's offer, and that he was in complete control of the situation. But there was no way of knowing what was going on inside him. His stomach churned with frustration and fear. He had to remove Samantha's image from his mind!

The carriage rolled over a bump, forcing Elise to grab the leather strap on her side of the seat, giving Lucien a chance to move away.

"Elise, you are a very interesting woman." He took out a cheroot, lighting it without her permission, and said, "Tell me more about yourself and your husband."

Lost in her favorite topic, Elise Fourier did not realize that Lucien had skillfully avoided her original invitation.

Much later, they laughed over wine and champagne. Lucien comfortably settled himself in Elise's parlor.

"Well, Lucien, at least I did not bring you into my bedroom. So," she lightly laughed, "it's not as if I am completely unfaithful."

She was wearing a dark red flowing robe which accented her dark beauty. Curling her legs beneath her, Elise could have fooled any man with her demure appearance. But beneath appearances was the heart of a harlot.

The pale blue cravat hung limply from Lucien's neck. Odd, he thought, but I feel relaxed. He had proved something to himself tonight: he could indeed enjoy another woman's company. Samantha would not intrude upon his actions—not this time.

"Darling, I do hope we can meet again—perhaps for

a longer, more private get-together." She watched his darkly handsome face as he laughed over her statement. Elise Fourier could have fallen in love with Lucien Fraser. If he had asked her then to abandon her husband and the security André's name provided, she would have, without the slighest hesitation.

His finely chiseled face, deep blue eyes, and wavy black hair affected her as no other man had. If his face weren't enough to move her, his lean muscular body reminded Elise of a sleek panther constantly alert . . . waiting . . . watching . . . making her feel like her bones would dissolve at his touch. His deep, cultured voice was like a rhapsody to her ears. And his rough, masculine manner was like symphonic drums beating at her heart. Elise would have him any way, any time he commanded.

"What would your pale wife Samantha do if she knew where you were?" It was a calculated question. Elise couldn't imagine Lucien and his red-haired wife enjoying a physical relationship. Elise simply needed to know how devoted Lucien was to his wife. But she was not prepared for his response.

Leaning forward in the armchair, Lucien grabbed Elise's forearm, causing her to wince from the pain. His dark blue eyes, previously filled with humor, were now filled with ice.

"My dear Elise. Do not ever, I repeat *ever*, mention my wife's name or ask about our relationship again. I will forgive you this time only."

Not a muscle in his face moved. His hard grip on her arm slowly loosened. This was incomprehensible. Why should he be so upset about her mentioning his wife's name? A more perceptive woman would have understood. But as Elise rubbed the red marks on her arm, all she could think about was that Lucien's arrangement with his wife must be just that, a formal arrangement—no love, no passion. Vainly, Elise could not consider that another woman, especially that empty-headed Southern belle, could keep a man like Lucien satisfied. Soon he shall be all mine, she thought as a self-satisfied grin crossed her face.

What appeared like ice to Elise was white hot fury to Lucien. Why the hell did she have to remind him about Samantha? Lucien's relationship with Samantha would never be subject to cross examination by anyone, let alone another woman. Lucien dimly recalled Samantha's generous gesture to give him his freedom if he wanted Caroline Prescott. How long ago was that? It felt like years instead of months. What would Samantha's reaction be now, after she learned about his liaison with Elise? Lucien had no doubt that Samantha would know. Some gossip, Major Gaspar or perhaps Elise herself, would see to that. Why didn't he tell her the truth? And what is the truth, a tiny voice asked? What are you trying to prove? That you really are a blackguard who cares nothing about Samantha's feelings? Does that truly make you feel more manly? Or are you a very confused man on the brink of an important discovery and too blind to acknowledge it?

Foolishly, Lucien refused to closely examine this matter. And that was his second biggest mistake of the day.

Chapter Twenty-Three

When he finally came home it was well past midnight. Elise had given him some information about André and the names of some business associates. It seemed they were in regular contact with the Spanish and the French. Elise jokingly spoke of a mysterious Spanish agent who had once appeared at their front door during a dinner party. Next time, Lucien decided, I will get the information I need on Gaspar, Wilkinson, and the whole bloody group. Oddly enough, no mention was made of Aaron Burr. Perhaps Samantha was right. Burr could have been set up by Wilkinson.

It didn't matter now. Maybe tomorrow. As he quietly entered his bedroom, his eyes immediately focused on the occupant in the big bed surrounded by a protective gauze curtain. Hair splayed across her back, shoulders, and over her head, her arms hugging the pillow as if it were her phantom lover, Samantha was lying on her stomach in the middle of the bed, leaving no room for Lucien. Perhaps she was not expecting me, the inexplicably sad thought flashed through his brain.

As he looked down at her, he felt a wave of pity and remorse engulf him. Tenderly, his hand reached out to push the hair away from her face. Why am I driven to hurt you? Does she really deserve this kind of treatment from me? Can I distinguish between my motives? Lucien had no answers, and cursed his weakness.

Quickly discarding his clothes, he climbed into his side of the bed, trying not to disturb Samantha. Yet instinctively, she must have sensed his presence. In her dreamy state she must have also forgotten her anger, for she molded her satin body into his, craving his warmth and protection. Lucien drank in the fragrance of her hair, but his ambivalence was the catalyst for a restless night.

A sharp jab to his ribs startled Lucien from a fitful sleep. Well, at least he had dozed off for a couple of hours. Quickly gathering his wits, Lucien looked up to see the stormiest pair of green eyes he had ever seen glaring down at him.

"What are you doing home, Lucien? Did Elise throw you out . . . or did her husband? How dare you come back into my bed with her fragrance all over you."

"Sensitive, aren't you," he calmly replied. Leaning against the headboard, his own hair mussed by a nearly sleepless night, Lucien smiled at his wife. "In the first place, this bed"—he patted the mattress—"is not yours exclusively. And no, I left Elise of my own free will."

"Get out of here, Lucien. I can't stand being near you." Her voice was dangerously low. "You destroyed something in me last night." She got off the bed to put on her dressing gown. Tying the sash with her back toward him so he could not see the hurt in her eyes, she continued. "I will never trust you again. You are a low, despicable animal. You shamed me in front of all those

314

people last night. And"—she moved to the bureau to brush her hair, finding it necessary to keep her hands busy—"you left me to fend for myself with both Gaspar and Wilkinson. You promised to protect me. Hah! You are a liar, dear husband!"

Spinning about to look directly at him, Samantha snarled, "Stay away from me. There is only one thing for you to remember: our purpose for being in this town. Do you? All you can seem to think about is dumpy Elise Fourier."

"Are you jealous?"

"Jealous? That's amusing. No! But just remember something I told you some time ago, dear husband"— she smiled tightly—"two can play this game."

"We shall see, Samantha, love. We shall see."

Tossing aside the netting, Lucien, who was stark naked, walked into the hall and shouted for Mrs. Wells to bring him hot water for a bath.

"Care to join me?" he taunted.

"I don't know what happened to you, Lucien. You aren't the same man I knew aboard the *Newport Wind*." Green eyes searched his for some kind of what? . . . Maybe remorse? Instead she saw a shuttered look. No hints—all secrets safely hidden from her.

Then she decided on a little compassion. "Is something wrong?" She moved toward him. "Why can't I help?"

A loud knock cut off what Samantha imagined to be a softening in his attitude. But the moment was forever lost. Two maids brought in the hot water and tub for Lucien's bath. After they departed he lost no time in climbing in and couldn't resist a barb of his own.

315

"Soon I shall smell only of sandalwood."

How can he smile at me like that, totally unconcerned about my feelings? Samantha wondered. Suppressing a desire to hurl everything in the room at his smug face, Samantha turned to her own ablutions and tried to dress quickly. The sooner she escaped his presence, the happier she would be. She was selecting her day dress from the small dressing room when he found her.

"Now, my love, I no longer can offend you," he murmured.

Surprised by his audacity, Samantha kept her back turned to him. Clinging to her dress, she forced her voice to reply coldly, "I do not take another woman's castoffs. Go back to your mistress, but *never* touch me again."

"Again, you are wrong, my love. You cannot stay away from me any more than I can resist your charms." His hand gently stroked her back, sending chills through her body.

"Stop it!" she commanded and turned to face him. "I do not want you. I . . . I will find another," she stammered. Why does he punish me? she asked herself.

Still damp and naked, he refused to remove his hand. "You will not find another to take my place. No one knows how to please you, where to touch you like I do."

He was too sure of himself and she was not going to submit—not this time—without a fight. Without thinking about it, Samantha quickly brought her knee up into him, causing him to howl with pain and surprise.

"There! I hope you're maimed for life." She felt satisfied as she left Lucien doubled over. However, Samantha got no further than the middle of the bedroom when Lucien caught up with her, yanking her by her streaming hair.

"Let go of me, you beast!" She was frightened, seeing a flash of that terrible time with Clinton. Lucien's recovery had been so quick that she could not finish dressing and escape the bedroom which was fast becoming her prison. He was hurting her, twisting her hair so that her only relief from the pain came when she stepped closer to him.

"Now, my love. I don't think that was very kind of you." His tone was ominous. Yanking harder, he forced her to face him and the hard glint in his eyes made her gasp.

"Please, not again." Her voice was barely audible.

He felt her fear. "I am sorry, sweetheart. I did not mean to remind you of that time."

Stiffening her body in expectation of some brutality, Samantha was totally unprepared for his soft kisses. With one part of his body he inflicted pain, while his mouth both enticed and tormented her at once. Exquisite torture. Lucien's left hand roamed along the contours of her chemise-clad body. Legs weakening, Samantha felt her body betray her will as she leaned closer to him.

"Lucien, please let me go . . . ," she whimpered.

"Once again, my love, you have to be tamed." His mouth was at her ear now. "You are such a wildcat. But," he began as he stroked her hair, "you still won't admit that you need me, want me, only me. Must I prove it to you again?"

Her legs felt like water. She knew he was pulling her toward the bed and she had no willpower left to fight him.

"Why, Lucien?" It was all she could manage before his mouth conquered hers and he dragged her onto the bed.

"You are mine . . . Do you hear me? And I will prove it to you every time you dare to challenge me!" His face was a portrait of so many emotions: passion, anger, pain, and confusion. Part of his mind was scolding him because he was treating the only woman he had ever felt protective about like a cheap prostitute. The other part told him how much she deserved this punishment because she had no right crawling under his skin, getting closer to his heart until he had no choice but to commit himself to her, body and soul.

"Damn you, Samantha." His voice sounded pained. Maybe he, too, has to fight himself and, if so, that is a small victory for me, Samantha realized.

Nothing else was said. Lucien's hands and mouth ran riot over her body. She was his slave. Her writhing body told him what her voice could not. The silken chemise lay in shreds on the floor, but she didn't care. What mattered was the moment. They were together, entwined in each other's bodies, captives of their emotions.

Lucien moved half off the bed, pulling her with him. Kneeling on the floor, he pulled her pliant legs closer until they locked around his shoulders. His mouth quickly found her liquid center while his hands sensuously stroked her breasts, delightfully teasing her nipples. He was driving her over the edge, but she could no longer hold back any more than she could deny the truth.

One thought became clear to Samantha seconds before all light and sound diminished: even after all this, she still loved him. Nails raking down his muscled back, she admitted total defeat once more. I still love you, Lucien, she told herself despairingly.

"Say it," he commanded. "Say my name."

"Lucien." It was the only word he needed to hear her cry passionately before he moved back onto the bed and moved into her welcoming body—before they both became lost in a comet's tail of heat and light.

Their relationship took on yet another facet after that morning. While Samantha thought Lucien would gloat over his reaffirmed domination of her, he did not.

"I will understand if you want to leave me" was his quiet, almost sad response to her question about whether or not he planned to continue his "friendship" with Elise Fourier. They were still entwined in each other's arms, exposing parts of their souls but not daring to reveal all.

"Do you want me to stay?" A stupid question, she berated herself. He is practically telling you he does not love you and wants you to leave him.

"Yes." He cradled her closer, half expecting her to laugh at him before she left him alone in bed. Inhaling the sweet, seductive fragrance of her, Lucien spoke into her tousled hair, "Damn! I don't know why, and I can't explain what you are doing to me."

To Samantha this had to be a beginning. Hope surged through her veins. Maybe . . . maybe if I hold on long enough, fight Elise and any other woman who dares to challenge me and help him fight his demons, he will need me, only me.

"I am not going anywhere," she said with conviction. She thought he sighed with relief, but perhaps it was only what she wanted to believe.

The days passed quickly with each one involved in sorting out private hells. Samantha knew Lucien still met Elise Fourier but pretended to ignore it. They did not mention Elise's name or Samantha's promise to stay. Most nights they slept together. However, on those nights Lucien went out alone, he did not say where he went, nor did he ever stay away the whole night. But when he came back, he did not join his wife in bed either. Instead, he remained in the library drinking, smoking, and eventually sleeping on the couch. Samantha always assumed that he had spent another passionate evening with his mistress and did not want to bring Elise's heady scent into their bedroom.

Other promises were kept, too. Samantha should have guessed that Lucien knew all about Adam's location and Gaspar's cleverly worded ransom demands.

Exactly two weeks after the night of the party, a ransom note was delivered:

If you still want to see the American agent, Adam Thornton, again, leave $10,000 in gold in the farmhouse near the Spanish border.

The note went on to explain the location of the farmhouse and the specific day and time when the exchange would take place.

"Ten days, Lucien. How can we get that much money in so short a time?" Samantha was nervous but excited about seeing Adam again.

"It will be arranged," Lucien said cryptically.

Roger Cole was in the room with them. He knew what Lucien meant. Although the men would always be good friends, Roger was annoyed with Lucien over his dalliance with Elise. But if Samantha chose to accept it, then who was he to object? After all, this was not his concern. Roger had his own problems now with the sweet young daughter of an American merchant.

"Roger, are you thinking about the lovely and fair-haired Nadine again?" Samantha couldn't resist teasing him. She had met the young girl and thought her quite charming.

Roger's blush covered every inch of his face in a red glow. "I think I'll bring her here for dinner tomorrow."

"Certainly, Roger, why don't you come for dinner tomorrow?" Lucien joined in teasingly. "Tomorrow may be our last day to relax anyway. After that we go west."

"What do you mean?" Samantha shot out of her seat, all humor gone. "We are going so soon?"

"Listen, you copper-haired spellbinder, don't you remember what I told you weeks ago?" Lucien was half serious. Reaching for her shoulders to steady her from jumping all over the room, Lucien calmly told her that "we" did not include Samantha.

"It will be too dangerous. What Roger and I have to

do is risky enough as it is. I do not want to have to worry about you."

"You will not know I am there, Lucien." She turned to meet his determined gaze with one of her own. "I am going whether you approve of it or not. I swear I will follow you if you go without me."

"The answer is still no," he insisted adamantly before turning away.

"I will dress in men's clothes. I won't complain about sleeping outdoors, or the weather, or the rough ride or," she gulped, "snakes or Indians."

Both men laughed at her last comment.

"Stop laughing at me, Lucien Fraser. I swear I am going. Even if I travel behind you . . . And I will, you know." She shook her finger at them. "And if anything happens to a poor, defenseless woman traveling alone—well," she caught her breath, "it will be your fault. Both of you," she petulantly wailed. Here were the uncontrolled rantings of a woman in a blind rage.

"Samantha, any Indian who sees one of your temper tantrums would run as far away as possible."

It's fun to tease her like this, he realized. We haven't acted this way in some time. She would probably tell me that's because of Elise Fourier. Oh hell! He still could not explain why he was doing half the things he had been. It might be nice to be with Samantha on the trails; away from New Orleans; away from Elise's company; away from the conspiracies of Wilkinson and Gaspar. It might be very interesting.

"All right, wench, you can come along. But"—he caught her as she hurled herself into his arms—"not one complaint. And you do whatever Roger and I tell you to do." He smiled at her cooperative air. "Agreed?"

"Anything. I'll even sleep with my clothes on and"—she touched the long unruly hairs at the base of his neck—"I'll even cut your hair for you."

At their sudden burst of laughter, Samantha smiled. This was an important decision. *She* was going to find Adam. And *she* would not have to share Lucien with Elise Fourier. At the thought of these opportunities her smile became a hearty laugh.

Chapter Twenty-Four

Not wanting to give Lucien an opportunity to change his mind, Samantha was packed and ready to go well before he was.

One look at her amount of baggage sent Lucien into another fit of laughter.

"Samantha sweet, are you serious?" he asked, eyes creasing with mirth. "This is not a pleasure trip. You cannot take more than one *small* bag that can be attached to the pack horse." Looking at the four neatly piled bags, he explained, "You have three bags too many." He saw her crestfallen face and added, "You probably didn't take the right clothing anyway."

A small "Oh" escaped her lips, and when her green eyes became watery, Lucien felt sorry about his comment. Putting his arms about her shoulders, he generously offered to help her repack.

"You will help me?" She was amazed. "You mean you won't stand there exhibiting impatience and leave without me?"

"Am I that harsh?"

"Always." Then she reconsidered. "Well, almost always."

The sweet smile was all he wanted to see. Lucien knew how hard she was trying to please him, and he was actually looking forward to being with her. Sitting on the floor, long legs folded, he proceeded to sort her clothing. Not knowing what else to do, Samantha gingerly sat down next to him and laughed with him over the items she had packed.

"Sweetheart, you are not going to an elegant mansion like Kingscote. Have you ever camped before?"

It was impossible to lie. Shaking her head in response to his question, he stupidly realized he should have known.

"This is going to be an experience for all of us," he groaned.

The weather was unusually hot and sticky for May. As the perspiration trickled down Samantha's chest, she wished they would stop and hopefully find a lake, brook, stream, anything that could provide relief. A bath would be so nice, she told herself. But she wouldn't tell Lucien or Roger.

You asked for this, Sam, she silently berated herself.

Her coppery tresses were securely pinned away from her face and neck. The breeches and cotton shirt offered some surcease from the hard ride and the wide-brimmed hat she had originally worn to New Orleans had also afforded some protection. But when Lucien presented her with a small version of his leather hat, she squealed with delight, then quickly sobered when he handed her a small pistol, grimly reminding her that she had better know how to use it and keep it on her

326

at all times.

"We look like army soldiers or like those wild settlers who trek across the country," she exclaimed.

But the gloves were truly a blessing. Her thin, flimsy cotton gloves would not have done and Lucien had known that, too. Maybe, she told herself, he really does not mind my being here—and he's being so thoughtful, too. What an enigma he is!

She had plenty of time to think about him. Lucien always looked well groomed and cool, in spite of the heat. He looked very much like the man she remembered aboard the *Newport Wind* in his black buckskin breeches, high leather boots, stark white shirt contrasting against his tan face, and that silly red scarf tied around his neck. Only the hat and gloves were different. How adaptable he is, she marveled. He's at home whether aboard his ship, in an elegant drawing room, or out in this wilderness. And women were drawn to him like plants drawn to sunlight.

The afternoon sun beat down on her head. Samantha tied her white scarf around her forehead to soak up the perspiration. The more she scrutinized her husband, the more she realized how difficult it would be to hold on to him for long. Lucien is so attractive, she thought, and I am so obviously unable to satisfy him. By the end of the day, she had almost convinced herself that she not only was not beautiful enough to keep him, but that some personality flaw of hers prevented him from returning her love. Insecurity washed over her like the humidity in the Louisiana bayou.

They stopped hours later, just before sundown. Every bone in her body ached. But a fire had to be built and some food eaten, so her chores were only

327

beginning. She was glad that Lucien had hired another man to join them. Manuel was originally from the Mexican Territory but somehow had ended up on the American side. Samantha suspected that Manual was another government "contact" of Lucien's, but she was too tired to ask.

Assuming command as usual, Lucien assigned the chores to everyone; no one was spared. There was a small stream, not deep enough for bathing but clean enough for Samantha to fill the now-empty canteens. Lucien wisely decided that she should not cook the rabbit Roger had caught. As soon as Samantha learned that the rabbit had to be skinned, her distaste for the procedure was apparent.

"Manuel will cook tonight, but you will have to learn if you want to be a part of this group." It was a small jibe but enough to damage Samantha's pride.

"I will do it tomorrow, Lucien," she replied crisply.

It was easy to see that Samantha was very uncomfortable. Perhaps that was what made Lucien so proud of her. He had not expected her to be this stoical about the discomforts of the trip. There was little conversation during the meal. Each person was either too tired to speak or too engrossed in private thoughts.

The night air was cooler than in New Orleans. The bright stars and milky-white full moon silhouetted the stark beauty of the vast land. The night sounds, not at all similar to the sounds of the city, were soothing to troubled minds.

"Lucien"—Samantha's tired voice broke the peaceful interlude—"when will we reach the farmhouse?" It was difficult keeping her eyes open. A blanket found its way around her hunched shoulders, and she wrapped herself tighter, seeking warmth. Unruly red-gold curls escaped the confines of the leather hat, but she couldn't lift her hands to brush the hair out of her eyes.

Gently, as if caring for a baby, Lucien reached for her folded form. Offering no resistance, she allowed her husband to remove the hat, and still gently, to smooth the hair away from her face and kiss her forehead.

"In two or three days, my love," he softly responded.

Why can't it always be like this? she asked herself. She certainly lacked the courage and the strength to say those words aloud. Allowing him to pull her closer to him, she leaned her head against his powerful chest and closed her eyes. Now the only peaceful sounds she heard were the steady beating of Lucien's heart and the crackling of the fire. Again, she felt his soft touch smoothing her hair once more then rubbing her sore neck. Sighing aloud, she snuggled deeply into his sheltering embrace and drifted into a peaceful slumber.

Too bad, Roger observed, that Samantha could not see her husband's loving look. Still playing with her hair, Lucien looked down at her innocent face and smiled. Such a peculiar smile, Roger thought. It was an odd combination of tenderness, wonder, and pain. It would have been inappropriate to call Lucien's attention to it. After all, he would have scoffed at Roger's suggestion that Lucien was totally captivated by his wife; that mere passion could not make a man look at a woman the way Lucien looked at her.

"So, Captain, how do you propose to keep your beautiful wife out of the way when we reach the house?"

"I have been thinking about that, Roger." His voice

was low so he wouldn't wake her. "I suppose I can insist she stay behind with the horses, but when does she ever listen? No"—he was absently stroking her hair—"I think I will have to send her on some errand."

"Won't she see through that?"

"Not if she goes with you. There is a small town not too far from the border. I think we will be in dire need of supplies by then," he smiled slyly. "She cannot refuse that chore—not when she's so intent on showing me that she can pull her own weight."

In hushed tones, Lucien and Roger went over their plans for the rescue for the fifth time. Each one knew what had to be done and how important split-second timing would be.

"Do you need help moving Samantha to her own bedroll, Lucien?" Roger was ready to turn in. Manuel had done so an hour earlier.

"No, thank you, Roger. I think I'll stay up a little longer. I can handle her myself." Only when she's sleeping, he silently amended.

For the next hour or so Lucien sat rigidly, ignoring the cramp in his left leg—which still bothered him occasionally—and watched her. What a paradox . . . this woman who can be a little girl, a firebrand, and so damned magnificent in bed! I want her, yet I push her away.

He was tiring of this charade with Elise but would never admit it to anyone. She was becoming too possessive; the nights he spent in Elise's house were entertaining, but Lucien found himself wondering about Samantha. Was she alone? Was she waiting up for him? Yet he also knew that if it weren't Elise Fourier, it would be someone else. That stupid demon again that controlled his urges. Once Adam was safely home Samantha would not need him. She would go to Stèfan Turreau or some other man eager to offer the love and tenderness that he could not . . . or would not give.

A small cry from Samantha startled him. He had been squeezing her hard, not realizing his self-directed anger had caused him to hurt her.

"I am sorry, sweetheart," he soothed. "I didn't mean to hurt you—I never mean to hurt you." He kissed her temple before carrying her to the bedroll next to his. Once more, she sought the security of his arms, and he welcomed it, abandoning all the other problems to the night.

By late morning they had almost made it to the Spanish border. It was not much cooler than the previous day, but Samantha's lethargy was not as pronounced as before. Perhaps it was because they were so close to Adam that a sense of urgency filled the air. Anxiety consumed Samantha. Would Adam be there? Was he in good health? Would there be any trouble with the exchange?

"Don't worry. I am sure Adam is fine." Sensing her fears, Lucien rode up beside her trying to reassure her.

"Am I that transparent?" She gave him a weak smile.

"Only to me, Samantha sweet." His deep blue eyes searched her face. A slight quiver ran through her. In the middle of this desert, in spite of these hardships, she wanted him as much as he wanted her. She could read it on his face—that knowing, hungry look.

"Everything will be all right," he repeated.

"Will it?" There was much more to her question. Did he understand? Or would he choose to ignore her?

"Señor Fraser, please come quick." Manuel's request was urgent.

His glance was fleeting as he smiled and touched her cheek. "Another time," he whispered wistfully and rode away. She was left with his back and her doubts.

They seemed to pass from one minor crisis to another that day. A more superstitious person would have refused to go on. Not Lucien. Hindered by a lame horse, a short but heavy rainstorm, and now the possibility of spoiled food, he pushed them on. At sundown the little troupe entered an area known as the "Neutral Ground." It was a site between the Sabine River and the Arroyo Hondo. Months before, the Americans under General Wilkinson's guidance had agreed with the Spanish to respect each other's borders. The Americans would not settle west of the Arroyo Hondo and the Spanish would not settle east of the Sabine River. The area in between became a neutral no man's land. The farm where the exchange was to take place was just west of the Sabine River on the Spanish side.

It had been decided earlier that Samantha would stay behind when the exchange took place. The men could easily pass for Mexicans—they spoke Spanish fluently—but Samantha, even dressed as a slim boy, would be a problem. That was the issue Lucien had raised earlier that day.

"Samantha, I cannot risk our being discovered because of you." Seeing her look of surprise, he pressed on, not wanting to lose the advantage. If she thought she might jeopardize the mission, she would unhesitatingly stay behind. But of that she was not convinced.

"But Lucien, I do not see what I have to do with this. How could I ruin things?" She hadn't believed that Lucien would keep her behind. Now, however, she was unsure.

"Look, I told you this before and you promised to listen to me." He sounded so impatient. Even his horse seemed uneasy. "You cannot come. It's too dangerous. We do not know if Herrera intends to trap us or how many men will be with him . . ." His voice droned on with determination and Samantha realized she could not oppose him.

"Anyway," he continued, "it is obvious that we are short of supplies. We will have to travel much faster on our return. You can save us time by going with Roger for the supplies, while I go on with Manuel."

"But why Roger? Don't you need him?"

"Yes, but Manuel is much more familiar with this area." Roger reluctantly agreed to be her escort, knowing that only two people could launch Lucien's plan successfully.

"Is this final, Lucien?" She looked up into his face, crestfallen.

"Yes. You and Roger will leave tomorrow at dawn." As he wheeled his skittish horse around, he added, "Manuel and I are going tonight."

There was no time to argue, for he was already shouting orders to the others.

*　　*　　*

"Roger, I want to know what is going on." She was determined to get the truth from him tonight. Lucien and Manuel had left two hours ago. There was nothing else to do. Chores were completed, the meal over, but it was not yet time for sleep. They sat by the fire drinking coffee and talking.

"I can't tell you anything, Sam. You know very well that if there were something Lucien wanted you to know, he would have told you himself. Besides"— Roger lowered his head so she couldn't see his face— "there is nothing to tell."

"Oh pooh," she snorted. "I don't believe you for one minute." She leaned against the saddle. Feeling perspired and dirty only increased her irritation. Her shirt was unbuttoned—Roger could see the lacy border of her chemise—long dirty curls were pulled high on her head, and even her boots were off. There was no respite from her physical and emotional discomfort.

"Roger, I am surprised that Lucien trusts me enough to spend the night with you," she laughed.

"You mean he trusts *me* enough. I know I would not have the use of any of my limbs if Lucien suspected I was even thinking of bedding you." He looked a little nervous as he made his claim.

Sipping the strong brew, she looked back up at him with a miserable smile. "Lucien really doesn't care about me, Roger. He just hates the idea of being cuckolded."

"Samantha Fraser, you have no idea how wrong you are. But"—he saw her about to disagree with him—"I know we do not agree on this subject, so . . . let's talk about something else."

"I can't wait to see Adam again," she murmured,

pulling her knees close to her chest, letting her chin rest on them. "There is so much to tell him. He does not know if he has a son or a daughter, or that Lucien and I are married."

"I am sure he'll be pleased on both accounts, Sam."

"Well, maybe he will be pleased about our marriage when he learns about it. But what will Adam think when he finds out the truth?"

They came back to her preoccupation again, the troubled look on her soft face revealing her deepest sentiments.

"Sam"—he reached for her hand—"do you need a temporary big brother, that is until Adam is back? I won't tell Lucien anything, if that's what concerns you."

"Oh, Roger." She looked so forlorn. "You do know. Everyone probably knows. I love him." It was easy to say those words to Roger. "But unless he sees through me the way the rest of you do, I will not tell him . . . not now . . . maybe not at all."

"As long as I have known Lucien, he has never stayed interested in any woman for more than a couple of months. Not so with you." He tried to make her smile. "And you know, Sam, Lucien *never* cared about his conquests. But he hates to let *you* out of his sight."

"But that is only because—"

"I know," he interrupted. "Because you are married," he finished for her. "Believe me . . . No, I can still see the doubting look on your face. What does Lucien have to do to tell you that he cares? He's had no other experience. Maybe, Sam, it is as hard for Lucien to accept things as it is for you."

"I don't know, Roger." Samantha only wished that

Roger spoke the truth. "Lucien has as much pride as a peacock, only his colors aren't so transparent." That comment held a special poignancy for her.

"You can be just as proud, Samantha. But I give you my word that I will not say anything to him. Lucien will have to find out for himself." Roger tossed her a blanket and helped her to her feet. "Let's try to get an early start. Tomorrow will be an interesting day," he prophesied.

It wasn't easy to fall asleep knowing Lucien's arms weren't comforting her. Samantha stared at the moonless sky, thinking. How would Lucien respond if he thought she were interested in another man? Would he give Elise up? Would he let her leave New Orleans without him? Would he want her to leave? Maybe it was time to appear as detached as he was.

"What can you lose, Sam? It can't get much worse," she said to the darkness.

They rose earlier than usual. The sky was only beginning to show signs of sunrise. But Roger insisted they still had another fifteen miles to go before they crossed the river. How they could ride into a town on the other side of the border without being seen still baffled her. Roger wasn't concerned. He merely smiled whenever she posed the question, chiding her for being so cynical.

"It is all arranged."

Fording the river was much easier than she had suspected. Roger seemed to know exactly which spot was the most shallow and effortlessly led them across.

"Well," she commented when they had paused to rest

briefly, "the land still looks the same as on the other side. The same brown. And just as hot, maybe hotter." She accepted the canteen Roger offered.

"How much farther?"

"Just a few more miles to the east. We'll give the horses a rest there."

The area Roger chose for them was a secluded spot, not far from a small village. She knew the village was nearby because she could hear the clanging of a bell through the trees.

"Sam, I want you to stay here with the horses." He led them into an area surrounded by rocks and trees. "You cannot be seen from here."

"Why can't we go together?"

"Because it will be hard enough explaining my presence to these people, let alone yours. I want them to think that I am carrying a message to the Herrera hacienda. But as you know, we are really here for supplies." His brown eyes twinkled with anticipation.

"Be a good girl, Sam. Stay put and stay ready. Who knows what kind of reception I'll get. If you see me fly past you, try to catch up and don't look back."

"Are you afraid of a few peasants?" she laughed.

"No, just their weapons."

Afraid to wander off, Samantha stayed close to the horses, reins held securely in her hand. He was gone almost an hour. Maybe I will have to go and get him, she thought. She was ready to do just that when Roger casually rode up, whistling.

"What the hell is wrong with you, Roger Cole? I

337

thought this was dangerous. And now you come sauntering up the road as if you had been on a picnic all day," she scolded, trying to keep her anger in check.

"Come on, Sam, we don't have too much time. They offered me some home-brewed whiskey. How could I refuse? My throat feels like it has been scorched," he grimaced. "Yet I was able to get most of the supplies we need. Come on, let's not give them a chance to doubt my story."

They rode swiftly to the east. Samantha did not have her bearings but sensed this was not quite right.

"Roger, do you know where we are going? Or did that poison you drank affect your brain?"

"Don't worry" was all he would say.

Almost two hours later Roger pointed to their destination, an old, deserted-looking stucco house.

"Are you out of your mind?" Samantha snapped. "What are we doing in such a God-forsaken place as this?" She jumped off her horse and looked around at the desolate area. There were a few trees, a house that looked like it hadn't been occupied for years, rickety fences, and dust. Everything blended into drab browns and grays.

"Roger, what are we doing here?" she insisted.

"Should have been here by now," was all she heard Roger say.

"Who? What are you talking about?"

"Come on." He pushed her inside. "Let's sit and wait. If no one shows up by tomorrow morning, we move on."

"Who are you talking about?" Planting her feet, Samantha snarled, "I am not budging, not one more

338

step, until you tell me what is going on."

Exasperated with her temper tantrum, Roger shrugged and replied, "Lucien is supposed to meet us here. He should have been here before us. But we agreed to wait until the following morning in case there was some difficulty."

Surprised and now worried by the change of plans, she asked, "Weren't we supposed to meet Lucien and Manuel near the house where the exchange was to take place?"

"Originally, yes. But Lucien had another idea. If it fails, we meet in the morning and proceed with the exchange."

"You are lying to me. Lucien lies to me. I know you're still not telling me everything, Roger. And from the way you look, you have no intention of telling me. So"—she sat in a dusty chair—"we wait."

"You can exhaust a person with your questions," Roger grumbled, seating himself across from her. "I feel sorry for Lucien. I don't know how he tolerates you."

"He doesn't," she replied.

Dinner that night was paltry. It was a combination of dried beef and raw vegetables. They ate, played cards, and finally, Samantha gave up and decided to get whatever sleep she could. Still dressed in the same pair of breeches she had been wearing for the last few days, Samantha settled herself in her bedroll. Earlier, she had refused Roger's suggestion that she sleep on what only those with a vivid imagination could call a bed.

339

"There are enough bugs on me already, Roger," she had commented.

The only luxuries Samantha allowed herself were washing her face with water—Roger had found an old well behind the house—and brushing her dirty hair.

"Nothing will help," she complained. "I may never be clean again."

Five minutes after she settled in the bedroll Samantha fell into a very deep sleep.

She must have been dreaming about Adam and Lucien because they kept appearing before her eyes. Voices, at first far off in different masculine tones, became clearer.

"Wake up, love, I have a surprise for you." It sounded like Lucien but how could it be? He was supposed to be somewhere else. She turned away from the voice.

"Samantha, wake up." It was still Lucien's voice, a little more insistent now. A hand massaged her shoulder. This is nice, she thought before a whack on her backside startled her from a moment of pleasure.

"What the . . . ?" She quickly turned to face her tormentor.

"Will you wake up? I have a surprise for you." Lucien smiled at her. He was crouching, his arm still resting on her backside. A wide grin, displaying his even white teeth, lit up his otherwise dark face.

"Lucien, I was trying to sleep so I could forget about worrying over you." She straightened up, brushing the hair out of her face. "Where have you been, and why didn't you tell me about the change in plans?"

she demanded.

"A shrew." Lucien turned to speak to someone behind him. "I married a shrew. This is what marriage did to your sister. My sister became sweeter with marriage, but not yours."

"Sister?" The word slowly registered. She looked into her husband's dirt-streaked face.

"Come on, get up. Someone is waiting to see you."

"Adam. Adam is here, with you?"

"Get up, Sam. I have waited a long time." It *was* Adam's voice. "Let me see what married life has done to you."

It was impossible to speak. Her voice was gone and her vision was blurred by tears.

"It is you. Oh, Adam . . ." She didn't need to say anything more. She leapt up into his arms and held on as if nothing else mattered and no one else was in the room watching the reunion.

Their tears mingled. They were tired and grimy, yet still they tenaciously clung to one another.

As she repeated his name, she released her hands and ran them over Adam's face, checking, touching, trying to convince herself that this was real, that Adam was real, not one of her many dreams.

Roger felt like an intruder. But he was an intruder moved by this loving reunion.

"Come on, Manuel," he croaked. "Let's see how the horses are doing."

Lucien just watched, wearing an ear-splitting grin, his own eyes strangely twinkling with happiness.

Chapter Twenty-Five

"I can't believe it," Samantha cried. "All these months of waiting, worrying, and finally . . ." She hugged Adam again.

"Did you know you are the father of an adorable son? And Meredith looks wonderful. Oh, his name is Jamie, I mean James . . ."

Samantha could not stop chattering. All Adam could do was smile and nod. Considering the circumstances of his disappearance, they all agreed that Adam looked surprisingly well. A bit thinner, perhaps, with darker circles under his hazel eyes, his auburn hair a shade darker, but healthy enough.

Since Lucien, Adam, and Manuel had ridden for the last two days with hardly a stop, they were overcome with exhaustion and aroused by the accomplishment of their mission.

"Come on," Roger insisted. "I surely won't be able to deal with you tomorrow if you don't sleep. You too, Sam. We will have plenty of time to talk."

"Roger's right," Lucien decided. "Those soldiers must be pursuing us by now. We will have to leave in a few hours." Turning to Roger and Samantha, Lucien added, "Manuel and I have agreed on a different route back to the American border. It will be longer and possibly more hazardous."

Samantha opened her mouth to question him, but Lucien cut her off with a wave of his hand. "Come on, wife. Let's try to sleep. Samantha and I will sleep outside tonight," he announced.

Adam knew what Lucien wanted—God, so did he. Sometimes Adam's longing for Meredith was so great, a deep physical pain in his loins made any movement uncomfortable. It was also difficult to adjust to the fact that his younger sister was a married woman—to Lucien, no less. Adam certainly would have accepted this match had he had a choice in the matter. He and Meredith had secretly believed that there was much more to Lucien's and Samantha's hostility and had hoped for their union. *I wonder how it happened?* Adam asked himself. Lucien had given him a partial description of their marriage, but not the antecedents. *Tomorrow, or the day after,* he thought as he yawned, *I will have plenty of time to find out. No guards, no beatings, no more carefully worded statements, no more invectives against his country. No more confinement.*

"I would love to sleep outside, if you two do not mind." He hinted to Roger and Manuel to join him. "Come on, friend." Adam grabbed Roger's shoulders. "I could use some fresh air."

Finally alone with her husband, Samantha felt a little awkward. Her first impulse was to rush into his arms and hug him for bringing her brother back safely, just as he had promised he would several months ago. Instead, she shyly looked up into his smiling face, a

344

lone tear sliding down her cheek, and whispered, "Thank you, Lucien. I should never have doubted your words, and . . . I am . . . sorry."

Why did she look so shy? he wondered. Seeing her smile warmly and lovingly at him was all he ever wanted.

"Come here, my love, and thank your husband properly."

Before she could protest, Samantha was engulfed in Lucien's arms, his lips searching for and finding hers. It was a delicious kiss. Her hands slowly reached up to encircle him and to feel the wavy hair at the nape of his neck. Within seconds, they were together on the narrow bed. There was a cover across it, probably Roger's doing, she thought absently, but at this moment she wouldn't have cared if they were making love in front of the whole Spanish army.

"I missed you," he whispered into her ear.

"Lucien, how did you free Adam?" she asked, trying to demonstrate a calm she did not feel.

"Later, love. I'll tell you anything you want to know." With lips claiming hers once more, his tongue probed for and sought hers. She went weak at his touch, yet demanded more of his caresses. Feeling bolder now, Samantha became the aggressor, pulling at his clothes so she could feel and taste the hot skin underneath.

"Wildcat," he laughed softly. "And unpredictable, too. I like the way you want me, Samantha."

Sliding his hand inside her breeches, he found her ready for him. Fumbling with the buttons, he cursed her clothes, threatening to tear them off. Helping him now, they shed each other's clothes until there was no protection from their unleashed passions. Abruptly, he stood up, taking her with him.

"Lucien, I am too heavy for you."

"Still modest, my love?" Pulling her body up and over his, he slowly lowered her onto his eager body, filling her with his uncontrollable desire. Moving her with his hands and body until he was sure that Samantha no longer felt self-conscious, he watched her eyes glaze with passion . . . and something else . . . before she rolled her head back moaning with unrestrained delight. Together they reached the heights of ecstasy, and ever so slowly descended.

"Lucien, do you think they heard us?" she inquired much later when rational thought returned.

"Not me. Only you were making those loud and passionate moans," he teased.

He felt so good and so tired. The last two days had been the culmination of methodical planning. However, the peace of mind he needed was not yet to be found. Somehow Lucien had to lead them safely out of this territory and onto American soil as fast as possible. The Spanish officers would not be as foolish as Herrera and his aides had been. Once they discovered how they were tricked into releasing Adam, they would come after the Americans with alacrity.

"Lucien," she murmured, "do you want to talk now? I'll understand if you want to sleep. You must be exhausted." Her silky voice was a balm to him. Long, tapered hands rubbed and circled his chest. Her right leg was flung casually across his.

"If you don't stop rubbing me, I'll tell you." Lightly kissing her temple as if to remind himself that she was in his arms, he began:

"Manuel and I arrived at the hacienda late last night. We were able to get some Spanish army uniforms before we left New Orleans. I thought that if we arrived in the middle of his camp, in the middle of the night, Herrera and his men would not suspect our presence.

"If we ever needed further proof of Gaspar's treachery, we found it last night. I said I was Gaspar's personal contact and that plans had to be changed. The ransom exchange would take place at daylight at a new location and we must take the prisoner right away in order to make up for lost time.

"Señor Herrera questioned us about Major Gaspar, trying unsuccessfully to find a flaw in our story. He asked, 'How do I know that you are really Gaspar's associate and not some imposter?' I said, 'Here, will this do?' It was that silver-handled riding quirt of Gaspar's. I don't know how Manuel managed to steal or duplicate it, but he did."

Lucien felt Samantha stiffen at the mention of the quirt. "Don't be upset, love. We got the best of him. Gaspar will know we were responsible, but he could never accuse us of it, now could he?" Pulling her head to his chest, he resumed:

"It was a matter of good timing and luck. I hollered so much, I almost believed my own lies. I said that Gaspar would be at this new site in the morning if the don wanted to talk to him then. But it would be well past the time set for the rendezvous and I hoped Señor Herrera would take full responsibility.

"Herrera finally accepted my argument and Adam was brought to me. I was sure that Adam, who had just been awakened, would reveal our true identities. But he did not show a flicker of recognition. I made my

347

explanations again for Adam's sake, and do you know what he did? He asked me if I could speak more slowly because his Spanish wasn't nearly as good as ours. I almost burst out laughing.

"We left immediately after that, giving Herrera enough gold to keep him intoxicated for a month. He asked me if we needed an escort to the border and I thanked him profusely for his generosity but told him I thought we would make better time alone. And that, my love, is all."

She sat up a little to examine his face, looking for some omission.

"Are you telling me everything? You are not just trying to spare me?" Leaning on her left elbow, her hair spilled over to one side, exposing the other side of her face. He nodded and, believing him, she relaxed.

There was no need to tell her about the man he had had to kill. Before leaving the hacienda's gates, they had to walk around a large fountain. At that moment they were stopped by a sergeant who asked several awkward questions. Lucien knew they had to move fast or risk discovery. Manuel looked at Lucien, inquiring with his eyes if Lucien wanted him to silence the soldier. All Lucien wished to do was to knock the man out, but the sergeant pulled a pistol, leaving Lucien with no recourse. Lucien deftly inched away from the weapon pointed at him and knocked the pistol out of his hand so swiftly that the soldier had no time to respond. Motioning Adam and Manuel to go on without him, Lucien now found himself facing the glint of a razor-sharp blade.

"Don't you know when to stop?" Lucien hissed in Spanish.

The burly soldier smiled menacingly at him. Lucien feinted to the right, then with his left hand grabbed the man's wrist and broke it with one shattering blow. The knife fell to the ground as both men lunged for the weapon. His senses heightened, Lucien grabbed the weapon and cut the soldier across the neck. Within seconds, the sergeant lay sprawled on the white tiles, his blood staining the floor.

Lucien swiftly moved on to join the others, not glancing back.

"I was so worried, Lucien . . . for all of you. I can't wait for this to be over." Her soft voice brought him back to the present.

"We have to reach the border first. Then I promise you the loudest family reunion New Orleans has ever seen."

What seemed to be minutes rather than hours later, Samantha was awakened by laughter. Whose voice was that? Turning toward Lucien, expecting to find him still beside her, Samantha found emptiness then heard the laughter again.

"Sam, for God's sake, where do you think you are— at Thornton Hill? You never could get up early."

It was Adam. Her head slowly cleared to recall the events of the preceding evening: Adam's safe return, Lucien's masterful lovemaking. Sighing loudly, she hugged the bedcover to her body. It reminded her of Lucien, the smell of leather, horses, and tobacco fusing into the manly scent that personified her husband. All man. And all hers for now.

"Sam, wake up!"

"All right," she shouted out the window. "I'll be there in ten minutes."

"Sister, dear, I have no desire to linger in this . . . this . . ." She thought she heard him say, "Make it five."

Where was Lucien? She saw Adam and Roger preparing for departure. But Lucien and Manuel were nowhere near and neither were their horses. Dressing with a speed she rarely displayed, Samantha stuffed her hair under her hat and stomped outside. The day was sure to be hot and damp.

Seeing her looking around, obviously for Lucien, Adam told her, "Lucien and Manuel decided to scout a bit before we left. That foolish husband of yours suggested that I let you sleep a little longer." He saw the color staining her cheeks. "I can't wait to hear about you two from Meredith," he told her.

"When are they coming back?"

"Any minute, Sam, so don't dawdle."

The horses were checked again, and by the time Samantha mounted hers, the sound of hoofbeats became clear.

Lucien rode as if the devil were behind him.

"Come on." He pulled the reins abruptly, making the animal snort with anger. "We must move fast. Herrera is not that stupid. We have a whole regiment after us."

Eyes evaluating the scene, making sure everything was ready, Lucien briefly looked at his wife.

"Keep your hat on at all times. Remember, you are a boy. And don't leave my side. You must keep up with me." His terse commands were devoid of any warmth.

There was no opportunity for her to reply. The little group left the area with as much speed as any hastily retreating army.

After an hour of the fast pace Lucien set, Samantha felt as if her eyes and mouth were filled with dust. There didn't seem to be any sign of pursuit, but she couldn't be sure. The one time she was able to glance at Lucien and not on the road ahead, Samantha saw cold blue eyes scanning the horizon, his mouth grimly set, his body rigid with expectation. They were riding far north of the original site near the Sabine River. They would cross the river from that point and crisscross their way back to the Louisiana Territory and eventually to New Orleans. Another four days had to be added to this trip. No one would feel safe until they reached the American territory and Samantha had no idea when that would be.

Finally, Lucien motioned for the group to stop. There was a thick area of trees and marsh ahead. Slowly winding their way through the mud, they stopped near a small stream.

Samantha did not know if she could get off her horse. As if reading her mind, Lucien's strong arms reached for her waist, helping her down. Her body slid along the length of his until he firmly set her on the ground. The tremors passed through both of them. Lucien never failed to arouse some emotion in her.

"I thought I might have been molded to that mare," she nervously blurted.

No one was paying any attention to them. Nonetheless, Samantha was acutely aware of the others and how their presence affected her actions with Lucien. She was uncomfortable because Adam had only known of their dislike for one another. What a shock it must have been to learn of their marriage and now to

351

see their embraces.

"Come on, my sweet, we don't have much time. Knowing you, I suspect you wish to refresh and"—he cleared his throat—"relieve yourself."

"My Lord! Being in the wilderness affects your manners. You're not supposed to mention such vulgarities," she drawled, glad for the playful exchange.

"Move, wench, or I promise to go with you."

She flicked the brim of his hat and sauntered off before he could catch her. "I wish we were home and in bed," he muttered to himself.

This time, Roger volunteered to scout for their pursuers. There was nothing else to do but wait for his return. Manuel immediately fell asleep; Samantha found a stream and tried to wash the mud off her face and arms; and Lucien and Adam fed the horses.

"Sam, refill the canteens," Adam called out to her.

It was so still. There was no breeze at all, but what the air lacked in movement it more than made up for in humidity. Samantha took off her hat, pinned her hair atop her head, and started washing her face. She was partially submerged in the water when a muffled crack was heard. Was it a pistol shot? No, it sounded far off. Now she could clearly hear rustling. She jerked up, looking around. Someone was here and she knew it wasn't Roger.

The small pistol Lucien insisted she keep with her at all times was tucked into her waistband. What should she do? Should she wait until Lucien called out to her? Another shot, closer now, startled her again. Creeping closer to the campsite, trying to make as little noise as possible, Samantha thought her legs would collapse. She heard voices—not anyone she knew. The words were firm and desperate—and in Spanish. How could they have been tracked so swiftly? Fighting the desire to give up and cry, Samantha hoped her nerves would not betray her presence. She had to see how many men were there. A sudden noise to her left made her gasp. Samantha got onto her stomach and crept toward some bushes close to the campsite.

She did not know what to make of the sight before her. Manuel was sprawled on the ground. Was he dead? Adam's arms were secured by one soldier and another stood before them, bayonet poised. Lucien was off to the right. There was a bloody gash on his temple. What almost made her cry out, however, was the way Lucien was favoring his left arm. Blood was trickling down. He seemed perfectly alert and so angry that Samantha assumed his wounds were slight.

As far as she could tell, there were only two soldiers. There was still a chance to overpower them and run.

"The others will be here soon, amigo, so don't try to escape. Of course, I don't mind killing another gringo."

The other joined in. "Our orders are to bring all of you back." He spit something onto the ground. "Alive. But accidents happen."

"We will wait for your two friends to return. Then we go back to meet the major."

The major! Surely they couldn't mean Gaspar— here! If they were brought to him, none of them would live long enough to reveal Gaspar's treachery. Of that Samantha was sure.

"I don't expect my friends at all, señor. They left this

353

morning and won't be back." Lucien sounded calm, but Samantha could sense his hostility. His hard blue eyes stared unflinchingly at the sergeant who held the fixed bayonet.

"Sam and Roger should be at the border by now, probably getting help. They wouldn't think of coming back. That would not make sense."

"Silence!" the man holding Adam ordered. "I want no more talk from either of you. Tie them up," he ordered the sergeant. "Maybe our friends left some food for us."

Of course Lucien wouldn't make it easy for his captor. The sergeant pushed him with a bayonet. Falling to his knees, Lucien caught himself before landing on his injured arm but was brutally kicked in his side. He groaned, as did Samantha.

Samantha knew she had to do something. Lucien's words were meant for her, warning her to stay clear until Roger came. But it might be too late. The way Lucien was glaring at that sergeant was an invitation for battle.

Drawing a deep breath, Samantha stood up, trying to be taller than her five and one-half feet.

"I wouldn't do that if I were you, señor." She was praying her voice sounded stern and steady.

"Over here, Roger," she shouted to no one and moved out of the bushes.

The soldiers were nonplussed. A little pistol was aimed at the sergeant's heart.

"Drop your weapons, señors. Unless"—she looked at the sergeant—"you don't mind my shooting you first."

The sergeant did not look convinced. With his

attention riveted on Samantha, he did not notice Lucien slowly inching toward him.

"I don't believe you, gringa. You won't shoot me, and"—he appeared to sneer beneath his heavy mustache—"I don't think that little pistol can shoot anything."

Panic seized her as the man stepped closer. If he grabbed her arm, she would surely let go of the pistol and lose their only chance for release.

"You're a beautiful lady. I think I shall keep you for myself after we kill the gringos." He moved closer. All he had to do was take two more steps before he reached her extended arm.

"Oh, no," she warned before closing her eyes and pulling the trigger. Her hand recoiled from the explosion. When she opened her eyes, the sergeant was staring at her in amazement. There was a hole in his stomach which was large enough to make his next few breaths his last.

"You . . . bitch," he gasped and fell forward.

Before the shock wore off on the other soldier, Lucien attacked. The lieutenant was thrown off balance, his own weapon falling out of his grasp. Adam dove for the weapon.

"Enough!" Adam shouted. "I think, lieutenant, you are outnumbered. Good work, Sam." He glanced at the frozen woman behind him.

Lucien struggled to his feet. The throbbing in his left arm was painful, and his side ached from the kick he had sustained.

"Tie him up, Adam. We will decide what to do with him later." Lucien looked at Samantha still holding the pistol, her mouth agape, her large green eyes staring at the body sprawled before her feet.

"You had to do it, my love, although I should be furious with you for disobeying my orders."

She appeared inattentive to his intentional barb.

"Disobey your what?" Her voice was not too steady.

"I told you to stay back, didn't I? You could have gotten us all killed."

"But I didn't. I saved *you*, you fool. You were practically begging this lout to shoot you." Steaming now, she shouted, "This man was going to stomp you to death. . . . If I hadn't stopped him when I did. . . ."

"She'll be okay now, Lucien." Adam walked over to where they stood. Samantha's face was flooded with anger, no longer expressionless with shock.

"Come on, my love, let's see if you are as good a nurse as you are a crack shot." With his arm extended in invitation, Samantha dismissed his sarcastic remarks. She moved easily to Lucien's chest, burying her body in his comforting warmth, and cried. Gently stroking her hair, he smiled at Adam.

"Samantha, if you hadn't shot him when you did, I swear I would have strangled him. His fate was sealed with he kicked me, but when he spoke to you like that I swore I would kill him no matter what happened to me." Lucien's voice was filled with venom.

"We still have some business to attend to," said Adam. "I think Manuel . . ."

"He was killed instantly. That bastard aimed at Manuel's back. Manuel never had a chance."

Samantha raised her head.

"Are you okay now, sweet?"

Nodding, she looked at Manuel's body. "He was a good friend to us. And I didn't really know anything

356

about him."

"I think, Adam, we should take Manuel back with us, at least as far as the American border, and bury him there."

"What about the other?"

"Let his amigo bury him—after we are gone."

Samantha was still clutching Lucien's sound arm. "We have some bandages, Lucien. Let's clean your wound."

"The bullet merely grazed me," he stated, dismissing the wound.

"Nevertheless, I will clean it. We have to wait for Roger anyway." There was more authority to her tone now.

"Yes, madam. You see, Adam, I told you your sister was a shrew." His smile was the familiar sardonic grin Samantha knew so well. This time she was pleased to see it.

Chapter Twenty-Six

New Orleans: Summer, 1807

"What is the point of staying in New Orleans all summer?"

"I need more proof, Adam. Both Jefferson and Madison are reluctant to accuse General Wilkinson of treason. They do not think that Gaspar's treachery is proof enough."

Lucien and Adam were in their office. They had been back in New Orleans for over a week now. Not wanting to waste any more time, Adam was planning to depart for Thornton Hill in two days. The uppermost thought on his mind was his reunion with his wife and the first meeting with his infant son.

"Then why don't you let Sam come home with me?"

"Home?" mocked Lucien. "She *is* home. With me, here, now and wherever else I decide to go." Roughly shoving his armchair aside, Lucien stood up and watched the activities of the busy port.

Things were deteriorating between Lucien and Samantha again. Almost as soon as they had come back to their little rented house, they each had seemed to reinstate the cool façades previously shed in the wilderness. Of course, outside pressures contributed to their states of mind.

Elise Fourier had known even before his own crew did, that Lucien was back. André was out of town for a few days and Elise was free to do as she wished. Lucien had decided weeks ago that he would sever his association with her, but that was not to be.

An invitation from Elise for a very late dinner had been awaiting him when he arrived that morning. As he was shredding the note, there was a soft knock at the door.

"Captain Fraser, this gentleman insists on seeing you. He says it's urgent."

A very short, balding man—probably in his late forties, Lucien surmised—entered behind Lucien's clerk. His dress was inappropriate for the hot weather of New Orleans. A dark brown velvet jacket and waistcoat, neatly trimmed shirt, cravat, and a silly brown hat made him appear much older than his age.

"I am terribly sorry to disturb you, Captain Fraser. But Mr. Madison said I must deliver this message to you as quickly as possible." A thick, brown envelope was handed to Lucien. "I am going back to Washington tomorrow. If you have a reply, please leave it at the hotel and I will deliver it to Mr. Madison."

"Why the urgency?"

The man doffed his hat. "Why, the trial, Captain."

"Trial?" How could he have overlooked something that sounded so important?

"Aaron Burr's trial, Captain. He is being tried in Richmond for treason." The man was a little smug. "I have a lot of witnesses to collect."

360

Annoyed by his superciliousness, Lucien said tersely, "Please don't let me keep you from your important duties. I will have a response for Mr. Madison tonight." He walked to the sturdy oak door, opened it, and smiled. "Good day, sir."

As soon as the little man had departed, Lucien lost no time in tearing the seal of the missive.

Adam quietly entered the room and let a few minutes pass before he spoke. The message could not have been good for Lucien's facial expression revealed consternation. Consternation for whom? Adam wondered.

"Well, are you going to sit there and frown or are you going to tell me the contents?"

"Dammit." Lucien crumpled the missive in his hand before flinging it across the room.

"Madison is almost ready to accept Wilkinson's part in Burr's conspiracy but not the general's involvement with the Spanish. And it appears as if the esteemed general's name has come up a number of times at Burr's trial."

"So why are you so angry? This is nothing new to you."

"Because Adam, Mr. Madison has reason to suspect—although he does not say what his reasons are—that André Fourier is a party to this 'conspiracy.' You know what that means, don't you?"

"What?"

"Don't you see? I must keep seeing Elise Fourier for the information she gives me."

Adam was as baffled as Roger Cole had been to learn of Lucien's relationship with Elise Fourier. Yet he wasn't ready to condemn him for it. This was obviously one of the reasons behind it.

"What is the quickest way to get the evidence I need?" He walked to the window, put his arms out in front of him, and buried his head. "This is a bloody mess. Samantha will never believe any explanation," he muttered. "Elise Fourier gives me eyes and ears in the enemy camp, and that, dear brother-in-law, means continuing a friendship—if you wish to call it that—I never should have started and would like to end."

"I had wondered about your good sense."

"I had to prove something to myself. But I don't think it was worth it, not if Samantha leaves me again." He smiled ruefully. "Adam, I am going to tell you something I shouldn't. But you of all people should know. Elise Fourier and I have never been lovers. And," he warned, "I will gladly slit your throat if you tell your sister the truth."

"Did you ever think of telling *her* the truth? Telling her you apologize for deceiving her; telling her that you need her?"

Lucien turned to face him. It was clear to Adam that Lucien loved his sister and that, more than anything else, gave Adam confidence that their relationship would endure.

"I cannot do that, Adam. Samantha really doesn't care. Who can blame her?" His tone was bitter.

"That is not true, Lucien. You have only to look at her face and see those adoring green eyes staring at you to know how much she cares."

"It's part of her act," Lucien replied, albeit with some hesitation. "Before this message, we might have had a chance to explore some of our problems. Not now, though. I cannot tell Samantha that the Secretary of State has ordered me to continue an illicit relationship, can I?"

"What else did Madison say?" He could not tolerate seeing Lucien this depressed.

"It gets better," he laughed. "The defense attorneys are going to call a lot of witnesses. Guess who might be summoned to Richmond, Virginia?"

"Stop the riddles."

"The two of you. You *and* Samantha. For different reasons I guess, but an interesting situation nonetheless. *I* must be on reserve for the prosecution."

"Lucien, I am leaving before anyone requests my attendance at the trial. Mr. Madison could not have received your note about my rescue yet. I am going home to my wife and son. After a nice long rest, maybe I will allow them to find me—if the trial is still on."

"I will tell them I never set eyes on you," Lucien joked, then quickly added, "Hell, I wish I had never met your sister."

"She does not believe Aaron Burr is guilty, does she?"

"No. I tell you, Adam, she almost has me believing it, too. The time she spent on that military ship with Bollman and Swartwout convinced her of Burr's innocence and Wilkinson's treachery. And, of course, there is still Major Gaspar."

"Yes, certainly I know better than anyone else what that bastard is capable of. Well"—Adam stood up—"maybe you should reconsider and force your wife to come with me to Thornton Hill. Perhaps she will forgive you for Elise Fourier. You can join us when you finish your uh . . . assignment. Think about it, Fraser. It might help. Stop insisting that she stay at your side while you are with someone else."

363

"I don't know." Lucien sounded thoughtful. "You have a point, Adam. I will think about it."

Much later, when quiet was restored to their home, Lucien realized his mistake. Telling Samantha that she had to leave with Adam had been enough to unleash a temper tantrum full of invectives that would make any man blush.

"Why are you so eager for me to leave, dear husband? Am I in your way? Is that it? What happened to your promise that you would never leave me again? Lies," she spat, "all lies. I never should have believed any of your syrupy sagas. They were nothing more than nonsense."

Pausing, her chest heaving with anxiety, Samantha glared at her husband. Never, she vowed to herself, would he know her true feelings. Thank God she had never told him. He and Elise would have had a grand time with that knowledge!

His long, tanned fingers reached for her shoulder, but she jerked away so quickly it felt as if he had encountered the recoil of a rifle shot.

"Don't you dare touch me, you . . . you . . . *canaille!* I will not make it easy for you and that mistress of yours, do you hear? You know"—she laughed, a bit hysterically now—"I could have sworn we had this same conversation months ago over Caroline Prescott. You could not be loyal to her either. You could not be loyal to any woman."

"Enough." His cold voice silenced her. Sitting on the bed trying hard to contain his fury at her wild accusation, he looked at her back and stated, "If you do not take my word, speak to Adam. And if that still does not convince you, madam, so be it. I am trying to protect you, whether you believe me or not."

"I don't. Never will I believe you again, Lucien Fraser." She waved her clenched fists, moving furiously around the bedroom.

"If you choose to stay, I will make no more apologies, no more attempts to reconcile our differences over this matter. Those are my terms. Do you accept, Samantha?"

He wasn't looking at her but at the street scene below their large bedroom window. "Well?" He did not turn around. Why, she wondered, did he make her feel like the one responsible for this argument?

"I told you, Lucien, I am staying." It was a pity she could not see the look of mingled frustration and pain cross his face.

"Fine. Then let me prepare you for something else." His voice sounded more controlled. "You are going to be asked to testify in Richmond at Aaron Burr's trial. For the defense."

"What!" Her green eyes sparkled with surprise. "Why me? What could I possibly say?"

"The truth, Samantha. I guess Bollman or Swartout thought you could tell about your 'voyage' to Washington with them."

"Well," she hesitated, "if it will help Mr. Burr, I will do it. Yes"—she sounded much more determined—"I will go."

"Hold on, sweetheart. You weren't asked to go yet, so don't start packing." The temptation to laugh was strong, but he knew it would have infuriated her. "Adam will probably be called, as will I." She looked surprised. "But by the other side."

"Oh. So what do we do?"

"*We*," he replied, mocking her, "will wait. Adam will stay at Thornton Hill until he is discovered. I have to finish up some business matters here."

"Yes, I am sure you do," she snapped, her voice full of sarcasm.

"You asked for it, love. Don't forget." Before she had time to protest, Lucien pulled her into his arms, pinning her hands to her sides. His mouth engulfed hers and he kissed her brutally. When he was finished, he released her, a dark, dangerous look in his eyes. "Just remember who owns you."

Her only answer was a stinging slap across his face. "Yes, I see you remember." He met her angry gaze, ignoring the red imprint on his cheek, then abruptly turned and walked out.

Standing in the middle of the room, Samantha had no idea how her look of hatred pained her husband. How they would get through the next month together, neither one would have dared to predict.

What Lucien could not possibly know was how much worse the situation would get.

Two days later, at a play the Frasers were attending at the St. Peter Street Theatre, the appearance of a certain patron created more havoc for Lucien and Samantha than either could have imagined.

It was intermission. Lucien went to get Samantha some cold champagne. Knowing that Elise Fourier was also in attendance, Samantha assumed Lucien wanted to sneak off for a tryst with his paramour. So absorbed in her self-misery, she failed to notice the movement behind her.

"Hello, *mon coeur*," a soft familiar voice cooed in her ear. "Have you missed me?"

Eyes closing in wishful anticipation, she whispered, "Stèfan, is it you? Are you here? Oh, I hope I am not dreaming."

As she turned to face him, his heart lurched at the sight of her exquisite beauty. Clasping his hands to her cheek, her bright emerald eyes revealed her happiness at seeing him again.

"This is my last stop before I go back to France. I thought I could make you change your mind and run away with me." He was teasing her, but his remark was tinged with seriousness.

"Oh, I just might. Where are you staying, Stèfan? How long will you be here? Is your father joining you?"

"Hold on, *ma petite*. One question at a time." He sat in the chair vacated by Lucien. "I am staying for a few weeks at some friends' home. Not mine, actually. The Fouriers are friends of my father's."

Samantha stiffened. "André and Elise Fourier?"

"Yes. Why do you look so strange?"

"Because, Stèfan . . ." She started to giggle. "This is really too much. This could make a better play than the one we are watching."

"You are beautiful, *chèrie*." Stèfan still looked as handsome and stylish as ever. His bright green jacket, quilted waistcoat and nankeen breeches hugged his body. His sun-bronzed skin matched his shining, golden brown eyes.

"I hope we can see each other before I depart."

"Believe me, we will," she replied enigmatically.

"We will what, love?" interrupted Lucien. Recognizing Stèfan's voice before he had stepped into the box, Lucien cursed his own bad luck. What an untimely arrival.

"Lucien, look who is here!" she enthusiastically announced.

"I can see that, madam." He extended his hand, albeit reluctantly, to Stèfan. "Staying long, Turreau?"

"A few weeks. I hope you will both be my guests for dinner one evening."

"Lucien," Samantha interrupted. "Guess where Stèfan is staying?" At his blank look, she hastily offered, "With your *dear* friends, André and Elise Fourier. Isn't that a coincidence? You may see Stèfan more often than I will."

Stèfan knew he had walked into another awkward situation. How these two had managed to stay together this long was miraculous. But of course Stèfan knew and could see the real reason for this marriage. Their veiled looks at one another were obvious, at least to him.

"Yes, I guess I will," was Lucien's subdued reply.

"Stèfan, please join us. I am dying to hear about your travels."

She was the most beautiful woman he had ever seen, Stèfan told himself. Her hair, arranged in long ringlets, swung freely whenever her head moved. A large diamond clip lay near the side of her hair, pulling the curls off her face. Oh, and what a delicately boned face; soft white skin, full mouth, high cheekbones with just a trace of a blush. The azure blue crepe dress had tiny blue and yellow flowers embroidered in the ribbon that tied below her bodice and trailed below the back of the dress. The same ribbon embroidery trimmed the base of her hem and the capped sleeves. Her ripened breasts appeared as voluptuous as ever. Such a beauty . . . and married, Stèfan warned himself. Lucien Fraser was not a man to be cuckolded

"You might as well stay, Turreau," Lucien grumbled. "I want to see what my wife finds so appealing in you."

Any other man would have been "called" for that remark. But Stèfan realized that Lucien was probably insanely jealous, an emotion that would be new to him.

"Thank you, I will. Perhaps the Fouriers can join us later for a light supper." Fraser, smartly dressed in various shades of beiges and browns accentuating his height and muscular frame, stiffened imperceptibly.

"Yes, that would be delightful. Wouldn't it, Lucien?" Samantha smiled with anticipation.

"Anything that pleases you, my love." He took her hand and squeezed it hard, almost causing her to gasp before he pulled it to his lips. "This should be interesting. Right, sweetheart?"

Elise certainly hid her surprise at being invited to dine with the Frasers by Samantha Fraser's former love . . . or lover, who ironically was her houseguest. From Elise's perspective, Lucien got more than he bargained for in a wife. Over the last several weeks, the two women had made a point of politely avoiding one another. What Elise knew of Samantha came from gossip mongers. Yet Elise also knew that Samantha was no ordinary woman. She was forced to recognize a worthy adversary and believed that if it were not for Lucien, she and Samantha could be friends.

André, probably sensing an uncomfortable situation, declined the supper invitation. Murmuring about some important business matter, he departed before the play ended.

369

So, the four of them dined together. It was an evening none of them would forget.

For Stèfan, a strange combination of hostilities, barbed comments, and forced gaiety comprised the scene. A thought had occurred to him when he had asked Elise Fourier to join them for supper. Her eyes had lit up at the mention of Lucien's name. By the end of the evening he was almost positive that Elise was Lucien's mistress. No wonder Samantha had said those cruel things to her husband earlier. She knew about it. Perhaps, Stèfan thought, there is hope for Samantha and me.

For Samantha, the late evening supper was a series of contradictions. Elise Fourier was on her best behavior. In fact, her own thoughts were not too different from Elise's. Samantha realized that Elise was trapped in a loveless marriage. Certainly, she, better than anyone, could emphathize. Elise was attractive and intelligent too, and her marriage was equally flawed.

But if anyone needed to be taught a lesson, it was Lucien. Samantha practically threw herself at Stèfan, drinking wine and champagne until she could no longer tell the difference. Giggling at all of Stèfan's stories, she pressed him for more. She appeared to hang on every word Stèfan uttered. After a while, Samantha no longer cared that Lucien and Elise were watching like indulgent parents. What a ridiculous notion! And she laughed all the harder.

"Stèfan, what is it like in Washington?" she asked.

"Well, everyone is traveling between Washington and Richmond, Virginia. This trial is a great spectacle. And it appears to be a social event."

370

Briefly forgetting his anger at his wife's outrageous behavior, Lucien asked, "What is the general feeling in Washington about this trial?"

"Well, there is a real split in opinion. Many people, my father among them, believe Mr. Burr to be innocent. In fact, it goes deeper than that."

"What do you mean?" Lucien was really interested now.

"It is said that the prosecution, headed by George Hay, is really controlled by the President, who is directing them from Washington."

"André says the same thing," added Elise, finding American politics interesting if not strange.

"Lucien and I are going to see first hand," blurted Samantha, a trifle too loudly. "We are going to be witnesses—on opposite sides, of course."

Why couldn't she keep her mouth shut? As Samantha gave more details, Lucien anxiously looked around the small restaurant. This conversation had surely been overheard by the people at the tables on either side of them. This could lead to trouble, his sixth sense warned, recognizing some of Fourier's questionable associates at the next table. Well, he told himself, now I will find out how deeply involved they are with Wilkinson and Gaspar.

All evening Lucien was tempted to render Samantha unconscious. He knew she was deliberately flaunting herself at Turreau, and a deep knot of fury festered within him. He remembered that time back at Thornton Hill when he had found Samantha laughing so gaily with Turreau. The same Turreau that loved her then still loved her now. But, Lucien kept asking himself all evening, am I not forcing my wife to

371

reconsider her own affections for Turreau when the woman Samantha thinks is my mistress is sharing our table? What a horrible joke this all is. When we get home tonight, I will thrash her lovely backside so she will not be able to sit for a week. I don't care if her brother witnesses it. As Lucien's mind raced with possibilities, his latent anger was barely contained. She will pay for embarrassing me, he vowed.

The evening ended with Samantha asking them all for tea to meet her brother before he left. Even if they had not heard Lucien groan, they saw he was surely surprised—and even more so when Elise accepted.

As soon as they were alone in the carriage, Samantha's giddiness disappeared. Looking ahead, her face expressionless, she refused to speak to Lucien. When they reached the house, she got out of the carriage without waiting for Lucien's assistance. Actually, he had had no intention of helping her.

Walking haughtily up the stairs, she reached the bedroom door and closed it before he could protest. Seemingly, Lucien did not care. He needed to be away from her to try to control his blazing anger. How could she be so spiteful! Perhaps it was a mistake to stay in the library by himself. While one part of his mind told him how furious he should be, another part recalled her scent and her glorious beauty—so much more beautiful than any woman he had ever known.

He wondered what would happen at tomorrow's "tea." Funny, he thought, Elise had acted more like an amused aunt than an angry lover. And she still had not given him all the information he needed about her husband. Somehow though, Lucien knew Elise would cooperate.

Striding over to his desk, Lucien noticed a note addressed to him from Adam. After reading it carefully, he smiled. There was no reason to remain secluded in this room all night, he decided. "Let's see what that termagant is up to now," he muttered aloud.

The door was locked. If Lucien had been of half a mind to forgive her outrageous behavior, the locking of the bedroom door changed that. Knocking firmly, he called to her.

"Samantha," his voice boomed, "if you do not open this door *now*, I will break it down."

No response. Was she asleep? He knocked louder and harder.

"Samantha," he warned, "open this door."

"Go away! Go to your mistress. And if she will not accept you, I am sure you will find another."

A thud, then a crunching sound. Suddenly the door burst open, wood scattering about the room. Lucien filled the doorway. If his rigid body did not warn her to be careful, the murderous blaze in his eyes did.

"I warned you."

The door slammed behind him. He placed a chair under the broken door knob. "Now, you flirtatious bitch. Are you ready to give me what you were obviously offering Turreau?" Slowly he walked toward her.

"Stay away from me, Lucien," she shouted back with no trace of fear. "I warn you I will scream for Adam."

"Adam left me a note, love. He is sleeping aboard the *Newport Wind* tonight. Lucky, aren't we? I believe, my dear wife, that you and I have to settle a few things."

373

"Why? Did you discuss your taking a lover with me? I do not recall giving my permission." Her lips curled into a forced smile. Still she retreated, trying to stay out of his reach.

"Don't rile me, Samantha. I told you before . . . you are mine. Do you understand? Or must I prove it to you once again?" Stepping closer, his eyes chips of blue ice, Lucien offered no comfort.

Fearing for her safety now, Samantha's hands frantically reached for something, anything, to halt Lucien's menacing progress. Her fingers curled around something. Yes, her silver-backed hairbrush. It was heavy enough to stun him, she thought. Her aim was surprisingly good as it struck him in the temple. He grunted but did not miss a step.

"You will pay for that." Then he grabbed her arm, cruelly twisting it behind her, forcing her closer to him so that her breasts pressed into his chest.

"I hate you, Lucien." She looked directly at him, trying not to show the pain.

"I know you do, love. But you are still mine." With that, he released his painful grip, yet she was still in the vise of his arms. Lucien's mouth nipped her exposed neck while his hands contemptuously roamed over her body.

Trying to hide any reaction to him, she forced herself to remain unresponsive. But he only chuckled a low, throaty sound that made her shiver.

"Ah, so you are now the ice maiden, are you, my sweet?"

Freeing one hand, Samantha made one last effort to protect herself. She clenched it into a tight fist and punched him with all her strength in his stomach. Only his exhalation of breath told her he had felt something.

"Very unwise, my love. I warned you this afternoon about raising your hands to strike me."

Before she could gather her wits, Lucien slapped her across the face. It wasn't a hard slap, yet it still brought tears to her eyes. And then, before Samantha fully comprehended the seriousness of her predicament, Lucien grabbed the low bodice of her gown and tore it from her.

"You wouldn't dare!" she gasped, clutching the torn material.

His response was the rending of her silk chemise. Lucien no longer seemed to be aware of her. Each time she protested, he lightly slapped her, but it was enough to stun her with his cruelty.

"Don't do this to me," she cried, ignoring her tears.

"You are going to learn to obey me, wife."

He methodically tore every bit of clothing from her body until the shreds lay scattered on the floor. Without giving her a chance to breathe, Lucien picked her up and abruptly tossed her onto the bed.

"Don't you dare move. Or so help me, I will tie you up and beat you."

This could not be the same man she loved, she told herself. But she was too frozen with shock and growing fear to move. And Lucien was beyond reasoning.

"That's better," he said when he saw her remaining still. He quickly removed his clothing and stood over her, forcing her to acknowledge his supremacy and his desire.

"Show me what a good lover you are," he demanded, then joined her on the bed.

Eyes closing against the pain and humiliation,

Samantha did not see the look of remorse he held for her. Lucien knew he was pushing her too far, but he could not stop himself. He had to teach her a lesson. And somewhere deep down, he had to vanquish that demon that told him he was a captive of this lovely creature.

And then she put his fear into words, bringing his thoughts into the open.

"You are jealous, Lucien. And you should be. For Stèfan will be my lover."

Blinded by his rage, he could only think of words that would hurt her in kind. "You are a bitch and will be treated like one."

Suddenly he was all over her, treating her not as a tender lover, but as a whore. He was ready; she was not. Lucien tore into her unprepared body with such force that she cried out. When he lowered his head to taste her mouth, she bit his lip so hard that she tasted his blood. Again he slapped her, making her face flame with anger and shame.

As soon as her mind adjusted to this new brutality, Lucien suddenly became the considerate lover. His pounding of her flesh slowed, his hands and lips traveled over her body, kissing the bruises he had inflicted. How could she take this? His brutality was one thing, but now Lucien wanted to make love to her and expected her to respond.

And damn her traitorous body, it was responding! Lucien pulled out of her and let his mouth travel all over her body, going lower and lower until he found the center of her being while his hands glided up her stomach, seeking her pink-tipped breasts. She shivered when his tongue entered her but tried to hide any other response. Her hands, trapped by Lucien's powerful grasp, were suddenly freed. And Samantha found to her dismay that they were now entwined in his black hair.

"No," she whimpered. But the word went unheeded.

When she felt she was ready to explode, Lucien positioned himself above her and asked, "Are you ready for me now, Samantha sweet?" She refused to answer.

He merely laughed as he slowly entered her wet, waiting body, spreading her legs with his powerful thighs. Pulling her legs higher, cradling them in his arms, he exposed all of her to his view. Leaning on his knees, his body above hers, his hand caressed her flushed face then moved lower to her erect nipples, roughly pinching them.

Eyes half opened, she saw him watching her. Samantha's hands began their own exploration of his hardened body, finally grasping his buttocks, pushing him deeper, harder into her, delighting in what he was giving her.

Groaning with passion, she asked, "Why, Lucien? Why the lover, not the rapist?"

"Because you need me as much as I need you. You crave my touch, the same way I crave yours. And you will never forget, my love, never."

There were no more words. Their bodies met, straining for the culmination, pounding each other. The feverish pitch reached a moment of volcanic explosion. A sigh of relief reached the heavens like an instant of tranquillity in the universe.

Chapter Twenty-Seven

The bright summer sunlight came through the curtains and settled on Samantha's sleeping face. When she tried to turn onto her side, a sharp pain forced her to awaken.

"Oh, Lord," she groaned. She placed her hands on her temples, praying for the pain to disappear. It did not affect her condition. Slowly, Samantha rolled on her side to face Lucien and the humiliation of the previous night.

He was gone! Angry at first, then secretly relieved, Samantha wondered if Lucien had anticipated her embarrassment and was wise enough to leave her alone. She didn't know how she could face him. I am no better than a common strumpet, she despaired silently. He knows he can have me—that I cannot resist his warm touch.

"What am I going to do now?" she lamented aloud. They no longer had a marriage and there was nothing she could do about it. The interlude in the Spanish Territory had been nothing but a deception—a brief and lovely memory. But it was over. Adam was free and Lucien was no longer bound by his promise to her.

He was still involved with another woman.

Testing her limbs to see if moving them would cause her pain, Samantha sat up. The sheet fell below her breasts and she felt chilled. She never had put on a nightgown last night. Lucien would have torn *it* the same way her clothes were shredded. She pondered her miserable predicament.

Maybe she should go away with Stèfan. Of course he had been only half-serious when he had asked her to leave with him yesterday. But even if Stèfan did not want her as his mistress, at least she would be in France, away from Lucien and his mistresses. Stèfan's intentions had always been honorable, and she believed he would help her if she asked him to. Yet, would it be fair to Stèfan? She did not love him—not the way she hopelessly loved Lucien. Stèfan deserved a woman who could return his love.

A knock on the door, which sounded like cannon-fire to Samantha, interrupted her thoughts.

"Come in but walk softly," she warned, not even liking the sound of her voice.

Harriet Wells bustled into the room balancing a breakfast tray.

"Good morning, dear. How was the play?" Harriet was about to ask Samantha something else about her husband, but one look at the scattered remains of Samantha's dress cautioned Harriet that this was not a time for idle chatter. Remembering the murderous look on Mr. Fraser's face early this morning before he had stormed out of the house, Harriet realized that something was awry. Whenever Lucien Fraser stomped about the house in that dark mood, it usually came after some altercation with his wife. Before he had stalked off, Lucien had told Harriet that Mrs. Fraser would definitely need strong Creole coffee and a hearty breakfast.

"She's going to have a terrible headache when she awakens. Let her try to sleep as long as she can, he had cautioned. Tell her I am sorry but I won't be back in time for her 'tea party.' Tell her I am sure she will have a better time without me."

That was quite a row they must have had last night, she thought, but Harriet was not the type to gossip and had no intention of asking Samantha.

"Harriet, I don't think I can eat. Ever. Perhaps some coffee . . ."

"Your husband said you should eat . . . that a full breakfast would cure your . . . ah . . . indisposition."

"Harriet, I may never drink again. My head feels as if it were made of cotton and metal. My mouth feels like I drank sour milk instead of wine. Ugh!" She lifted her red-rimmed eyes. "Did my husband have any messages for me?"

"Yes." Harriet placed the tray in front of Samantha, despite her grimace and groan. "He said he was sorry, but he had some important business to attend to today and that he wouldn't be back in time for your tea."

"Hmm, so the great lion is really a kitten after all. Is that all?"

"No." Harriet hesitated a bit here. "Mr. Fraser said, 'I am sure she will have a better time without me.' And then he left."

"Why, that no good, miserable . . . oh!" Samantha yelled, then held her throbbing head. "I suppose this is his way of getting even with me," she whispered to herself. "I hope Stèfan and Adam show up. Otherwise

381

Elise and I may have a very stimulating conversation."

It was more than she expected. Elise arrived with Stèfan and looked her usual stunning self. She wore a high-necked, short-sleeved muslin day dress that was the most interesting shade of peach. The color enhanced her dark beauty. Samantha felt awkward standing next to her since she was so much taller than Elise. Her own cream-colored dress, with delicate lace trimming, made Samantha feel like a mere child. At that moment she thought, no wonder Lucien is so attracted to Elise.

The afternoon passed quite pleasantly. Adam, who was so excited about leaving, was in an incredibly funny mood and practically entertained the three of them by himself. Stèfan instantly liked Adam, and his rendition of Samantha's experiences in Paris added to the pleasure of the day.

"Your sister captured more hearts in one afternoon just by strolling through the Tuileries, than other women acquire in a lifetime of flirtation. I had to fight off many heartsick suitors. But you see, *mon ami*, through it all this charming lady would only blush— just like she is doing now."

"Oh, Stèfan, don't embarrass me." She did not want Elise to think that she was an innocent adolescent.

"But she did not want me. Instead, she marries your partner." Stèfan's laugh sounded a bit hollow to Adam. But it was Elise Fourier who was the most perceptive member of the little group.

Of course she could not help but notice the way Samantha blushed at Stèfan's jests. But at the mention

382

of Lucien's name or any reference to their marriage, Samantha lowered her green eyes and stared at her hands. It was very interesting. Samantha's expression revealed disappointment and anger.

Elise had never come into contact with the "other woman." Most of her lovers were unattached. She never felt remorse for either betraying André or being involved with a married man. But now she had this funny twinge in her stomach. Could it be that she had finally discovered a conscience? It was unfortunate that Elise liked Samantha Fraser and loved her husband. Since last night, Elise had had time to ponder the strange relationship of the Frasers. *Could I break up their marriage? Perhaps Lucien only wanted his freedom. Would Samantha graciously concede her husband? More importantly, would Lucien leave his wife for her? Why did Lucien avoid her advances yet choose to visit her at such odd hours that naturally Samantha and everyone else in New Orleans believed them to be lovers? Why did Lucien want his wife to think that he had a lover?*

Elise had hoped to see the Frasers together again today so she could find some answers by observing their relationship, but she would have to wait for that opportunity. Watching Samantha had already left Elise with many more doubts and questions. But the big unresolved question was whether Samantha could be in love with her husband.

Then, of course, there was Stèfan, dear Stèfan. Too bad he was leaving for Paris so soon. If she had to find a replacement for Lucien, Stèfan would do nicely. Elise's brown eyes gleamed with the prospect. Stèfan was still infatuated with Samantha, but he could be made to see the hopelessness of the situation. Leaning back on the white wicker lawn chair, Elise smiled. Yes, she thought things might untangle themselves yet.

Long before Lucien came back, Samantha bade a tearful farewell to her brother. Adam made her promise to contact him if she needed him, but Samantha had no intention of disturbing her brother's reunion with his family.

"Sam, your crazy husband can care for you better than any man. Understand? And"—his hazel eyes searched her tear-stained face—"he cares for you, more than anyone else. Don't give up on him yet. Love is a new concept for him, too."

"He will have to prove it to me now. He deserves to feel uneasy. I only wish he were half as desolate as I am."

"Lord, you are stubborn, Sam. Probably from Mother's side of the family. No matter what happens though, Lucien has promised to get you out of this town before August. Yellow fever, once it spreads, cannot be stopped. So take care, little sister."

"I almost wish I were going with you, Adam."

"But"—he tweaked her nose—"you don't want to leave your man behind."

Lucien slammed his way into his office. Nothing was right today. Angered and confused by his wife's outrageous then passionate behavior last night, Lucien began the day in an unpleasant mood. Adam was leaving and taking the *Newport Wind* with him, which meant that Lucien still had a lot of work to do before the schooner returned. And he had no more than two weeks in which to accomplish it. Two weeks to get the evidence against André Fourier, Gaspar, and Wilkinson. Two weeks and then they would leave New Orleans. "That damn trial," he cursed. He and Samantha couldn't possibly settle their differences in the midst of all this intrigue. When, if ever, would that happen?

Lucien settled himself in his dark Moroccan leather armchair. Funny, he thought, no matter how bad things were between them, he could not consider leaving without his wife. Adam and Roger were convinced he was in love with her.

Me? he mused. In love with that coquette? I never have a moment's peace with Samantha. She is unpredictable, beautiful, stubborn, and so passionate. His body warmed at the memory of her body against his.

"Oh, Samantha, damn you, what are you doing to me?" he asked aloud. "I don't want you in my blood, do you hear? I don't want to spend half my time wondering where you are and who you are with." Picking up a glass paperweight, Lucien angrily flung it across the room, ignoring the sound of the crash.

Stomping outdoors, Lucien barked a few last-minute orders to the crew loading the *Newport Wind*. At least he was able to attend to some business matters. This latest shipment of rice, sugar, and tobacco would bring an enormous profit since there was never any difficulty in finding prospective buyers.

Since he did not plan to go home until Samantha's "tea" was long over, Lucien knew he had time today to meet with Governor Claiborne. He sent a message to the governor, asking him if he would be Lucien's lunch guest, a request which was greeted by a positive reply within the hour.

Lucien was hoping that Claiborne would help him in gathering information. Certainly the governor was not very fond of General Wilkinson or Major Gaspar. However, he did seem to be on friendly terms with André Fourier. Elise had once noted that the governor often asked André for advice.

They met in one of the new restaurants, not far from the Vieux Carré. Claiborne was always punctual so Lucien made a point of getting there early. As Lucien guessed, the governor arrived promptly and inconspicuously.

"Governor, it was kind of you to meet me on such short notice." Lucien rose as he extended his hand.

"I must say, Fraser, you caused me quite a bit of concern when you first arrived in New Orleans. But now"—the governor settled in his chair—"I think I understand."

"Understand what, sir?"

The governor gave him a friendly smile. "While you were away I had to make a short trip to Washington— about the Burr affair, you know. I met with a number of your friends—Mr. Madison in particular—and he explained your 'assignment.' Personally, I am not convinced that Mr. Burr was involved in treasonous activities. But"—he pounded his fist on the table—"I cannot say the same thing about Major Gaspar, General Wilkinson, or some other distinguished gentlemen of this town."

Visibly relaxed now that there was no need for artifice with the governor, Lucien asked the question that was plaguing him. "When you refer to certain respectable gentlemen, do you mean André Fourier?"

"Why, yes. You see, Mr. Fraser, I believe that Fourier and a few of his associates, including Wilkinson, concocted this scheme, somehow got Mr. Burr involved, then when they saw how unprofitable the scheme was, well . . . you know the rest."

"Governor, I need proof. I know Major Gaspar is involved—perhaps more deeply than the others—but I need proof that these men are being paid by the Spanish or any other government to instigate trouble here in New Orleans. Can you help me?"

"Most people are equally suspicious, sir, but getting the evidence you need is next to impossible. These men have been involved in this for quite a few years. They have not been sloppy before, so why now?"

Lucien was sure the governor was overlooking some fact—however trivial it seemed to him. "Look, I don't have much time. Tell me who their associates are, where they meet, where their offices are, and who can discreetly cooperate with me."

What Lucien was not ready to reveal to Governor Claiborne was his alternate plan. Although Lucien would be publicly censured by Madison if caught, he had to get into André's personal files. And Lucien knew exactly where they were located. Of course if André caught him, Lucien would be shot. But he was ready to take the chance, and Samantha would have to help him. The governor talked on while Lucien half listened, planning his next move. Samantha was going to give a dinner party. They would invite the Fouriers, Turreau, and Governor Claiborne and General Wilkinson.

"Look, Governor," he interrupted, "would you be

willing to come to a party my wife and I are hosting next Saturday?"

"Yes, I think so." He looked as perplexed as he sounded. Suddenly he brightened. "Fraser, if you are up to anything that is the least bit, uh, shall we say out of the ordinary, please do not tell me until it is over."

"Absolutely," he grinned. "If, in the meantime, you should come across any useful information, you know where to find me."

For the rest of the afternoon Lucien wondered about how much he should tell Samantha. She was so angry with him, he doubted she would willingly cooperate. However, if he did not tell her of his plans, she could unknowingly walk into a trap. No matter what was wrong between them, Lucien knew that Samantha wanted him to finish this assignment so they could leave New Orleans. Besides, her own sense of fair play and justice would militate against her obstinacy. Getting her to listen to him, however, would be another problem.

She was not at home when he returned later that evening. Harriet explained that at the last minute Samantha had decided to attend a charity ball sponsored by a local women's group. *I wonder if Elise had something to do with this?* he thought grimly.

"Oh, Mr. Fraser, Samantha said you might be interested in a letter your mother sent. It arrived this morning, after you left," Harriet informed him.

He knew his mother was well and back at Kingscote. What could Samantha possibly think was so interesting? As he walked up the stairs to the bedroom, he scanned the contents and burst out laughing.

"That minx," he smiled. Did Samantha really think he would be heartbroken upon learning of Caroline Prescott's marriage? To a New York banker, no less. Well, at least Caroline would not be interfering in their lives once they got back to Kingscote.

At the thought of Kingscote, Lucien felt a pang of homesickness. He missed his home, Newport, and his shipping business. Feeling weary, he sat on the edge of the bed and thought of his future. Would Samantha stay with him? Or would she leave with Turreau or go back to Thornton Hill? Lucien did not think he could let her go; she was a part of him now. He would gladly give up anything she asked, if only she could tell him she loved him, needed him—the way he needed and wanted her. "Do you love her?" Adam had kept asking him. "Why are you so afraid to admit it? Do not wait until it is too late, Lucien." Those were Adam's parting words today. Why can't I say it? he asked himself.

Suddenly a more immediate issue entered his thoughts. Samantha had not left alone this evening. She must have had an escort.

"Mrs. Wells!" he shouted as he ran down the steps. "Harriet, where are you?"

"Here, Mr. Fraser. Is something wrong?"

"Yes, I mean no. Tell me who escorted Mrs. Fraser tonight."

"It was Mr. Turreau."

Of course, Lucien had already known the answer. "Where is this charity ball?"

She told him, and within the hour Lucien was on his

way. What a pleasant surprise my wife will have, he smiled to himself.

It was not too difficult to locate Samantha, even in a crowded room. Lucien looked for a circle of men and knew his wife was in the middle. As he purposefully strode across the room nodding his greetings to some people, Lucien could hear her soft, infectious laughter—and Turreau's voice. The man's a leech, he decided.

"Oh, come now, Stèfan. I did not say that to the emperor." He heard her laugh again. "These gentlemen will think I am so bold."

They are all charmed by now, Lucien thought. The combination of her beauty and coquetry is enough to make the most devout free man her slave . . . including me.

"Gentlemen." He pushed his way through the little group. "I thank you for taking such good care of my wife until I arrived. I hope my lateness did not inconvenience any of you." He smiled broadly, but Samantha knew that it was a false smile, that underneath he was angry, perhaps jealous, as she secretly hoped.

"Your wife, monsieur," said a young, foppish-looking gentleman, "is the most charming woman here."

"In all of New Orleans," piped another.

Samantha sat on a satin settee near the French windows. Only a small, humid breeze blew through them, barely flickering the many candles in the room. Lucien's sailing experience led him to believe that a

390

storm was approaching. He studied his wife who was holding a beautifully carved Chinese fan—one of his Christmas gifts to her, he realized—and gently caressed it across her lovely face. The repaired diamond bracelet moved with her wrist. Her green eyes shone brightly over the white fan. Her flushed face and the almost sheer, red-gold dress she was wearing were practically the exact shade of her hair. A confection of curls framed her head, giving her a peaceful, angelic look, but those eyes were flashing surprise and anger.

"Hello, my love. I hope you are not angry with your tardy husband." His hand reached out for hers, causing her immediate annoyance. Lucien turned toward Stèfan. "It seems, Turreau, I again must thank you for bringing my wife and keeping her company until I arrived."

Stèfan bowed and replied, "We cannot always depend on your arrival. It is indeed a pleasure to be of service to the lovely Samantha."

"I believe, Turreau, that in the future your cooperation will not be required."

"We shall see," Stèfan responded, his intentions somewhat obvious.

It was ridiculous continuing these barely concealed barbs in front of other people. Lucien calmly turned back to his wife, whose face registered mild shock at the underlying threats Lucien and Stèfan passed to one another.

"My love, I did not realize the party was starting so early. My business made me neglect quite a few things today." Staring into her emerald green eyes, he thought he saw a flicker of what? . . . passion, or love? No, he dismissed it, for as soon as he turned away, that angry look replaced the mysterious one.

"How can you act so . . . so . . ." she sputtered, unable to finish.

"Samantha, love, not in front of your friends." He whispered so low that only she could hear. "But I haven't greeted you properly, love, have I?" Warm lips lightly touched hers. But it was enough to remind the men near them to whom she was married.

Taking her by the elbow, Lucien led her onto the dance floor where a lively waltz began. Before she could bid Stèfan adieu, Samantha's red-gold silk dress swirled around her slender body.

"To borrow a phrase from one of your admirers, 'You are the most beautiful woman in New Orleans, *Mrs.* Fraser.' I emphasize the word *Mrs.* lest you forget, my love." Mockery and admiration made his voice appear husky.

"I am not the one who forgets, dear husband. By the way, I am sorry to hear about Caroline Prescott's marriage. She should have informed you."

"Thank you for the kind sentiments. Your concern is most touching," he replied flatly. For a man who had even less sleep than she, Lucien radiated vitality and a sensuality most women could not ignore. Lucien appeared oblivious to the looks of admiration the women gave him as they twirled around the dance floor. Before she could say another word, he whisked her outside onto the jasmine-scented terrace.

"Lucien," she feebly protested. "Please! Stèfan will be looking for us." She could not have said anything more antagonizing.

"I don't give a damn if the President and my mother are looking for us! Samantha, I want you." It was a statement and a command. With little effort, Lucien pulled his wife into his hard embrace and scorched her mouth with his. Was it the humid, hot, night air or Lucien's proximity that made her weaken, her body flowing into his like molten lava? Whenever he touched her like this, Samantha lost all ability to remain unemotional.

"Not again," she moaned. As his mouth nibbled her ear, his hand caressed her face then lowered to her inviting breasts which spilled over the high-waisted gown.

"I hope you are enjoying yourself this evening, my love."

Samantha was only partially attentive to his words. Her thoughts were filled with the passion she had known with him before.

"Hmm."

"We won't have many more New Orleans nights," his deep voice hummed in her ears. "So I hope you won't mind making our farewell dinner party next Saturday. We do owe a few invitations, sweetheart."

"Yes." She swayed. All of a sudden his words cut through her rising desire and she jerked away.

"What are you talking about? And how dare you use me like . . . like . . . a servant!"

It pained her to know he had not responded to her; not the way she had succumbed to him. No, never that way, she realized.

Was she angry because her pride had been slightly bruised? he wondered. The moonlight highlighted her flushed face. So tempting, he told himself, and so vulnerable.

"Samantha, do you want to help me or not?"

Lucien's voice was harsher than he had meant it to be. But one look at her was enough to distract him from his plan and make him want to take her home to bed.

"Oh, I don't know." Automatically her hands smoothed the dress then her stray curls. She needed the time to regain control of herself. Exhaling a long breath, she said in a much calmer and resigned tone, "What do you want me to do? What does any of this have to do with a dinner we are making?"

He had to move away from her to think clearly. Pretending to be absorbed in finding a light for his cheroot, Lucien leaned against the white balustrade.

"I am running out of time. We are expected to leave New Orleans any time now." The light from the cheroot outlined the profile of his hardened jawline and nose. "The defense attorneys for Aaron Burr have probably sent someone to call on you as a witness. I know"—he noticed she was about to interrupt—"you want to testify. But if I am going to get you to Richmond in time, I have to get the information for which I came."

"And what is that?" Samantha asked, stepping into the moonlight.

"I want to prove their treachery," he quickly responded. "Wilkinson, Gaspar, Fourier, all of them."

Of course, she thought. Wouldn't it be wonderful if André Fourier were arrested. Poor Elise would need someone to comfort her.

Not more than twenty minutes after they returned to the ballroom, Samantha couldn't help but notice Lucien dancing with Elise Fourier. Seeing their heads so close in an intimate conversation as if they were the only couple in the room made Samantha's heart bleed

394

nce again. A lot of grief could have been spared if she ad been privy to the discussion, but when she saw ucien smile at Elise and lovingly pat her arm, Samantha knew her emotions could not stand the train. Frantically, she searched for Stèfan. She needed is comfort now more than at any other time before. If e wanted her to leave with him tonight, she would, nd to hell with Lucien's schemes.

As soon as she reached Stèfan, dinner was announced. Since there were so many guests, the hostess uggested that dinner would be served as a buffet. Tureens of gumbo, cold dishes of shrimp, lobster, oysters, and hot platters of ham, turkey, and all kinds f meat, adorned the long tables at the end of the dining all.

Seeing her distress, Stèfan volunteered to get Samantha a plate of food and a cold drink while she vaited for him. They found a private spot—a window eat large enough for two—toward the rear of the allroom. Knowing she could observe others before hey could see her, Samantha calmly looked about for ucien and found him occupied with Governor Claiborne and, of course, Elise. He did not bother to ee if I was still here, she thought miserably. A small igh escaped her lips. She was so unhappy. This had een her permanent state since she had married Lucien, he told herself. Eyes closing to hide the heartbreak and ears forming, Samantha was unaware that she was not alone. Sensing a shadowy figure before her, Samantha quickly opened her eyes and gasped.

"Good evening, Mrs. Fraser." His silver eyes flashed at her. "If you are waiting for your husband, I think he s occupied elsewhere." Major Gaspar moved directly in front of her, blocking her view of the room. "It would be a pleasure indeed, Samantha, if I could get you some food and join you."

"Thank you, but no, Major Gaspar." She turned her clammy hands nervously. "I already have a dinner companion. Another time, perhaps?" She smiled deceptively at his cold, expressionless face as she tried to remind herself that there was no reason to fear this man. After all, didn't she and Lucien have enough proof against him?

"Do you find me so far beneath you, Samantha, that you put me off with only a pretty smile? Oh no, my dear." Henri Gaspar leaned down to her. He was too close, but Samantha refused to show her fear. "I am well aware of your husband's activities. He does leave you alone too much." Gaspar picked up one of her stray curls, bringing it to his face. "A woman like you needs to be pampered, to have constant companionship, to have a real lover." His voice was controlled, but Samantha sensed the underlying passion and cruelty.

"That is none of your concern, Major," she snapped, angered at the liberties he was taking.

"But it is, my dear. You see, you will be mine." Her body chilled at his outrageous vow. "I know your husband thinks he has evidence to have me arrested"—his hand returned to the curl, then rested on her bare arm—"but he will be dead long before he has a chance to prove anything, my dear. And you"—his eyes murderously glinted—"will be a lonely, grieving widow who will need a man to protect her." He applied some modest pressure to her arm, causing Samantha to groan. "I assure you, I will have you in my bed within the month."

"How dare you!" she snarled, raising her hand to strike him as hard as she could. She almost connected, but Gaspar's reflexes were much quicker than hers. Grabbing her hand, he laughingly said, "That's what I like about you, Samantha—your spirit. And *I* will be the one to break it."

"I would kill myself first, Major. Anything would be better than submitting to you." Her eyes searched for and thankfully found Stèfan coming toward them.

"We will have plenty of time to discuss this, Mrs. Fraser, after your husband's timely demise."

"Lucien will kill you first, Major. But"—she forced a laugh—"I would rather see you on trial and convicted of treason."

"We shall see, my dear." He bowed stiffly. The candles' glow from the ornate crystal chandelier made his dark head look like blue-black lights. Reaching to kiss her hand, he renewed his vow. "You will be mine. Perhaps I will allow your fearless husband to watch me as I take you. Then"—he kissed her hand before he continued—"I will kill him . . . very slowly." He laughed—a deep, throaty sound. "Yes, I like that."

"Sam, I am sorry . . ." Stèfan did not finish, noticing she was not alone. "Pardon me, Major." He half-bowed somewhat disrespectfully.

"I was just leaving, Monsieur Turreau. I was keeping this beautiful lady company until you returned. Good evening."

"Sam, what's going on? Are you all right? You look pale. You are shivering, you know."

No, she had not known she was shivering. But one look at her trembling hands confirmed it. "Oh God," she moaned, leaning her head against the curtained window frame. "That man terrifies me, Stèfan."

"Tell me what happened." He sat beside her looking concerned. "But first, drink this champagne."

She told him everything Gaspar had said, pausing only to sip the drink. "Stèfan"—she looked up at him, her eyes bright with unshed tears—"what should I do? I cannot tell Lucien about the threat. Lucien will not wait for Gaspar to come looking for him. I know it, Stèfan. And I do not believe that either one of them would settle for a duel behind St. Anthony's Square." A lone tear traveled down her cheek. "I cannot let anything happen to Lucien. I thought I had lost him once, because of an explosion . . . ," she said absently as those memories flooded her mind, causing Samantha to wince from the remembered hours of terror. "I cannot let it happen."

If Stèfan had had any doubts about Samantha's feelings for her husband, he had none now. In her highly agitated state, Samantha was revealing those feelings that had been so carefully camouflaged. The woman was so in love with Lucien that Stèfan marveled at how she could think of anything else. Once more Stèfan had to come to grips with rejection and his futile pursuit of Samantha. She would never leave Lucien. But damn Lucien Fraser if he hurt her any more than he had already. Stèfan could at least show Samantha that he would always remain her loyal friend.

"Sam, try to forget this. I don't believe that you should tell Lucien or anyone else of Gaspar's words. It is just an idle threat, *ma chère*. You will be leaving New Orleans soon, and I cannot imagine Major Gaspar having the time to follow you." Stèfan patted her cold hand reassuringly.

"Perhaps you are right, Stèfan." Samantha looked across the room, settling her eyes on Lucien, who was lifting his glass in some toast. "I hope he never knows how much it cost to protect his unfaithful life."

A few moments before Samantha had located Lucien, he and Elise had been involved in a very serious conversation.

"Lucien dear, spare me the explanations. I think I know what you have been trying to say all evening. Frankly"—she fanned herself for added effect—"if you had not raised the subject of your marriage, I would have."

Her bold announcement almost caused Lucien to laugh with relief. All night he had been trying to tell Elise that their charade had to stop, but he could not find the right words. Elise did not deserve a callous rejection; in spite of her strange amorous tastes, she had many redeeming qualities.

"I did not realize I was so obvious." He laughed, and reaching into the pocket of his silver brocade waistcoat, Lucien pulled out another cheroot.

"I do not wish to discuss this issue again. It is beginning to bore me. I assume"—she smiled, a trifle sadly Lucien thought—"that your wife does not know the truth yet. You really are a cad, Lucien Fraser, if you don't tell her. Oh, by the way, André and I are probably taking a trip to Paris."

"You did not tell me that you were going to Paris." He was more than a little interested. If Lucien wanted to trap André, he would have to work fast.

"Oh," she giggled, "are you jealous? We are going to Paris because André says we must. He has some family to see and I am sure some business to conduct with the emperor."

So, Lucien thought, if André were ready to leave for France, he had nearly completed his assignments in New Orleans. Perhaps André was not working solely on his private interests but was under Napoleon's orders. The proof against Wilkinson and Gaspar would undoubtedly emerge from this discovery. The sooner he could view André's papers, the happier he would be.

"How often does André receive letters from Paris?"

"Lucien, I know what you are looking for." Elise playfully touched his sleeve. "And," she saucily added, "this is my farewell gift to you. About once a month André receives a few letters from various 'members of the family.' But I do not know why you are so fascinated with French politics."

"Another hobby of mine," he replied drily. "Tell me, Elise, when do you leave?"

"Oh, probably not for a couple of months. *Mon Dieu*, Lucien, it will take me that long to pack." She chuckled. Lifting her champagne glass, she suggested, "Lucien, let's toast *l'amour*. You must be magnificent. It will take me a long time to find anyone like you." Elise would not let Lucien know how difficult it was for her to remain cheerful. But no man had ever done to her what this handsome rogue had. And yet, she could only wish for his happiness. Better to reach a stalemate with Lucien, she felt, and at least salvage her pride—and reputation.

"To future success, Elise." He smiled warmly at her,

totally unaware that Samantha could see this touching scene.

Elise noticed Samantha's cold glare on the other side of the room. "Lucien, I fear you will have much to make amends for with Samantha. Tomorrow, I shall curse myself for drinking so much champagne, but honestly, my dear man, you two are congruent parts. Do not let anything stand in the way of making your marriage successful. I would have given so much to have a love like yours." Her tone became wistful.

"The last thing I need now is sage advice from you. Let's dance for the last time, my dear."

Chapter Twenty-Eight

What a strange week it has been, marveled Samantha, as she made the final preparations for tonight's dinner party.

First of all, Lucien could not have been more charming and attentive to her needs. Keeping her company most of the week, helping her with the dinner plans, staying home in the evenings for several quiet dinners, were all actions so uncharacteristic of him. They had even dared to approach a topic that neither of them had had the courage to discuss before: the future. It had started so matter-of-factly that neither of them realized what they were doing until the conversation was almost over.

"Samantha, love, since that fellow representing Burr's defense handed you the request today, we should make arrangements for our departure." He leaned back in the Sheraton-designed armchair with a snifter of brandy in his hand. His white shirt was unbuttoned to the middle of his chest, and he was wearing a pair of dark brown buckskin breeches.

Neither of them had bothered to dress formally for their dinners; Samantha believed it was compatible with their intimacy.

"The letter from Mr. Burr's attorney, John Wickham, asked that I be at the trial before the end of this month. Today is the 15th of July, so we don't have much time."

"The *Newport Wind* should be back in port by the end of next week. Let's plan on leaving then. Is that all right with you, green eyes?"

Not only was he asking for her opinion, but he sounded so affectionate.

"I can be ready, Lucien." She was afraid to tamper with the amiability they were sharing. "Are you unhappy to leave?" What she wanted to ask was if he were sad about leaving Elise and would he be coming back for her?

"Absolutely not!" he firmly answered. "New Orleans is a lovely town, but I would rather be here in the fall or winter months, not in this unbearable summer heat. And not under these political circumstances." Suddenly Lucien leaned forward, extending his hand to hers. "You know my love, we have not had a honeymoon. Do you want to come back to New Orleans?" There was amusement in his azure eyes.

"Heavens no!" she exclaimed. "Anywhere but here for a honeymoon. Unless"—she lowered her eyes—"you have other reasons for coming back."

"There is no reason for me to return, if you are referring to certain former acquaintances. It is finished, Samantha." It was all he would say, not revealing the whole truth.

Relief swept over her, but Samantha dared not show it or ask him to elaborate on his remark. The fact that Lucien had bothered to mention the end of his affair with Elise was a small victory she could relish. Looking up from her dinner plate, she stole a look at his face. He looked as if a heavy curtain suddenly had dropped before his eyes, preventing any emotion from showing.

"What do you think it's like in Washington and in Richmond?" she asked, changing the subject.

"We shall soon see. I hope we can use Harold's house again in Washington. I have some business to attend to there, and then we can go to Richmond."

"How long will that take?" Samantha really didn't care, but she was so happy to discuss a neutral topic with him that she asked several questions.

"It's not more than an overnight trip, if one rides all day. But"—his eyes took in her serene face—"we need not rush. Two nights will be fine. And once we get to Richmond, we should not have to stay longer than another two nights."

"I hope not. I am anxious to get away from this whole ugly imbroglio." She wanted to add "and go home with you," but she refrained from doing so!

"I hear Richmond is like a side show. People arrive daily to see the trial. If they can't get in, they are happy to gawk at the witnesses who come and go. Burr seems to be taking all of this in stride. He is amused by this attention he is attracting.

"Most people simply want to hear the great orators, most notably Chief Justice John Marshall. I am afraid, Samantha, that the President is displeased for more than one reason."

"Oh, am I one of them?" It saddened her to think Mr. Jefferson would be angry with her.

"I am almost sure of it. But"—he grinned broadly—"Mr. Madison would not consider saying something like that to me, knowing how quickly I would rise to defend my wife against *anyone*."

"You are making fun of me again."

Reaching over to touch her hand, he said softly, "I mean every word of it."

A servant came in at that moment. The tenderness had come and gone like a beam of sunlight through the clouds. But while it was there it had shed such a pleasant light.

"Come, my love, let's go to the library to continue our chat." Helping her to rise, he added, "Perhaps I shall let you beat me in a game of chess tonight."

"I win fairly, dear. You simply hate to admit you might be bested. You take the pleasure out of winning, you know."

"Do I?" Lucien said absently and went back to discussing the trial. "Did you know that women are not allowed in the courtroom? That you, even as a witness, will cause a minor sensation? We shall be the subject of gossip in both Richmond and Washington for weeks after your appearance." He led her out of the room, his arm securely wrapped about her waist. "While we are safely reinstated in our home back at Kingscote, the gossip mongers will still be regaling the townspeople with stories of the mysterious and lovely Samantha Fraser."

How could Samantha take issue with his light teasing, especially after he had told her he was taking her home? "Yes, my love, I quite agree. Of course no mention will be made of the darkly handsome Mr. Fraser—who looks more like a pirate than a gentleman—and his involvements in this intrigue."

"On second thought, my sweet, I suddenly feel quite

tired." Lucien turned to lead her toward the staircase. "I think we should go to bed." His hand moved up her waist to the soft, rounded swell of her breast, and all Samantha could do was nod her assent.

Once or twice, Samantha had felt compelled to tell Lucien how much she loved him and that their marriage could be wonderful if he could love her—even if he loved her only a little. When she had begun to speak, she imagined that he was trying to pry the words from her. His deep blue eyes had seemed strangely innocent as he whispered, "Are you holding something back from me, love?"

It had been impossible to give her heart permission to be honest. When they were together in their bedroom with no outside influences, when they lay naked in each other's arms, and when Lucien looked at her as if she were the only woman in the world, Samantha was ready to trust him. But the memories of the past did not quickly fade. It had been the same just the night before—their next-to-last night in New Orleans—and the passion they had shared after closing their bedroom door to the world had brought them no closer to revealing their love for each other.

Settling herself in the large copper tub, Samantha leaned her head against the high back, inhaling the fragrance of the warm, lavender-scented bath water. Mentally, she checked off the details for tonight and calculated how many extra trunks she would need to pack for their departure. She had so many new clothes for herself, gifts for everyone at Thornton Hill and at Kingscote, and a few new pieces of furniture for their bedroom. Samantha hadn't thought about buying them, but one afternoon she and Harriet had found a small shop with the most beautifully carved lounge chairs upholstered in a rich, rose-brocaded satin, a light cherry wood dressing table, and matching highboy dressers. Reluctant to tell Lucien—fearing he would tell her that she was not returning to Kingscote with him—Samantha talked the kindly shopowner into holding the pieces until the *Newport Wind* was ready to sail. Smiling to herself, Samantha wondered how Lucien would react to the extra weight in the schooner's hold. She doubted she could convince Roger to place the items aboard surreptitiously.

"What are you smiling at, wench?" His amused voice startled her.

"Don't you ever knock? Or do you enjoy barging in on ladies while they bathe?" Her stern tone was tinged with laughter.

"I only barge in on coppery-haired, sharp-tongued, enchanting wives," Lucien said, still dressed in his pirate's outfit. Removing the white frilled shirt, he stepped closer to the tub, stuck his hand in the water, and grabbed the wash cloth.

"Need some help, love?" His dark head lowered to nibble her ear lobe. "Here, let me rub your back."

"Lucien, do you want to be downstairs when our guests arrive? Stop that," she scolded. "You're tickling me." Dissolving into loud giggles, she tried to stop his hands from tickling her sides. She reached for his neck and playfully tugged, harder than she realized. With a loud guffaw and a louder splash, he ended up in the tub with her.

Quickly divesting himself of his breeches, he sat back

in the tub lightly kissing her face and said with a smile, "I wonder if our guests will think your husband is turning into a lavender-scented fop."

Reaching for the soap, Samantha looked directly into his dark blue eyes and smiled slyly, "May I?"

"Of course, my sweet." Although all of him could not possibly fit into the tub, Lucien lowered his body, letting his long, muscular legs hang over the opposite end of the tub.

Beginning at his shoulders, Samantha slowly rubbed her soapy hands along the breadth of his upper torso, watching his black, curly chest hairs turn white with suds. Continuing the motion, she directed her hands lower to his stomach then around his waist, and just when he expected her to go much lower, she raised her hands out of the water to rub his neck, gently massaging the stiff muscles.

"Ah, it feels so good."

"Would you prefer a back rub?"

"Not now, sweetheart. Continue your exploration."

And she did, moving her hands and the lavender soap up and down his body.

When she finally lowered her hands into the water, she did not need any guidance. Lucien did not know which he was enjoying more—what she was doing with her hands or the sensual look on her lovely face. Her mouth parted slightly, her tongue occasionally wetting her dry lips. And there was a slight widening of her leaf-green eyes which darkened with desire and wonder as she felt him hardening. The heat caused tiny droplets of perspiration to form along her high brow, curling the tendrils of coppery locks surrounding her face. This woman . . . his woman . . . abandoning all inhibitions because she wanted him. He reveled in the knowledge of what her hands could do to him. She was all passion and she was his. A low groan escaped his lips.

"I cannot wait any longer." Within seconds Lucien stood up, lifted her water-slicked body into his arms, and lowered her onto the Turkish rug.

"Samantha, I can never get enough of you."

Positioning himself above her, Lucien cupped her face in his hands. "You are so beautiful, my love." His voice was husky with desire. His mouth found hers, and before Lucien entered her waiting body he kissed her with such a curious combination of tenderness and passion that Samantha almost believed it was love.

It was a close call, but they made it downstairs in time for the arrival of their first guests. After their quick yet sensuous lovemaking, Lucien had insisted on helping her dress. However, after a few tries at the delicate pearly buttons on the back of her sapphire blue dress, he cursed without restraint.

"Lucien, dear. You may be adept at a lot of things, but helping ladies dress is not one of them." Her eyes glowed with satisfaction as she turned to look at his face which feigned disappointment and inadequacy.

"I'll do this if we have to stay here all night," he snapped. "Besides"—his face softened into a boyish smile—"I am better at helping ladies undress."

"Oh, you rogue!" She stamped her foot in mock anger.

The guests—a small group of twelve—all knew each other, so conversation was easy. General Wilkinson, neatly dressed in his army uniform, was as charming as usual. Looking at this seemingly friendly group, it was difficult to believe that such mystery lay just beneath their gay façade.

"We will miss you, cousin," Armand Bonnard said. "I hope you both come back to New Orleans again."

"Perhaps," she replied noncommittally. "But come, let us enjoy our last evening together. Shall we go in to dinner now?"

Gracefully, she led her cousin into the dining room while Lucien escorted Elise Fourier. Strange, Samantha thought upon seeing them together, that she no longer felt any jealousy or animosity toward Elise. Samantha knew Lucien had told her the truth about the end of his liaison. Earlier that evening, when the two women had been alone, Elise touched Samantha's arm and said, "I wish you good fortune . . . together, Samantha. I mean it. I am sorry if I caused you any trouble." Her voice was sincere.

"Why, thank you, Elise." She was nonplussed.

"André and I are leaving for Paris in a few weeks. You won't mind if I visit your friend Stèfan, will you?"

"No." Samantha laughed. "Stèfan can certainly take care of himself."

"Your husband loves you" was the last remark Elise made before Governor Claiborne claimed her attention.

Almost immediately after the soup was served, Harriet Wells interrupted Lucien's dinner with an urgent message.

Samantha could not look up from her wine glass for fear of showing the concern in her eyes. She had known

411

this was going to happen. She just did not know when Lucien had planned the emergency.

"I am so sorry, my friends," he announced, "but I must go to my office. There is trouble with one of my ships. I hope it's not the *Newport Wind*, love." He patted Samantha's shoulder reassuringly. "Roger is supposed to be bringing the schooner in tomorrow." No one noticed the light squeeze he gave her before he bent to kiss her cheek. "I'll be back as soon as the problem is settled. Governor"—Lucien turned to a suspicious-looking Claiborne—"would you act as host until I return?"

Disguising her anxiety took extraordinary acting ability which Samantha had not known she possessed. Silently she prayed for Lucien's safe return before the end of the party.

Since Lucien had experience stealthily entering and leaving the Fouriers' house, his only concern was prying open the lock of Fourier's desk in order to find the evidence he sought. The room was dark; only a single candle served as his guide. Muffling the curses and ignoring the beads of perspiration forming on his brow, Lucien persisted with the uncooperative lock. There was no way of knowing how much time had elapsed. Five, ten, or twenty minutes? Finally, he heard a click and the drawer opened. The papers were neatly piled in three rows. What he wanted was not among them.

Yet Lucien surmised that the telling evidence was in this room. He pulled the drawer out. And then he saw a small package which had been cleverly concealed beneath the drawer. There were a few sheets of paper, all written in French. Quickly reading the contents, he smiled with satisfaction. Withdrawing the incriminating document, Lucien folded it and put it in his pocket while neatly placing the others back in the exact location they had been before; then he quietly departed.

Mr. Madison would truly covet this. Lucien knew Madison had suspected all along that the esteemed Emperor Napoleon was not quite content to relinquish all of the Territory of Louisiana. The question of statehood had become an increasingly heated issue—not just in New Orleans—but all over the Southwest. If the Territory of Louisiana decided not to join the Union, a new set of political machinations would begin. The Territory could become an independent nation—which was what Aaron Burr had been accused of inspiring; or the Spanish government could add the Territory to its Spanish empire. But Napoleon had the most to gain: a stronghold in the new world, freely chosen by people who would be loyal to the French Emperor.

Incredible, Lucien marveled. If André Fourier were arrested and tried for treason, how embarrassing it would be for Napoleon Bonaparte and his elaborate scheme.

Lucien was so pleased with himself that he failed to notice the man behind him as he turned up Poydras Street toward his home.

"Good evening, Mr. Fraser. Why aren't you home entertaining your guests?" It was a dark night, the moon hidden behind rainclouds. Lucien wondered how long Henri Gaspar had been following him.

Thankfully, Lucien was still dressed in his dark evening clothes, having discarded an earlier notion to disguise himself completely before entering the Fouriers' home.

"Major Gaspar." He slowly turned toward Gaspar, trying hard to conceal his hatred for the man. "Do you know everything that happens in New Orleans? Then you must know I had trouble this evening with some of the cargo for my ship. Or"—Lucien smiled coldly—"was that something you arranged?"

"Nonsense. You accuse me falsely . . . yet again. One does not continually make false accusations without facing some form of retaliation. Don't you agree?" Gaspar looked as if he were reaching for his pistol, but Lucien knew it was another bluff.

"I would invite you in for dessert, but I am afraid you would be most odd and unlucky, our thirteenth . . ."— he flicked an imaginary piece of lint off his dark blue jacket—"guest." He tried not to choke on the last word. Before Lucien reached the wrought iron gate in front of the house, he said in a menacing voice, "I will see you in Richmond."

Gaspar, left alone outside the house, once again swore to kill Lucien Fraser, no matter what it took. Unfortunately, Lucien did not hear his muffled threat or the ugly, bone-chilling laughter that filled the night air.

Relief and joy brightened Samantha's face as soon as Lucien walked into the library. When the dinner had ended, Samantha and Governor Claiborne had decided to forego the usual custom of splitting into two groups—the men to the library to smoke and drink brandy while the ladies retreated to the upstairs parlor—and all adjourned to the library. Moreover, the responsibility for conversation would not be Samantha's alone—not with Stèfan and William Claiborne by her side. The governor knew about Lucien's activities, Samantha realized. Perhaps Stèfan suspected something too, but certainly Lucien would not have confided in Stèfan.

There seemed to be a tacit understanding between Samantha and Stèfan not to mention her marriage or her marital problems. Lighthearted discussion and jokes about Samantha leaving Lucien for Stèfan had ceased the night of the charity ball. Stèfan knew a lost cause when he saw one and he did not feel the need to put either Samantha or himself through another painful discussion. Maybe he would have had a chance if Samantha had never met Lucien. But that was wishful thinking.

Stèfan planned his departure, hoping he might someday see Samantha again but knowing, however, that she would stay with her husband. Stèfan's roving eye had delighted in visually ravishing the luscious Elise Fourier more than once during the evening. Her mouth seemed to part each time Stèfan smiled at her. She had said they would be in Paris soon, and if her cues were any indication, he would have her—under his own roof or wherever else he decided. What a curious sense of humor we French have, Stèfan mused.

Sensing Samantha's agitation, Stèfan set aside his thoughts of future seduction and stayed by her side after dinner. General Wilkinson was asking many questions about Lucien's relationship with President Jefferson. Of course she parried his questions well, but

Stèfan knew these political matters were disorienting for her.

"Sam, did I tell you about your old friend, David Parker? Oh"—Stèfan looked shame-faced and his voice slurred—"I apologize for the interruption, General."

"No need, sir. I see Armand trying to determine whose portrait that is." His blue eyes twinkled. "Don't worry about your husband, dear. I am sure the problem has been rectified." Wilkinson spoke to her like a dear old uncle. "By the way"—he turned back to them—"I believe we shall see each other again in Richmond. I am going to testify at the trial, too, you know."

"That man knows everything, Stèfan," she whispered. "He probably knows the dress I'll be wearing to the trial."

"Don't concern yourself about him, *ma petite*. You won't be here much longer."

"No, thank God." She absently looked out the window for the tenth time.

"He'll be back soon, Sam. Here"—he handed her a glass of sherry—"this should calm your nerves."

"You are so good to me." She smiled sweetly at him.

"Yes, yes, I know. Promise me one thing, Sam." Stèfan earnestly searched her beautiful face. "If you ever need a friend, you will remember me. Promise?"

"Yes, I promise."

The outside door slammed shut at that very moment and Samantha closed her eyes and silently thanked God that her worst fears had not been realized. Restraining herself from greeting him, she remained

416

stationary and commanded, "Just talk, Stèfan, about anything. I don't care."

"I did not finish telling you about David Parker. He sends his warmest regards. You know the last time I saw him, David was enamored with the lovely young daughter of a prominent minister. She has almost the same color hair as yours." He laughed.

"Stop teasing me," she ordered. "David was a good friend, nothing more. But give him my love." Stèfan talked on, but Samantha only half-listened, her eyes focusing on the door.

Finally, Lucien walked into the room, his eyes imploringly seeking hers. She looks so happy to see me, or is it her companion and the sherry making her look that way? he wondered jealously. Nevertheless, he made his way toward her and clasped her waist.

"Miss me, sweet?" He smiled engagingly.

"Yes," she breathed, loving his touch. Then in a louder voice she asked, "Is everything all right?"

"All is well." He looked into her bright eyes. "I am sorry it took a little longer than expected. One of the tobacco merchants had decided my offer was too low and wanted to renegotiate. He could not wait until morning. But it is settled now."

Why did Turreau always have to be by her side? he fumed. Well, he won't have many more opportunities for this.

"Lucien, Stèfan is going back to France the day after we leave. Do you remember David Parker?" She chattered nervously, wishing the night would end.

"Yes, of course—another one of your admirers," he curtly replied.

417

"Stèfan says that David may stay in France a little longer than he planned. At least until he gets permission to marry a young lady." Her voice sounded rather stilted.

Why would she want to tell me this? Am I supposed to know all her former beaus or lovers are safely out of the way? Is she interested in acquiring new ones? Or will she want only me?

"I am pleased to hear that, love. That leaves only your husband. Is that enough for you?"

"Yes," she replied, "more than enough."

"Good." Relieved but unconvinced, he bent to whisper in her ear. "Get rid of our guests," he ordered. "I am tired."

Finally, after what seemed like hours of conversation, their guests left. Samantha did not know how much longer she could have kept her charming little smile frozen in place when underneath she had been so eager to be alone with Lucien. Lucien had tried hard not to show how enervated he was. He drank enough brandy to make up for his early departure, but this only added to his fatigue.

As soon as the front door closed, they collapsed into each other's arms and slowly made their way upstairs.

"So"—she couldn't wait for him to begin—"what happened? Did it go well? Did you find what you were searching for? Can we leave this city?"

"Hold on, my love." He grinned. "One question at a time . . . and relax. Everything is fine." Closing the bedroom door behind them, he settled himself on the settee and told her exactly what had transpired. Samantha found an outlet for her tension in the furious brushing of her hair.

"Do you think André Fourier will discover the letter is missing?" She now had something new to fret over.

Lucien saw her nervously biting her lip and calmly replied, "There is nothing to worry about, Samantha. By the time André discovers that anything is amiss, we will be safely aboard the *Newport Wind*. Were any of our guests suspicious about my emergency?"

"Only Stèfan and Governor Claiborne. But Stèfan would never say anything."

"I hope you are correct about the loyalty of your former beau." His voice hardened.

"No more than I hope you are about your former acquaintances."

"I ran into Gaspar on my way home," he stated, changing the subject.

Her hand stopped in midair. Should she tell him now of Gaspar's threat? No, she would tell him once they were safely aboard the ship.

"I hate him, Lucien. Henri Gaspar is dangerous. I hope he hangs for his crimes." Thinking about Gaspar gave her goose bumps.

"He will be stopped. I swear."

"Promise me something, Lucien." She turned in her seat to face him directly, her voice rising with fear. "Do not ever be alone with that snake. There is no telling what he might do."

"Sweetheart"—he rose to touch the soft outline of her face—"I can assure you that I am not afraid of men like Major Gaspar. I can fight his way, too."

"Promise me," she insisted. He did not immediately respond. His dark eyes studied her graceful beauty, and, somewhere between the kisses which followed, Lucien gave her his promise.

419

His kisses were like live ashes swirling in the wind, igniting her skin with a burning, desperate desire to feel his passion all over.

As her arms lovingly wound around his neck, Lucien placed his arm under her knees, lifted her, and carried her to the bed. Her eyes, half-closed in anticipation of their lovemaking, never left his. Lucien slowly undid the tie of Samantha's dark purple satin wrapper and deliberately ran his hands over her belly, then lower until her breath came in shallow gasps. Hurriedly, he reached for the buttons of his breeches, eager to tear them off, but she stayed his hand.

"No, let me."

Samantha leaned onto her side, motioning for Lucien to stand in front of her. With agonizing slowness, Samantha undid each button of his breeches while running her free hand along his firm thighs. His groan spurred her to even greater daring. Opening his breeches, she found his engorged manhood eager for release. She lowered her head to where her hands firmly caressed him, kissed his length and took him into her mouth. Oh, how she wanted to give him the same kind of white-hot passion he had always given her.

Unable to resist her overtures, Lucien felt himself caught in a maelstrom of emotion over which he had no control. She guided him onto the bed and he mounted her, eager to share the growing affinity in their relationship. This marriage of convenience, which had used sex as a diversion, underwent a change so dramatic that their passion now became an outgrowth of their unspoken love.

When he entered her, they both felt a new, deeper

sensation—one that was surprisingly glorious and profound. They instinctively knew that the disagreements, which had separated them in the past could no longer sever their growing bond. And as they reached in unison the heights of rapture, they remained entwined in the warm glow of their love.

Chapter Twenty-Nine

Washington: Late Summer, 1807

Seeing the city of Washington come into view was one of the happier moments Samantha had experienced in the past few weeks.

The trip had been halcyonic. The crew was as happy as she to leave New Orleans for their first stop on their trip home. Roger brought letters from Robert Thornton describing the fabulous homecoming of his son and the latest events at Thornton Hill. Meredith and Adam wrote separate letters, each brimming with happiness and extreme delight at being reuinted. Unfortunately, Lucien had not understood what Meredith meant by the words, "Emotional separation is the great gulf between people that only a bridge of perseverance can overcome."

The only near disaster had been caused by the arrival of the furniture on the New Orleans dock. Samantha was already in their cabin when Lucien pounded on the door and with clenched teeth tried to inquire—in as calm a voice as he could muster considering his anger—about the heavy furniture Mrs. Fraser specifically had requested to be delivered that morning.

"Oh, that," she lamely responded. "You did say I could purchase a few things. I hope you do not mind," she added in a honeyed tone.

"Don't mind!" he thundered. "Do you have any idea how much that weighs? Do you?" He noticed the way her head lowered a bit as she mumbled a response. Immediately feeling contrite for screaming at her, he said in a much softer tone, "Well, I guess we can manage. It is a short trip." Still, she refused to look at him. Reaching for her arm, he asked, "How much did this cost us, Samantha?"

When she told him, it took a tremendous amount of willpower not to explode again.

"I hope, madam, that the profits from the sale of the cargo you almost displaced will cover the cost."

"I am sorry I did not check with you first. But Lucien"—she held her head higher in a defiant gesture—"you were not around to discuss these matters."

"Well, next time I insist on accompanying you." He tried to smile, but it was more of a grimace.

Unspoken understanding began to emerge and was the magic adhesive that held their marriage together. There were words about the future, their future . . . together; things they would do together, places they would go. And not once were either of them courageous enough to cross over the personal boundary where excessive pride, jealousy, and anger could be flung to the wind and replaced by a commitment based on love and trust.

Washington was unusually crowded this summer, probably because of the Aaron Burr trial and the unsettling political events abroad and at home, thought Samantha.

The federal city looked more like a mining town than the capital of the United States. The master plan for the new city was still in its early stages of development. The streets were so muddy that even the wooden planks used as sidewalks could not disguise the mess. Pennsylvania Avenue looked more like a country road than the most important avenue in the capital, yet many people were brave enough to start building homes, knowing how important land would become once the new federal buildings were completed. A community was finally developing as families began settling in the federal city and the surrounding areas. Until the last few years most of the newly elected members of Congress had come to Washington alone, leaving their families at home, staying only as long as Congress was in session. It was too great a risk for wives and children to accompany the gentlemen, for the health and safety conditions of the city were repellent. Ironically, quite a few of these gentlemen were leaving beautiful, opulent homes to reside temporarily in an inn or as a guest in someone's house. The conditions of some of the inns were no better than the hold of a ship.

Georgetown was becoming more popular for the new residents. One could escape the noise, the activity caused by carpenters and stonemasons, and the filth, yet still be within thirty minutes of the Capitol building.

Lucien decided it would be more convenient to stay in Washington for the two nights. Having no idea of how often or when he could see Madison, he once again borrowed the same house he and Samantha had used on their wedding night. Its owner, Lucien's friend from school, was back at the family plantation in Mississippi for the summer. There never was a problem, for Lucien and Harold often shared and exchanged residences. The staff in the house on Maryland Street knew Lucien Fraser and always made him feel comfortable during his stays.

The last time they had been there Samantha had hardly noticed the house, its furnishings, or even the location. The quaint two-story house with sloping roof and dormer windows enchanted her. Walking into the upstairs bedroom brought a blush to her cheeks at the remembrances of their marriage night together. Could things have turned out better if they had begun their relationship differently—on any other level but as adversaries?

She walked over to the bed decorated with a golden damask coverlet and touched the fine material. Lost in her daydream, Samantha did not see Lucien who was quietly leaning against the doorframe watching her, instinctively knowing what she was thinking about—for the same thought had crossed his mind more than once today. As he remembered the circumstances of their marriage, how he had blamed her for trapping him, a wave of guilt and remorse washed over him. Whenever he thought of Samantha lately, he experienced queer twinges and pains as if his heart sporadically beat rapidly and then not at all.

"It is unfortunate, sweet, that we did not start out as the happily married couple." His voice sounded odd. There was a bit of sarcasm in it, but Samantha also thought he sounded wistful.

Without knowing what possessed her to do this, she said, "Do you think it is too late to try?" Her voice was barely audible.

Clearly taken off guard by her blunt question, Lucien was actually at a loss for the right words. He opened his arms for her, and as she eagerly settled into his loving embrace he was touched as never before. "I would love to try. More than anything. I want you with me, Samantha, but I know there is much you have to forgive me for. Or"—he chuckled—"to put it more appropriately, there is so much I have to apologize for."

She lifted her face to his. Silent crystal tears ran down her cheeks onto his hand. "Lucien, we have to talk. I know there is no time right now—I saw Roger come in with you—and I know we are expected at the Madisons' for dinner tonight. But there is so much I need to tell you, no matter how you feel about me . . . I mean us," she quickly corrected herself.

Lucien tenderly lifted her chin so he could kiss tear-filled eyes, her nose, and finally drink in the warmth of her lips.

"Let's leave early and settle ourselves in this room to talk all night and all day tomorrow, if necessary." His warm, loving smile was the most beautiful sight Samantha had seen in a long time.

"Agreed, green eyes?"

"Agreed."

But it was not meant to be.

Dinner was a most uncomfortable experience for the Frasers. It was a small party of eight people, including

President Jefferson. Neither Lucien nor Samantha had any idea how Thomas Jefferson would receive them. Officially, Lucien was still working for the Secretary of State and Jefferson. Lucien had submitted his letter of resignation earlier in the day, promising to follow through on the Southwest Conspiracy—he no longer thought of this as the Burr Conspiracy—but he would not take on new assignments. It was precisely because Lucien and a more determined Samantha believed Aaron Burr innocent in this conspiracy that Jefferson may have felt alienated from them. The Frasers believed the real treachery lay with Wilkinson, Gaspar, Fourier, and others in New Orleans. But Jefferson was adamant.

Dolley Madison, well known as Washington's best hostess, tried to avoid the sensitive topic. However, Jefferson would not oblige.

"I tell you, Aaron Burr is guilty," he casually but firmly announced after the first course was served. "I read your report, Lucien, and I accept some of your evidence against this fellow Fourier and Major Gaspar, but I do not believe Wilkinson was behind all of their actions. It has to be Aaron Burr."

Samantha almost choked on her wine. "Please, this is preposterous! Lucien and I were there—we saw what General Wilkinson and his cohorts were doing. We heard enough from people who know Wilkinson. Didn't you speak to Governor Claiborne? Why can't you accept this information as fact or at least substantial?"

Her anger erased all proprieties from her bearing. She noticed the way Lucien glared at her with that look of admonition in his eyes.

"Samantha, dear, when General Wilkinson arrives and testifies, your theory will be set to rest. He has promised to bring along a very reliable witness who can support the general's claims," Jefferson said calmly, ignoring her outburst. "I also have in my possession a very incriminating letter in Burr's hand," he emphasized, "which clearly spells out his treasonous plan."

Both Lucien and Samantha had never seen such an intractable Thomas Jefferson. In the past, he had given them the impression that he was a sensible, open, and easy-going man whose ideals and love for his country took precedence over everything else in his life.

"A man does not gather an army—as Burr did on Blennerhassett's Island—for the sheer pleasure of it. No, friends, this was not a casual hobby. Burr meant to undermine me and our government."

"Mr. Burr has some staunch supporters. You know Andrew Jackson is planning to testify on Burr's behalf." Lucien was trying hard to sound diplomatic but he was sorely tempted to throttle Samantha for arousing them.

"It does not mean anything. How can Jackson know what happened in New Orleans or on Blennerhassett's Island? I am telling you there is written evidence that Burr was planning treason, either with the Spanish or French."

"I'll tell you who is guilty of treason. It is Major Henri Gaspar and André Fourier. That's who." Samantha's voice etched her frustration. "Why don't you give Lucien a chance to demonstrate this?"

"Sweetheart, I will tell them all about it later. This is not suitable dinner conversation, now is it?"

Underneath the table Samantha felt Lucien's boot strike her ankle admonishingly. Calm now, she sweetly smiled at Lucien, placing her hand across the table to reach him. Firmly digging her nails into his hand, she replied, "You are absolutely right, dear." She turned to Jefferson. "Forgive me."

The tension was so great that the guests found surcease in the ample quantity of wine that was offered. The topic was not brought up again, but somehow the anger remained just beneath the surface. Words were so carefully chosen that pleasant conversation was not possible.

Samantha was ready to leave by ten o'clock but did not do anything until other guests said it was time for them to go home. Before she had a chance, however, Lucien came to her side and whispered, "Jefferson and Madison want to talk tonight, after everyone leaves. If I can get this over with, we are free to leave whenever you want to go to Richmond. And Samantha, after tonight I won't have to be a part of this government's intrigue. My job is finished."

She was as disappointed as he about not having this night to have their overdue talk. They walked away from the little group before she could tell him her innermost thoughts.

"I guess I understand. We've waited this long. Another day won't matter."

"I may not be back tonight, so don't wait up for me. But we will have tomorrow to be together."

Their parting kiss was the sweet reminder Samantha needed for the days ahead.

*   *   *

At least James Madison was convinced that André Fourier was spying for the French Government.

"Before the end of next week, Lucien, Monsieur Fourier will be on his way to Washington under armed guard. This letter you 'borrowed' should interest the French Ambassador."

"I wonder if Fourier realizes that something is missing." Lucien absentmindedly played with the stem of the wine glass and flicked the ashes from his cheroot. It was almost dawn and all he could think about was his wife sleeping alone in that large tester bed waiting for his return.

How could he miss her after only a few hours apart? Yet Lucien did. The need to feel her body and hear her voice was so great he did not think he could stay in this stuffy, smoke-filled room any longer. Rising from the chair, Lucien walked to the window to see the sky's colors change from dark shades of blue and purple to pale tones. In his mind he envisioned Samantha languorously rising from bed wearing a sheer night-gown, and he felt his blood stir. Little scenes captivated his imagination, like the time Samantha had sat next to four large travel bags overstuffed with clothes, waiting for Lucien to take her with him on their trek into the Spanish Territory. He smiled. She had been so primly dressed that day, Lucien could not help but laugh at her. Or the time she had pulled him into the stream at Thornton Hill, her infectious laughter making him forget he was angry at her for splashing him.

I don't believe this. The words that had previously made him anxious suddenly crystallized in his thoughts before they burst into consciousness.

"I love her." The words no longer frightened him.

"What did you say, Lucien?" asked Madison. "You seem so preoccupied."

He ran his fingers through his dark, wavy hair. "What . . . Oh, yes, sir." Then he broke into a long, loud laugh. "I'll be . . ."

"Lucien, what is wrong?" Madison was clearly concerned for Lucien's state of mind.

"Oh, I am perfectly all right, sir." He blithely stepped toward Madison, a wide grin on his face. "I just realized something I should have known months ago."

"May I ask what that is?"

"I love my wife. And you, Mr. Secretary of State, are the first to know it." Lucien clutched Madison's shoulders.

"Oh, no I am not. Nor am I blind to your wife's adoration of you."

"Do you really think so?"

Sometimes Lucien felt that she cared for him, maybe loved him somewhat. But then something would happen and he could almost see Samantha withdraw her affection.

"Well, I hope so. And I think it's time I told her so."

"Fine, son, fine. Now that we have settled that matter, can we complete the other issue?" he asked wryly.

Since Lucien was so eager to leave, the meeting progressed rapidly. Fourier was going to be questioned about his activities for the French Government, brought to Washington, and eventually tried for treason.

"Major Gaspar will be immediately relieved of his command. But," Madison continued, "Gaspar will have to face two trials; the first, a military court martial."

"How soon will that happen?" Lucien looked forward to Gaspar's dismissal. "Isn't General Wilkinson the highest commanding officer?"

"He won't be," Madison calmly replied. "The general is temporarily relieved of his duties so that he may come to Washington."

"Good. Perhaps Fourier believed he owed some allegiance to the French, but Gaspar"—Lucien's lip curled with distaste—"cares for no one but himself."

"Lucien, you have done an extremely fine job. Perhaps someday, after you tire of your sedate life in the shipping business and feel the need for a little adventure, you can be lured into public service again."

"With my wife, I doubt I will ever be bored. But"— he rose to shake Madison's hand—"thank you. Who knows? Maybe Samantha will decide I should return after she tires of me."

"Good luck. And don't worry about our President. He will expect you to visit Monticello as if nothing had ever happened," Madison prophesied.

As soon as Lucien walked into the house on Maryland Street, he felt his spirits soar. Samantha would be waiting or him, and he would sweep her into his arms before he told her all that had transpired.

Since it was still early morning, he knew Samantha would be in bed. He was hungry and felt as if he needed

433

both a bath and a shave but not until he saw her. Quickly he ran up the stairs and quietly entered the bedroom. She was not there.

Where the devil can she be at this hour? he wondered. Lucien dropped his jacket and cravat on the bed and ran back downstairs calling her name, searching the dining room, kitchen, and finally the library.

She was lying on the sofa, sound asleep, a leather-bound book on the floor beside her. She was still wearing her nightgown and peignoir. It seemed she had slept in this room all night. As always, long, red-gold curls were spread across her breast and hung over the side of the sofa. Walking softly toward her—he wasn't ready to wake her yet—Lucien took the opportunity to study her carefully. There was no doubt in his mind that Samantha was the most beautiful, sensuous, and loving woman he had ever known. And the most temperamental, too.

Bending on one knee, Lucien placed a feathery kiss on her forehead.

"Wake up, green eyes. You cannot spend the rest of the day asleep on this sofa. Anyway"—he smiled—"you snore!"

The emerald eyes came to sparkling life as her broad smile tugged at his heart.

"Have you been here all night?"

"No," she whispered, unable to find her voice. "I . . . I could not sleep," she stammered, and he loved her all the more for her shyness.

"Why?" His hand stroked her face. She shifted her body and the peignoir opened, revealing that pink

434

sheer nightgown he had imagined in his fantasy, exposing her firm breasts.

"I cannot sleep alone any more." She was still sleepy and could not even think about guarding her words.

"Will anyone do?"

"No."

"Turreau then?"

"No. You know I mean you," she snapped, becoming more irritable. He was surely mocking her. Lucien looked even more disheveled than she. His light blue silk shirt was open to the middle of his chest, exposing a curly black mat of hair, and his unshaven face gave him a sinister look. His eyes were half closed, a condition that Samantha associated with his drinking. But there was only a slight hint of alcohol on his breath. From the way his dark, wavy hair fell about his forehead, it looked as if he had continually run his hand through his hair. Yet he did not seem angry; in fact, from the way he was grinning, he looked as if something wonderful had happened.

"Lucien"—she struggled on one elbow to sit up—"are you feeling well?"

"Better than ever."

"Why are you acting so . . . strangely? Did your talk with Mr. Madison go well? Did Jefferson stay the night, too?"

He sat down next to her reclining body and rested his head against her chest. Automatically, Samantha's hand reached to play with the curling hair at the nape of his neck, a response he had come to expect.

"This is heavenly," he sighed. "To be finished with my assignment for Madison and secure in the arms of the woman I love."

There was no response, but he could hear the quickening of her heart. In fact, in the silence that followed, all he heard were her short breaths.

Finally she breathlessly asked, "What did you say, Lucien?"

He raised his head level with hers and said the words again, this time slower.

"I said, Samantha, I love you." There was no mockery to his tone. He looked serious, his eyes shining boldly.

It was hard to comprehend the words she had waited to hear for what seemed to be her whole life. Samantha had imagined the ways and circumstances in which Lucien would reveal his overwhelming love for her. But not like this, when she looked a frightful mess and her mind was clouded by sleep. They were not aboard the *Newport Wind*, or in their large bed at Kingscote, or anywhere she knew and felt at ease.

"Well, did you hear me? Here, I will say it again. I love you, Samantha Thornton Fraser." He did indeed seem earnest.

Her response was not what he had expected. Samantha threw her arms about his neck, half choking him, and burst into tears. Loud sobs escaped her and Lucien felt her tears staining his neck.

"Samantha, can't you respond by telling me that you love me? Do your tears mean you are sorry but you can't reciprocate?" He steeled himself for her rejection.

Sniffling, with tears streaming down her cheeks, she vigorously shook her head.

"I love you too, Lucien," she answered in a small voice. "I always have."

"That's all I ever wanted to hear."

Scooping her into his arms, Lucien kissed her in a reaffirmation of their words and carried her up to bed.

They could not see the shrouded figure clutching a silver riding quirt, who stood on Maryland Street watching the house and waiting.

Chapter Thirty

The rest of the morning passed in passionate moans, laughter, and promises. Still a bit wary of each other, they did not reveal all. But they both knew there would be plenty of time for revelations.

"Come on." Lucien playfully slapped her naked bottom. "Get dressed. I promised you a picnic lunch and a long ride. Let's go before I forget I made that promise in a moment of passion." He swung his long legs out of bed. "But first, I need a bath."

"And a shave," she teased and hugged him lovingly. "Oh, Lucien, I am so happy."

"I hope you feel that way later, after you have had a chance to reflect on our discussion."

And later, Samantha could not remember a time when she had enjoyed herself as much. It was as if all the shadows in her life had disappeared with Lucien's simple declaration. The nagging insecurities that had plagued her these last few months no longer existed. She felt beautiful and confident. Nothing could go wrong again.

They made plans to go directly to Kingscote after their appearance at the Aaron Burr trial. After a few months of getting their business affairs in order, Lucien promised to take her to Thornton Hill before they sailed to France for their long-delayed honeymoon.

When Lucien and Samantha came back from their lovely afternoon sojourn, there was a note from Roger waiting for them.

"It's not serious," he told her. "There seems to be a mix-up with the cargo orders. But if I leave now, I know I can quickly settle the problem and be back by dinner."

"I'll go with you."

"It isn't necessary. Why don't you pack our things so we can leave early tomorrow." Lucien smiled lovingly at her. "What's the matter, my love? Don't you trust me?"

"Of course I do. I just want to be with you. But . . . I suppose I can take a hint. I would rather take a bath and read a book then watch you admonish your crew," she chided. "Besides, I probably would not give the mean Captain Fraser a chance to settle his problems with dispatch, for I might order him to his cabin."

"What a siren you are, madam."

"Lucien, you can invite Roger to dinner. I don't mind sharing you for a little while."

By five o'clock Samantha had finished her chores and was dressed and ready for Lucien and Roger to return. The off-white India muslin dress edged with gold embroidery and the full skirt only hinted at the lovely body underneath. The short sleeves trimmed with tiny gold buttons were cool enough for this hot Washington climate, but the deep square neckline did not hide the tempting swell of her breasts. Imagining Lucien's response to her almost demure attire made her flush with desire.

There were only two servants working this evening. Samantha happily informed the others they could have the night off. The cook had prepared a very simple meal so there was nothing left for Samantha to do but wait. Taking the novel she had started the day before, she went to the library where she was sure to hear Lucien's return.

Barely fifteen minutes passed when Samantha heard a loud knocking at the door. How odd, she thought, that the sounds of a carriage or the closing of the gate were not heard. She was on her feet by the time one of the servants timidly knocked on the library door.

"Mrs. Fraser, there is a gentleman to see you. He would not give his full name," she nervously stammered, "but insisted I let him in."

A strange chill crept over her.

"Tell him I will not be receiving anyone until my husband and his friends return." She hoped the "visitor" could hear.

"That is too bad, Samantha. I was hoping your husband would not return at all. In fact, the message I sent should delay him."

She was too numb and afraid to respond. She saw his steely gray eyes examining her.

"Major Gaspar, you are not welcome here. So please get out before I call the rest of the staff to throw you out."

His low laugh exacerbated her fear. "Samantha, you cannot fool me. I have seen the servants leave. There are only three of you here now. The cook, I am afraid, will not be available tonight."

"What did you do to her?"

441

"Nothing too serious. Although she will have a terrible headache in the morning. And you"—he turned to the cringing servant, a girl no older than Samantha—"are going to join her."

Before either of the women could scream, Major Gaspar hit the frightened girl and dragged her unconscious body out of the room. Samantha watched in paralyzing fear.

"Now my dear, why don't you sit over there"—he motioned to a large wing chair—"while I sit close to the door and wait for your husband to arrive."

Determined not to show her terror, she defiantly walked to the window and sat on another chair.

"Do not make me use this weapon sooner than I intend to, my dear." The ominous click of his pistol echoed throughout the room.

"Listen to me, Major"—her mind desperately sought the right words—"if you leave now, before my husband returns, I will not mention this to anyone, I swear. And I will see to it that the servants stay quiet."

"So will I," he laughed. "So will I. You are going to be my property just as soon as I settle a little matter with your husband." As he slowly stepped toward her, he reached out, grabbing her waist, then felt her body go limp. "You will be mine, my whore, to do with as I please. Only when . . . and if I decide I have tired of you will I free you."

He lifted the silver riding quirt, making Samantha gasp. Instead of striking her, he purposely placed the quirt on her shoulder then slowly ran it down her arm.

Every muscle in her body strained. She wanted to scream and run as fast as she could, but she knew she could not escape. Yet she had to convince him to leave

442

before Lucien returned. Lucien would not stand a fair chance if Gaspar surprised him. Knowing that Gaspar's intent was not to fight honorably, Samantha knew she had to protect Lucien at any cost.

"Major." She tried to smile, but her lips only slightly curved. "Why don't we leave now, before Lucien returns? I promise not to resist you. I will write Lucien a note telling him not to follow me . . . only . . . please"—she hated begging him—"please leave my husband out of this."

"What a wonderful performance, my dear, but I am afraid I have made up my mind. I do not intend to change it." Again the quirt traveled up and down her arm, this time digging into her soft flesh. He quickly flicked the sleeve of the dress, scattering the tiny gold buttons about the room.

"I will do anything you ask if we leave now—alone." She swallowed hard, recognizing the hysterical edge in her voice.

Don't come back, Lucien, she repeated to herself. Don't come back.

"Now, I did ask you to sit over here"—again he motioned to the chair—"so sit."

Her mouth felt dry, but her hands and body felt so clammy Samantha wished she would faint. But if she did, she would not hear Lucien's carriage. Somehow she had to warn her husband that danger awaited him. What could she do? Silently she racked her brain, selecting then quickly discarding a variety of plans.

"I believe I shall help myself to a drink." Gaspar was not wearing his military uniform. Perhaps, Samantha thought, he had already been court-martialed.

As if he had read her mind, he said, "I am no longer

in the Army. I decided to resign before the inquiries went any further. I must thank your husband for that, too. As soon as I have finished my business here, you and I are going south to the Spanish Territory. So," Gaspar sneered, "you will not make an appearance at the trial tomorrow."

How this man managed to know everything, she could not guess. Gaspar sat as if he were an invited guest, not the cold-blooded killer planning his revenge. His face looked much thinner, making each of his almost-handsome features aquiline. Being in the same room with this man gave Samantha the feeling that the walls were closing in on her. Mindlessly, her hand closed on the crystal wine decanter placed on the table to her right. Hurling it at him, she stunned Gaspar enough to dart past him and out into the hallway. But she never made it out the front door.

"Your aim is very poor, dear Samantha," he commented dryly seconds before he cruelly slapped her face.

Out of breath, shocked, and pained by his brutality, Samantha felt herself sag against the doorframe. The desperation was clearly written on her face.

As Gaspar started to drag her back into the room, the sounds of a carriage rounding the street corner became louder as it approached the house.

Gaspar shoved Samantha onto the sofa, retrieved the pistol, smoothed his jet-black hair, and smiled a smile so full of malice that once more Samantha prayed for Lucien. Ignoring the painful swelling of her bruised face, she tearfully looked at him and pleaded, "Don't do it. We can still leave together. I'll tell him I don't love him, that it is you I want." Feeling filthier by the

444

second, Samantha reached for his arm. "Please?"

Another slap across her face was his only response.

"Say one word, and I kill him the moment he walks into the house." Checking the pistol to make sure it was primed, he added, "I am looking forward to this."

Fighting the blackness that threatened to overtake her, Samantha vainly tried to stand up.

"Don't move," he warned.

Hearing Lucien's voice outside made her heart stop. As the gate closed, Lucien shouted something to the coachman then laughed at his response. She heard the large oak door open. I cannot allow him to be caught unaware, she thought. Gaspar, still smiling, was half turned away from Samantha, his pistol raised and pointed.

Nothing would matter to her if Lucien were killed. She knew she could not survive without him. At the very least she had to give Lucien a chance, a fighting chance, even if it meant sacrificing herself. Surely Lucien was stronger than Gaspar. He simply needed a warning. Her thoughts of self-preservation were meaningless in the face of her love. Her one desire, her only thought, was to protect Lucien. Without him there would be no life for her anyway.

"Lucien, don't," she screamed. "Gaspar will kill you!" She forced herself to stand.

"That was very unwise, my dear." Gaspar glared at her murderously for an instant and then focused his attention on Lucien who was now standing frozen in place. Gaspar aimed the pistol directly at Lucien's heart.

"Come in, Mr. Fraser."

Lucien quickly assessed the situation.

445

"Leave her alone, Major. Let her go. Do what you will with me, but let her go."

"My, you two certainly think alike. Move Fraser next to your wife. I want her to see you grovel before you die."

"What have you done to her?" He saw the ugly bruises on her face. Yet he did not move. He thought that Samantha would have a better opportunity to escape if she stayed on the other side of the room.

"You have ruined me, but you know that. Your sworn affidavit took care of that, Fraser. I am going to enjoy my revenge," he said ruthlessly.

"No," she screamed, "I won't let you kill him!"

But Gaspar paid no attention to her. Still facing Lucien, his pistol was poised and cocked. With a renewed energy born of fear for the man she unabashedly loved, Samantha ran toward Lucien. She meant to stand in front of him, as a shield from his tormentor, but just before she reached him, Gaspar whirled, instinctively sensing danger, and without hesitation released the trigger.

She couldn't feel anything. Her right side felt numb and she stared down at the ripples of red on her white dress. Did I spill something? Her mind could not accept the bullet in her chest. From far off she thought she heard Lucien scream, "No," but it was such a strange sound—more like an animal cry than a man shouting. Her legs could not support her and a sharp ache overwhelmed her senses.

"Lucien, help me" were her last words before she sank to the floor unconscious.

For a few seconds, Gaspar and Lucien stood motionless, but it was Lucien who reacted first. He would not let Henri Gaspar escape unharmed for his dastardly act.

"You bastard!" he growled and lunged for his throat. The pistol was useless, but Gaspar threw it at Lucien. However, it was as effective as dust landing on a table. Lucien only saw her blood pouring from the wound, her life ebbing away. And he could not help her, for this murdering son of a bitch was in the way.

A deep, menacing cry left his lips as his hands closed around Gaspar's throat. Gaspar was strong but he was no match for Lucien in his frenzied state. Lucien had one goal: to kill the man who had shot and probably murdered Samantha.

From out of his boot Gaspar took a small dagger. Lucien saw the glint of the blade from the corner of his eye as Gaspar, now fighting for air, lifted his arm to strike.

"Oh no. I will see you in hell." Lucien's superior strength held Gaspar's arm. He was so obsessed with anger and revenge that he did not hear the sound of an approaching horse.

Firmly grasping Gaspar's wrist, Lucien fought in a blind and relentless wrestle for life.

As Samantha moaned, Lucien found the strength to turn Gaspar's knife into his stomach, striking the fatal blow. Lucien twisted the dagger and whispered, "And now we are even."

Henri Gaspar made an ugly, gurgling sound. And then nothing.

The front door slammed shut. Roger entered the room and looked in horror at the carnage. Major Henri Gaspar's lifeless body lay sprawled before him, a dagger protruding from his stomach. In the center of the room lay Samantha. Roger could see the stark contrast of the off-white dress and the bright red bloodstain on her chest. Lucien gathered her limp form into his arms, a look of anguish on his every feature.

"No, my love, not you . . . No!" he bellowed, his voice unnaturally loud with his anguish.

"Lucien, how did this happen?" Roger was dumbfounded.

"I am not sure." His hand swept his dark hair. "I'll explain later, but first help me. Get a doctor, find the two servants, and have them get water and bandages. I don't think I should move her, Roger."

"How badly wounded is she?"

"She was shot in the chest—on the right side. Roger"—he looked up at his friend, a strange brightness in his eyes—"that bullet was meant for me. For me, Roger. She deliberately took that bullet to protect me. My God!"

They looked at the unconscious Samantha in Lucien's arms. Mercifully she could not feel the pain. But her face was whiter than her dress and Lucien wished he could kill Gaspar again.

"The bullet is still lodged in her chest. There is no exit hole. Damn," he repeated to no one in particular, "why did she do it?"

"She loves you" came Roger's simple reply.

"I love her! So what? If she dies, how can I ever show her, tell her how much I need her? It's not fair," he cried. "Go on. Get help. I will watch over her."

And watch over her he did. Lucien did not leave Samantha's side. When the doctor and a federal marshal arrived thirty minutes later, Lucien described the events of the last several hours. But he would not leave Samantha's side.

The doctor, upon seeing the distraught husband, ordered Lucien to leave with the marshal while he examined Samantha, but Lucien insisted on staying and did indeed remain in the room.

"First see to my wife, Doctor. Tell me what can be done to remove the bullet and how to keep her alive. Then, and only then, will I leave her. Do you understand, gentlemen?" Lucien would not be denied. He was once again the captain in command, even though his future rested with fate, with Samantha's fate, not his own actions.

When the doctor informed him it was essential to remove the bullet, Lucien insisted that Samantha be brought upstairs to the large bedroom. Gently, he lifted her still body, kissed her cheek, and slowly took her to the room. The young servant, recovered by now from Gaspar's blow, prepared the bed. As the other servants returned from their night off, they eagerly did whatever Lucien and the doctor prescribed, anything to help the lovely Mrs. Fraser.

Dr. Warren removed the bullet, but it was arduous surgery. Because the pistol had been fired at such close range, the bullet was deeply lodged in her chest. But Dr. Warren was afraid of damaging Samantha's vital organs and spine while removing it, so he decided to operate from the front. Lucien agreed, even though he knew the operation could scar her badly. His only concern was that she live.

Holding her hand throughout the ordeal, Lucien watched the surgical knife pierce her flesh. He fervently wished he could change places with her. She looked so fragile, so lost in the big bed, and so still. More than a few times Lucien watched the slow rise and fall of her chest which was the only assurance that she was alive— barely alive. At last, after uncounted hours, he thought the ordeal had ended when he saw Dr. Warren remove the bullet. But this was simply a new and difficult stage in the nightmare.

"It's not over yet. This is a dangerous period. She is going to have a fever. If it's very high and lasts more than a week, well . . ." his voice trailed off.

"Well what?" he shouted, more out of fear for Samantha's life than anger.

"I don't know. Not many survive such a trauma."

"My wife will!" He squeezed her hand. "I will give her the will to go on."

Late that night Samantha's body was racked by alternating bouts of chills and heat. Lucien did not leave her side. No matter how much Roger pleaded with him to sleep, Lucien obstinately refused.

At daybreak Lucien agreed to talk to the federal marshal who had been waiting patiently downstairs in order to learn of the events of the night before. But as soon as the marshal left, Lucien raced upstairs to sit with her.

For three days Samantha did not move; her eyes were shut, but she was not in peaceful slumber. Lucien looked almost as pale as she. Wearing the same clothes he had been wearing since that fateful night, he looked unkempt and haggard. His only meals were comprised of an occasional bite of whatever was placed in front of him.

There was plenty of time—so many hours to think about Samantha: the attractive and flirtatious young

450

woman who challenged Lucien to kiss her; the beautiful woman in a French chateau waiting for "Mr. Smith," the government agent; the stubborn, passionate, and oh-so-loving woman who gave herself to him willingly and unwillingly so many times. All these months he had loved her but could not admit it to himself, afraid it was not manly to lose his heart to a woman, afraid that by giving his heart to another he was no longer independent. What foolishness. Now here she was, lying so still, fighting for her life. She had given herself for him. Wasn't this the ultimate act of love? Hadn't Samantha shown him more courage and love than he had ever shown her?

"Yes, yes, you did!" he fiercely whispered to her. "Everything I did was designed to resist your love for me. Even the day I told you my true feelings—it was not enough. Not enough, Samantha. I am a fool. But I swear to you, never again, my love."

He told her so much—all his innermost thoughts: how afraid he had been of losing her; the first time he had realized she was a part of him; how angry and jealous she had made him; everything he should have told her months before, not while she lay unconscious and barely alive.

Lucien could not keep track of time. How many days ago had she been shot? Three? Four? Only Roger Cole seemed to be the ballast in his life. Roger handled all the business and personal matters, glad to be of some assistance. Day after day Roger looked in on Lucien. The image of Lucien sitting in a chair close to the bed, his eyes revealing all the anguish of the days past— holding her hand, talking to her as if engaged in normal conversation but looking disconsolate—was permanently etched in Roger's thoughts. Lucien did ask Roger to contact the family at Thornton Hill and apprise them of Samantha's condition. He also remembered that Adam and Meredith were planning to surprise Samantha at Richmond.

"I took care of it, Lucien," Roger told him. "I sent Hooper to Richmond. They should be here any day. Oh, and the Madisons want to come by, Lucien. I think you should see them."

"Yes, all right," he responded without enthusiasm. Then he looked at Roger and said, "Roger, you are a good friend. I'll never forget this." Lucien's voice cracked. That was happening a lot lately, whenever he thought about recent events in his life. When Roger left their room, Lucien could not restrain himself any longer. Hot tears scalded his cheeks while deep sobs escaped his lips, and he could not stop himself from praying and crying; "Please God, please help her! Please let her live!"

"Lucien? Where are you? I cannot see you." Samantha heard his crying voice. It could not be Lucien. Why was he crying?

She was back in New Orleans, dancing with Lucien. Her head ached—she must have had too much champagne. Lucien swirled her around the room. She was so dizzy and exhilarated. As he swirled her again, the candles almost went out from the breeze. Samantha looked at Lucien, imploring him to stop spinning her about. But it wasn't his face she saw—it was Gaspar's! He was laughing, touching her face, poking at her chest with that ugly quirt, and defying her requests.

She pulled away from him, looking for a place to which she could escape. But before she could leave, Gaspar was there at the doorway and Clinton Davis was next to him.

"*You are dead. Leave me be. No, Clinton, don't touch me. Lucien, where are you?*" Her cry for assistance was greeted by the other people in the room with inattention, as if they were marble statues. Gaspar got closer, raising one hand to strike her and holding a pistol in his other hand.

"*Go ahead, shoot me! I don't want to live if Lucien dies. Don't you understand?*" Lucien ran toward her, then held her in his arms, kissed her cheek, and said some soothing words.

"You are here with me, my love. No one will ever harm you again. Remember I promised you that long ago. I swear."

"*Go away, Lucien. He will kill you!*" She wildly thrashed about in his arms. Her body felt like it was on fire . . . Fire! . . . The fire! Lucien was trapped in the *Seafarer.* It was so hot, an inferno at sea. Where was the doctor? Someone had to help Lucien.

"*Where is Dr. Bentley? Someone has to help Lucien. Lucien is hurt. Please*"—the tears rolled onto her gown—"*why won't someone help? He cannot die!*"

"I am here, sweetheart. I am fine. Oh God, please give her strength."

"*Lucien? Oh, I love you! I've always loved you. But I ruined your plans. I kept you from Caroline Prescott. I am sorry, my darling. I never want to stand in your way. If you still want Elise, I will leave. I swear I won't*

453

bother you ever again. I want you to be happy! I love you! Why can't you love me?"

"I do love you, with all my heart. Please, I only want *you.* I need you, Samantha. Can't you hear me—I need you!"

The chills were severe. She felt as if she were outside in the snow, not far from Kingscote. All alone. But nothing looked familiar. She felt the cold wind against her skin. Her clothes were wet from the snow which became a blizzard, blinding her to any familiar sights. But she thought she heard a carriage. Then she saw it. A man and a woman were in the coach. Was it? Yes, it was Lucien and Elise!

"Lucien, wait! Wait for me. Why are you laughing at me? I know I am not as beautiful as you, Elise. But Lucien, you are my husband. Don't leave me. Please, I am so cold. Don't leave me!"

But the carriage swept past her. The snow kept falling and she slipped. She was unable to get up. It was strange; she felt warm despite the snow. There was something covering her. The snow? A shadowy figure spooned some hot broth into her parched lips.

"Here. Take some, my love. It will comfort you!"

He sounded like Lucien. But it wasn't. There were those cold, gray, penetrating eyes. He raised his hand and there was a pistol aimed at her.

"No!" She slapped the hand away. *"No! No! Help me!"* she screamed. But when she opened her eyes again, he was gone. There was a man before her. Not Major Gaspar. It was Lucien. But he looked so pale, so unhappy. His eyes looked as if they had sunk into his head. His face glistened from tears. Her hand tried to touch his cheek, but the searing pain in her chest made

454

her recoil. She could not move her arm. The pain was excruciating.

"I don't know how much longer she can hold on." Lucien tried to explain what had happened to Adam and Meredith. They had rushed to Washington, not bothering to stay overnight at an inn in Richmond.

When Hooper met them in Richmond with a message from Lucien, Meredith tearfully held Adam, asking, "When will they ever have a chance? It's not fair, Adam. Neither my brother nor Samantha deserve this."

Seeing Lucien confirmed their worst fears. For the first time in her life Meredith worried about her brother's emotional state. She was able to get him out of the bedroom for short intervals to take him somewhere to talk and where he might not be completely preoccupied with Samantha's recovery.

"I cannot lose her, Meredith. I will not let her die," he vowed. "Not now. She does not know how much I love her, how sorry I am for what I have done to her!"

"Lucien"—she placed her arms around him—"you are too harsh on yourself. She does not blame you for anything."

"You have heard her crying, Meredith. You heard her call out in her delirium for me to help. But I disappointed her. Dammit!" He pounded his fist against the wall, oblivious to the pain.

"Lucien, I think she will make it. Her wound seems to be healing. And you know, brother, I have the strangest feeling that Samantha does hear your voice or at least senses your presence."

His face almost brightened. "Funny, I had that feeling, too. But I thought it was wishful thinking."

"Adam told me that when you left the room earlier today Samantha appeared agitated and called for you."

Knowing what he was about to say she countered, "Listen, if you think you can thrive solely by watching her every move, you are mistaken. It is not healthy. Look at you"—her voice rose—"you look awful. When was the last time you shaved? Or had a decent meal? Do you know what's going on out there? Did you know that the Aaron Burr trial is over? Do you know . . . oh, what's the use," she lamented.

For the first time in days Lucien allowed Meredith's words to make an impression on him. Looking down at his unkempt clothes and feeling scruffy, he finally realized what a disservice he was doing to himself and the others who cared about him.

"Christ! I am a sight," he snorted. "If my nephew saw me, he would howl with fright."

Lucien finally agreed to have dinner with Adam, Meredith, and Roger, provided that Dr. Warren stay with Samantha. They answered all his questions about the last few days.

"Wait until Samantha hears this," he proclaimed after listening to the most interesting political peccadillo. "If"—he sobered—"she lives."

Meredith's eyes felt teary, but there weren't any tears left to shed. She hated to see her brother so anguished.

That night Lucien took his usual post by Samantha's bedside. Her color had improved slightly. Dr. Warren said she was not as restless as she had been the last two days. Nor did she appear to have those horrible nightmares. Maybe there was a reason to be hopeful. Tenderly, Lucien kissed her brow. It did not feel as warm as before.

"Please, Samantha, hear me. You must get well. I need you."

But she did not stir. Lucien watched her for the next few hours. His eyes fought to remain open, but he lost the battle late in the night. Leaning his head on his folded arms, Lucien fell asleep half-lying on the bed and the armchair.

There was something different in the air this evening. There was an aura of relief. Then he felt it, her hand lightly brushing his hair.

He did not want to open his eyes to another illusion. Lifting his groggy head, he realized this was real. Samantha was awake and there was the trace of a smile on her angelic face, a face that had seen the other side of life.

"Lucien," she managed to say, "I knew you were here with me."

"Welcome back, my love." His radiant smile was not half as bright as his blue eyes. "I missed you terribly, and Samantha"—he cupped her face in his hand—"I love you so much. I did not know how I could go on without you." His voice broke with pent-up emotion.

"I love you too!" She started to say something but could not summon the strength. Finally, she sighed, "Sleep with me, Lucien. Here." She motioned to the empty side of the bed. "I . . . missed you."

Carefully easing himself onto the bed, Lucien murmured contentedly, "I want your warmth."

"Hold me," she replied.

"With pleasure, madam," and he placed her head

457

into the crook of his arm. She could have asked anything of him and he would have complied.

"Adam, come quickly," Meredith called softly. "You must see this."

There they were together again, Samantha softly wrapped in Lucien's arms, deep in the healing sleep of one who had returned to life, while Lucien, in an exhausted slumber, was at peace with the world.

Chapter Thirty-One

"Another week, madam, and that's final," he chided. "Was I as impossible a patient as you are?"

"Worse," she laughed. "But Lucien, tell me when I can leave this bed."

"I said another week. Do you think I enjoy being your nursemaid?"

"Tell me again about your nursing me," she pressed. "I wish I could have seen you brushing my hair and sponging my body."

"I will do it again tonight," he promised. "But I must admit, it will be more difficult this time, especially if you start to purr. It's too soon to ravish you." Even in her weakened state, his playful banter was thrilling.

"I asked Dr. Warren about *that*, and he said, 'Soon, my dear.' I hope he means next week." She captured his hands in hers and kissed his fingers.

"Tell you what, my sweet. Tonight I will carry you downstairs and you can have dinner with all of us."

"Wonderful." She clapped her hands. "I really feel fine, you know."

"I know. But you gave me such a scare, I would rather you indulge yourself for a while. I don't mind being the solicitous husband."

It was a wonderful dinner. Lucien, in the best of spirits, joked and shared stories with the men.

Samantha, looking like a porcelain doll in a pale lavender dressing gown and colorful Chinese silk shawl, looked lovingly at her husband and family, thankful she could be among them.

"I love you all." She raised her wine glass. "Thank you. And thank you for putting up with my incorrigible spouse."

"Life would not be worth living without you, my love." He too lifted his glass, looking into her beautiful eyes. Long, unbound red-gold hair loosely framed her face. "You are beautiful. To my wife."

The magic in their lives was immutable. They both knew that now. Lucien dismissed all her fears. Of course he loved her and never regretted marrying her. The morning after she awoke from her first deep, trouble-free sleep in a week, Lucien told her the truth about Elise Fourier, his guilt, his torment, and his desire for her. Just looking at his earnest, loving face told her all she wanted to know.

"Can you forgive me for being such a fool? It should have been me, you know. Gaspar wanted to shoot me."

It did not pain her to talk about Gaspar's insane attack any longer. But more than anything, Samantha did not want Lucien to blame himself for her injury.

"Lucien, I never blamed you for anything. Please, let's try to forget." As his lips warmly claimed hers, she believed they would forget.

Gradually, Lucien, Adam, and Roger apprised her of recent political events.

"You realize, Sam, you missed the whole trial?"

Adam laughed. "And so did I."

"But it seems that Mr. Burr did not need your cooperation," added Roger.

"You mean . . ."

"Not guilty, Sam. They could not prove Aaron Burr was guilty of treason. There was never any substantial proof. After all, there was no overt act of war," replied Roger.

"Jefferson is furious," Lucien explained. "Perhaps you were right, Samantha. Many people are saying that Jefferson tried to influence this trial, that the prosecution—under the President's orders—tried to bribe witnesses. He has publicly denounced Burr and is enraged that General Andrew Jackson supported him."

"And Jackson publicly accused Jefferson of illegally arresting Burr and his supporters," Roger added.

Samantha was delighted by the outcome. "What about General Wilkinson?" Samantha hoped he had gotten what he deserved.

"The President still stands by him. He has to," Adam said. "Jefferson's case rested entirely on General Wilkinson's testimony. It has become a matter of pride, I think."

"Nevertheless," her husband interrupted, "Wilkinson will no longer be such a powerful force in the Army. I have heard that an investigation into his activities is about to be launched."

"Lucien, tell Sam about the Fouriers." Meredith's statement was innocent enough, but Lucien saw his wife stiffen at the name.

"Gone. Off to France. They managed to leave before Madison's men could reach André Fourier. I guess

André and Elise will have to like living in France, for they will not be welcome here."

"Good," she said under her breath. Everyone and everything was accounted for.

Later, in the early evening, Lucien sat on the edge of the bed holding Samantha's hand.

The sun was setting, allowing the last of its rays to brighten the room. The turmoil of the last few weeks had taken its toll, but they both felt purged. A warm breeze filtered through the open window, giving them a sense of life's vitality. They were captives of a new emotion—a love born of suffering, shared experience, and passion. Instinctively, each knew that brighter tomorrows awaited them as long as they were together. Lucien's figure cast a long shadow over the bed, providing Samantha with a blanket of comfort in his nearness. Their spirits merged as one, creating an essence of hope. The light of the sun was gone and a new day awaited them. Lucien kissed Samantha's forehead lovingly and murmured, "It's time to go home."

I hope you enjoyed reading about the adventures of Samantha and Lucien. I would love to hear from my readers. I will personally answer all my mail. Please write to me at:

P.O. Box #1
Bay Station
Brooklyn, N.Y. 11235

—Victoria London